"My God! Look!" cried
the communications officer.

The RG 132, torpid, massive, was rolling
away from the docking station, drives
blaring at full power.

Auson dropped, unheeded, from Miles's
attention. "The RG 132, loaded, has four
times the mass of that pocket dreadnought," he breathed.

"Which is why it flies like a pig and
costs a fortune in fuel to move!" yelled
Auson. "That pilot officer of yours is crazy
if he thinks he can outrun Tung—"

Then, almost in slow motion, with a kind
of crazy majesty, the RG 132 lumbered
into the warship—and kept going. The
dreadnought was nudged into the huge
smeltery. Projecting equipment and surface
housings snapped and spun off in all
directions. Smashed edges of the dreadnought were caught up on the smeltery,
thoroughly entangled. Gaudy chemical fires
gouted here and there into the vacuum.

The RG 132 drifted off. Miles stood
before the tactics-room screen and stared
in stunned fascination as half the freighter's
outer hull delaminated and peeled into
space.

For
Lillian Stewart Carl

LOIS McMASTER BUJOLD

THE WARRIOR'S APPRENTICE

BAEN
SCIENCE FICTION
BOOKS

THE WARRIOR'S APPRENTICE

Copyright © 1986 by Lois McMaster Bujold

A Baen Books Original

Baen Publishing Enterprises
260 Fifth Avenue
New York, N.Y. 10001

First printing, August 1986

ISBN: 0-671-65587-6

Cover art by Alan Gutierrez

Printed in the United States of America

Distributed by
SIMON & SCHUSTER
TRADE PUBLISHING GROUP
1230 Avenue of the Americas
New York, N.Y. 10020

CHAPTER ONE * * *

The tall and dour non-com wore Imperial dress greens and carried his communications panel like a field marshall's baton. He slapped it absently against his thigh and raked the group of young men before him with a gaze of dry contempt. Challenging.

All part of the game, Miles told himself. He stood in the crisp autumn breeze and tried not to shiver in his shorts and running shoes. Nothing to put you off balance like being nearly naked when all about you look ready for one of Emperor Gregor's reviews although, in all fairness, the majority here were dressed the same as himself. The non-com proctoring the tests merely seemed like a one-man crowd. Miles measured him, wondering what conscious or unconscious tricks of body language he used to achieve that air of icy competence. Something to be learned there . . .

"You will run in pairs," the non-com instructed. He did not seem to raise his voice, but somehow it was pitched to carry to the ends of the lines. Another effective trick, Miles thought; it reminded him of that habit of his father's, of dropping his voice to a whisper when speaking in a rage. It locked attention.

"The timing of the five kilometer run begins immediately upon completion of the last phase of the obstacle course; remember it." The non-com began counting off pairs.

The eliminations for officers candidacy in the Barrayaran Imperial Military Service took a grueling week. Five days of written and oral examinations were behind Miles now. The hardest part was over, everybody said. There was almost an air of relaxation among the young men around him. There was more talking and joking in the group, exaggerated complaints about the difficulty of the exams, the withering wit of the examining officers, the poor food, interrupted sleep, surprise distractions during the testing. Self-congratulatory complaints, these, among the survivors. They looked forward to the physical tests as a game. Recess, perhaps. The hardest part was over—for everyone but Miles.

He stood to his full height, such as it was, and stretched, as if to pull his crooked spine out straight by force of will. He gave a little upward jerk of his chin, as if balancing his too-large head, a head meant for a man over six feet, on his just-under-five-foot frame, and narrowed his eyes at the obstacle course. It began with a concrete wall, five meters high, topped with iron spikes. Climbing it would be no problem, there was nothing wrong with his muscles, it was the coming down that worried him. The bones, always the damn bones . . .

"Kosigan, Kostolitz," the non-com called, passing in front of him. Miles's brows snapped down and he gave the non-com a sharp upward glance, then controlled his gaze to a blank straightness. The omission of the honorific before his name was policy, not insult. All classes stood equal in the Emperor's service now. A good policy. His own father endorsed it.

Grandfather bitched, to be sure, but that unreconstructed old man had begun his Imperial service when its principle arm was horse cavalry and each officer trained his own military apprentices. To have addressed him in those days as Kosigan, without the Vor, might have resulted in a duel. Now his grandson sought entrance to a military academy, off planet style, and training in the tactics of energy weapons, wormhole exits, and planetary defense. And stood shoulder to shoulder with boys who would not have been permitted to polish his sword in the old days.

Not quite shoulder to shoulder, Miles reflected dryly,

stealing a sidelong glance up at the candidates on either side of him. The one he had been paired with for the obstacle course, what's his name, Kostolitz, caught the glance and looked back down with ill-concealed curiosity. Miles's eye level gave him a fine opportunity to study the fellow's excellent biceps. The non-com signalled fall out for those not running the obstacle course immediately. Miles and his companion sat on the ground.

"I've been seeing you around all week," offered Kostolitz. "What the hell is that thing on your leg?"

Miles controlled his irritation with the ease of long practice. God knew he did stand out in a crowd, particularly this crowd. At least Kostolitz did not make hex signs at him, like a certain decrepit old countrywoman down at Vorkosigan Surleau. In some of the more remote and undeveloped regions on Barrayar, like deep in the Dendarii Mountains in the Vorkosigans' own district, infanticide was still practiced for defects as mild as a harelip, despite sporadic efforts from the more enlightened centers of authority to stamp it out. He glanced down at the pair of gleaming metal rods paralleling his left leg between knee and ankle that had remained secretly beneath his trouser leg until this day.

"Leg brace," he replied, polite but unencouraging.

Kostolitz continued to stare. "What for?"

"Temporary. I have a couple of brittle bones there. Keeps me from breaking them, until the surgeon's quite sure I'm done growing. Then I get them replaced with synthetics."

"That's weird," commented Kostolitz. "Is it a disease, or what?" Under the guise of shifting his weight, he moved just slightly farther from Miles.

Unclean, unclean, thought Miles wildly; should I ring a bell? I ought to tell him it's contagious—I was six-foot-four this time last year . . . He sighed away the temptation. "My mother was exposed to a poison gas when she was pregnant with me. She pulled through all right, but it wrecked my bone growth."

"Huh. Didn't they give you any medical treatment?"

"Oh, sure. I've had an Inquisition's worth. That's why

I can walk around today, instead of being carried in a bucket."

Kostolitz looked mildly revolted, but stopped trying to sidle subtly upwind. "How did you ever get past the medicals? I thought there was a minimum height rule."

"It was waived, pending my test results."

"Oh." Kostolitz digested this.

Miles returned his attention to the test ahead. He should be able to pick up some time on that belly-crawl under the laser fire; good, he would need it on the five kilometer run. Lack of height, and a permanent limp from a left leg shorter, after more fractures than he could remember, by a good four centimeters than his right, would slow him down. No help for it. Tomorrow would be better; tomorrow was the endurance phase. The herd of long-legged gangling boys around him could unquestionably beat him on the sprint. He fully expected to be anchor man on the first 25 kilometer leg tomorrow, probably the second as well, but after 75 kilometers most would be flagging as the real pain mounted. *I am a professional of pain, Kostolitz,* he thought to his rival. *Tomorrow, after about kilometer 100, I'll ask you to repeat those questions of yours—if you have the breath to spare. . . .*

Bloody hell, let's pay attention to business, not this dink. A five meter drop—perhaps it would be better to go around, take a zero on that part. But his overall score was bound to be relatively poor. He hated to part with a single point unnecessarily, and at the very beginning, too. He was going to need every one of them. Skipping the wall would cut into his narrow safety margin—

"You really expect to pass the physicals?" asked Kostolitz, looking around. "I mean, above the 50th percentile?"

"No."

Kostolitz looked baffled. "Then what the hell's the point?"

"I don't have to pass it; just make something near a decent score."

Kostolitz's eyebrows rose. "Whose ass do you have to kiss to get a deal like that? Gregor Vorbarra's?"

There was an undercurrent of incipient jealousy in his tone, class-conscious suspicion. Miles's jaw clamped. Let us not bring up the subject of fathers . . .

"How do you plan to get in without passing?" Kostolitz persisted, eyes narrowing. His nostrils flared at the scent of privilege, like an animal alert for blood.

Practice politics, Miles told himself. That too should be in your blood, like war. "I petitioned," Miles explained patiently, "to have my scores averaged instead of taken separately. I expect my writtens to bring up my physicals."

"That far up? You'd need a damn near perfect score!"

"That's right," Miles snarled.

"Kosigan, Kostolitz," another uniformed proctor called. They entered the starting area.

"It's a little hard on me, you know," Kostolitz complained.

"Why? It hasn't got a thing to do with you. None of your business at all," Miles added pointedly.

"We're put in pairs to pace each other. How will I know how I'm doing?"

"Oh, don't feel you have to keep up with me," Miles purred.

Kostolitz's brows lowered with annoyance.

They were chivvied into place. Miles glanced across the parade ground at a distant knot of men waiting and watching; a few military relatives, and the liveried retainers of the handful of Counts' sons present today. There was a pair of hard-looking men in the blue and gold of the Vorpatrils'; his cousin Ivan must be around here somewhere.

And there was Bothari, tall as a mountain and lean as a knife, in the brown and silver of the Vorkosigans. Miles raised his chin in a barely perceptible salute. Bothari, 100 meters away, caught the gesture and changed his stance from at ease to a silent parade rest in acknowledgment.

A couple of testing officers, the non-com, and a pair of proctors from the course were huddled together at a distance. Some gesticulations, a look in Miles's direction; a debate, it seemed. It concluded. The proctors returned to their stations, one of the officers started the next pair of boys over the course, and the non-com approached Miles and his companion. He looked uneasy. Miles schooled his features to cool attention.

"Kosigan," the non-com began, voice carefully neutral. "You're going to have to take off the leg brace. Artificial aids not permitted for the test."

A dozen counter-arguments sprang up in Miles's mind. He tightened his lips on them. This non-com was in a sense his commanding officer; Miles knew for certain that more than physical performance was being evaluated today. "Yes, sir." The non-com looked faintly relieved.

"May I give it to my man?" asked Miles. He threatened the non-com with his eyes—if not, I'm going to stick you with it, and you'll have to cart it around the rest of the day—see how conspicuous it makes *you* feel . . .

"Certainly, sir," said the non-com. The "sir" was a slip; the non-com knew who he was, of course. A small wolfish smile slid across Miles's mouth, and vanished. Miles gave Bothari a high sign, and the liveried bodyguard trotted over obediently. "You may not converse with him," the non-com warned.

"Yes, sir," acknowledged Miles. He sat on the ground and unclipped the much-loathed apparatus. Good; a kilo less to carry. He tossed it up to Bothari, who caught it one-handed, and squirmed back to his feet. Bothari, correctly, offered him no hand up.

Seeing his bodyguard and the non-com together, the non-com suddenly bothered Miles less. The proctor looked shorter, somehow, and younger; even a little soft. Bothari was taller, leaner, much older, a lot uglier, and considerably meaner-looking. But then, Bothari had been a non-com himself when this proctor had been a toddler.

Narrow jaw, hooked beak of a nose, eyes of a nondescript color set too close together; Miles looked up at his liveried retainer's face with a loving pride of possession. He glanced toward the obstacle course and let his eyes pass over Bothari's. Bothari glanced at it too, pursed his lips, tucked the brace firmly under his arm, and gave a slight shake of his head directed, apparently, at the middle distance. Miles's mouth twitched. Bothari sighed, and trotted back to the waiting area.

So Bothari advised caution. But then, Bothari's job was to keep him intact, not advance his career—no, unfair, Miles chided himself. No one had been of more service in the preparations for this frantic week than Bothari. He'd spent endless time on training, pushing Miles's body to its too-soon-found limits, unflaggingly devoted to his charge's passionate obsession. My first command, thought Miles. My private army.

Kostolitz stared after Bothari. He identified the livery at last, it seemed, for he looked back at Miles in startled illumination.

"So, that's who you are," he said, with a jealous awe. "No wonder you got a deal on the tests."

Miles smiled tightly at the implied insult. The tension crawled up his back. He groped for some suitably scathing retort, but they were being motioned to the starting mark.

Kostolitz's deductive faculty crunched on, it seemed, for he added sardonically, "And so that's why the Lord Regent never made the bid for the Imperium!"

"Time mark," said the proctor, "now!"

And they were off. Kostolitz sprinted ahead of Miles instantly. You'd better run, you witless bastard, because if I can catch you, I'm going to kill you—Miles galloped after him, feeling like a cow in a horse race.

The wall, the bloody wall—Kostolitz was grunting halfway up it when Miles arrived. At least he could show this working class hero how to climb. He swarmed up it as if the tiny toe and finger holds were great steps, his muscles powered—over-powered—by his fury. To his satisfaction, he reached the top ahead of Kostolitz. He looked down, and stopped abruptly, perched gingerly among the spikes.

The proctor was watching closely. Kostolitz caught up with Miles, his face suffused with effort. "A Vor, scared of heights?" Kostolitz gasped, with a grinning glare over his shoulder. He flung himself off, hit the sand with an authoritative impact, recovered his balance, and dashed off.

Precious seconds would be wasted climbing down like some arthritic little old lady—perhaps if he hit the ground rolling—the proctor was staring—Kostolitz had already reached the next obstacle—Miles jumped.

Time seemed to stretch itself, as he plummeted toward the sand, especially to allow him the full sick savor of his mistake. He hit the sand with the familiar shattering crack.

And sat, blinking stupidly at the pain. He would not cry out—at least, the detached observer in the back of his brain commented sardonically, you can't blame it on the brace—this time you've managed to break both of them.

His legs began to swell and discolor, mottled white and flushed. He pulled himself along until they were stretched out straight, and bent over a moment, hiding his face in his knees. Face buried, he permitted himself one silent rictus scream. He did not swear. The vilest terms he knew seemed wholly inadequate to the occasion.

The proctor, awakening to the fact that he was not going to stand up, started toward him. Miles pulled himself across the sand, out of the path of the next pair of candidates, and waited patiently for Bothari.

He had all the time in the world, now.

Miles decided he definitely didn't like the new antigrav crutches, even though they were worn invisibly inside his clothing. They gave his walk a slithery uncertainty that made him feel spastic. He would have preferred a good old-fashioned stick, or better yet a swordstick like Captain Koudelka's that one could drive into the ground with a satisfying thunk at each step, as if spearing some suitable enemy—Kostolitz, for example. He paused to gather his balance before tackling the steps to Vorkosigan House.

Minute particles in their worn granite scintillated warmly in the autumn morning light, in spite of the industrial haze that hung over the capital city of Vorbarr Sultana. A racket from farther down the street marked where a similar mansion was being demolished to make way for a modern building. Miles glanced up to the high-rise directly across the street; a figure moved against the roofline. The battlements had changed, but the watchful soldiers still stalked along them.

Bothari, looming silently beside him, bent suddenly to retrieve a lost coin from the walkway. He placed it carefully in his left pocket. The dedicated pocket.

One corner of Miles's mouth lifted, and his eyes warmed with amusement. "Still the dowry?"

"Of course," said Bothari serenely. His voice was deep bass, monotonous in cadence. One had to know him a long time to interpret its expressionlessness. Miles knew every minute variation in its timbre as a man knows his own room in the dark.

"You've been pinching tenth-marks for Elena as long as I can remember. Dowries went out with the horse cavalry, for God's sake. Even the Vor marry without them these days. This isn't the Time of Isolation." Miles made his mockery gentle in tone, carefully fitted to Bothari's obsession. Bothari, after all, had always treated Miles's ridiculous craze seriously.

"I mean her to have everything right and proper."

"You ought to have enough saved up to buy Gregor Vorbarra by now," said Miles, thinking of the hundreds of small economies his bodyguard had practiced before him, over the years, for the sake of his daughter's dowry.

"Shouldn't joke about the Emperor." Bothari depressed this random stab at humor firmly, as it deserved. Miles sighed and began to work his way cautiously up the steps, legs stiff in their plastic immobilizers.

The painkillers he'd taken before he'd left the military infirmary were beginning to wear off. He felt unutterably weary. The night had been a sleepless one, sitting up under local anesthetics, talking and joking with the surgeon as he puttered endlessly, piecing the minute shattered fragments of bone back together like an unusually obstreperous jigsaw puzzle. *I put on a pretty good show*, Miles reassured himself; but he longed to get off stage and collapse. *Just a couple more acts to go.*

"What kind of fellow are you planning to shop for?" Miles probed delicately during a pause in his climb.

"An officer," Bothari said firmly.

Miles's smile twisted. So that's the pinnacle of your ambition, too, Sergeant? he inquired silently. "Not too soon, I trust."

Bothari snorted. "Of course not. She's only ..." He paused, the creases deepening between his narrow eyes. "Time's gone by ..." his mutter trailed off.

Miles negotiated the steps successfully, and entered Vorkosigan House, bracing for relatives. The first was to be his mother, it seemed; that was no problem. She appeared at the foot of the great staircase in the front hall as the door was opened for him by a uniformed servant-cum-guard. Lady Vorkosigan was a middle-aged woman, the fiery red of her hair quenched by natural grey, her height neatly disguising a few extra kilos weight. She was breathing a bit heavily; probably had run downstairs when he was spotted approaching. They exchanged a brief hug. Her eyes were grave and unjudgemental.

"Father here?" he asked.

"No. He and Minister Quintillian are down at headquarters, arm-wrestling with the General Staff about their budget this morning. He said to give you his love and tell you he'd try to be here for lunch."

"He, ah—hasn't told Grandfather about yesterday yet, has he?"

"No—I really think you should have let him, though. It's been rather awkward this morning."

"I'll bet." He gazed up at the stairs. It was more than his bad legs that made them seem mountainous. Well, let's get the worst over with first ... "Upstairs, is he?"

"In his rooms. Although he actually took a walk in the garden this morning, I'm glad to say."

"Mm." Miles started working his way upstairs.

"Lift tube," said Bothari.

"Oh, hell, it's only one flight."

"Surgeon said you're to stay off them as much as possible."

Miles's mother awarded Bothari an approving smile, which he acknowledged blandly with a murmured, "Milady." Miles shrugged grudgingly and headed for the back of the house instead.

"Miles," said his mother as he passed, "don't, ah ... He's very old, he's not too well, and he hasn't had to be polite to anybody in years—just take him on his own terms, all right?"

"You know I do." He grinned ironically, to prove how unaffected he proposed to be. Her lips curved in return, but her eyes remained grave.

He met Elena Bothari, coming out of his grandfather's chambers. His bodyguard greeted his daughter with a silent nod, and won for himself one of her rather shy smiles.

For the thousandth time Miles wondered how such an ugly man could have produced such a beautiful daughter. Every one of his features was echoed in her face, but richly transmuted. At eighteen she was tall, like her father, fully six feet to his six-and-a-half; but while he was whipcord lean and tense, she was slim and vibrant. His nose a beak, hers an elegant aquiline profile; his face too narrow, hers with the air of some perfectly-bred aristocratic sight-hound, a borzoi or a greyhound. Perhaps it was the eyes that made the difference; hers were dark and lustrous, alert, but without his constantly shifting, unsmiling watchfulness. Or the hair; his greying, clipped in his habitual military burr, hers long, dark, straight-shining. A gargoyle and a saint, by the same sculptor, facing each other across some ancient cathedral portal.

Miles shook himself from his trance. Her eyes met his briefly, and her smile faded. He straightened up from his tired slouch and produced a false smile for her, hoping to lure her real one back. Not too soon, Sergeant ...

"Oh, good, I'm so glad you're here," she greeted him. "It's been gruesome this morning."

"Has he been crotchety?"

"No, cheerful. Playing Strat-O with me and paying no attention—do you know, I almost beat him? Telling his war stories and wondering about you—if he'd had a map of your course, he'd have been sticking pins in it to mark your imaginary progress . . . I don't have to stay, do I?"

"No, of course not."

Elena twitched a relieved smile at him, and trailed off down the corridor, casting one disquieted look back over her shoulder.

Miles took a breath, and stepped across General Count Piotr Vorkosigan's inner threshold.

CHAPTER TWO ✳ ✳ ✳

The old man was out of bed, shaved and crisply dressed for the day. He sat up in a chair, gazing pensively out the window overlooking his back garden. He glanced up with a frown at the interruptor of his meditations, saw that it was Miles, and smiled broadly.

"Ah, come, boy . . ." He gestured at the chair Miles guessed Elena had recently vacated. The old man's smile became tinged with puzzlement. "By God, have I lost a day somewhere? I thought this was the day you were out on that 100 kilometer trot up and down Mt. Sencele."

"No, sir, you haven't lost a day." Miles eased into the chair. Bothari set another before him and pointed at his feet. Miles started to lift them, but the effort was sabotaged by a particularly savage twinge of pain. "Yeah, put 'em up, Sergeant," Miles acquiesced wearily. Bothari helped him place the offending feet at the medically correct angle and withdrew, strategically Miles thought, to stand at attention by the door. The old Count watched this pantomime, understanding dawning painfully in his face.

"What have you done, boy?" he sighed.

Let's make it quick and painless, like a beheading . . . "Jumped off a wall in the obstacle course yesterday and broke both my legs. Washed myself out of the physical tests completely. The others—well, they don't matter now."

"So you came home."

13

"So I came home."

"Ah." The old man drummed his long gnarled fingers once on the arm of the chair. "Ah." He shifted uncomfortably in his seat and thinned his lips, staring out the window, not looking at Miles. His fingers drummed again. "It's all the fault of this damned creeping democratism," he burst out querulously. "A lot of imported off-planet nonsense. Your father did not do Barrayar a service to encourage it. He had a fine opportunity to stamp it out when he was Regent—which he wasted totally, as far as I can see . . ." he trailed off. "In love with off-planet notions, off-planet women," he echoed himself more faintly. "I blame your mother, you know. Always pushing that egalitarian tripe . . ."

"Oh, come on," Miles was stirred to object. "Mother's as apolitical as you can get and still be conscious and walking around."

"Thank God, or she'd be running Barrayar today. I've never seen your father cross her yet. Well, well, it could have been worse . . ." The old man shifted again, twisting in his pain of spirit as Miles had in his pain of body.

Miles lay in his chair, making no effort to defend the issue or himself. The Count could be trusted to argue himself down, taking both parts, in a little time.

"We must bend with the times, I suppose. We must all bend with the times. Shopkeepers' sons are great soldiers, now. God knows, I commanded a few in my day. Did I ever tell you about the fellow, when we were fighting the Cetagandans up in the Dendarii Mountains back behind Vorkosigan Surleau—best guerilla lieutenant I ever had. I wasn't much older than you, then. He killed more Cetagandans that year . . . His father had been a tailor. A tailor, back when it was all cut and stitched by hand, hunched over all the little detailing . . ." He sighed for the irretrievable past. "What was the fellow's name . . ."

"Tesslev," supplied Miles. He raised his eyebrows quizzically at his feet. *Perhaps I shall be a tailor, then. I'm built for it. But they're as obsolete as Counts, now.*

"Tesslev, yes, that was it. He died horribly when they

caught his patrol. Brave man, brave man ..." Silence fell between them for a time.

The old Count spotted a straw, and clutched at it. "Was the test fairly administered? You never know, these days—some plebian with a personal ax to grind. . ."

Miles shook his head, and moved quickly to cut this fantasy down before it had a chance to grow and flower. "Quite fair. It was me. I let myself get rattled, didn't pay attention to what I was doing. I failed because I wasn't good enough. Period."

The old man twisted his lips in sour negation. His hand closed angrily, and opened hopelessly. "In the old days no one would have dared question your right . . ."

"In the old days the cost of my incompetence would have been paid in other men's lives. This is more efficient, I believe." Miles's voice was flat.

"Well ..." the old man stared unseeingly out the window. "Well—times change. Barrayar has changed. It underwent a world of change between the time I was ten and the time I was twenty. And another between the time I was twenty and forty. Nothing was the same . . . And another between the time I was forty and eighty. This weak, degenerate generation—even their sins are watered down. The old pirates of my father's day could have eaten them all for breakfast and digested their bones before lunch . . . Do you know, I shall be the first Count Vorkosigan to die in bed in nine generations?" He paused, gaze still fixed, and whispered half to himself, "God, I've grown weary of change. The very thought of enduring another new world dismays me. Dismays me."

"Sir," said Miles gently.

The old man looked up quickly. "Not your fault, boy, not your fault. You were caught in the wheels of change and chance just like the rest of us. It was pure chance, that the assassin chose that particular poison to try and kill your father. He wasn't even aiming for your mother. You've done well despite it. We—we just expected too much of you, that's all. Let no one say you have not done well."

"Thank you, sir."

The silence lengthened unbearably. The room was growing warm. Miles's head ached from lack of sleep, and he felt nauseous from the combination of hunger and medications. He clambered awkwardly to his feet. "If you'll excuse me, sir . . ."

The old man waved a hand in dismissal. "Yes, you must have things to do . . ." He paused again, and looked at Miles quizzically. "What are you going to do now? It seems very strange to me. We have always been Vor, the warriors, even when war changed with the rest of it . . ."

He looked so shrunken, down in his chair. Miles pulled himself together into a semblence of cheerfulness. "Well, you know, there's always the other aristocratic line to fall back on. If I can't be a Service grunt, I'll be a town clown. I plan to be a famous epicure and lover of women. More fun than soldiering any day."

His grandfather fell in with his humor. "Yes, I always envied the breed—go to, boy . . ." He smiled, but Miles felt it was as forced as his own. It was a lie anyway— "drone" was a swear word in the old man's vocabulary. Miles collected Bothari and made his own escape.

Miles sat hunched in a battered armchair in a small private parlor overlooking the street side of the great old mansion, feet up, eyes closed. It was a seldom used room; there was a good chance of being left alone to brood in peace. He had never come to a more complete halt, a drained blankness numb even to pain. So much passion expended for nothing—a lifetime of nothing stretching endlessly into the future—because of a split second's stupid, angry self-consciousness . . .

There was a throat-clearing noise behind him, and a diffident voice; "Hi, Miles."

His eyes flicked open, and he felt suddenly a little less like a wounded animal hiding in its hole. "Elena! I gather you came up from Vorkosigan Surleau with Mother last night. Come on in."

She perched near him on the arm of another chair. "Yes, she knows what a treat it is for me to come to the capital. I almost feel like she's my mother, sometimes."

"Tell her that. It would please her."

"Do you really think so?" she asked shyly.

"Absolutely." He shook himself into alertness. Perhaps not a totally empty future . . .

She chewed gently on her lower lip, large eyes drinking in his face. "You look absolutely smashed."

He would not bleed on Elena. He banished his blackness in self-mockery, leaning back expansively and grinning. "Literally. Too true. I'll get over it. You, ah—heard all about it, I suppose."

"Yes. Did, um, it go all right with my lord Count?"

"Oh, sure. I'm the only grandson he's got, after all. Puts me in an excellent position—I can get away with anything."

"Did he ask you about changing your name?"

He stared. "What?"

"To the usual patronymic. He'd been talking about, when you—oh." She cut herself off, but Miles caught the full import of her half revelation.

"Oh, ho—when I became an officer, was he finally planning to break down and allow me my heir's names? Sweet of him—seventeen years after the fact." He stifled a sick anger beneath an ironic grin.

"I never understood what that was all about."

"What, my name—Miles Naismith, after my mother's father, instead of Piotr Miles, after both? It all goes back to that uproar when I was born. Apparently, after my parents had recovered from the soltoxin gas and they found out what the fetal damage was going to be—I'm not supposed to know this, by the way—Grandfather was all for an abortion. Got in a big fight with my parents—well, with Mother, I suppose, and Father caught in the middle—and when my father backed her up and faced him down, he got huffy and asked his name not be given me. He calmed down later, when he found I wasn't a total disaster." He smirked, and drummed his fingers on the chair arm. "So he was thinking of swallowing his words, was he? Perhaps it's just as well I washed out. He might have choked." He closed his teeth on further bitterness, and wished he could call back his last speech. No point in being more ugly in front of Elena than he already was.

"I know how hard you studied for it. I—I'm sorry."

He feigned a surface humor. "Not half as sorry as I am. I wish you could have taken my physicals. Between us we'd make a hell of an officer."

Something of the old frankness they had shared as children escaped her lips suddenly. "Yes, but by Barrayaran standards I'm more handicapped than you—I'm female. I wouldn't even be permitted to petition to take the tests."

His eyebrows lifted in wry agreement. "I know. Absurd. With what your father's taught you, all you'd need is a course in heavy weapons and you could roll right over nine-tenths of the fellows I saw out there. Think of it—Sergeant Elena Bothari."

She chilled. "Now you're teasing."

"Just speaking as one civilian to another," he half-apologized.

She nodded dark agreement, then brightened with remembered purpose. "Oh. Your mother sent me to get you for lunch."

"Ah." He pushed himself to his feet with a sibilant grunt. "There's an officer no one disobeys. The Admiral's Captain."

Elena smiled at the image. "Yes. Now, she was an officer for the Betans, and no one thinks she's strange, or criticizes her for wanting to break the rules."

"On the contrary. She's so strange nobody even thinks of trying to include her in the rules. She just goes on doing things her own way."

"I wish I were Betan," said Elena glumly.

"Oh, make no mistake—she's strange by Betan standards, too. Although I think you would like Beta Colony, parts of it," he mused.

"I'll never get off planet."

He eyed her sapiently. "What's got you down?"

She shrugged. "Oh, well, you know my father. He's such a conservative. He ought to have been born two hundred years ago. You're the only person I know who doesn't think he's weird. He's so paranoid."

"I know—but it's a very useful quality in a body-guard. His pathological suspiciousness has saved my life twice."

"You should have been born two hundred years ago, too."

"No, thanks. I'd have been slain at birth."

"Well, there is that," she admitted. "Anyway, just out of the blue this morning he started talking about arranging my marriage."

Miles stopped abruptly, and glanced up at her. "Really. What did he say?"

"Not much," she shrugged. "He just mentioned it. I wish—I don't know. I wish my mother were alive."

"Ah. Well . . . There's always my mother, if you want somebody to talk to. Or—or me. You can talk to me, can't you?"

She smiled gratefully. "Thanks." They came to the stairs. She paused; he waited.

"He never talks about my mother anymore, you know? Hasn't since I was about twelve. He used to tell me long stories—well, long for him—about her. I wonder if he's beginning to forget her."

"I shouldn't think so. I see him more than you do. He's never so much as looked at another woman," Miles offered reassuringly.

They started down the stairs. His aching legs did not move properly; he had to do a kind of penguin shuffle to achieve the steps. He glanced up at Elena self-consciously, and grasped the rail firmly.

"Shouldn't you be taking the lift tube?" she asked suddenly, watching his uncertain placement of his feet.

Don't you start treating me like a cripple, too . . . He glanced down the railing's gleaming helix. "They told me to stay off my legs. Didn't specify how . . ." He hopped up on the bannister, and shot her a wicked grin over his shoulder.

Her face reflected mixed amusement and horror. "Miles, you lunatic! If you fall off that, you'll break every bone in your body—"

He slid away from her, picking up speed rapidly. She cantered down the stairs after him, laughing; he lost her around the curvature. His grin died as he saw what awaited him at the bottom. "Oh, hell . . ." He was going too fast to brake . . .

"What the—"

"Watch out!"

He tumbled off the railing at the bottom of the staircase into the frantic clutch of a stocky, grey-haired man in officer's dress greens. They both scrambled to their feet as Elena arrived, out of breath, on the tessellated pavement of the front hall. Miles could feel the anguished heat in his face, and knew it was scarlet. The stocky man looked bemused. A second officer, a tall man with captain's tabs on the collar of his uniform, leaned on a walking stick and gave a brief surprised laugh.

Miles collected himself, coming more-or-less to attention. "Good afternoon, Father," he said coolly. He gave a little aggressive lift to his chin, defying anyone to comment on his unorthodox entrance.

Admiral Lord Aral Vorkosigan, Prime Minister of Barrayar in the service of Emperor Gregor Vorbarra, formerly Lord Regent of same, straightened his uniform jacket and cleared his throat. "Good afternoon, son." Only his eyes laughed. "I'm, ah—glad to see your injuries were not too serious."

Miles shrugged, secretly relieved to be spared more sardonic comments in public. "The usual."

"Excuse me a moment. Ah, good afternoon, Elena. Koudelka—what did you think of those ship cost figures of Admiral Hessman's?"

"I thought they went by awfully fast," replied the Captain.

"You thought so too, eh?"

"Do you think he's hiding something in them?"

"Perhaps. But what? His party budget? Is the contractor his brother-in-law? Or sheer slop? Peculation, or merely inefficiency? I'll put Illyan on the first possibility—I want you on the second. Put the squeeze on those numbers."

"They'll scream. They were screaming today."

"Don't believe it. I used to do those proposals myself

when I was on the General Staff. I know how much garbage goes into them. They're not really hurting until their voices go up at least two octaves."

Captain Koudelka grinned, and bowed himself out with a brief nod at Miles and Elena, and a very sketchy salute.

Miles and his father were left looking at each other, neither wishing to be the first to open the issue that lay between them. As if by mutual agreement, Lord Vorkosigan said only, "Well, am I late for lunch?"

"Just been called, I think, sir."

"Let us go in, then . . ." He made a little abortive lift of his arm, as if to offer his injured son assistance, but then clasped his hands tactfully behind his back. They walked on side by side, slowly.

Miles lay propped up in bed, still dressed for the day, with his legs stretched out correctly before him. He eyed them distastefully. Rebellious provinces—mutinous troops—quisling saboteurs . . . He should get up one more time, and wash and change to night clothes, but the effort required seemed heroic. No hero he. He was reminded of that fellow Grandfather told about, who accidentally shot his own horse out from under himself in the cavalry charge—called for another, and then did it again.

So his own words, it appeared, had set Sergeant Bothari thinking in just the channel Miles least desired. Eleana's image turned before his inner eye—the delicate aquiline profile, great dark eyes—cool length of leg, warm flare of hip—she looked, he thought, like a Countess in a drama. If only he could cast her in the role in reality . . . But such a Count!

An aristocrat in a play, to be sure. The deformed were invariably cast as plotting villains in Barrayaran drama. If he couldn't be a soldier, perhaps he had a future as a villain. "I'll carry the wench off," he muttered, experimentally dropping his voice half an octave, "and lock her in my dungeon."

His voice returned to its normal pitch with a regretful sigh. "Except I haven't got a dungeon. It would have to be the closet. Grandfather's right, we are a reduced generation. Anyway, they'd just rent a hero to rescue her. Some tall piece of meat—Kostolitz, maybe. And you know how those fights always come out—"

He slid to his feet and pantomimed across the room, Kostolitz's swords against—say—Miles's morningstar. A morningstar was a proper villainous weapon. It gave the concept of one's personal space some real authority. Stabbed, he died in Elena's arms as she swooned in grief—no, she'd be in Kostolitz's arms, celebrating.

Miles's eye fell on an antique mirror, clasped in a carven stand. "Capering dwarf," he growled. He had a sudden urge to smash it with his naked fists, shattered glass and blood flying—but the sound would bring the hall guard, and packs of relatives, and demands for explanation. He jerked the mirror around to face the wall instead, and flopped onto the bed.

Lying back, he gave the problem more serious attention. He tried to imagine himself, rightly and properly, asking his father to be his go-between to Sergeant Bothari. Horrific. He sighed, and writhed vainly for a more comfortable position. Only seventeen, too young to marry even by Barrayaran standards, and quite unemployed, now—it would be years, probably, before he would be in a sufficiently independent position to offer for Elena against parental backing. Surely she would be snapped up long before then.

And Elena herself . . . What was in it for her? What pleasure, to be climbed all over by an ugly, twisted shrimp—to be stared at in public, in a world where native custom and imported medicine combined ruthlessly to eliminate even the mildest physical deformity—doubly stared at, because of their ludicrous contrast? Could the dubious privileges of an obsolete rank more drained of meaning with each passing year make up for that? A rank totally without meaning off Barrayar, he knew—in eighteen years of residence here, his own mother had never come to regard the Vor system as anything other than a planet-wide mass hallucination.

There came a double rap upon his door. Authoritatively firm; courteously brief. Miles smiled ironically, sighed, and sat up.

"Come in, Father."

Lord Vorkosigan poked his head around the carved doorframe. "Still dressed? It's late. You should be getting some rest." Somewhat inconsistently, he let himself in and pulled up a desk chair, turning it around and sitting astride it, arms comfortably athwart its back. He was still dressed himself, Miles noted, in the dress greens he wore every working day. Now that he was but Prime Minister, and not Regent and therefore titular commander of the armed forces, Miles wondered if the old Admiral's uniform was still correct. Or had it simply grown to him?

"I, ah," his father began, and paused. He cleared his throat, delicately. "I was wondering what your thinking was now, for your next step. Your alternate plans."

Miles's lips tightened, and he shrugged. "There never were any alternate plans. I'd planned to succeed. More fool I."

Lord Vorkosigan tilted his head in negation. "If it's any consolation, you were very close. I talked to the selection board commander today. Do you—want to know your score on the writtens?"

"I thought they never released those. Just an alphabetical list: in or out."

Lord Vorkosigan spread his hand, offering. Miles shook his head. "Let it go. It doesn't matter. It was hopeless from the beginning. I was just too stiff-necked to admit it."

"Not so. We all knew it would be difficult. But I would never have let you put that much effort on something I thought impossible."

"I must have inherited the neck from you."

They exchanged a brief, ironic nod. "Well, you couldn't have had it from your mother," Lord Vorkosigan admitted.

"She's not—disappointed, is she?"

"Hardly. You know her lack of enthusiasm for the military. Hired killers, she called us once. Almost the first thing she ever said to me." He looked fondly reminiscent.

Miles grinned in spite of himself. "She really said that to you?"

Lord Vorkosigan grinned back. "Oh, yes. But she married me anyway, so perhaps it wasn't all that heartfelt." He grew more serious. "It's true, though. If I had any doubts about your potential as an officer—"

Miles stiffened inwardly.

"—it was perhaps in that area. To kill a man, it helps if you can first take away his face. A neat mental trick. Handy for a soldier. I'm not sure you have the narrowness of vision required. You can't help seeing all around. You're like your mother, you always have that clear view of the back of your own head."

"Never knew you for narrow, sir."

"Ah, but I lost the trick of it. That's why I went into politics." Lord Vorkosigan smiled, but the smile faded. "To your cost, I'm afraid."

The remark triggered a painful memory. "Sir," asked Miles hesitantly, "is that why you never made the bid for the Imperium that everyone was expecting? Because your heir was—" a vague gesture at his body silently implied the forbidden term, "deformed".

Lord Vorkosigan's brows drew together. His voice dropped suddenly to near a whisper, making Miles jump. "Who has said so?"

"Nobody," Miles replied nervously.

His father flung himself out of his chair and snapped back and forth across the room. "Never," he hissed, "let anyone say so. It is an insult to both our honors. I gave my oath to Ezar Vorbarra on his deathbed to serve his grandson—and I have done so. Period. End of argument."

Miles smiled placatingly. "I wasn't arguing."

Lord Vorkosigan looked around, and gave vent to a short chuckle. "Sorry. You just hit my jitter trigger. Not your fault, boy." He sat back down, controlled again. "You know how I feel about the Imperium. The witch's christening gift, accursed. Try telling *them* that, though . . ." He shook his head.

"Surely Gregor can't suspect you of ambition. You've

done more for him than anyone, right through Vordarian's Pretendership, the Third Cetagandan War, the Komarr Revolt—he wouldn't even be here today—"

Lord Vorkosigan grimaced. "Gregor is in a rather tender state of mind at the moment. Just come to full power—and by my oath, it is real power—and itching, after sixteen years of being governed by what he refers to privately as 'the old geezers', to try its limits. I have no wish to set myself up as a target."

"Oh, come on. Gregor's not so faithless."

"No, indeed, but he is under a great many new pressures that I can no longer protect—" he cut himself off with a fist-closing gesture. "Just alternate plans. Which brings us, I hope, back to the original question."

Miles rubbed his face tiredly, pressing fingertips against his eyes. "I don't know, sir."

"You could," said Lord Vorkosigan neutrally, "ask Gregor for an Imperial order."

"What, shove me into the Service by force? By the sort of political favoritism you've stood against all your life?" Miles sighed. "If I were going to get in that way, I should have done it first, before failing the tests. Now—no. No."

"But," Lord Vorkosigan went on earnestly, "you have too much talent and energy to waste on idleness. There are other forms of service. I wanted to put an idea or two to you. Just to think on."

"Go ahead."

"Officer, or not, you will be Count Vorkosigan someday." He held up a hand as Miles opened his mouth to object. "Someday. You will inevitably have a place in the government, always barring revolution or some other social catastrophe. You will represent our ancestral district. A district which has, frankly, been shamefully neglected. Your grandfather's recent illness isn't the only reason. I've been taken up with the press of other work, and before that we both pursued military careers—"

Tell me about it, Miles thought wearily.

"The end result is, there is a lot of work to be done there. Now, with a bit of legal training—"

"A *lawyer*?" Miles said, aghast. "You want me to be a lawyer? That's as bad as being a tailor—"

"Beg pardon?" asked Lord Vorkosigan, missing the connection.

"Never mind. Something Grandfather said."

"Actually, I hadn't planned to mention the idea to your grandfather." Lord Vorkosigan cleared his throat. "But given some ground in government principles, I thought you might, ah, deputize for your grandfather in the district. Government was never all warfare, even in the Time of Isolation, you know."

Sounds like you've been thinking about it for a while, Miles thought resentfully. Did you ever *really* believe I could make the grade, Father? He looked at Lord Vorkosigan more doubtfully. "There's not anything you're not telling me, is there, sir? About your—health, or anything?"

"Oh, no," Lord Vorkosigan reassured him. "Although in my line of work, you never know from one day to the next."

I wonder, thought Miles warily, what else is going on between Gregor and my father? I have a queasy feeling I'm getting about ten percent of the real story . . .

Lord Vorkosigan blew out his breath, and smiled. "Well. I'm keeping you from your rest, which you need at this point." He rose.

"I wasn't sleepy, sir."

"Do you want me to get you anything to help . . . ?" Lord Vorkosigan offered, cautiously tender.

"No, I have some painkillers they gave me at the infirmary. Two of those and I'll be swimming in slow motion." Miles made flippers of his hands, and rolled his eyes back.

Lord Vorkosigan nodded, and withdrew.

Miles lay back and tried to recapture Elena in his mind. But the cold breath of political reality blown in with his father withered his fantasies, like frost out of season. He swung to his feet and shuffled to his bathroom for a dose of his slow-motion medicine.

Two down, and a swallow of water. All of them, whispered something from the back of his brain, and you could come to a complete stop . . . He banged the nearly-full container back onto the shelf.

His eyes gave back a muted spark from the bathroom mirror. "Grandfather is right. The only way to go down is fighting."

He returned to bed, to re-live his moment of error on the wall in an endless loop until sleep relieved him of himself.

CHAPTER THREE   *   *   *

Miles was awakened in a dim grey light by a servant apprehensively touching his shoulder.

"Lord Vorkosigan? Lord Vorkosigan?" the man murmured.

Miles peered through slitted eyes, feeling thick with sleep, as though moving under water. What hour—and why was the idiot miscalling him by his father's title? New, was he? No . . .

Cold consciousness washed over him, and his stomach knotted, as the full significance of the man's words penetrated. He sat up, head swimming, heart sinking. "What?"

"The—y—your father requests you dress and join him downstairs immediately." The man's tumbling tongue confirmed his fear.

It was the hour before dawn. Yellow lamps made small warm pools within the library as Miles entered. The windows were blue-grey cold translucent rectangles, balanced on the cusp of night, neither transmitting light from without nor reflecting it from within. His father stood, half-dressed in uniform trousers, shirt, and slippers, talking in a grave undertone with two men. Their personal physician, and an aide in the uniform of the Imperial Residence. His father—Count Vorkosigan? —looked up to meet his eyes.

"Grandfather, sir?" asked Miles softly.

The new Count nodded. "Very quietly, in his sleep,

about two hours ago. He felt no pain, I think." His father's voice was low and clear, without tremor, but his face seemed more lined than usual, almost furrowed. Set, expressionless; the determined commander. Situation under control. Only his eyes, and only now and then, through a passing trick of angle, held the look of some stricken and bewildered child. The eyes frightened Miles far more than the stern mouth.

Miles's own vision blurred, and he brushed the foolish water from his eyes with the back of his hand in a brusque, angry swipe. "God damn it," he choked numbly. He had never felt smaller.

His father focused on him uncertainly. "I—" he began. "He's been hanging by a thread for months, you know that . . ."

And I cut that thread yesterday, Miles thought miserably. I'm sorry . . . But he said only, "Yes, sir."

The funeral for the old hero was nearly a State occasion. Three days of panoply and pantomime, thought Miles wearily; what's it all for? Proper clothing was produced, hastily, in somber correct black. Vorkosigan House became a chaotic staging-area for forays into public set-pieces. The lying-in-state at Vorhartung Castle, where the Council of Counts met. The eulogies. The procession, which was nearly a parade, thanks to the loan from Gregor Vorbarra of a military band in dress uniform and a contingent of his purely decorative horse cavalry. The interment.

Miles had thought his grandfather was the last of his generation. Not quite, it seemed, for the damndest set of ancient croaking martinets and their crones, in black like flapping crows, came creeping from whatever woodwork they'd been lurking in. Miles, grimly polite, endured their shocked and pitying stares when introduced as Piotr Vorkosigan's grandson, and their interminable reminiscences about people he'd never heard of, who'd died before he was born, and of whom—he sincerely hoped—he would never hear again.

Even after the last spadeful of dirt had been packed down, it was not ended. Vorkosigan House was invaded, that afternoon and evening, by hordes of—you couldn't call them well-wishers, exactly, he reflected—but friends, acquaintances, military men, public men, their wives, the courteous, the curious, and more relatives than he cared to think about.

Count and Countess Vorkosigan were nailed downstairs. Social duty was always yoked, for his father, to political duty, and so was doubly inescapable. But when his cousin Ivan Vorpatril arrived, in tow of his mother Lady Vorpatril, Miles determined to escape to the only bolt-hole left not occupied by enemy forces. Ivan had passed his candidacy exams, Miles had heard; he didn't think he could tolerate the details. He plucked a couple of gaudy blooms from a funeral floral display in passing, and fled by lift tube to the top floor, and refuge.

Miles knocked on the carved wood door. "Who's there?" Elena's voice floated through faintly. He tried the enamel-patterned knob, found it unlocked, and snaked a hand waving the flowers around the door. Her voice added, "Oh, come in, Miles."

He bobbed around the door, lean in black, and grinned tentatively. She was sitting in an antique chair by her window. "How did you know it was me?" Miles asked.

"Well, it was either you or—nobody brings me flowers on their knees." Her eye lingered a moment on the doorknob, unconsciously revealing the height scale used for her deduction.

Miles promptly dropped to his knees and quick-marched across the rug, to present his offering with a flourish. "Voila!" he cried, surprising a laugh from her. His legs protested this abuse by going into painful cramping spasms. "Ah . . ." He cleared his throat, and added in a much smaller voice, "Do you suppose you could help me up? These damn grav-crutches . . ."

"Oh, dear." Elena assisted him on to her narrow bed, made him put his legs out straight, and returned to her chair.

Miles looked around the tiny bedroom. "Is this closet the best we can do for you?"

"I like it. I like the window on the street," she

assured him. "It's bigger than my father's room here."
She tested the flowers' scent, a musty green odor. Miles
immediately regretted not sorting through to find some
of the more perfumy kind. She looked up at him in
sudden suspicion. "Miles, where did you get these?"

He flushed, faintly guilty. "Borrowed 'em from Grandfather. Believe me, they'll never be missed. It's a jungle
down there."

She shook her head helplessly. "You're incorrigible."
But she smiled.

"You don't mind?" he asked anxiously. "I thought
you'd get more enjoyment from them than he would, at
this point."

"Just so nobody thinks I filched them myself!"

"Refer them to me," he offered grandly. He jerked up
his chin. She was gazing into the flowers' delicate structure more somberly. "Now what are you thinking? Sad
thoughts?"

"Honestly, my face might as well be a window."

"Not at all. Your face is more like—like water. All
reflections and shifting lights—I never know what's lurking in the depths." He dropped his voice at the end, to
indicate the mystery of the depths.

Elena smiled derisively, then sighed seriously. "I was
just thinking—I've never put flowers on my mother's
grave."

He brightened at the prospect of a project. "Do you
want to? We could slip out the back—load up a cart or
two—nobody'd notice . . ."

"Certainly not!" she said indignantly. "This is quite
bad enough of you." She turned the flowers in the light
from the window, silvered from the chill autumn cloud-
iness. "Anyway, I don't know where it is."

"Oh? How strange. As fixated as the Sergeant is on
your mother, I'd have thought he'd be just the pilgrimmage type. Maybe he doesn't like to think about her
death, though."

"You're right about that. I asked him about it once, to
go and see where she's buried and so on, and it was like
talking to a wall. You know how he can be."

"Yes, very like a wall. Particularly when it falls on

someone." A theorizing gleam lit Miles's eye. "Maybe it's guilt. Maybe she was one of those rare women who die in childbirth—she did die about the time you were born, didn't she?"

"He said it was a flyer accident."

"Oh."

"But another time he said she'd drowned."

"Hm?" The gleam deepened to a persistent smoulder. "If she'd ditched her flyer in a river or something, they could both be true. Or if he ditched it . . ."

Elena shivered. Miles caught it, and castigated himself inwardly for being an insensitive clod. "Oh, sorry. Didn't mean to—I'm in a gruesome mood today, I'm afraid," he apologized. "It's all this blasted black." He flapped his elbows in imitation of a carrion bird.

He lapsed into introspective quiet for a time, meditating on the ceremonies of death. Elena fell in with his silence, gazing wistfully down on the darkly glittering throng of Barrayar's upper class, passing in and out four floors below her window.

"We could find out," he said suddenly, startling her from her reverie.

"What?"

"Where your mother's buried. And we wouldn't even have to ask anyone."

"How?"

He grinned, swinging to his feet. "I'm not going to say. You'd go all wobbly on me, like that time we went spelunking down at Vorkosigan Surleau and found the old guerilla weapons cache. You'll never get another chance in your life to drive one of those old tanks, you know."

She made doubtful noises. Apparently her memory of the incident was vivid and awful, even though she had avoided being caught in the landslide. But she followed.

They entered the darkened downstairs library cautiously. Miles paused to brace the duty guard outside it with an off-color smirk, lowering his voice confidentially. "Suppose you could sort of rattle the door if anyone comes, Corporal? We'd, ah— rather not have any surprise interruptions."

The duty guard's return smirk was knowing. "Of course, Lord Mi—Lord Vorkosigan." He eyed Elena with fresh speculation, one eyebrow quirking.

"Miles," Elena whispered furiously as the door swung closed, cutting off the steady murmur of voices, clink of glass and silver, soft tread of feet from Piotr Vorkosigan's wake that penetrated from nearby rooms. "Do you realize what he's going to think?"

"Evil to him who evil thinks," he flung gaily over his shoulder. "Just so he doesn't think of this . . ." He palmed the lock to the comconsole, with its double-scrambled links to military headquarters and the Imperial Residence, that sat incongruously before the carved marble fireplace. Elena's mouth fell open in astonishment as its force screen parted. A few passes of his hands brought the holovid plates to life.

"I thought that was top security!" she gasped.

" 'Tis. But Captain Koudelka was giving me a little tutoring on the side, before, when I was—" a bitter smile, a jerk of the wrist, "studying. He used to tap into the battle computers—the real ones, at headquarters— and run simulations for me. I thought he might not have remembered to unkey me . . ." he was half-absorbed, entering a tattoo of complex directions.

"What are you doing?" she asked nervously.

"Entering Captain Koudelka's access code. To get military records."

"Ye gods, Miles!"

"Don't worry about it." He patted her hand. "We're in here necking, remember? Nobody's likely to come in here tonight but Captain Koudelka, and he won't mind that. We can't miss. Thought I'd start with your father's Service record. Ah, here . . ." The holovid plate threw up a flat screen and began displaying written records. "There's bound to be something about your mother on it, that we can use to unravel," he paused, sitting back puzzled, "the mystery . . ." He flipped through several screens.

"What?" Elena agitated.

"Thought I'd peek into near the time you were born—I thought he'd quit the Service just before, right?"

"Right."

"Did he ever say he was involuntarily medically discharged?"

"No . . ." She peered over his shoulder. "That's funny. It doesn't say why."

"Tell you what's funnier. His entire record for most of the preceding year is sealed. Your time. And the code on it—very hot. I can't crack it without triggering a double-check, which would end—yes, that's Captain Illyan's personal mark. I definitely don't want to talk to him." He quailed at the thought of accidentally summoning the attention of Barrayar's Chief of Imperial Security.

"Definitely," croaked Elena, staring at him in fascination.

"Well, let's do some time-travelling," Miles pattered on. "Back, back . . . Your father doesn't seem to have gotten along too well with this Commodore Vorrutyer fellow."

Elena perked with interest. "Was that the same as the Admiral Vorrutyer who was killed at Escobar?"

"Um . . . Yes, Ges Vorrutyer. Hm." Bothari had been the commodore's batman, it appeared, for several years. Miles was surprised. He'd had the vague impression that Bothari had served under his father as a ground combat soldier since the beginning of time. Bothari's service with Vorrutyer ended in a constellation of reprimands, black marks, discipline parades, and sealed medical reports. Miles, conscious of Elena staring over his shoulder, whipped past these quickly. Oddly inconsistent. Some, bizarrely petty, were marked with ferocious punishments. Others, astonishingly serious—had Bothari really held an engineering tech at plasma-arc-point in a lavatory for sixteen hours? and for God's sake, why? —disappeared into the medical reports and resulted in no discipline at all.

Going farther into the past, the record steadied. A lot of combat in his twenties. Commendations, citations for being wounded, more commendations. Excellent marks in basic training. Recruiting records. "Recruiting was a lot simpler in those days," Miles said enviously.

"Oh! Are my grandparents on that?" asked Elena eagerly. "He never talks about them, either. I gather his mother died when he was rather young. He's never even told me her name."

"Marusia," Miles sounded out, peering. "Fuzzy photostat."

"That's pretty," said Elena, sounding pleased. "And his father's?"

Whoops, thought Miles. The recopied photostat was not so fuzzy that he couldn't make out the blunt, uncapitalized "unknown" printed in some forgotten clerk's hand. Miles swallowed, realizing at last why a certain insulting epithet seemed to get under Bothari's skin when all others were allowed to roll off, patiently disdained.

"Maybe I can make it out," Elena offered, misinterpreting his delay.

The screen went blank at a twitch of his hand. "Konstantine," Miles declared firmly, without hesitation. "Same as his. But both his parents were dead by the time he joined the Service."

"Konstantine Bothari junior," Elena mused. "Hm."

Miles stared into the blank screen, and suppressed an urge to scream with frustration. Another damned artificial social wedge driven between himself and Elena. A father who was a bastard was about as far from being "right and proper" for a young Barrayaran virgin as anything he could think of. And it was obviously no secret—his father must know, and God knew how many hundreds of other people besides. Equally obviously, Elena did not. She was rightfully proud of her father, his elite service, his position of high trust. Miles knew how painfully hard she struggled sometimes for some expression of approval from the old stone carving. How strange to realize that pain might cut both ways—did Bothari then dread the loss of that scarcely-acknowledged admiration? Well, the Sergeant's semi-secret was safe with him.

He flipped, fast-forward, through the years of Bothari's

life. "Still no sign of your mother," he said to Elena.
"She must be under that seal. Damn, and I thought this
was going to be easy." He stared thoughtfully into space.
"Try hospital records. Deaths, births—you sure you were
born here in Vorbarr Sultana?"

"As far as I know."

Several minutes of tedious search produced records
on a fair number of Botharis, none related to the Sergeant or Elena in any way. "Ah ha!" Miles broke out
suddenly. "I know what I haven't tried. Imp Mil!"

"They don't have an obstetrics department," Elena
said doubtfully.

"But if an accident—soldier's wife and all that—maybe
she was rushed to the nearest facility, and the Imperial
Military Hospital was it . . ." He crooned over the machine. "Searching, searching . . . huh!"

"Did you find me?" she asked excitedly.

"No—I found me." He flipped over screen after screen
of documentation. "What a scramble it must have been,
making military research clean up after its own prod-
uct. Lucky for me they'd imported those uterine replicators—yes, there they are—they could never have tried
some of those treatments *in vivo*, they'd have killed
Mother. There's good old Dr. Vaagen—ah ha! So he was
in military research, before. Makes sense—I guess he
was their poison expert. I wish I'd known more about
this when I was a kid, I could have agitated for two
birthdays, one when Mother had the cesarian, and one
when they finally popped me out of the replicator."

"Which did they choose?"

"Cesarian day. I'm glad. Makes me only six months
younger that you are. Otherwise you'd be nearly a year
older—and I've been warned about older women . . ."
This babble won a smile at last, and he relaxed a little.

He paused, staring at the screen with slitted eyes,
then entered another search query. "That's weird," he
muttered.

"What?"

"A secret military medical research project—with my
father as project director, no less."

"I never knew he was in research too," said Elena, sounding enormously impressed. "He sure got around."

"That's what's curious. He was a Staff tactician. Never had anything to do with research, as far as I know." A by-now-familiar code appeared at his next inquiry. "Blast! Another seal. Ask a simple question, get a simple brick wall . . . There's Dr. Vaagen, hand-in-rubber-glove with Father. Vaagen must have been doing the actual work, then. That explains that. I want under that seal, damn it . . ." He whistled a soundless tune, staring into space, fingers drumming.

Elena began to look dampened. "You're getting that mulish look," she observed nervously. "Maybe we should just let it go. It doesn't really matter by now."

"Illyan's mark's not on this one. It might be enough . . ."

Elena bit her lip. "Look, Miles, it's not really—" but he was already launched. "What are you doing?"

"Trying one of Father's old access codes. I'm pretty sure of it, all but a few digits."

Elena gulped.

"Jackpot!" Miles cried softly, as the screen began disgorging data at last. He read avidly. "So that's where those uterine replicators came from! They brought them back from Escobar, after the invasion failed. The spoils of war, by God. Seventeen of them, loaded and working. They must have seemed like really high tech, in their day. I wonder if we looted them?"

Elena paled. "Miles—they weren't doing human experiments or, or anything like that, were they? Surely your father wouldn't have countenanced . . ."

"I don't know. Dr. Vaagen can be pretty, um, one track, about his research . . ." Relief eased his voice. "Oh, I see what was going on. Look here . . ." The holoscreen began scrolling yet another file in midair; he waved his fingers through it. "They were all sent to the Imperial Service Orphanage. They must have been some children of our men killed at Escobar."

Elena's voice tensed. "Children of *men* killed at Escobar? But where are their mothers?"

They stared at each other. "But we've never had any

women in the Service, except for a few civilian medtechs," began Miles.

Elena's long fingers closed urgently on his shoulder.
"Look at the dates."

He scrolled the file again.

"Miles," she hissed.

"Yes, I see it." He stopped the screen. "Female infant
released to the custody of Admiral Aral Vorkosigan. Not
sent to the orphanage with the rest."

"The date—Miles, that's my birthday!"

He unpeeled her fingers. "Yes, I know. Don't crush
my collarbone, please."

"Could it be me? Is it me?" Her face tightened with
hope and dismay.

"I—it's all numbers, you see," he said cautiously.
"But there's plenty of medical identification—footprints,
retinal, bloodtype—stick your foot over here."

Elena hopped about, removing shoes and hose. Miles
helped her place her right foot over the holovid plate.
He restrained himself with a twitching effort from running a hand up that incredible silken length of thigh,
blooming from her rumpled skirts. Skin like an orchid
petal. He bit his lips; pain, pain would help him to
focus. Damn tight trousers anyway. He hoped she
wouldn't notice . . .

Setting up the optical laser check helped his focus
rather better. A flickering red light played over her sole
for a few seconds. He set the machine to comparing
whorls and ridges. "Allowing for the change from infant
to adult—my God, Elena, it is you!" He preened. If he
couldn't be a soldier, perhaps he had a future as a
detective . . .

Elena's dark gaze transfixed him. "But what does it
mean?" Her face congealed suddenly. "Don't I have—
was I—am I some kind of clone, or manufactured?" She
blinked suddenly liquid eyes, and her voice trembled. "I
don't have a mother? No mother, and it was all just—"

The triumph of his successful identification seeped
out of him at her distress. Clod! Now he'd turned her
dream mother into a nightmare—no, it was her own
flying imagination that was doing that. "Uh, uh—no,

certainly not! What an idea! You're obviously your father's daughter—no insult intended—it just means your mother was killed at Escobar, instead of here. And furthermore," he sprang up to declaim dramatically, "this makes you my long-lost sister!"

"Huh?" said Elena, bewildered.

"Sure. Or—anyway, there's a 1/17th chance that we came out of the same replicator." He spun about her, conjuring farce against her terrors. "My 1/17th twin sister! It must be Act V! Take heart, this means you're bound to marry the Prince in the next scene!"

She laughed through her tears. The door rattled ominously. The corporal outside declaimed with unnecessary volume, "Good evening, sir!"

"Shoes! My shoes! Give me back my stockings!" hissed Elena.

Miles thrust them at her, killed the comconsole, and sealed it with one frantic, fluid motion. He catapulted onto the sofa, grabbed Elena about the waist and carrying her down with him. She giggled and swore at him, struggling with her second shoe. One tear was still making a glistening track down her cheek.

He slipped a hand up into her shining hair, and bent her face toward his. "We better make this look good. I don't want to arouse Captain Koudelka's suspicions." He hesitated, his grin fading into seriousness. Her lips melted onto his.

The lights flicked on; they sprang apart. He peered up over her shoulder, and forgot for a moment how to exhale.

Captain Koudelka. Sergeant Bothari. *And* Count Vorkosigan.

Captain Koudelka looked suffused, a slight upward curl escaping from one corner of his mouth as if from enormous inward pressure. He glanced sideways at his companions, and tamped it out. The Sergeant's craggy face was icy. The Count was darkening rapidly.

Miles finally found something to do with all the air he'd taken in. "All right," he said in a firm didactic tone, "Now, after 'Grant me this boon,' on the next line you say, 'With all my heart; and much it joys me too, to see you are become so penitent.' " He glanced up most impenitently at his father. "Good evening, sir. Are we taking up your space? We can go practice elsewhere . . ."

"Yes, let's," Elena squeaked, picking up her cue with alacrity. She produced a rather inane smile for the three adults as Miles towed her safely past. Captain Koudelka returned the smile with all his heart. The Count somehow managed to smile at her and frown menacingly at Miles at the same time. The Sergeant's frown was democratically universal. The duty guard's smirk broadened to a muffled snicker as they fled down the hall.

"Can't miss, eh?" Elena snarled out of the corner of her mouth at Miles as they rose up the lift tube.

He executed a pirouette in midair, shamelessly. "A strategic withdrawal in good order; what more can you ask for being out-gunned, out-numbered, and out-ranked? We were just practicing that old play. Very cultural. Who could possibly object? I think I'm a genius."

"I think you're an idiot," she said fiercely. "My other stocking is hanging over the back of your shoulder."

"Oh." He twisted his neck for a look, and plucked off the filmy, clinging garment. He held it out to her with a sickly, apologetic smile. "I guess that didn't look too good."

She glared at him and snatched it back. "And now I'm going to get lectured at—he treats every male that comes near me like a potential rapist anyway—he'll probably forbid me to speak to you, too, now. Or send me back to the country forever . . ." Her eyes were swimming for their lives. They reached the door. "And on top of that, he's—he's *lied* to me about my mother—"

She fled into her bedroom, slamming the door so hard that she came close to taking off a few fingers from the hand Miles was raising in protest. He leaned against the door and called through the heavy carved wood anxiously. "You don't know that! There's undoubtedly some perfectly logical explanation—I'll get it figured out—"

"Go AWAY!" her muffled wail came back.

He shuffled uncertainly around the hall for a few

more minutes, hoping for a second chance, but the door remained uncompromisingly blank and silent. After a time he became conscious of the stiff figure of the floor duty guard at the end of the corridor. The man was politely not looking at him. The Prime Minister's security detail was, after all, among the most discreet, as well as the most alert, available. Miles swore under his breath, and shuffled back to the lift tube.

CHAPTER FOUR ✳ ✳ ✳

Miles ran into his mother in the back passage downstairs.

"Have you seen your father lately, heart?" Countess Vorkosigan asked him.

"Yes," unfortunately, "he went into the library with Captain Koudelka and the Sergeant."

"Sneaking off for a drink," she analyzed wryly, "with his old troopers. Well, I can't blame him. He's so tired. It's been a ghastly day. And I know he hasn't gotten enough sleep." She looked him over penetratingly. "How have you been sleeping?"

Miles shrugged. "All right."

"Mm. I'd better go catch him before he has more than one—ethanol has an unfortunate tendency to make him blunt, and that egg-sucker Count Vordrozda just arrived, in company with Admiral Hessman. He'll have trouble ahead if those two are getting in bed together."

"I shouldn't think the far right could muster that much support, with all the old soldiers solidly behind Father."

"Oh, Vordrozda's not a rightist at heart. He's just personally ambitious, and he'll ride any pony that's going his way. He's been oozing around Gregor for months ..." Anger sparked in her grey eyes. "Flattery and innuendo, oblique criticisms and these nasty little barbs stuck in all the boy's self doubts—I've watched him at work. I don't like him," she said positively.

42

Miles grinned. "I never would have guessed. But surely you don't have to worry about Gregor." His mother's habit of referring to the Emperor as if he were her rather backward adopted child always tickled him. In a sense it was true, as the former Regent had been Gregor's personal as well as political guardian during his minority.

She grimaced. "Vordrozda's not the only one who wouldn't hesitate to corrupt the boy in any area he could sink his claws into—moral, political, what you will—if he thought it would advance himself one centimeter, and damn the long range good of Barrayar—or of Gregor, for that matter." Miles recognized this instantly as a quote from his mother's sole political oracle, his father. "I don't know why these people can't write a constitution. Oral law—what a way to try and run an interstellar power." This was homegrown opinion, pure Betan.

"Father's been in power so long," said Miles equably. "I think it would take a gravity torpedo blast to shift him out of office."

"That's been tried," remarked Countess Vorkosigan, growing abstracted. "I wish he'd get serious about retiring. We've been lucky so far," her eye fell on him wistfully, "—mostly."

She's tired too, Miles thought.

"The politicking never stops," she added, staring at the floor. "Not even for his father's funeral." She brightened wickedly. "Nor do his relations. If you see him before I do, tell him Lady Vorpatril's looking for him. That'll make his day—no, better not. We'd never be able to find him, then."

Miles raised his brows. "What dooo Aunt Vorpatril want him to do for her now?"

"Well, ever since Lord Vorpatril died she's been expecting him to stand in loco parentis to that idiot Ivan, which is fine, up to a point. But she nailed me a while ago, when she couldn't find Aral—seems she wants Aral to stand the boy up in a corner somewhere and brace him for—er—swiving the servant girls, which ought to embarrass them both thoroughly. I've never understood why these people won't clip their kids' tubes and turn them loose at age twelve to work out their own damnation, like sensible folk. You may as well try to stop a sandstorm with a windsock ..." She went off toward the library, muttering her favorite swear-word under her breath, "Barrayarans!"

Wet darkness had fallen outside, turning the windows into dim mirrors of the subdued and mannered revelry within Vorkosigan House. Miles stared into his own reflection in passing; dark hair, grey eyes, pale shadowed face, features too sharp and strongly marked to satisfy aesthetics. And an idiot, to boot.

The hour reminded him of dinner, probably cancelled due to the press of events. He determined to forage among the canapes, and collect enough to sustain a strategic retreat back to his bedroom for the rest of the evening. He peered around a hall arch, to be sure none of the dreaded geriatric set were nearby. The room appeared to contain only middle-aged people he didn't know. He nipped over to a table, and began stuffing food into a fine fabric napkin.

"Stay away from those purple things," a familiar, affable voice warned in a whisper. "I think they're some kind of seaweed. Is your mother on a nutrition kick again?"

Miles looked up into the open, annoyingly handsome face of his second cousin, Ivan Vorpatril. Ivan too held a napkin, filled close to capacity. His eyes looked slightly hunted. A peculiar bulge interrupted the smooth lines of his brand-new cadet's uniform jacket.

Miles nodded toward the bulge, and whispered in astonishment, "Are they letting you carry a weapon already?"

"Hell, no." Ivan flicked the jacket open after a conspiratorial glance around, probably for Lady Vorpatril. "It's a bottle of your father's wine. Got it from one of the servants before he'd poured it into those itty-bitty glasses. Say—any chance of you being my native guide to some out-of-the-way corner of this mausoleum? The duty guards don't let you wander around by yourself, upstairs. The wine is good, the food is good, except for those purple things, but my God, the company at this party! . . ."

Miles nodded agreement in principle, even though he was inclined to include Ivan himself in the category of "my God the company." "All right. You pick up another bottle of wine," that should be enough to anesthetize him to tolerance, "and I'll let you hide out in my bedroom. That's where I was going anyway. Meet you by the lift tube."

Miles stretched out his legs on his bed with a sigh as Ivan pooled their picnic and opened the first bottle of wine. Ivan emptied a generous third of the bottle into each of the two bathroom tumblers, and handed one to his crippled cousin.

"I saw old Bothari carrying you off the other day." Ivan nodded toward the injured legs, and took a refreshing gulp. Grandfather, Miles thought, would have had a fit to see that particular vintage treated so cavalierly. He took a more respectful sip himself, by way of libation to the old man's ghost, even though Grandfather's tart assertion that Miles couldn't tell a good vintage from last Tuesday's washwater was not far off the mark. "Too bad," Ivan went on cheerfully. "You're really the lucky one, though."

"Oh?" muttered Miles, closing his teeth on a canape.

"Hell yes. Training starts tomorrow, y'know—"

"So I've heard."

"—I've got to report to my dormitory by midnight at the latest. Thought I was going to spend my last night as a free man partying, but instead I got stuck here. Mother, y'know. But tomorrow we take our preliminary oaths to the Emperor, and by God! if I'll let her treat me like a boy after that!" He paused to consume a small stuffed sandwich. "Think of me, out running around in the rain at dawn tomorrow, while you're tucked away all cozy in here . . ."

"Oh, I will." Miles took another sip, and another.

"Only two breaks in three years," Ivan rambled on between bites. "I might as well be a condemned prisoner. No wonder they call it service. Servitude is more like it." Another gulp, to wash down a meat-stuffed pastry. "But your time is all your own—you can do whatever you want with it."

"Every minute," agreed Miles blandly. Neither the Emperor nor anyone else demanded his service. He couldn't sell it—couldn't give it away . . .

Ivan, blessèdly, fell silent for a few minutes, refueling. After a time he said hesitantly. "No chance of your father coming up here, is there?"

Miles jerked his chin up. "What, you're not afraid of him, are you?"

Ivan snorted. "The man turns entire General Staffs to pudding, for God's sake. I'm just the Emperor's rawest recruit. Doesn't he terrify you?"

Miles considered the question seriously. "Not exactly, no. Not in the way you mean."

Ivan rolled his eyes heavenward in disbelief.

"Actually," added Miles, thinking back to the recent scene in the library, "if you're trying to duck him this might not be the best place, tonight."

"Oh?" Ivan swirled his wine in the bottom of his cup. "I've always had the feeling he doesn't like me," he added glumly.

"Oh, he doesn't mind you," said Miles, taking pity. "At least as you appear on his horizon at all. Although I think I was fourteen before I found out that Ivan wasn't your middle name." Miles cut himself off. That-idiot-Ivan was beginning a lifetime of Imperial service tomorrow. Lucky-Miles was emphatically not. He took another gulp of wine, and longed for sleep. They finished the canapes, and Ivan emptied the first bottle and opened the second.

There came an authoritative double knock on the door. Ivan sprang to his feet. "Oh, hell, that's not him, is it?"

"A junior officer," said Miles, "is required to stand and salute when a senior officer enters. Not hide under the bed."

"I wasn't thinking of hiding under the bed!" said Ivan, stung. "Just in the bathroom."

"Don't bother. I guarantee there'll be so much cover-

ing fire you'll be able to retreat totally unnoticed."
Miles raised his voice. "Come!"

It was indeed Count Vorkosigan. He pinned his son
with eyes cold and grey as a glacier on a sunless day,
and began without preamble, "Miles, what did you do
to make that girl cr—" He broke off as his gaze passed
over Ivan, standing at attention like a man stuffed.
Count Vorkosigan's voice returned to a more normal
growl. "Oh, hell. I was hoping to avoid tripping over
you tonight. Figured you'd be getting safely drunk in a
corner on my wine—"

Ivan saluted nervously. "Sir. Uncle Aral. Did, um, did
my mother speak with you, sir?"

"Yes," Count Vorkosigan sighed. Ivan paled. Miles
realized Ivan did not see the amusement in the hooded
set of his father's eyelids.

Miles ran a finger pensively around the lip of the
empty wine bottle. "Ivan has been commiserating me
upon my injuries, sir." Ivan nodded confirmation.

"I see," said Count Vorkosigan dryly—and Miles felt
he really did. The coldness sublimated altogether. Count
Vorkosigan sighed again, and addressed Ivan in a tone
of gentle, rhetorical complaint. "Going on fifty years of
military and political service, and what am I? A boogey-
man, used to frighten boys into good behavior—like the
Baba Yaga, who only eats the bad little children." He
spread his arms, and added sardonically, "Boo. Consider yourself chastized, and take yourself off. Go, boy."

"Yes, sir." Ivan saluted again, looking decidedly
relieved.

"And stop saluting me," Count Vorkosigan added more
sharply. "You're not an officer yet." He seemed to notice Ivan's uniform for the first time. "As a matter of
fact—"

"Yes, sir. No, sir." Ivan began to salute again, stopped
himself, looked confused, and fled. Count Vorkosigan's
lips twitched.

And I never thought I'd be grateful to Ivan, Miles
mused. "You were saying, sir?" he prompted.

It took Count Vorkosigan a moment to collect his
thoughts after the diversion provided by his young rela-

tive. He opened again, more quietly. "Why was Elena crying, son? You weren't, ah, harassing her, were you?"

"No, sir. I know what it looked like, but it wasn't. I'll give you my word, if you like."

"Not necessary." Count Vorkosigan pulled up a chair. "I trust you were not emulating that idiot Ivan. But, ah—your mother's Betan sexual philosophy has its place—on Beta Colony. Perhaps here too, someday. But I should like to emphasize that Elena Bothari is not a suitable test case."

"Why not?" said Miles suddenly. Count Vorkosigan raised his eyebrows. "I mean," Miles explained quickly, "why should she be so—so constrained. She gets duenna'd to death. She could be anything. She's bright, and she's, she's good-looking, and she could break me in half— why shouldn't she get a better education, for instance? The Sergeant isn't planning any higher education for her at all. Everything he's saved is for dowry. And he never lets her go anyplace. She'd get more out of travel— hell, she'd appreciate it a thousand times more than any other girl I know." He paused, a little breathless.

Count Vorkosigan pursed his lips, and ran his hand thoughtfully across the chair back. "This is all very true. But Elena—means enormously more to the Sergeant than I think you are aware. She is a symbol to him, of everything he imagines . . . I'm not sure how to put this. She is an important source of order in his life. I owe it to him to protect that order."

"Yes, yes, right and proper, I know," said Miles impatiently. "But you can't owe everything to him and nothing to her!"

Count Vorkosigan looked disturbed, and began again. "I owe him my life, Miles. And your mother's. In a very real sense, everything I've been and done for Barrayar in the last eighteen years is owed to him. And I owe him your life, twice over, since then, and so my sanity— what there is of it, as your mother would say. If he chooses to call in that debt, there's no bottom to it." He rubbed his lips introspectively. "Also—it won't hurt to emphasize this anyway—I'd much prefer to avoid any kind of scandal in my household at the moment. My adversaries are always groping for a handle on me, some lever to move me. I beg you will not let yourself become one."

And what the hell is going on in the government this week? Miles wondered anew. Not that anybody's likely to tell me. Lord Miles Naismith Vorkosigan. Occupation: security risk. Hobbies: falling off walls, disappointing sick old men to death, making girls cry ... He longed to patch things up with Elena, at least. But the only thing he could think of that might put her imagination-generated terrors to rest would be actually finding that blasted grave, and as near as he could figure, it had to be on Escobar, mixed in with those of the six or seven thousand war dead left behind so long ago.

Between opening his mouth, and speaking, the plan possessed him. The result was that he forgot what he'd been about to say, and sat with his mouth open a moment. Count Vorkosigan raised his eyebrows in courteous inquiry. What Miles finally said instead was, "Has anyone heard from Grandmother Naismith lately?"

Count Vorkosigan's eyes narrowed. "Curious that you should mention her. Your mother has spoken of her quite frequently in the last few days."

"Makes sense, under the circumstances. Although Grandmother's such a healthy old bird—all Betans expect to live to be 120, I guess. They think it's one of their civil rights."

Miles's Betan grandmother, seven wormhole jumps and three weeks travel time away by the most direct route— via Escobar. A carefully chosen commercial passenger liner might well include a layover at Escobar. Time for a little tourism—time for a little research. It could be done subtly enough, even with Bothari hanging over his shoulder. What could be more natural than for a boy interested in military history to make a pilgrimmage to the cemeteries of his Emperor's soldiers, maybe even burn a death offering? "Sir," he began, "do you suppose I could—"

And, "Son," Count Vorkosigan began at the same moment, "How would you like to deputize for your mother—"

"I beg your pardon," and "Go ahead, sir."

"I was about to say," continued the Count, "that this might be a very opportune time for you to visit your Grandmother Naismith again. It's been what, almost two years since you were to Beta Colony? And while Betans may expect to live to be 120—well, you never know."

Miles untangled his tongue, and managed not to lurch. "What a wonderful idea! Uh—could I take Elena?"

There went the eyebrows again. "What?"

Miles swung to his feet, and shuffled back and forth across the room, unable to contain his outpouring of schemes in stillness. Give Elena a trip off-planet? My God, he'd be a hero in her eyes, a sheer two meters tall, like Vorthalia the Bold. "Yes, sure—why not? Bothari will be with me anyway—who could be a more right and proper chaperone than her own father? Who could object?"

"Bothari," said Count Vorkosigan bluntly. "I can't imagine him warming to the thought of exposing Elena to Beta Colony. After all, he's seen it. And coming from you, ah, just at the moment, I'm not at all sure he'd perceive it as a proper invitation."

"Mm." Shuffle, turn, shuffle. Flash! "Then I won't invite her."

"Ah." Count Vorkosigan relaxed. "Wise, I'm sure . . ."

"I'll have Mother invite her. Let's see him object to that!"

Count Vorkosigan emitted a surprised laugh. "Underhanded, boy!" But his tone was approving. Miles's heart lifted.

"This trip idea was really hers, wasn't it, sir?" Miles said.

"Well—yes," Count Vorkosigan admitted. "But in fact, I was glad she suggested it. It would—ease my mind, to have you safe on Beta Colony for the next few months." He rose. "You must excuse me. Duty calls. I have to go feel up that rampant creeper Vordrozda, for the greater glory of the Empire." His expression of distaste spoke volumes. "Frankly, I'd rather be getting drunk in a corner with that idiot Ivan—or talking to you." His father's eyes were warm upon him.

"Your work comes first, of course, sir. I understand that."

Count Vorkosigan paused, and gave him a peculiar look. "Then you understand nothing. My work has been a blight on you from the very beginning. I'm sorry, sorry it made such a mess for you—"

Mess of you, thought Miles. Say what you really mean, damn it.

"—I never meant it to be so." A nod, and he withdrew.

Apologizing to me again, thought Miles miserably. For me. He keeps telling me I'm all right—and then apologizing. Inconsistent, Father.

He shuffled back and forth across the room again, and his pain burst into speech. He flung his words against the deaf door, "I'll make you take back that apology! I am all right, damn it! I'll make you see it. I'll stuff you so full of pride in me there'll be no room left for your precious guilt! I swear by my word as Vorkosigan. I swear it, Father," his voice fell to a whisper, "Grandfather. Somehow, I don't know how . . ."

He took another turn around his chamber, collapsing back into himself, cold and desperately sleepy. A mess of crumbs, an empty wine bottle, an open full one. Silence.

"Talking to yourself in an empty room again, I see," he whispered. "A very bad sign, you know."

His legs hurt. He cradled the second bottle, and took it with him to lie down.

CHAPTER FIVE   *   *   *

"Well, well, well," said the sleek Betan customs agent, in sarcastic simulation of good cheer. "If it isn't Sergeant Bothari of Barrayar. And what did you bring me this time, Sergeant? A few nuclear antipersonnel mines, overlooked in your back pocket? A maser cannon or two, accidentally mixed up with your shaving kit? A gravitic imploder, slipped somehow into your boot?"

The Sergeant answered this sally with something between a growl and a grunt.

Miles grinned, and dredged his memory for the agent's name. "Good afternoon, Officer Timmons. Still working the line, are you? I thought for sure you'd be in administration by now."

The agent gave Miles a somewhat more courteous nod of greeting. "Good afternoon, Lord Vorkosigan. Well, civil service, you know." He sorted through their documents and plugged a data disc into his viewer. "Your stunner permits are in order. Now if you will please step, one at a time, through this scanner?"

Sergeant Bothari frowned at the machine glumly, and sniffed disdain. Miles tried to catch his eye, but he was studiously finding something of interest in midair somewhere. On the suspicion, Miles said, "Elena and I first, I think."

Elena passed through with a stiff uncertain smile like a person holding still too long for a photograph, then continued to look eagerly around. Even if it was only a

52

rather bleak underground customs entry port, it was another planet. Miles hoped Beta Colony would make up for the disappointing fizzle of the Escobar layover.

Two days of records searches and trudging through neglected military cemetries in the rain, pretending to Bothari a passion for historical detail, had produced no maternal grave or cenotaph after all. Elena had seemed more relieved than disappointed by the failure of their covert search.

"You see?" she had whispered to Miles. "Father *didn't* lie to me. You have a hyper imagination."

The Sergeant's own bored reaction to the tour clinched the argument; Miles conceded. And yet . . .

It was his hyper imagination, maybe. The less they found the more queasy Miles became. Were they looking in the wrong army's cemetery? Miles's own mother had changed allegiances to return to Barrayar with his father; maybe Bothari's romance had not taken so prosperous a turn. But if that were so, should they even be looking in cemeteries? Maybe he should be hunting Elena's mother in the comm link directory . . . He did not quite dare suggest it.

He wished he had not been so intimidated by the conspiracy of silence surrounding Elena's birth to refrain from pumping Countess Vorkosigan. Well, when they returned home he would screw up his courage and demand the truth of her, and let her wisdom guide him as to how much to pass on to Bothari's daughter.

For now, Miles stepped after Elena through the scanner, enjoying her air of wonder, and looking forward like a magician to pulling Beta Colony out of a hat for her delight.

The Sergeant stepped through the machine. It gave a rude blat.

Agent Timmons shook his head and sighed. "You never give up, do you, Sergeant?"

"Ah, if I may interrupt," said Miles, "the lady and I are cleared, are we not?" Receiving a nod, he retrieved their stunners and his own travel documentation. "I'll show Elena around the shuttleport, then, while you two are discussing your, er, differences. You can bring the luggage when he gets done with it, Segeant. Meet you in the main concourse."

"You will not—" began Bothari.

"We'll be perfectly all right," Miles assured him airily. He grasped Elena's elbow and hustled her off before his bodyguard could marshall further objections.

Elena looked back over her shoulder. "Is my father really trying to smuggle in an illegal weapon?"

"Weapons. I expect so," said Miles apologetically. "I don't authorize it, and it never works, but I guess he feels undressed without deadly force. If the Betans are as good at spotting everyone else's goods as they are at spotting ours, we really don't have anything to worry about."

He watched her, sideways, as they entered the main concourse, and had the satisfaction of seeing her catch her breath. Golden light, at once brilliant and comfortable, spun down from a huge high vault upon a great tropical garden, dark with foliage, vibrant with flowers and birds, murmurous with fountains.

"It's like stepping into a giant terrarium," she commented. "I feel like a little horned hopper."

"Exactly," he agreed. "The Silica Zoo maintains it. One of their extended habitats."

They strolled toward an area given over to small shops. He steered Elena carefully along, trying to pick out things she might enjoy, and avoid catastrophic culture shock. That sex-aids shop, for example, was probably a little too much for her first hour on the planet, no matter how attractive the pink when she blushed. However, they spent a pleasant few minutes in a most extraordinary pet store. His good sense barely restrained him from making her an awkward present of a large ruffed Tau Cetan beaded lizard, bright as jewelry, that caught her eye. It had rather strict dietary requirements, and besides, Miles was not quite sure if the 50 kilo beast could be housebroken. They wandered along a balcony overlooking the great garden, and he bought them rational ice creams, instead. They sat on the bench lining the railing to eat.

"Everything seems so free, here," Elena said, licking

her fingers and looking around with shining eyes. "You don't see soldiers and guards all over the place. A woman—a woman could be anything here."

"Depends on what you mean by free," said Miles. "They put up with rules we'd never tolerate at home. You should see everyone fall into place during a power outage drill, or a sandstorm alarm. They have no margin for—I don't know how to put it. Social failures?"

Elena gave him a baffled smile, not understanding. "But everyone arranges their own marriages."

"But did you know you have to have a permit to have a child here? The first one is free, but after that . . ."

"That's absurd," she remarked absently. "How could they possibly enforce it?" She evidently felt her question to be rather bold, for she took a quick glance around, to be sure the Sergeant was nowhere near.

Miles echoed her glance. "Permanent contraceptive implants, for the women and hermaphrodites. You need the permit to get it removed. It's the custom, at puberty—a girl gets her implant, and her ears pierced, and her, er, um—" Miles discovered he was not immune to pinkness himself—he went on in a rush, "her hymen cut, all on the same visit to the doctor. There's usually a family party—sort of a rite of passage. That's how you can tell if a girl's available, the ears . . ."

He had her entire attention, now. Her hands stole to her earrings, and she went not merely pink, but red. "Miles! Are they going to think *I'm*—"

"Well, it's just that—if anyone bothers you, I mean if your father or I aren't around, don't be afraid to tell them to take themselves off. They will. They don't mean it as an insult, here. But I figured I'd better warn you." He gnawed a knuckle, eyes crinkling. "You know, if you intend to walk around for the next six weeks with your hands over your ears . . ."

She replaced her hands hastily in her lap, and glowered at him.

"It can get awfully peculiar, I know," he offered apologetically. A scorching memory of just how peculiar disturbed him for a moment.

He had been fifteen on his year-long school visit to

Beta Colony, and he'd found himself for the first time in his life with what looked like unlimited possibilities for sexual intimacy. This illusion had crashed and burned very quickly, as he found the most fascinating girls already taken. The rest seemed about equally divided among good samaritans, the kinky/curious, hermaphrodites, and boys.

He did not care to be an object of charity, and he found himself too Barrayaran for the last two categories, although Betan enough not to mind them for others. A short affair with a girl from the kinky/curious category was enough. Her fascination with the peculiarities of his body made him, in the end, more self-conscious than the most open revulsion he had experienced on Barrayar, with its fierce prejudice against deformity. Anyway, after finding his sexual parts disappointingly normal, the girl had drifted off.

The affair had ended, for Miles, in a terrifying black depression that had deepened for weeks, culminating at last late one night in the third, and most secret, time the Sergeant had saved his life. He had cut Bothari twice, in their silent struggle for the knife, exerting hysterical strength against the Sergeant's frightened caution of breaking his bones. The tall man had finally achieved a grip that held him, and held him, until he broke down at last, weeping his self-hatred into the Sergeant's bloodied breast until exhaustion finally stilled him. The man who'd carried him as a child, before he first walked at age four, then carried him like a child to bed. Bothari treated his own wounds, and never referred to the incident again.

Age fifteen had not been a very good year. Miles was determined not to repeat it. His hand tightened on the balcony railing, in a mood of objectless resolve. Objectless, like himself; therefore useless. He frowned into the black well of this thought, and for a moment even Beta Colony's glitter seemed dull and grey.

Four Betans stood nearby, arguing in a vociferous undertone. Miles turned half around, to get a better view of the speakers past Elena's elbow. Elena began to speak, something about his abstraction. He shook his head, and held up a hand, begging silence. She subsided, watching him curiously.

"Damn it," a heavy man in a green sarong was saying, "I don't care how you do it, but I want that lunatic pried out of my ship. Can't you rush him?"

The woman in the uniform of Betan Security shook her head. "Look, Calhoun, why should I risk my people's lives for a ship that's practically scrap anyway? It's not as if he was holding hostages or something."

"I have a salvage team tied up waiting that's collecting time-and-a-half for overtime. He's been up there three days—he's got to sleep sometime, or take a leak or some goddamn thing," argued the civilian.

"If he's as hopped-up crazy as you claim, nothing would be more likely to trigger his blowing it than a rush. Wait him out." The security woman turned to a man in the dove-grey and black uniform of one of the larger commercial spacelines. Silver hair in his sideburns echoed the triple silver circles of his pilot's neurological implant on midforehead and temples. "Or talk him out. You know him, he's a member of your union, can't you do anything with him?"

"Oh, no you don't," objected the pilot officer. "You're not shoving this one off on me. He doesn't want to talk to me anyway, he's made that clear."

"You're on the Board this year, you ought to have some authority with him—threaten to revoke his pilot's certification or something."

"Arde Mayhew may still be in the Brotherhood, but he's two years in arrears on his dues, his license is on shaky ground already, and frankly, I think this episode is going to cook it. The whole point of this bananarama in the first place is that once the last of the RG ships goes for scrap," the pilot officer nodded toward the bulky civilian, "he isn't going to be a pilot anymore. He's been medically rejected for a new implant—it wouldn't do him any good even if he had the money. And I know damn well he doesn't. He tried to borrow rent money from me last week. At least, he said it was for rent. More likely for that swill he drinks."

"Did you give it to him?" asked the woman in the blue uniform of shuttleport administration.

"Well—yes," replied the pilot officer moodily. "But I told him it was absolutely the last. Anyway ..." he frowned at his boots, then burst out, "I'd rather see him go out in a blaze of glory than die of being beached! I know how I'd feel if I knew I'd never make a jump again ..." He compressed his lips, defensive-aggressive, at the shuttleport administration.

"All pilots are crazy," muttered the security woman. "Comes from getting their brains pierced."

So Miles eavesdropped, shamelessly fascinated. The man they were discussing was a fellow-freak, it seemed, a loser in trouble. A wormhole jump pilot with an obsolete coupler system running through his brain, soon to be technologically unemployed, holed up in his old ship, fending off the wrecking crews—how? Miles wondered.

"A blaze of traffic hazards, you mean," complained the shuttleport administrator. "If he makes good on his threats, there'll be junk pelting all through the inner orbits for days. We'd have to shut down—clean it up—" she turned to the civilian, completing the circle, "and you'd better believe it won't be charged to my department! I'll see your company gets the bill if I have to take it all the way to JusDep."

The salvage operator paled, then went red. "Your department permitted that hot-wired freak-head access to my ship in the first place," he snarled.

"He said he'd left some personal effects," she defended. "We didn't know he had anything like this in mind."

Miles pictured the man, huddled in his dim recess, stripped of allies, like the last survivor of a hopeless seige. His hand clenched unconsciously. His ancestor, General Count Selig Vorkosigan, had raised the famous seige of Vorkosigan Surleau with no more than a handful of picked retainers, and subterfuge, it was said.

"Elena," he whispered fiercely, stilling her restlessness, "follow my lead, and say nothing."

"Hm?" she murmured, startled.

"Ah, good, Miss Bothari, you're here," he said loudly,

as if he had just arrived. He gathered her up and marched up to the group.

He knew he confused strangers as to his age. At first glance, his height led them to underestimate it. At second, his face, slightly dark from a tendency to heavy beard growth in spite of close shaving, and prematurely set from long intimacy with pain, led them to overestimate. He'd found he could tip the balance either way, at will, by a simple change of mannerisms. He summoned ten generations of warriors to his back, and produced his most austere smile.

"Good afternoon, ladies, gentlemen," he hailed them. Four stares greeted him, variously nonplussed. His urbanity almost crumpled under the onslaught, but he held the line. "I was told one of you could tell me where to find Pilot Officer Arde Mayhew."

"Who the devil are you?" growled the salvage operator, apparently voicing the thought of them all.

Miles bowed smoothly, barely restraining himself from swirling an imaginary cape. "Lord Miles Vorkosigan, of Barrayar, at your service. This is my associate, Miss Bothari. I couldn't help overhearing—I believe I might be of assistance to you all, if you will permit me ..." Beside him, Elena raised puzzled eyebrows at her new, if vague, official status.

"Look, kid," began the shuttleport administrator. Miles glanced up from lowered brows, shooting her his best imitation General Count Piotr Vorkosigan military glare.

"—sir" she corrected herself. "Just, uh—just what do you want with Pilot Officer Mayhew?"

Miles gave an upward jerk of his chin. "I have been commissioned to discharge a debt to him." Self-commissioned, about ten seconds ago ...

"Somebody owes money to Arde?" asked the salvage operator, amazed.

Miles drew himself up, looking offended. "Not money," he growled, as though he never touched the sordid stuff. "It's a debt of honor."

The shuttleport administrator looked cautiously impressed; the pilot officer, pleased. The security woman looked dubious. The salvage operator looked extremely dubious. "How does that help me?" he asked bluntly.

"I can talk Pilot Officer Mayhew out of your ship," said Miles, seeing his path opening before him, "if you'll provide me with the means of meeting him face to face." Elena gulped; he quelled her with a narrow, sideways flick of a glance.

The four Betans looked, one to another, as if responsibility could be shuffled off by eye contact. Finally the pilot officer said, "Well, what the hell. Does anybody have a better idea?"

In the control chair of the personnel shuttle the greyhaired senior pilot officer spoke—once again—into his comconsole. "Arde? Arde, this is Van. Answer me, please? I've brought up somebody to talk things over with you. He's going to come on board. All right, Arde? You're not going to do anything foolish now, are you?"

Silence was his sole reply. "Is he receiving you?" asked Miles.

"His comconsole is. Whether he's got the volume turned up, or is there, or awake, or—or alive, is anybody's guess."

"I'm alive," growled a thick voice suddenly from the speaker, making them both start. There was no video. "But you won't be, Van, if you try to board my ship, you double-crossing son of a bitch."

"I won't try," promised the senior pilot officer. "Just Mister, uh, Lord Vorkosigan, here."

There was a moody silence, if the static-spattered hiss could be so described. "He doesn't work for that bloodsucker Calhoun does he?" asked the speaker suspiciously.

"He doesn't work for anybody," Van soothed.

"Not for the Mental Health Board? Nobody's going to get near *me* with a damn dart gun—I'll blow us all to hell, first . . ."

"He's not even Betan. He's a Barrayaran. Says he's been looking for you."

Another silence. Then the voice, uncertain, querulous, "I don't owe any Barrayarans—I don't think . . . I don't even know any Barrayarans."

There was an odd feeling of pressure, and a gentle click from the exterior of the hull, as they came in contact with the old freighter. The pilot waved a finger by way of signal at Miles, and Miles made the hatch connections secure. "Ready," he called.

"You sure you want to do this?" whispered the pilot officer.

Miles nodded. It had been a minor miracle, escaping the protection of Bothari. He licked his lips, and grinned, enjoying the exhilaration of weightlessness and fear. He trusted Elena would prevent any unnecessary alarm, planetside.

Miles opened the hatch. There was a puff of air, as the pressure within the two ships equalized. He stared into a pitch-dark tunnel. "Got a hand light?"

"On the rack there," the pilot officer pointed.

Provided, Miles floated cautiously into the tube. The darkness skulked ahead of him, hiding in corners and cross corridors, and crowding in behind him as he passed. He threaded his way toward the Navigation and Communications Room, where his quarry was presumed to be lurking. The distance was actually short—the crew's quarters were small, most of the ship being given over to cargo space—but the absolute silence gave the journey a subjective stretch. Zero-gee was now having its usual effect on making him regret the last thing he'd eaten. Vanilla, he thought; I should have had vanilla.

There was a dim light ahead, spilling into the corridor from an open hatch. Miles cleared his throat, loudly, as he approached. It might be better not to startle the man, all things considered.

"Pilot Officer Mayhew?" he called softly, and pulled himself to the door. "My name is Miles Vorkosigan, and I'm looking for—looking for—" what the devil was he looking for? Oh, well. Wing it. "I'm looking for desperate men," he finished in style.

Pilot Officer Mayhew sat strapped in his pilot's chair in a mournful huddle. Clutched in his lap were his pilot's headset, a half-full liter squeeze bottle of a gurgling liquid of a brilliant and poisonous green, and a box hastily connected by a spaghetti-mass of wiring to a half-gutted control panel and topped by a toggle switch. Quite as fascinating as the toggle box was a dark, slender, and by Betan law very illegal little needle gun. Mayhew blinked puffed and red-rimmed eyes at the apparition in his doorway, and rubbed a hand—still holding the lethal needler—over a three-day beard stubble. "Oh, yeah?" he replied vaguely.

Miles was temporarily distracted by the needler. "How did you ever get that through Betan customs?" he asked in a tone of genuine admiration. "I've never been able to carry so much as a sling-shot past 'em."

Mayhew stared at the needler in his hand as if he'd just discovered it, like a wart grown unnoticed. "Bought it at Jackson's Whole once. I've never tried to take it off the ship. I suppose they'd take it away from me, if I tried. They take everything away from you, down there." He sighed.

Miles eased into the room, and arranged himself cross-legged in midair, in what he hoped was a nice, non-threatening sort of listening posture. "How did you ever get into this fix?" he asked, with a nod around that included the ship, the situation, and Mayhew's lap-full of objects.

Mayhew shrugged. "Rotten luck. I've always had rotten luck. That accident with the RG 88—it was the moisture from those busted amphor tubes that soaked those dal bags that swelled and split the bulkhead and started the whole thing. The 'port cargo master didn't even get a slap on the wrist. Damn it, what I did or didn't have to drink wouldn't have made a damn bit of difference!" He sniffed, and drew a sleeve across his flushed face, looking alarmingly as if he were about to weep. It was a very disturbing thing to see in a man pushing, Miles estimated, forty years of age. Mayhew took a swig from his bottle instead, then with some dim remnant of courtesy offered it to Miles.

Miles smiled politely and took it. Should he grab this chance to dump it out, in the interests of sobering Mayhew up? There were drawbacks to the idea, in free fall. It would have to be dumped into something else, if he were not to spend his visit dodging flying blobs of whatever-it-was. Hard to make it look like an accident. While he mulled, he sampled it, in the interests of scientific inquiry.

He barely managed not to choke it into free fall, atomized. Thick, green herbal, sweet as syrup—he nearly gagged on the sweetness—perhaps 60% pure ethanol. But what was the rest of it? It burned down his esophagus, making him feel suddenly like an animated display of the digestive system, with all the different parts picked out in colored lights. Respectfully, he wiped the mouthpiece on his sleeve and handed the bottle to its owner, who tucked it back under his arm.

"Thanks," Miles gasped. Mayhew nodded. "So how," Miles aspirated, then cleared his throat to a more normal tone, "what are you planning to do next? What are you demanding?"

"Demanding?" said Mayhew. "Next? I don't—I'm just not going to let that cannibal Calhoun murder my ship. There isn't—there isn't any text." He rocked the box with the toggle switch on his lap, a miserable madonna. "Have you ever been red?" he asked suddenly.

Miles had a confused vision of ancient Earth political parties. "No, I'm Vor," he said, not sure if that was the right response. But it seemed not to matter. Mayhew soliliquized on.

"Red. The color red. Pure light I was, once, on the jump to some little hole of a place called Hespari II. There's no experience in life like a jump. If you've never ridden the lights in your brain—colors no man's ever put a name to—there are no words for it. Better than dreams, or nightmares—better than a woman—better than food or drink or sleep or breath—and they pay us for it! Poor deluded suckers, with nothing under their skulls but protoplasm . . ." He peered blurrily at Miles. "Oh, sorry. Nothing personal. You're just not a pilot. I never took a cargo to Hespari again." He focused on Miles a little more clearly. "Say, you're a mess, aren't you?"

"Not as much of a mess as you are," Miles replied frankly, nettled.

"Mm," the pilot agreed. He passed his bottle back.

Curious stuff, thought Miles. Whatever was in it seemed to be counteracting the usual effect ethanol had on him of putting him to sleep. He felt warm and energetic, as if it flowed right down to his fingers and toes. It was probably how Mayhew had kept awake for three days, alone in this deserted can.

"So," Miles went on scornfully, "you haven't got a battle plan. You haven't asked for a million Betan dollars in small unmarked slips, or threatened to drop the ship through the roof of the shuttleport, or taken hostages, or—or *anything* constructive at all. You're just sitting up here, killing time and your bottle, and wasting your opportunities, for want of a little resolve, or imagination, or something."

Mayhew blinked at this unexpected point of view. "By God, Van told the truth for once. You're *not* from the Mental Health Board . . . I could take you hostage," he offered placatingly, swinging the needler toward Miles.

"No, don't do that," said Miles hastily. "I can't explain, but—they'd overreact, down there. It's a bad idea."

"Oh." The needler's aim drifted off. "But anyway, don't you see," he tapped his headset, attempting to explain, "what I want, they can't give me? I want to ride the jumps. And I can't, not any more."

"Only in this ship, I gather."

"This ship is going for scrap," his despair was flat, unexpectedly rational, "just as soon as I can't stay awake any more."

"That's a useless attitude," scoffed Miles. "Apply a little logic to the problem, at least. I mean like this. You want to be a jump pilot. You can only be a jump pilot for an RG ship. This is the last RG ship. Ergo, what you need is this ship. So get it. Be a pilot-owner. Run your own cargos. Simple, see? May I have some more of that stuff, please?" One got used to the ghastly taste quite quickly, Miles found.

Mayhew shook his head, clutching his despair and his toggle box to him like a familiar, comforting child's toy. "I tried. I've tried everything. I thought I had a loan. It folded, and anyway, Calhoun outbid me."

"Oh." Miles passed the bottle back, feeling deflated.

He gazed at the pilot, to whom he was now floating at right angles. "Well, all I know is, you can't give up. Shur—surrender besmirches the honor of the Vor." He began to hum a little, a snatch of some half-remembered childhood ballad; "The Seige of Silver Moon". It had a Vor lord in it, he recalled, and a beautiful witch-woman who rode in a magic flying mortar; they had pounded their enemies' bones in it, at the end. "Gimme another drink. I want to think. 'If thou wilt swear thyself to me, thy leige lord true to thee I'll be . . .' "

"Huh?" said Mayhew.

Miles realized he'd been singing aloud, albeit softly. "Nothing, sorry." He floated in silence a few minutes longer. "That's the trouble with the Betan system," he said after a time. "Nobody takes personal responsibility for anyone. It's all these faceless fictional corporate entities—government by ghosts. What you need is a leige lord, to take sword in hand and slice through all the red tape. Just like Vorthalia the Bold and the Thicket of Thorns."

"What I need is a drink," said Mayhew glumly.

"Hm? Oh, sorry." Miles handed the bottle back. An idea was forming up in the back of his mind, like a nebula just starting to contract. A little more mass, and it would start to glow, a proto star . . . "I have it!" he cried, straightening out suddenly, and accidently giving himself an unwanted spin.

Mayhew flinched, nearly firing his needler through the floor. He glanced uncertainly at the squeeze bottle. "No, I have it," he corrected.

Miles overcame the spin. "We'd better do this from here. The first principle of strategy—never give up an advantage. Can I use your comconsole?"

"What for?"

"I," said Miles grandly, "am going to buy this ship. And then I shall hire you to pilot it."

Mayhew stared in bewilderment, looking from Miles to the bottle and back. "You got that much money?"

"Mm . . . Well, I have assets . . ."

* * *

A few minutes work with the comconsole brought the salvage operator's face on the screen. Miles put his proposition succinctly. Calhoun's expression went from disbelief to outrage.

"You call that a compromise?" he cried. "At cost! And backed by—I'm not a damned real estate broker!"

"Mr. Calhoun," said Miles sweetly, "may I point out, the choice is not between my note and this ship. The choice is between my note and a rain of glowing debris."

"If I find out you're in collusion with that—"

"Never met him before today," Miles disclaimed.

"What's wrong with the land?" asked Calhoun suspiciously. "Besides being on Barrayar, I mean."

"It's like fertile farm country," Miles answered, not quite directly. "Wooded—100 centimeters of rain a year—" that ought to fetch a Betan, "barely 300 kilometers from the capital."

Downwind, fortunately for the capital. "And I own it absolutely. Just inherited it from my grandfather recently. Go ahead and check it through the Barrayaran Embassy. Check the climate plats."

"This rainfall—it's not all on the same day or something, is it?"

"Of course not," replied Miles, straightening indignantly. Not easy, in free fall. "Ancestral land—it's been in my family for ten generations. You can believe I'll make every effort to cover that note before I'll let my home ground fall from my hands—"

Calhoun rubbed his chin irritably. "Cost plus 25%," he suggested.

"Ten percent."

"Twenty."

"Ten, or I'll let you deal directly with Pilot Officer Mayhew."

"All right," groaned Calhoun, "ten percent."

"Done!"

It was not quite that easy, of course. But thanks to the efficiency of the Betans' planetary information network, a transaction that would have taken days on Barrayar was completed in less than an hour, right from Mayhew's control room. Miles was cannily reluctant to give up the tactical bargaining advantage possession of the toggle box gave them, and Mayhew, after his first astonishment had worn off, became silent and loathe to leave.

"Look, kid," he spoke suddenly, about halfway through the complicated transaction. "I appreciate what you're trying to do, but—but it's just too late. You understand, when I get downside, they're not going to just be laughing this off. Security'll be waiting at the docking bay, with a patrol from the Mental Health Board right beside 'em. They'll slap a stun-net over me so fast—you'll see me in a month or two, walking around smiling. You're always smiling, after the M.H.B. gets done . . ." He shook his head helplessly. "It's just too late."

"It's never too late while you're breathing," snapped Miles. He did the free-fall equivalent of pacing the room, shoving off from one wall, turning in midair, and shoving off from the opposite wall, a few dozen turns, thinking.

"I have an idea," he said at last. "I'll wager it would buy time, time enough at least to come up with something better—trouble is, since you're not Barrayaran, you're not going to understand what you're doing, and it's serious stuff."

Mayhew looked thoroughly baffled. "Huh?"

"It's like this." Thump, spin, turn straighten, thump. "If you were to swear fealty to me as an Armsman simple, taking me for your leige lord—it's the most straightforward of our oath relationships—I *might* be able to include you under my Class III diplomatic immunity. Anyway, I know I could if you were a Barrayaran subject. Of course, you're a Betan citizen. In any case, I'm pretty sure we could tie up a pack of lawyers and several days, trying to figure out which laws take precedence. I would be legally obligated for your bed, board, dress, armament—I suppose this ship could be classed as your armament—your protection, in the event of challenge by any other leigeman—that hardly applies, here on Beta Colony—oh, there's a passel of stuff, about your family, and—do you have a family, by the way?"

Mayhew shook his head.

"That simplifies things." Thump, spin, turn, straighten,

thump. "Meanwhile, neither Security nor the M.H.B. could touch you, because legally you'd be like a part of my body."

Mayhew blinked. "That sounds screwy as hell. Where do I sign? How do you register it?"

"All you have to do is kneel, place your hands between mine, and repeat about two sentences. It doesn't even need witnesses, although it's customary to have two."

Mayhew shrugged. "All right. Sure, kid."

Thump, spin, turn, straighten, thump. "All-right-sure-kid. I thought you wouldn't understand it. What I've described is only a tiny part of my half of the bargain, your privileges. It also includes your obligations, and a ream of rights I have over you. For instance—just one for-instance—if you were to refuse to carry out an order of mine in the heat of battle, I would have the right to strike off your head. On the spot."

Mayhew's jaw dropped. "You realize," he said at last, "the Mental Health Board's going to drop a net over you, too . . ."

Miles grinned sardonically. "They can't. Because if they tried, I could cry havoc to my leige lord for protection. And I'd get it, too. He's pretty touchy about who does what to his subjects. Oh, that's another angle. If you become a leigeman to me, it automatically puts you into a relationship with *my* leige lord, kind of a complicated one."

"And his, and his, and his, I suppose," said Mayhew. "I know all about chains of command."

"Well, no, that's as far as it goes. I'm sworn directly to Gregor Vorbarra, as a vassal secundus." Miles realized he might as well be talking gibberish, for all the meaning his words were conveying.

"Who's this Greg-guy?" asked Mayhew.

"The Emperor. Of Barrayar." Miles added, just to be sure he understood.

"Oh."

Typical Betan, thought Miles, they don't study anybody's history but Earth's and their own. "Think about it, anyway. It's not something you should just jump into."

When the last voice-print had been recorded, Mayhew carefully disconnected the toggle box—Miles held his breath—and the senior pilot officer returned to convey them planetside.

The senior pilot officer addressed Miles with a shade more respect in his voice. "I had no idea you were from such a wealthy family, Lord Vorkosigan. That was a solution to the problem I certainly hadn't anticipated. But perhaps one ship is just a bauble, to a Barrayaran lord."

"Not really," said Miles. "I'm going to have to do some hustling to cover that note. My family used to be well off, I admit, but that was back in the Time of Isolation. Between the economic upheavals at the end of it, and the First Cetagandan War, we were pretty much wiped out, financially." He grinned a little. "You galactics got us coming and going. My great-grandfather on the Vorkosigan side, when the first galactic traders hit us, thought he was going to make a killing in jewels— you know, diamonds, rubies, emeralds—the galactics seemed to be selling them so cheaply. He put all his liquid assets and about half his chattels into them. Well, of course they were synthetics, better than the naturals and cheap as dirt—uh, sand—and the bottom promptly dropped out of the market, taking him with it. I'm told my great-grandmother never forgave him." He waved vaguely at Mayhew who, becoming conditioned, passed over his bottle. Miles offered it to the senior pilot officer, who rejected it with a look of disgust. Miles shrugged, and took a long pull. Amazingly pleasant stuff. His circulatory system, as well as his digestive, now seemed to be glowing with rainbow hues. He felt he could go days without sleep.

"Unfortunately, most of the land he sold was around Vorkosigan Surleau, which is pretty dry—not by your standards, of course—and the land he kept was around Vorkosigan Vashnoi, which was the better."

"What's unfortunate about that?" asked Mayhew.

"Well, because it was the principal seat of govern-

ment for the Vorkosigans, and because we owned about
every stick and stone in it—it was a pretty important
industrial and trade center—and because the Vorkosigans
were, uh, prominent in the Resistance, the Cetagandans
took the city hostage. It's a long story, but—eventually,
they destroyed the place. It's now a big glass hole in the
ground. You can still see a faint glow in the sky, on a
dark night, twenty kilometers off."

The senior pilot officer brought the little shuttle
smoothly into its dock.

"Hey," said Mayhew suddenly. "That land you had
around Vorkosigan whatever-you-said—"

"Vashnoi. Have. Hundreds of square kilometers of it,
and mostly downwind, yes?"

"Is that the same—" his face was lighting, like the
sun coming up after a long, dark night, "is that the
same land you mortgaged to—" he began to laugh,
delightedly, under his breath; they disembarked. "Is
that what you pledged to that sand-crawler Calhoun in
return for my ship?"

"Caveat emptor," bowed Miles. "He checked the climate plat; he never thought to check the radioactivity
plat. He probably doesn't study anybody else's history
either."

Mayhew sat down on the docking bay, laughing so
hard that he bent his forehead nearly to the floor. His
laughter had more than an edge of hysteria—several
days without sleep, after all ... "Kid," he cried, "have
a drink on me!"

"I mean to pay him, you understand," explained Miles.
"The hectares he chose would make an unaesthetic hole
in the map for some descendant of mine, in a few hundred years, when it cools off. But if he gets greedy, or
pushy about collecting—well, he'll get what he deserves."

Three groups of people were bearing down upon them.
Bothari had escaped customs at last, it appeared, for he
led the first group. His collar was undone, and he looked
decidedly ruffled. Uh oh, thought Miles, it looks like
he's had a strip-search—that's guaranteed to put him in
a ferocious mood. He was followed by a new Betan
security patrolman, and a limping Betan civilian Miles

had never seen before, who was gesticulating and complaining bitterly. The man had a livid bruise on his face, and one eye was swelling shut. Elena trailed, seeming on the verge of tears.

The second group was led by the shuttleport administrator, and included now a number of other officials. The third group was headed by the Betan security woman. She had two burly patrolmen and four medical types in her wake. Mayhew glanced from right to left, and sobered abruptly. The Betan security men had their stunners in hand.

"Oh, kid," he muttered. The security men were fanning out. Mayhew scrambled to his knees. "Oh, kid . . ."

"It's up to you, Arde," said Miles quietly.

"Do it!"

The Botharis arrived. The Sergeant opened his mouth. Miles, dropping his voice, cut across his beginning roar—by God, it *was* an efffective trick—"Attention, please, Sergeant. I require your witness. Pilot Officer Mayhew is about to make oath."

The Sergeant's jaw tightened like a vise, but he came to attention.

"Put your hands between mine, Arde—like that—and repeat after me. I, Arde Mayhew—is that your full legal name? use that, then—do testify I am an unsworn freeman, and take service under Lord Miles Naismith Vorkosigan as an Armsman simple— go ahead and say that part—" Mayhew did so, rolling his eyes from left to right. "And will hold him as my leige commander until my death or his releases me."

That repeated, Miles said, rather quickly as the crowd closed in, "I, Miles Naismith Vorkosigan, vassal secundus to Emperor Gregor Vorbarra, do accept your oath, and pledge you the protection of a leige commander; this by my word as Vorkosigan. All done—you can get up now."

One good thing, thought Miles, it's diverted the Sergeant completely from whatever he was about to say. Bothari found his voice at last. "My lord," he hissed, "you can't swear a Betan!"

"I just did," Miles pointed out cheerfully. He bounced

a bit, feeling quite unusually pleased with himself. The Sergeant's glance passed across Mayhew's bottle, and narrowed on Miles.

"Why aren't you asleep?" he growled.

The Betan patrolman gestured at Miles. "Is this the man?"

The Betan security officer from the original shuttleport group approached. Mayhew had remained on his knees, as if plotting to crawl off under cover of the fire overhead. "Pilot Officer Mayhew," she cried, "you are under arrest. These are your rights: you have a right to—"

The bruised civilian interrupted, pointing at Elena. "Screw him! This woman assaulted me! There were a dozen witnesses. Damn it, I want her charged. She's vicious."

Elena had her hands over her ears again, lower lip stuck out but trembling slightly. Miles began to get the picture. "Did you hit him?"

She nodded. "But he said the most horrible thing to me . . ."

"My lord," said Bothari reproachfully, "it was very wrong of you to leave her alone in this place—"

The security woman began again. "Pilot Officer Mayhew, you have a right—"

"I think she cracked the orbit of my eye," moaned the bruised man. "I'm going to sue . . ."

Miles shot Elena a special reassuring smile. "Don't worry, I'll take care of it."

"You have a right—" yelled the security woman.

"I beg your pardon, Officer Brownell," Miles interrupted her smoothly. "Pilot Officer Mayhew is now my leigeman. As his leige commander, any charges against him must be addressed to me. It will then be my duty to determine their validity and issue the orders for the appropriate punishments. He has no rights but the right to accept challenge in single combat for certain categories of slander which are a bit complicated to go into now—" Obsolete, too, since dueling was outlawed by Imperial edict, but these Betans won't know the difference—"So unless you happen to be carrying two pairs of swords and are prepared to, say, offer an insult to

Pilot Officer Mayhew's mother, you will simply have to—ah—contain yourself."

Timely advice; the security woman looked as if she were about to explode. Mayhew gave a hopeful nod, smiling weakly. Bothari stirred uneasily, eyes flicking on an inventory of men and weapons in the mob. Gently, thought Miles; let's take it gently. "Get *up*, Arde . . ."

It took some persuading, but the security officer finally checked with her superiors about Miles's bizarre defense of Pilot Officer Mayhew. At that point, as Miles had hoped and forseen, proceedings broke down in a morass of untested interplanetary legal hypotheses that threatened to engulf the Barrayaran Embassy and the Betan State Department on ever-ascending levels of personnel.

Elena's case was easier. The outraged Betan was directed to take his case to the Barrayaran Embassy in person. There, Miles knew, it would be swallowed up in an endless moebius loop of files, forms, and reports, kept especially for such occasions by the extremely competent staff. The forms included some particularly creative ones that had to be round-tripped on the six-week journey back to Barrayar itself, and were guaranteed to be sent back several times for minor errors in execution.

"Relax," Miles whispered in an aside to Elena. "They'll bury that guy in files so deep you'll never see him again. It works great with Betans—they're perfectly happy, because all the time they think they're doing something to you. Just don't kill anybody. My diplomatic immunity doesn't go that far."

The exhausted Mayhew was swaying on his feet by the time the Betans gave way. Miles, feeling like an old sea raider after a successful looting spree, bore him off.

"Two hours," muttered Bothari. "We've only been in this bloody place two bloody hours . . ."

CHAPTER SIX   *   *   *

"Miles, dear," his grandmother greeted him with a peck on the cheek as regulation as a salute. "You're rather late—trouble in Customs again? Are you very tired from your trip?"

"Not a bit." He bounced on his heels, missing free fall and its unconstrained motion. He felt like taking a fifty kilometer run, or going dancing, or something. The Botharis looked weary, though, and Pilot Officer Mayhew was nearly green. The pilot officer, after the briefest introduction, was shipped off to the spare bedroom in Mrs. Naismith's apartment to wash, take his choice of too-small or too-large borrowed pajamas, and fall unconscious across the bed as though slugged with a mallet.

Miles's grandmother fed the survivors dinner, and as Miles had hoped seemed quite taken with Elena. Elena was having an attack of shyness in the presence of the admired Countess Vorkosigan's mother, but Miles was fairly sure the old woman would soon bring her out of it. Elena might even pick up a little of her Betan indifference to Barrayaran class distinctions. Might it ease the oppressive constraint that seemed to have been growing between himself and Elena ever since they had ceased to be children? It was the damn Vor-suit he wore, Miles thought. There were days it felt like armor; archaic, clanking, encrusted and spiked. Uncomfortable to wear, impossible to embrace. Give her a can opener, and let her see what a pale soft miserable slug this gaudy shell encloses—not that that would be any less repellent—his thoughts buried themselves in the dark fall of Elena's hair, and he sighed. He realized his grandmother was speaking to him. "I beg your pardon, ma'am?"

"I said," she repeated patiently between bites, "one of my neighbors—you remember him, Mr. Hathaway, who works at the recycling center—I know you met him when you were here to school—"

"Oh, yeah, sure. Him."

"He has a little problem that we thought you might be able to help with, being Barrayaran. He's sort of been saving it for you, since we knew you were coming. He thought, if you weren't too tired, you might even go with him tonight, since it *is* starting to be rather disturbing . . ."

"I really can't tell you all that much about him myself," said Hathaway, staring out over the vast domed arena that was his special charge. Miles wondered how long it would take to get used to the smell. "Except that he says he's a Barrayaran. He disappears from time to time, but he always comes back. I've tried to persuade him to go to a Shelter, at least, but he didn't seem to like the idea. Lately, I haven't been able to get near him. You understand, he's never tried to *hurt* anybody or anything, but you never know, what with his being a Barrayaran and all—oh, sorry . . ."

Hathaway, Miles, and Bothari picked their way across the treacherous and uneven footing. Odd-shaped objects in the piles tended to turn unexpectedly, tripping the unwary. All the detritus of high tech, awaiting apotheosis as the next generation of Betan ingenuity, gleamed out amid more banal and universal human rubbish.

"Oh, damn it," cried Hathaway suddenly, "he's gone and lit a fire again." A small curl of grey smoke was rising a hundred meters away. "I hope he's not burning wood this time. I just *cannot* convince him how valuable—well, at least it makes him easy to find . . ."

A low place in the piles gave an illusion of a sheltered

space. A thin, dark-haired man in his late twenties was hunched glumly over a tiny fire, carefully arranged in the bottom of a shallow parabolic antenna dish. A makeshift table that had started life as a computer desk console was evidently now the man's kitchen, for it held some flat pieces of metal and plastic now doing duty as plates and platters. A large carp, its scales gleaming red-gold, lay gutted and ready for cooking upon it.

Dark eyes, black smudges of weariness beneath them, flashed up at the clank of their approach. The man scrambled to his feet, grabbing what appeared to be a home-made knife; Miles couldn't tell what it was made of, but it was clearly a good one, if it had done the job on the fish. Bothari's hand automatically checked his stunner.

"I think he *is* a Barrayaran," muttered Miles to Bothari. "Look at the way he moves."

Bothari nodded agreement. The man held his knife properly, like a soldier, left hand guarding the right, ready to block a snatch or punch an opening for the weapon. He seemed unconscious of his stance.

Hathaway raised his voice. "Hey, Baz! I brought you some visitors, all right?"

"No."

"Uh, look," Hathaway slid down a pile of rubble, closer but not too close. "I haven't bothered you, have I? I let you hang around in my center for days on end, it's all right as long as you don't carry anything out— that's not wood, is it? oh, all right . . . I'll overlook it this time, but I want you to talk to these guys. I figure you owe me. All right? Anyway, they're Barrayarans."

Baz glanced up at them sharply, his expression a strange mixture of hunger and dismay. His lips formed a silent word. Miles read it, Home. I'm silhouetted, thought Miles; let's get down where he can see the light on my face. He picked his way down beside Hathaway.

Baz stared at him. "You're no Barrayaran," he said flatly.

"I'm half Betan," Miles replied, feeling no desire to go into his medical history just then. "But I was raised on Barrayar. It's home."

"Home," whispered the man, barely audibly.

"You're a long way from home." Miles upended a plastic casing from something-or-other—it had some wires hanging out of it, giving it a sad disembowelled air—and seated himself. Bothari took up position above on the rubble within comfortable pouncing distance. "Did you get stuck here or something? Do you, ah—need some help getting home?"

"No." The man glanced away, frowning. His fire had burned down. He placed a metal grill from an air conditioner over it and laid his fish on top.

Hathaway eyed these preparations with fascination. "What are you going to do with that dead goldfish?"

"Eat it."

Hathaway looked revolted. "Look, mister—all you have to do is report to a Shelter and get Carded, and you can have all the protein slices you want—any flavor, clean and fresh from the vats. Nobody has to eat a dead animal on this planet, really. Where'd you get it, anyway?"

Baz replied uneasily, "Out of a fountain."

Hathaway gasped in horror. "Those displays belong to the Silica Zoo! You can't eat an exhibit!"

"There were lots of them. I didn't think anybody would miss one. It wasn't stealing. I caught it."

Miles rubbed his chin thoughtfully, gave a little upward jerk of his head, and pulled Pilot Officer Mayhew's green bottle, which he had brought along on a last-minute impulse, from under his jacket. Baz started at the movement, then relaxed when he saw it was no weapon. By Barrayaran etiquette, Miles took a swallow first—he made it a small one, this time—wiped the mouthpiece on his sleeve, and offered it to the thin man. "Drink, with dinner? It's good—makes you feel less hungry—dries up your sinuses, too. Tastes like horse-piss and honey."

Baz frowned, but took the bottle. "Thanks." He took a drink, and added in a strangled whisper, "Thanks!"

Baz slipped his dinner onto a cover plate from a tube-car wheel, and sat cross-legged amid the junk to pick out the bones. "Care for any?"

"No, thanks, just had dinner."

"Dear God, I should think not!" cried Hathaway.

"Ah," said Miles. "Changed my mind. Just a taste . . ."
Baz held out a morsel on the point of his knife;
Bothari's hands twitched. Miles lipped it off, camp-
fashion, and chomped it down with a sardonic smile at
Hathaway. Baz waved the bottle at Bothari.

"Would your friend. . .?"

"He can't," excused Miles. "He's on duty."

"Bodyguard," whispered Baz. He looked again at Miles
with that strange expression, fear, and something else.
"What the hell are you?"

"Nothing you need be afraid of. Whatever you're hiding from, it isn't me. You can have my word on that, if
you wish."

"Vor," breathed Baz. "You're Vor."

"Well, yes. And what the hell are you?"

"Nobody." He picked rapidly at his fish. Miles wondered how long it had been since his last meal.

"Hard, to be nobody, in a place like this," Miles observed. "Everybody has a number, everybody has a place
to be—not many interstices, to be nobody in. It must
take a lot of effort and ingenuity."

"You said it," Baz agreed around a mouthful of goldfish. "This is the worst place I've ever been. You've got
to keep moving around all the time."

"You do know," said Miles tentatively, "the Barrayaran
Embassy will help you get home, if you want. Of course,
you have to pay it back later, and they're pretty strict
about collecting—they're not in the business of giving
free rides to hitchhikers—but if you're really in trouble—"

"No!" It was almost a cry. It echoed faintly across the
enormous arena. Baz lowered his voice self-consciously.
"No, I don't want to go home. Sooner or later, I'll pick
up some kind of job at the shuttleport, and ship off
someplace better. There's got to be something turn up
soon."

"If you want work," said Hathaway eagerly, "all you
have to do is register at—"

"I'll get something my own way," Baz cut him off
harshly.

The pieces were falling into place. "Baz doesn't want to register anywhere," Miles explained to Hathaway, coolly didactic. "Up until now, Baz is something I thought impossible on Beta Colony. He's a man who isn't here. He's passed across the information network without a blip. He never arrived—never passed through Customs, and I'll bet that was one hell of a neat trick—as far as the computers are concerned, has not eaten, or slept, or purchased—or Registered, or been Carded—and he would rather starve than do so."

"For pity's sake, why?" asked Hathaway.

"Deserter," commented Bothari laconically from above. "I've seen the look."

Miles nodded. "I think you've hit it, Sergeant."

Baz sprang to his feet. "You're Service Security! You twisty little bastard—"

"Sit down," Miles overrode him, not stirring. "I'm not anybody. I'm just not quite as good at it as you are."

Baz hesitated. Miles studied him seriously, all the pleasure suddenly gone out of the excursion in a wash of cold ambiguity. "I don't suppose—Yeoman?—no. Lieutenant?"

"Yes," growled the man.

"An officer. Yes." Miles chewed his lip, disturbed. "Was it in the heat?"

Baz grimaced reluctantly. "Technically."

"Hm." A deserter. Strange beyond comprehension, for a man to trade the envied splendor of the Service for the worm of fear, riding in his belly like a parasite. Was he running from an act of cowardice? Or another crime? Or an error, some horrible, lethal mistake? Technically, Miles had a duty to help nail the fellow for Service Security. But he had come here tonight to help the man, not destroy him . . .

"I don't understand," said Hathaway. "Has he committed a crime?"

"Yes. A bloody serious one. Desertion in the heat of battle," said Miles. "If he gets extradited home, the penalty's quartering. Technically."

"That doesn't sound so bad," Hathaway shrugged.

"He's been quartered in my recycling center for two months. It could hardly be worse. What's the problem?"

"Quartering," said Miles. "Uh—not domiciled. Cut in four pieces."

Hathaway stared, shocked. "But that would kill him!" He looked around, and wilted under the triple, unified, and exasperated glares of the three Barrayarans.

"Betans," said Baz disgustedly. "I can't stand Betans."

Hathaway muttered something under his breath; Miles caught, "— bloodthirsty barbarians . . ."

"So if you're not Service Security," Baz finished, sitting back down, "you may as well shove off. There's nothing you can do for me."

"I'm going to have to do something," Miles said.

"Why?"

"I'm—I'm afraid I've inadvertantly done you a disservice, Mr., Mr.—you may as well tell me your name . . ."

"Jesek."

"Mr. Jesek. You see, I'm, un, under the scrutiny of Security myself. Just by meeting you, I've endangered your cover. I'm sorry."

Jesek paled. "Why is Service Security watching you?"

"Not the S.S. Imperial Security, I'm afraid."

The breath went out of the deserter as from a body blow, and his face drained utterly. He bent over, his head pressed to his knees, as if to counteract a wave of faintness. A muffled whimper—"God . . ." He stared up at Miles. "What did you *do*, boy?"

Miles said sharply, "I haven't asked you that question, Mr. Jesek!"

The deserter mumbled some apology. I can't let him know who I am, thought Miles, or he'll be off like a shot and run straight into my Security so-called safety net— even as it is, Lt. Croye or his minions from the Barrayaran Embassy Security staff are going to start looking this guy over. They'll go wild when they find he's the invisible man. No later than tomorrow, if they give him the routine check. I've just killed this man—no! "What did you do in the Service, before?" Miles groped for time and thought.

"I was an engineer's assistant."

"Construction? Weapons systems?"

The man's voice steadied. "No, jump ship engines. Some weapons systems. I try to get tech work on private freighters, but most of the equipment I'm trained in is obsolete in this sector. Harmonic impulse engines, Necklin color drive—hard to come by. I've got to get farther out, away from the main economic centers."

A small, high "Hm!" escaped Miles. "Do you know anything about the RG class freighters?"

"Sure. I've worked a couple. Necklin drive. They're all gone now, though."

"Not quite." A discordant excitement shivered through Miles. "I know one. It's going to be making a freight run soon, if it can get a cargo, and crew."

Jesek eyed him suspiciously. "Is it going someplace that doesn't have an extradition treaty with Barrayar?"

"Maybe."

"My lord," Bothari's voice was edged with agitation, "you're not considering *harboring* this deserter?"

"Well . . ." Miles voice was mild. "Technically, I don't know he's a deserter. I've merely heard some allegations."

"He admitted it."

"Bravado, perhaps. Inverted snobbery."

"Are you hankering to be another Lord Vorloupulous?" asked Bothari dryly.

Miles laughed, and sighed; Baz's mouth twisted. Hathaway begged to be let in on the joke.

"It's Barrayaran law again," Miles explained. "Our courts are not kindly disposed to those who maintain the letter of the law and violate its spirit. The classic precedent was the case of Lord Vorloupulous and his 2000 cooks."

"Did he run a chain of restaurants?" asked Hathaway, floundering. "Don't tell me that's illegal on Barrayar too . . ."

"Oh, no. This was at the end of the Time of Isolation, almost a hundred years ago. Emperor Dorca Vorbarra was centralizing the government, and breaking the power of the Counts as separate governing entities—there was a civil war about it. One of the main things he did was eliminate private armies, what they used to call livery and maintenance on old Earth. Each Count was stripped down to twenty armed followers—barely a bodyguard.

"Well, Lord Vorloupulous had a feud going with a few neighbors, for which he found this allotment quite inadequate. So he hired on 2000 'cooks', so-called, and sent them out to carve up his enemies. He was quite ingenious about arming them, butcher knives instead of short swords and so on. There were plenty of recently unemployed veterans looking for work at the time, who weren't too proud to give it a try . . ." Miles's eyes glinted amusement.

"The Emperor, naturally, didn't see it his way. Dorca marched his regular army, by then the only one on Barrayar, on Vorloupulous and arrested him for treason, for which the sentence was—still is—public exposure and death by starvation. So the man with 2000 cooks was condemned to waste away in the Great Square of Vorbarr Sultana. And to think they always said Dorca Vorbarra had no sense of humor . . ."

Bothari smiled grimly, and Baz chuckled; Hathaway's laugh was more hollow. "Charming," he muttered.

"But it had a happy ending," Miles went on. Hathaway brightened. "The Cetagandans invaded us about that point, and Lord Vorloupulous was released."

"By the Cetagandans? Lucky," commented Hathaway.

"No, by Emperor Dorca, to fight the Cetagandans. You understand, he wasn't pardoned—the sentence was merely delayed. When the First Cetagandan War was over, he would have been expected to show up to complete it. But he died fighting, in battle, so he had an honorable death after all."

"That's a happy ending?" Hathaway shrugged. "Oh, well."

Baz, Miles noted, had become silent and withdrawn again. Miles smiled at him, experimentally; he smiled back awkwardly, looking younger for it. Miles made his decision.

"Mr. Jesek, I'm going to make you a proposition, which you can take or leave. That ship I mentioned is the RG 132. The jump pilot officer's name is Arde Mayhew. If you can disappear—I mean *really* disappear—

for the next couple of days, and then get in touch with him at the Silica shuttleport, he'll see that you get a berth on his ship, outbound.''

"Why should you help me at all, Mr.—Lord—"

"Mr. Naismith, for all practical purposes." Miles shrugged. "Call it a fancy for seeing people get second chances. It's something they're not very keen on, at home.''

Home, Baz's eyes echoed silently again. "Well—it was good to hear the accent again, for a little time. I might just take you up on that," he remembered to be cagey, "or I might not.''

Miles nodded, retrieved his bottle, motioned to Bothari, and withdrew. They threaded their way back across the recycling center with an occasional muted clank. When Miles looked back, Jesek was a shadow, melting toward another exit.

Miles became conscious of a profound frown from Sergeant Bothari. He smiled wryly, and kicked over a control casing from some junked industrial robot, lying skeletally athwart a mound of other rubble. "Would you have had me turn him in?" he asked softly. "But you're Service to the bone, I suppose you would. So would my father, I guess—he's so all-fired stringent about the law, no matter how ghastly the consequences.''

Bothari grew still. "Not always, my lord." He retreated into a suddenly neutral silence.

"Miles," whispered Elena, detouring from a nocturnal trip to the bathroom from the bedroom she was sharing with Mrs. Naismith, "aren't you ever going to bed? It's almost morning.''

"Not sleepy." He entered yet another inquiry on his grandmother's comconsole. It was true; he still felt fresh, and preternaturally alert. It was just as well, for he was plugged into a commercial network of enormous complexity. Ninety percent of success seemed to lie in asking the right questions. Tricky, but after several hours work he seemed to be getting the hang of it. "Besides, with Mayhew in the spare bedroom, I'm doomed to the couch.''

"I thought my father had the couch."

"He ceded it to me, with a smile of grim glee. He hates the couch. He slept on it all the time I went to school here. He's blamed every ache, twinge, and lower back pain he's had ever since on it, even after two years. It couldn't possibly be old age creeping up on him, oh, no . . ."

Elena strangled a giggle. She leaned over his shoulder for a look at the screen. The light from it silvered her profile, and the scent of her hair, falling forward, dizzied him. "Finding anything?" she asked.

Miles entered three wrong directions in a row, swore, and refocused his attention. "Yes, I think so. There were a lot more factors to be taken into account than I realized, at first. But I think I've found something—" He retrieved his fumbled data, and waved his finger through the holoscreen. "*That* is my first cargo."

The screen displayed a lengthy manifest. "Agricultural equipment," she analyzed. "Bound for—whatever is Felice?"

"It's a country on Tau Verde IV, wherever *that* is. It's a four-week run—I've been cost-calculating fuel, and supplies, and the logistics of it in general—everything from spare parts to toilet paper. That's not what's interesting, though. What's interesting is that with that cargo I can pay for the trip *and* clear my debt to Calhoun, well inside the time limit on my note." His voice went small. "I'm afraid I, uh, underestimated the time I'd need for the RG 132 to run enough cargos to cover my note, a little. A lot. Well, quite a lot. Badly. The ship costs more to run than I'd realized, when I finally went to add up all the real numbers." He pointed to a figure. "But that's what they're offering for transport, C.O.D. Felice. And the cargo's ready to go immediately."

Her eyebrows drew down in awed puzzlement. "Pay for the whole ship in one run? But that's wonderful! But . . ."

He grinned. "But?"

"But why hasn't somebody else snapped up this cargo? It seems to have been sitting in the warehouse a long time."

"Clever girl," he crooned encouragingly. "Go on."

"I see they only pay on delivery. But maybe that's normal?"

"Yes . . ." he spread the word out, like butter. "Anything else?"

She pursed her lips. "Something's weird."

"Indeed." His eyes crinkled. "Something is, as you say, weird."

"Do I have to guess? Because if I do, I'm going back to bed . . ." She stifled a yawn.

"Ah. Well—Tau Verde IV is in a war zone, at the moment. It seems there is a planetary war in progress. One of the sides has the local wormhole exit blocked—not by their own people, it seems to be a somewhat industrially backward place—they've hired a mercenary fleet. And why has this cargo been mouldering in a warehouse so long? Because none of the big shipping companies will carry into a war zone—their insurance lapses. That goes for most of the little independents, as well. But since I'm not insured, it does not go for me." He smirked.

Elena looked doubtful. "Is it dangerous, crossing the blockade? If you cooperate on their stop-and-search—"

"In this case, I think so. The cargo happens to be addressed to the other side of the fray."

"Would the mercenaries seize it? I mean, robotic combines or whatever couldn't be classed as contraband—don't they have to abide by interstellar conventions?" Her doubt became wariness.

He stretched, still smiling. "You've almost got it. What is Beta Colony's most noted export?"

"Well, advance technology, of course. Weapons and weapons systems—" her wariness became dismay. "Oh, Miles . . ."

" 'Agricultural equipment'," he snickered. "I'll bet! Anyway, there's this Felician who claims to be the agent for the company purchasing the equipment—that's another tip-off, that they should have a man personally shepherding this cargo through—I'm going to go see him first thing in the morning, as soon as the Sergeant wakes up. And Mayhew, I'd better take Mayhew . . ."

CHAPTER SEVEN ✷ ✷ ✷

Miles reviewed his troops, before pressing the buzzer to the hotel room. Even in civilian dress, there was no mistaking the Sergeant for anything but a soldier. Mayhew—washed, shaved, rested, fed, and dressed in clean new clothes—looked infinitely better than yesterday, but still . . .

"Straighten up, Arde," advised Miles, "and try to look professional. We've just got to get this cargo. I thought Betan medicine was advanced enough to cure any kind of hangover. It's bound to make a bad impression on this guy if you walk around clutching your stomach."

"Grm," muttered Mayhew. But he did return his hands to his sides, and come more-or-less to attention. "You'll find out, kid," he added in a tone of bitter clairvoyance.

"And you're going to have to stop calling me 'kid'," Miles added. "You're my Armsman now. You're supposed to address me as 'my lord'."

"You really take that stuff seriously?"

One step at a time. "It's like a salute," Miles explained. "You salute the uniform, not the man. Being Vor is—is like wearing an invisible uniform you can never take off. Look at Sergeant Bothari—he's called me 'my lord' ever since I was born. If he can, you can. You're his brother-in-arms, now."

Mayhew looked up at the Sergeant. Bothari looked back, his face saturnine in the extreme. Miles had the impression that had Bothari been a more expressive man, he would have made a rude noise at the concept of Mayhew as his brother-in-arms. Mayhew evidently received the same impression, for he straightened up a little more, and bit out, "Yes, my lord."

Miles nodded approval, and pressed the buzzer.

The man who answered the door had dark almond eyes, high cheekbones, skin the color of coffee and cream, and bright copper-colored hair, tightly curled as wire, cropped close to his head. His eyes searched the trio anxiously, widening a little at Miles; he had only seen Miles's face that morning, over the viewscreen. "Mr. Naismith? I'm Carle Daum. Come in."

Daum closed the door behind them quickly, and fussed at the lock. Miles deduced they'd just passed through a weapons scan, and the Felician was sneaking a peek at his readout. The man turned back with a look of nervous suspicion, one hand automatically touching his right hip pocket. His gaze did not linger elsewhere in the little hotel room, and Bothari's lips twitched satisfaction at Daum's unconscious revelation of the weapon he must watch for. Legal stunner, most likely, thought Miles, but you never know.

"Won't you sit down?" the Felician invited. His speech had a soft and curious resonance to Miles's ear, neither the flat nasal twang, heavy on the r's, of the Betans, nor the clipped cold gutturals of Barrayar. Bothari indicated he would prefer to stand, and took up position to Daum's right, uncomfortably far over in the Felician's peripheral vision. Miles and Mayhew sat before a low table. Daum sat across from them, his back to a "window", actually a viewscreen, bright with a panorama of mountains and a lake from some other world. The wind that really howled far overhead would have scoured such trees to sticks in a day. The window silhouetted Daum, while revealing his visitors' expressions in full light; Miles appreciated the choice of views.

"Well, Mr. Naismith," began Daum. "Tell me something about your ship. What is its cargo capacity?"

"It's an RG class freighter. It can easily handle twice the mass of your manifest, assuming those figures you put into the com system are quite correct. . .?"

Daum did not react to this tiny bait. Instead he said, "I'm not very familiar with jump ships. Is it fast?"

"Pilot Officer Mayhew?" Miles prodded.

"Huh? Oh. Uh, do you mean acceleration? Steady, just steady. We boost a little longer, and get there nearly as fast in the end."

"Is it very maneuverable?"

Mayhew stared. "Mr. Daum, it's a freighter."

Daum's lips compressed with annoyance. "I know that. The question is—"

"The question is," Miles interrupted, "can we either outrun or evade your blockade. The answer is no. You see, I've done my homework."

Frustration darkened Daum's face. "Then we seem to be wasting each other's time. So much time lost ..." He began to rise.

"The next question is, is there another way to get your cargo to its destination? Yes, I believe," said Miles firmly.

Daum sat back, tense with mistrust and hope. "Go on."

"You've done as much yourself already, in the Betan's comm system. Camouflage. I believe your cargo can be camouflaged well enough to pass a blockade inspection. But we'll have to work together on it, and somewhat more frankly—ah ..." Miles made a calculation, based on the Felician's age and bearing, "Major Daum?"

The man twitched. Ah ha, thought Miles, nailed him on the first try. He compressed this internal crow to a suave smile.

"If you're a Pelian spy, or an Oseran mercenary, I swear I'll kill you—" Daum began. Bothari's eyelids drooped, in a pose of deceptive calm.

"I'm not," said Miles, "although it would be a great ploy, if I were. Load up you and your weapons, take you halfway, and make you get out and walk—I appreciate your need for caution."

"What weapons?" said Daum, attempting belatedly to regain his cover.

"What weapons?" echoed Mayhew, in a frantic, near-silent whisper to Miles's ear.

"Your plowshares and pruning hooks, then," said Miles tolerantly. "But I suggest we end the game and get to work. I am a professional—" and if you buy that, I have this nice farmland on Barrayar for sale, "and so, obviously, are you, or you wouldn't have gotten this far."

Mayhew's eyes widened. Under the guise of shifting in his seat, Miles kicked him preemptively in the ankle. Make a note, he thought; next time, wake him earlier and brief him better. Although getting the pilot officer functional that morning had been rather like trying to raise the dead. Miles was not sure he could have succeeded, earlier.

"You're a mercenary soldier?" said Daum.

"Ah . . ." said Miles. He had meant to imply, a professional shipmaster—but might this be even more attractive to the Felician? "What do you think, Major?"

Bothari stopped breathing a moment. Mayhew, however, looked suddenly dismayed. "So that's what you meant yesterday," he murmured. "Recruiting . . ."

Miles, who had meant nothing of a kind in his facetious crack about looking for desperate men, murmured back, "Of course," in a tone of maximum off-handedness. "Surely you realized . . ."

Daum looked doubtfully at Mayhew, but then his gaze fell on Bothari. Bothari maintained parade rest and an expression of remarkable blankness. Belief hardened in Daum's eyes. "By God," he muttered, "if the Pelians can hire galactics, why can't we?" He raised his voice. "How many troops are in your outfit? What ships do you have?"

Oh, hell—now what? Mile's extemporized like mad. "Major Daum, I didn't mean to mislead you—" Bothari breathed, gratefully, Miles saw from the corner of his eye, "I'm, uh—detached from my outfit at the moment. They're tied up on another contract. I was just visiting Beta Colony for, uh, medical reasons, so I have only myself and, ah, my immediate staff, and a ship my fleet could spare, here to offer you. But we're expected to operate independently, in my bunch," exhale, Sergeant, please exhale, "so since it will be a little time yet before

I can rejoin them, and I find your problem tactically interesting, my services are yours."

Daum nodded slowly, "I see. And by what rank should I address you?"

Miles nearly appointed himself Admiral on the spot. Captain? Yeoman? he wondered wildly. "Let's just leave it at Mr. Naismith, for now," he suggested coolly. "A centurion without his hundred men is, after all, a centurion in name only. At the moment, we need to be dealing with realities." Do we ever . . .

"What's the name of your outfit?"

Miles free-associated frantically. "The Dendarii Mercenaries." It fell trippingly from the tongue, at least.

Daum studied him hungrily. "I've been tied down in this damn place for two months, looking for a carrier that would haul me, that I could trust. If I wait much longer, could be delay will destroy the purpose of my mission as certainly as any betrayal. Mr. Naismith, I've waited long enough—too long. I'm going to take a chance on you."

Miles nodded satisfaction, as if he had been concluding such transactions all of a somewhat longer life than he actually possessed. "Then Major Daum, I undertake to get you to Tau Verde IV. My word on it. The first thing I need is more intelligence. Tell me all you know about the Oseran Mercenaries' blockade procedures . . ."

"It was my understanding, my lord," said Bothari severely as they left Daum's hotel for the slidewalk, "that Pilot Officer Mayhew here was to transport your cargo. You didn't tell me anything about going along yourself."

Miles shrugged, elaborately casual. "There are so many variables, so much at stake—I've just got to be on the spot. It's unfair to dump it all on Arde's shoulders. I mean, would you?"

Bothari, apparently caught between his disapproval of his leige lord's get-rich-quick scheme and his low opinion of the pilot officer, gave a noncommittal grunt, which Mayhew chose not to notice.

Miles's eyes glinted. "Besides, it'll put a little excitement in your life, Sergeant. It has to be dull as dirt, following me around all day. I'd be bored to tears."

"I like being bored," said Bothari morosely.

Miles grinned, secretly relieved at not being taken more strictly to task for his "Dendarii Mercenaries" outbreak. Well, the brief moment of fantasy was probably harmless enough.

The three of them found Elena stalking back and forth across Mrs. Naismith's living room. Two bright spots of color burned in her cheeks, her nostrils flared, and she was muttering under her breath. She transfixed Miles with an angry glare as he entered. "Betans!" she bit out in a voice of loathing.

This only let him half off the hook. "What's the matter?" he inquired cautiously.

She took another turn around the room, stiff-legged, as if trampling bodies underfoot. "That awful holovid," she glowered. "How can they—oh, I can't even describe it."

Ah ha, she found one of the pornography channels, thought Miles. Well, it had to happen eventually. "Holovid?" he said brightly.

"How could they permit such horrible slanders on Admiral Vorkosigan, and Prince Serg, and our forces? I think the producer should be taken out and shot! And the actors—and the scriptwriter—we would at home, by God . . ."

Not the pornography channel, evidently. "Uh, Elena—just what have you been looking at?"

His grandmother was seated, with a fixed nervous smile, in her float chair. "I tried to explain that it's fictionalized—you know, to make the history more dramatic . . ."

Elena gave vent to an ominous rattling hiss; Miles gave his grandmother a pleading look.

"*The Thin Blue Line*," Mrs. Naismith explained cryptically.

"Oh, I've seen that one," said Mayhew. "It's a rerun."

Miles recalled the docudrama vividly himself; it had first been released two years ago, and had contributed its mite to making his school visit to Beta Colony the sometimes surreal experience it had been. Miles's father, then-Commodore Vorkosigan, had begun the aborted Barrayaran invasion of Beta Colony's ally Escobar 19 years ago as a Staff officer. He had ended, upon the catastrophic deaths of the co-commanders Admiral Vorrutyer and Crown Prince Serg Vorbarra, as commander of the armada. His brilliant retreat was still cited as exemplary, in the military annals of Barrayar. The Betans naturally took a different view of the affair. The blue in the title of the docudrama referred to the color of the uniform worn by the Betan Expeditionary Force, of which Captain Cordelia Naismith had been a part.

"It's—it's . . ." Elena turned to Miles. "There isn't any truth in it—is there?"

"Well," said Miles, equable from years of practice in coming to terms with the Betan version of history, "some. But my mother says they never wore the blue uniforms until the war was practically over. And she swears up and down, privately, that she didn't murder Admiral Vorrutyer, but she won't say who did. Protests too much, I think. All my father will ever say about Vorrutyer is that he was a brilliant defensive strategist. I've never been quite sure what to make of that, since Vorrutyer was in charge of the offense. All my mother says about him is that he was a bit strange, which doesn't sound too bad, until I reflect that she's a Betan. They've never said a word against Prince Serg, and Father was on his staff and knew him, so I guess the Betan version of him is mainly a crock of war propaganda."

"Our greatest hero," cried Elena. "The Emperor's father—how dare they—"

"Well, even on our side, consensus seems to be that we were overreaching ourselves, to try and take Escobar, on top of Komarr and Sergyar."

Elena turned to her father, as the resident expert. "You served with my lord Count at Escobar, sir! Tell *her*—" a toss of her head indicated Mrs. Naismith, "it isn't so!"

"I don't remember Escobar," replied the Sergeant stonily, in a tone unusually flat and unencouraging even for him. "No point to that—" he jerked one large hand, thumb hooked in his belt, toward the holovid viewer. "It was wrong for you to see that."

The tension in Bothari's shoulders disturbed Miles, and the set look about his eyes. Anger? Over an ephemeral holovid which he had seen before, and ignored as readily as Miles had?

Elena paused, diverted and confused. "Don't remember? But . . ."

Something clicked in Miles's memory—the medical discharge, at last accounted for? "I didn't realize—were you wounded at Escobar, Sergeant?" No wonder he's twitchy about it, then.

Bothari's lips moved about the beginning of the word, wounded. "Yes," he muttered. His eyes shifted away from Miles and Elena.

Miles gnawed his lip. "Head wound?" he inquired in a burst of surmise.

Bothari's gaze shifted back to Miles, quellingly. "Mm."

Miles permitted himself to be quelled, hugging this new prize of information to himself. A head wound would account for much, that had long bemused him in his leigeman.

Taking the hint, Miles changed the subject firmly. "Be that as it may," he swept Elena a courtly bow—whatever happened to plumed hats, for men?—"I got my cargo."

Elena's irritation vanished instantly in pleased interest. "Oh, grand! And have you figured out how to get it past the blockade yet?"

"Working on it. Would you care to do some shopping for me? Supplies for the trip. Put the orders in to the ship chandlers—you can do it from here on the comconsole, Grandmother'll show you how. Arde has a standard list. We need everything—food, fuel cells, emergency oxygen, first-aid supplies—and at the best price you can get. This thing is going to wipe out my travel allowance, so anything you can save—eh?" He gave his draftee his most encouraging smile, as if the offer of two full days locked in struggle with the electronic labyrinth of Betan business practices was a high treat.

Elena looked doubtful. "I've never outfitted a ship before."

"It'll be easy," he assured her airily. "Just bang into it—you'll have it figured out in no time. If I can do it, you can do it." He zipped lightly over this argument, giving her no time to reflect on the fact that he had never outfitted a ship either. "Figure for Pilot Officer, Engineer, the Sergeant, me, and Major Daum, for eight weeks, and maybe a little margin, but not too much—remembering the budget. We boost the day after tomorrow."

"All right—when. . .?" she snapped to full alertness, thunder in the crimp of her black winging eyebrows. "What about me? You're not leaving me behind while you—"

Metaphorically, Miles slunk behind Bothari and waved a white flag. "That's up to your father. And Grandmother, of course."

"She's welcome to stay with me," said Mrs. Naismith faintly. "But Miles—you just got here . . ."

"Oh, I still mean to make my visit, ma'am," Miles reassured her. "We'll just reschedule our return to Barrayar. It's not like I had to—to get back in time for school or anything."

Elena stared at her father, tight-lipped with silent pleading. Bothari blew out his breath, his gaze turning calculatingly from his daughter to Mrs. Naismith to the holovid viewer, then inward to what thoughts or memories Miles could not guess. Elena barely restrained herself from hopping up and down in agitation. "Miles—my lord—you can order him to—"

Miles flicked a hand palm-out, and gave a tiny shake of his head, signalling, wait.

Mrs. Naismith glanced at Elena's anxiety, and smiled thoughtfully behind her hand. "Actually, dear, it would be lovely having you all to myself for a time. Like having a daughter again. You could meet young people— go to parties—I have some friends over in Quartz who could take you desert-trekking. I'm too old for the sport myself, now, but I'm sure you'd enjoy it . . ."

Bothari flinched. Quartz, for example, was Beta Colony's principle hermaphrodite community, and although Mrs. Naismith herself typified hermaphrodites as "people who are pathologically incapable of making up their minds," she bristled in patriotic Betan defense of them at Bothari's open Barrayaran revulsion to the sex. And Bothari had personally carried Miles home unconscious from more than one Betan party. As for Miles's nearly-disastrous desert-trek . . . Miles shot his grandmother a look of thanks from crinkling eyes. She acknowledged it with a puckish nod, and smiled blandly at Bothari.

Bothari was unamused. Not ironically unamused, befitting the interplay, as his guerilla warfare with Mrs. Naismith on the subject of Miles's cultural mores usually was; but genuinely enraged. An odd knot formed in Miles's stomach. He came to a species of attention, querying his bodyguard with puzzled eyes.

"She goes with us," Bothari growled. Elena nearly clapped her hands in triumph, although Mrs. Naismith's list of proposed treats had plainly eroded her resolve not to be left sitting in the baggage train when the troops moved out. But Bothari's eyes raked past his daughter unresponsively, lingered for a last frown at the holovid, and met Miles's—beltbuckle.

"Excuse me, my lord. I'll—patrol the hall, until you're ready to leave again." He exited stiffly, great hands, all bone and tendon, vein and corded muscle, held half-curled by his sides.

Yes, go, thought Miles, and see if you can patrol up your self-control out there. Overreacting a tad, aren't you? Admittedly, nobody likes having their tail twisted.

"Whew," said Mayhew, as the door closed. "What bit him?"

"Oh, dear," said Mrs. Naismith. "I hope I didn't offend him." But she added under her breath, "the hypocritical old stick . . ."

"He'll come down," Miles promised. "Just leave him alone for a while. Meantime, there's work to do. You heard the man, Elena. Supplies for a crew of two and a supercargo of four."

*   *   *

The next 48 hours were a blur of motion. To prepare an eight-week run for the old ship within that time limit would have been mind-boggling for an ordinary cargo, but crammed atop that were extras needed for the camouflage scheme. These included a partial cargo of hastily purchased items to provide them with a real manifest in which to embed the false, and supplies needed for rearranging the cargo hold bulkheads, flung aboard to wait the actual work to be done en route. Most vital, and correspondingly expensive, were the extremely advanced Betan mass detector jammers, to be run off the ship's artificial gravity and with which, Miles hoped, they would foil the Oseran Mercenaries' cargo check. It had taken all the simulated political weight Miles could muster on the basis of his father's name to convince the Betan company representative that he was a qualified purchaser of the new and still partially classified equipment.

The mass jammers came with an astonishingly lengthy file of instructions. Miles, studying them in bewilderment, began to have qualms over Baz Jesek's qualifications as an engineer. These gave way, as the hours passed, to even more frantic doubts about whether the man was going to show at all. The level of liquid in Mayhew's green bottle, now wholly expropriated by Miles, dropped steadily, and Miles sweated sleeplessly.

The Betan shuttleport authorities, Miles found, were not sympathetic to the suggestion that their stiff usage fees be paid on credit. He was forced to strip himself of his entire travel allowance. It had seemed a wildly generous one, back on Barrayar, but in the suction of these new demands it vanished literally overnight. Growing creative, Miles turned in his first-class return ticket to Barrayar upon one of the better-known commercial spacelines for a third-class one. Then Bothari's. Then Elena's. Then all three were exchanged for tickets on a line Miles had never heard of; then, with a low, guilty mutter of "I'll buy everybody new ones when we get back—or run a cargo to Barrayar on the RG 132," he cashed them in entirely. At the end of two days he found himself teetering atop a dizzying financial structure compounded of truth, lies, credit, cash purchases, advances on advances, shortcuts, a tiny bit of blackmail, false advertising, and yet another mortgage on some more of his glow-in-the-dark farmland.

Supplies were loaded. Daum's cargo, a fascinating array of odd-shaped anonymous plastic crates, was put aboard. Jesek showed. Systems were checked, and Jesek was instantly put to work jury-rigging vital repairs. Luggage, scarcely opened, was stuffed back together and sent back up. Some good-byes were said; others carefully avoided. Miles had dutifully reported to Bothari that he'd talked to Lieutenant Croye; it wasn't Miles's fault if Bothari neglected to ask what he'd said. At last, they stood in Silica Shuttleport Docking Bay 27, ready to go.

"Waldo handling fee," stated the Betan shuttleport cargo master. "Three-hundred-ten Betan dollars; foreign currencies not accepted." He smiled pleasantly, like a very courteous shark.

Miles cleared his throat nervously, stomach churning. He mentally reviewed his finances. Daum's resources had been stripped in the last two days; indeed, if something Miles had overheard was correct, the man was planning to leave his hotel bill unpaid. Mayhew had already put everything he had into emergency repairs on the ship. Miles had even floated one loan from his grandmother. Courteously, she'd called it her "investment". Just like the *Golden Hind*, she'd said. Some kind of ass, anyway, Miles had reflected in a moment of quavering doubt. He had accepted, rawly embarrassed, but too harried to forgo the offer.

Miles swallowed—perhaps it was pride going down that made that lump—took Sergeant Bothari aside, and lowered his voice. "Uh, Sergeant—I know my father made you a travel allowance . . ."

Bothari's lips twisted thoughtfully, and he gave Miles a penetrating stare. He knows he can kill this scheme right here, Miles realized, and return to his life of boredom—God knows my father'd back him up. He loathed wheedling Bothari, but added, "I could repay you in eight weeks, two for one—for your left pocket? My word on it."

Bothari frowned. "It's not necessary for you to redeem your word to me, my lord. That was pre-paid, long ago." He looked down at his leige lord, hesitated a long moment, sighed, then dolefully emptied his pockets into Miles's hands.

"Thanks." Miles smiled awkwardly, turned away, then turned back. "Uh—can we keep this between you and me? I mean, no need to mention it to my father?"

An involuntary smile turned one corner of the Sergeant's mouth. "Not if you pay me back," he murmured blandly.

And so it was done. What a joy, Miles thought, to be a military ship captain—just bill it all to the Emperor. They must feel like a courtesan with a charge card. Not like us poor working girls.

He stood in the Nav and Com room of his own ship and watched Arde Mayhew, far more alert and focused than Miles had ever seen him before, complete the traffic control checklist. In the screen the glimmering ochre crescent of Beta Colony turned beneath them.

"You are cleared to break orbit," came the voice of traffic control. A wave of dizzy excitement swept through Miles. They were really going to bring this off . . .

"Uh, just a minute, RG 132," the voice added. "You have a communication."

"Pipe it up," said Mayhew, settling under his headset.

This time a frantic face appeared on the viewscreen. Not one Miles wanted to see. He braced himself, quelling guilt.

Lieutenant Croye spoke urgently, tense. "My lord! Is Sergeant Bothari with you?"

"Not just this second. Why?" The Sergeant was below, with Daum, already beginning to tear out bulkheads.

"Who is with you?"

"Just Pilot Officer Mayhew and myself." Miles found he was holding his breath. So close . . .

Croye relaxed just a little. "My lord, you could not have known this, but that engineer you hired is a deserter from Imperial Service. You must shuttle down immediately, and find some pretext for him to accompany you. Make sure the Sergeant is with you—the man must be regarded as dangerous. We'll have a Betan Security patrol waiting at the docking bay. And also," he glanced aside at something, "what the devil did you do to that Tav Calhoun fellow? He's here at the Embassy, howling for the ambassador . . ."

Mayhew's eyes widened in alarm.

"Uh . . ." said Miles. Tachycardia, that's what it was called. Could 17-year-olds have heart attacks? "Lieutenant Croye, that transmission was extremely garbled. Could you repeat?" He shot Mayhew an imploring glance. Mayhew gestured at a panel. Croye began his message again, starting to look disturbed. Miles opened the panel and stared at a spidery maze of wires. His head seemed to swim dizzily in panic. So close . . .

"You're still garbled, sir," said Miles brightly. "Here, I'll fix it. Oh, damn." He pulled six tiny wires at random. The screen dissolved in sparkling snow. Croye was cut off in mid-sentence.

"Boost, Arde!" cried Miles. Mayhew needed no urging. Beta Colony wheeled away beneath them.

Quite dizzy. And nauseated. Blast it, this wasn't free fall. He sat abruptly on the deck, weak from the near-disaster. No, it was something more. He had a paranoid flash about alien plagues, then realized what was happening to him.

Mayhew stared, looking first alarmed, then sardonically understanding. "It's about time that stuff caught up with you," he remarked, and keyed the intercom. "Sergeant Bothari? Would you report to Nav and Com, please? Your, uh, lord needs you." He smiled acidly at Miles, who was beginning to seriously repent some of the harsh things he'd said to Mayhew three days ago.

The Sergeant and Elena appeared. Elena was saying, "— everything's so dirty. The medical cabinet doors just came off in my hands, and—" Bothari snapped to alertness at Miles's hunched huddle, and quizzed Mayhew with angry eyes.

"His creme de meth just wore off," Mayhew explained. "Drops you in a hurry, doesn't it, kid?"

Miles mumbled, an inarticulate groan. Bothari growled something exasperatedly under his breath about "deserve", picked him up, and slung him unceremoniously over his shoulder.

"Well, at least he'll stop bouncing off the walls, and give us all a break," said Mayhew cheerfully. "I've never seen anybody overrev on that stuff the way he did."

"Oh, was that liquor of yours a stimulant?" asked Elena. "I wondered why he didn't fall asleep."

"Couldn't you tell?" chuckled Mayhew.

"Not really."

Miles twisted his head to take in Elena's upside-down worried face, and smile in weak reassurance. Sparkly black and purple whirlpools clouded his vision.

Mayhew's laughter faded. "My God," he said hollowly, "you mean he's like that *all the time*?"

CHAPTER EIGHT ✳ ✳ ✳

Miles extinguished his welding tool, and pushed back his safety goggles. Done. He glanced with pride back up the neat seam that sealed the last false bulkhead into place. If I can't be a soldier, he thought, perhaps I have a future as an engineer's assistant. About time I got some use out of being a shrimp ... He called back over his shoulder, "You can pull me out now."

Hands grasped his booted ankles, and dragged him out of the crawl space. "Try your black box now, Baz," he suggested, sitting up and stretching cramped muscles. Daum watched anxiously over the engineer's shoulder as he began, once again, to dry-run the check procedure. Jesek walked back and forth beside the bulkhead, scanning. At last, finally, for the first time in seven trials, all the lights on his probe remained green.

A smile lit his tired face. "I think we've done it. According to this, there's nothing behind that wall but the next wall."

Miles grinned at Daum. "I gave you my word I'd get it together in time, did I not?"

Daum grinned back, relieved. "You're lucky you don't own a faster ship."

The intercom buzzed in the cargo hold. "Uh, my lord?" came Mayhew's voice. It had an edge that popped Miles instantly to his feet.

"Trouble, Arde?"

"We're coming up on the jump to Tau Verde in about

two hours. There's something out here I think you and the Major ought to have a look at."

"Blockaders? This side of the exit? They'd have no legal authority—"

"No, it's a buoy, of a sort." Mayhew sounded distinctly unhappy. "If you were expecting this, I think you might have told me . . ."

"Back in a few minutes, Baz," Miles promised, "and we'll help you rearrange the cargo in here more artistically. Maybe we could pile up a bunch against that first seam I welded."

"It's not that bad," Jesek reassured him. "I've seen professional work with more slop."

In Nav and Com Miles and Daum found Mayhew staring, aggrieved, at a screen readout.

"What is it, Arde?" asked Miles.

"Oseran warning buoy. They have to have it, for the regular merchant shipping lanes. It's supposed to prevent accidents, and misunderstandings, in case anybody doesn't know what's going on on the other side—but this time there's a twist. Listen to this." He flipped on the audio.

"Attention. Attention. To all commercial, military, or diplomatic shipping planning to enter Tau Verde local space, warning. You are entering a restricted military area. All entering traffic, without exception, is subject to search and seizure for contraband. Any non-cooperation will be construed as hostile, and the vessel subjected to confiscation or destruction without further warning. Proceed at your own risk.

"Upon emergence into Tau Verde local space, all vessels will be approached and boarded for inspection. All wormhole jump Pilot Officers will be detained at this time, until their vessel completes its contact with Tau Verde IV and returns to the jump point. Pilot Officers will be permitted to rejoin their vessels upon completion of the outbound inspection . . ."

"Hostages, damn it," groaned Daum. "They're taking hostages now."

"And a very clever choice of hostages," added Miles

through his teeth. "Especially for a cul-de-sac like Tau Verde, taking your jump pilot traps you like a bug in a bottle. If you're not a good little tourist there, you just might not be allowed to go home. This is new, you say?"

"They weren't doing it five months.ago," said Daum. "I haven't had word from home since I got out. But this means the fighting must still be going on, at.least." He stared intently into the viewscreen, as if he could see through the invisible gateway to his home.

The message went on into technicalities, and ended, "By order of Admiral Yuan Oser, Commanding, Oseran Free Mercenary Fleet, under contract to the legal government of Pelias, Tau Verde IV."

"Legal government!" Daum spat angrily. "Pelians! Damned self-aggrandizing criminals . . ."

Miles whistled soundlessly and stared into the wall. If I really were a nervous entrepreneur trying to unload that odd-lot of crap down there, what would I do? he wondered. I wouldn't be happy about dropping my pilot, but—I sure wouldn't be arguing with a disruptor bell-muzzle. Meek. "We are going to be meek," said Miles forcefully.

They hesitated half a day on the near side of the exit, to put the finishing touches on the arrangement of the cargo, and rehearse their roles. Miles took Mayhew aside for a closed debate, witnessed by Bothari alone. He opened bluntly, studying the pilot's unhappy face.

"Well, Arde, do you want to back out?"

"Can I?" the pilot asked hopefully.

"I'm not going to order you into a hostage situation. If you choose to volunteer, I swear not to abandon you in it. Well, I'm already sworn, as your leige lord, but I don't expect you to know—"

"What happens if I don't volunteer?"

"Once we jump to Tau Verde local space, we'd have no effective way of resisting a demand for your surrender. So I guess we apologize to Daum for wasting his time and money, turn around, and go home." Miles sighed. "If Calhoun was at the Embassy for the reason I think when we left, he's probably started legal procedings to reposses the ship by now." He tried to lighten his voice. "I expect we'll end up back where we began the day I met you, only more broke. Maybe I can find some way to make up Daum's losses to him . . ." Miles trailed off in penitent thought.

"What if—" began Mayhew. He looked at Miles curiously. "What if they'd wanted, say, Sergeant Bothari instead of me? What would you have done then?"

"Oh, I'd go in," said Miles automatically, then paused. The air hung empty, waiting for explanation. "That's different. The Sergeant is—is my leige-man."

"And I'm not?" asked Mayhew ironically. "The State Department will be relieved."

There was a silence. "I'm your leige lord," replied Miles at last, soberly. "What you are is a question only you can answer."

Mayhew stared into his lap, and rubbed his forehead tiredly, one finger unconsciously caressing a silver circle of his implant contact. He looked up at Miles then, an odd hunger in his eyes that reminded Miles for a disquieting instant of the homesick Baz Jesek. "I don't know what I am anymore," said Mayhew finally. "But I'll make the jump for you. And the rest of the horsing around."

A queasy wavering dizziness—a few seconds static in the mind—and the wormhole jump to Tau Verde was done. Miles hovered impatiently in Nav and Com, waiting for Mayhew, whose few seconds had been biochemically stretched to subjective hours, to crawl out from under his headset. He wondered again just what it was pilots experienced threading a jump that their passengers did not. And where did they go, the one ship in ten thousand that jumped and was never seen again? "Take a wormhole jump to hell" was an old curse one almost never heard in a pilot's mouth.

Mayhew swung his headset, stretched, and let out his breath. His face seemed grey and lined, drained from the concentration of the jump. "That was a shit-kicker," he muttered, then straightened, grinned, and met Miles's eye. "That'll never be a popular run, let me tell you, kid. Interesting, though."

Miles did not bother to correct the honorific. Letting Mayhew rest, he slid into the comconsole himself and punched up a view of the outside world. "Well ..." he muttered after a few moments, "where are they? Don't tell me we got the party ready and the guest of honor's not coming—are we in the right place?" he demanded anxiously of Mayhew.

Mayhew raised his eyebrows. "Kid, at the end of a wormhole jump you're either in the right place or you're a bucket of quarks smeared between Antares and Oz." But he checked anyway. "Seems to be ..."

It was a full four hours before a blockade ship finally approached them. Miles's nerves stretched taut. Its slow approach seemed freighted with deliberate menace, until voice contact was made. The mercenary communication officer's tone of sleepy boredom then put it in its true light; they were sauntering. Desultorily, a boarding shuttle was launched.

Miles hovered in the shuttle hatch corridor, scenarios of possible disasters flashing through his mind. *Daum has been betrayed by a quisling. The war is over, and the side we're expecting to pay us has lost. The mercenaries have turned pirate and are going to steal my ship. Some klutz has dropped and broken their mass detector, and so they're going to physically measure all our interior volumes, and they won't add up* ... This last notion, once it occurred to him, seemed so likely that he held his breath until he spotted the mercenary technician in charge of the instrument among the boarders.

There were nine of them, all men, all bigger than Miles, and all lethally armed. Bothari, unarmed and unhappy about it, stood behind Miles and inspected them coldly.

There was something motley about them. The grey-and-white uniforms? They weren't particularly old, but some were in disrepair, others dirty. But were they too busy to waste time on non-essentials, or merely too lazy to keep up appearances? At least one man seemed out-of-focus, leaning against a wall. Drunk on duty? Recovering from wounds? They bore an odd variety of weapons, stunners, nerve disruptors, plasma arcs, needlers. Miles tried to add them up and evaluate them the way Bothari would. Hard to tell their working condition from the outside.

"All right," a big man shouldered through the bunch. "Who's in charge of this hulk?"

Miles stepped forward. "I'm Naismith, the owner, sir," he stated, trying to sound very polite. The big man obviously commanded the boarders, and perhaps even the cruiser, judging from his rank insignia.

The mercenary captain's eyes flicked over Miles; a quirk of an eyebrow, a shrug of contemptuous dismissal, clearly categorized Miles as No Threat. *That's just what I want*, Miles reminded himself firmly. *Good.*

The mercenary heaved a sigh of ennui. "All right, Shorty, let's get this over with. Is this your whole crew?" He gestured to Mayhew and Daum, flanking Bothari.

Miles lidded his eyes against a flash of anger. "My engineer's at his station, sir," he said, hoping he was achieving the right tone of a timid man anxious to please.

"Search 'em," the big man directed over his shoulder. Bothari stiffened; Miles met his look of annoyance with a quelling shake of his head. Bothari submitted to being pawed over with an obvious ill-grace that was not lost on the mercenary captain. A sour smile slid over the man's face.

The mercenary captain split his crew into three search parties, and gestured Miles and his people ahead of him to Nav and Com. His two soldiers began spot-checking everything that would come apart, even disassembling the padded swivel chairs. Leaving all in disarray, they went on to the cabins, where the search took on the nature of a ransacking. Miles clenched his teeth and smiled meekly as his personal effects were dumped pell-mell on the floor and kicked through.

"These guys have got *nothing* worth having, Captain

Auson," muttered one soldier, sounding savagely disappointed. "Wait, here's something . . ."

Miles froze, appalled at his own carelessness. In collecting and concealing their personal weapons, he had overlooked his grandfather's dagger. He had brought it more as a memento than a weapon, and half-forgotten it at the bottom of a suitcase. It was supposed to date back to Count Selig Vorkosigan himself; the old man had cherished it like a saint's relic. Although clearly not a weapon to tip the balance of the war on Tau Verde IV, it had the Vorkosigan arms inlaid in cloisonne, gold, and jewels on the hilt. Miles prayed the pattern would be meaningless to a non-Barrayaran.

The soldier tossed it to his captain, who withdrew it from its lizard skin sheath. He turned it in the light, bringing out the strange watermark pattern on the gleaming blade—a blade that had been worth ten times the price of the hilt even in the Time of Isolation, and was now considered priceless for its quality and workmanship, among connoisseurs.

Captain Auson was evidently not a connoisseur, for he merely said, "Huh. Pretty," resheathed it—and jammed it in his belt.

"Hey!" Miles checked himself halfway through a boiling surge forward. Meek. Meek. He tamped his outrage into a form fitting his supposed Betan persona. "I'm not insured for this sort of thing!"

The captain snorted. "Tough luck, Shorty." But he mulled on Miles in a moment of curious doubt.

Backpedal, thought Miles. "Don't I at least get a receipt?" he asked plaintively.

Auson snickered. "A receipt! That's a good one." The soldiers grinned nastily.

Miles controlled his ragged breathing with an effort. "Well . . ." he choked out, "at least don't let it stand wet. It'll rust if it's not properly dried after each use."

"Cheap pot metal," growled the mercenary captain. He ticked it with a fingernail; it rang like a bell. "Maybe I can get a good stainless blade put on that fancy hilt." Miles went green.

Auson gestured to Bothari. "Open that case there."

Bothari, as usual, glanced at Miles for confirmation. Auson frowned irritably. "Stop looking at Shorty. You 'ake your orders from me."

Bothari straightened, and raised an eyebrow. "Sir?" he inquired dulcetly of Miles.

Meek, damn it, Sergeant, Miles thought, and sent the message by a slight compression of his lips. "Obey this man, Mr. Bothari," he replied, a little too sharply.

Bothari smiled slightly. "Yes, sir." Having established the pecking order in a form more to his taste, he at last unlocked the case, with precise, insulting deliberation. Auson swore under his breath.

The mercenary captain herded them to a final rendezvous, in what the Betans called the rec room and the Barrayarans called the wardroom. "Now," he said, "you will produce all your off-planet currency. Contraband."

"What!" cried Mayhew, outraged. "How can *money* be contraband?"

"Hush, Arde," hissed Miles. "Just do it." Auson might well be telling the truth, Miles realized. Foreign currency was just what Daum's people needed to buy such things as off-planet weaponry and military advisors. Or it might simply be the hold-up it appeared. No matter—judging from the lack of excitement of all hands, Daum's cargo had escaped them, and that was all that counted. Miles secreted triumph in his heart, and emptied his pockets.

"That's *all*?" said Auson disbelievingly, as they placed their final offerings in a little pile on the table before him.

"We're a little shor—broke, at the moment," Miles explained, "until we get to Tau Verde and make some sales."

"Shit," muttered Auson. His eyes bored exasperatedly into Miles, who shrugged helplessly and produced his most inane smile.

Three more mercenaries entered, pushing Baz and Elena before them.

"Got the engineer?" said the captain tiredly. "I suppose he's bro—short, too." He glanced up and saw Elena. His look of boredom vanished instantly, and he came smoothly to his feet. "Well, *that's* better. I was beginning to think they were all freaks and fright masks here. Business before pleasure, though—you carrying any non-Tau Verdan currency, honey?"

Elena glanced uncertainly at Miles. "I have some," she admitted, looking surprised. "Why?"

"Out with it, then."

"Miles?" she queried.

Miles unclenched his aching jaw. "Give him your money, Elena," he ordered in a low tone.

Auson glowered at Miles. "You're not my frigging secretary, Shorty. I don't need you to transmit my orders. I don't want to hear any more back-chat from you, hear?"

Miles smiled and nodded meekly, and rubbed one sweating palm against his trouser seam where a holster wasn't.

Elena, bewildered, laid five hundred Betan dollars on the table. Bothari's eyebrows drew down in astonishment.

"Where'd you get all that?" whispered Miles as she stepped back.

"Countess—your mother gave it to me," she whispered back. "She said I should have some spending money of my own on Beta Colony. I didn't want to take so much, but she insisted."

Auson counted it, and brightened. "So, you're the banker, eh, honey? That's a bit more reasonable. I was beginning to think you folks were holding out on me." He cocked his head, looking her over and smiling sardonically. "People who hold out on me always come to regret it." The money vanished, along with a meager haul of other small, valuable items.

He checked their cargo manifest. "This right?" he asked the leader of the party who had come in with Elena and Baz.

"All the cases we busted open checked," replied the soldier.

"They made the most awful mess down there," Elena gritted under her breath to Miles.

"Sh. Never mind."

The mercenary captain sighed, and began sorting

through their various identification files. At one point he grinned, and glanced up at Bothari, then Elena. Miles sweated. Auson finished the check, and leaned back casually in his seat before the computer console, regarding Mayhew glumly.

"You the pilot officer, eh?" he inquired unenthusiastically.

"Yes, sir," replied Mayhew, well-coached in meekness by Miles.

"Betan?"

"Yes, sir."

"Are you—never mind. You're Betan, that answers the question. More frigging weirds per capita than any other . . ." he trailed off. "You ready to go?"

Mayhew glanced at Miles uncertainly.

"Damn it!" cried Auson. "I asked you, not Shorty! Bad enough that I'll have to look at you over the breakfast table for the next few weeks. He'd give me indigestion. Yeah, smile, you little mutant—" this last to Miles, "I bet you'd like to cut my liver out."

Miles smoothed his face, worried. He had been so sure he'd looked meek. Maybe it was Bothari. "No, sir," he said brightly, blinking for a meek effect.

The mercenary captain glared at him a moment, then muttered, "Aw, the hell with it," and rose.

His eye fell on Elena again, and he smiled thoughtfully. Elena frowned back. Auson looked around.

"Tell you what, Shorty," he said, in a benevolent tone. "You can keep your pilot. I've had about all the Betans I can take, lately."

Mayhew sighed relief under his breath. Miles relaxed, secretly delighted.

The mercenary captain waved at Elena. "I'll take her, instead. Go pack your things, honey."

Frozen silence.

Auson smiled at her, invitingly. "You won't be missing a thing by not seeing Tau Verde, believe me. You be a good girl, you might even get your money back."

Elena turned dilated eyes toward Miles. "My lord . . . ?" she said in a small, uncertain voice. It was not a slip of the tongue; she had a right to call for protection from her leige lord. It grieved him that she had not called "Miles," instead. Bothari's stillness was utter, his face blank and hard.

Miles stepped up to the mercenary captain, his meekness slipping badly. "The agreement was you were to hold our pilot officer," he stated in a flat voice.

Auson grinned wolfishly. "I make my own rules. She goes."

"She doesn't want to. If you don't want the pilot officer, choose another."

"Don't worry about it, Shorty. She'll have a good time. You can even have her back on the way out—if she still wants to go with you."

"I said choose another!"

The mercenary captain chuckled and turned away. Miles's hand closed around his arm. The other mercenaries, watching the show, didn't even bother to draw weapons. Auson's face lit with happiness, and he swung around. He's been itching for this, Miles realized. Well, so have I . . . .

The contest was brief and unequal. A clutch, a twist, a ringing blow, and Miles was slammed face-down on the deck. The metallic tang of blood filled his mouth. As an afterthought, a deliberately-aimed boot to his belly doubled him over where he lay, and assured that he wouldn't be rebounding to his feet in the immediate future.

Miles curled in agony, cheek pressed to the friction matting. Thank God it wasn't the ribcage, he thought incoherently through a haze of rage, pain, and nausea. He squinted at the boots, spread aggressively beyond his nose. Toes must be steel-lined . . .

The mercenary captain wheeled around, hands on hips. "Well?" he demanded of Miles's crew. Silence and stillness; all looked to Bothari, who might have been stone.

Auson, disappointed, spat disgustedly—either he wasn't aiming at Miles, or he missed—and muttered, "Aw, the hell with it. This tub's not worth confiscating anyway. Lousy fuel efficiency . . ." He raised his voice to his crew. "All right, load up, let's go. Come on, honey," he added to Elena, taking her firmly by the upper arm.

The five mercenaries unhinged themselves from their various postures of languid observation, and prepared to follow their captain out the door.

Elena glanced back over her shoulder, to meet Miles's flaming eyes; her lips parted in a little "Ah," of understanding, and she stared at Auson with cold calculation.

"Now, Sergeant!" cried Miles, and launched himself at his chosen mercenary. Still shaken from his encounter with the captain, in an inspiration of rare prudence he picked the one he had seen propping up the wall earlier. The room seemed to explode.

A chair, which no one had seen the Sergeant unfasten from its moorings, flew across the room to smash into the mercenary carrying the nerve disruptor before he even began to draw. Miles, occupied with his own tackle, heard but did not see the Sergeant's second victim go down with a meaty, resonating "Unh!" Daum, too, reacted instantly, disarming his man neatly and tossing the stunner to an astonished Mayhew. Mayhew stared at it a second, woke up and fumbled it right way round, and fired. Unfortunately, it was out of charge.

A needler went off, wildly; its projectile exploded against a far wall. Miles put his elbow with all his strength into his man's stomach, and had his earlier hypothesis confirmed when the man folded, gagging and retching. Unquestionably drunk. Miles dodged emesis, and at last achieved a strangle hold. He put the pressure on full power for the first time in his life. To his surprise, the man jerked but a few times and went still. Is he surrendering? Miles wondered dizzily, and pulled the head back by the hair for a look at the face. The man was unconscious.

A mercenary, bouncing off Bothari, stumbled past Mayhew who at last found a use for the stunner, blackjacking the man to his knees. Mayhew hit him a couple more times, rather experimentally. Bothari, hurtling past, paused to say disgustedly, "Not like that!", grab the stunner, and smash the man flat with one accurately-placed blow.

The Sergeant then proceeded to assist Daum with his second, and it was over, but for some yelling by the door accompanying a muffled cracking noise. The mercenary captain, his nose gouting blood, was down on the floor with Elena atop him.

"That's enough, Elena," said Bothari, placing the bell-muzzle of a captured nerve disruptor against the man's temple.

"No, Sergeant!" Miles cried. The yelling stopped abruptly, and Auson rolled fear-whitened eyes toward the gleaming weapon.

"I want to break his legs, too!" cried Elena angrily. "I want to break every bone in his body! I'll Shorty him! When I'm done he's going to be one meter tall!"

"Later," promised Bothari. Daum found a functioning stunner, and the Sergeant put the mercenary captain temporarily out of his misery, then proceeded systematically around the room to make sure of the rest. "We still have three more out there, my lord," he reminded Miles.

"Unh," Miles acknowledged, crawling to his feet. And the eleven or so in the other ship, he thought. "Think you and Daum can ambush and stun 'em?"

"Yes, but . . ." Bothari hefted the nerve disruptor in his hand. "May I suggest, my lord, that it may be preferable to kill soldiers in battle than prisoners after?"

"It may not come to that, Sergeant," said Miles sharply. The full chaotic implications of the situation were just beginning to dawn on him. "Stun 'em. Then we'll—figure out something else."

"Think quickly, my lord," suggested Bothari, and vanished out the door, moving with uncanny silence. Daum chewed his lip worriedly, and followed.

Miles was already starting to think. "Sergeant!" he called after them softly. "Keep one conscious for me!"

"Very good, my lord."

Miles turned back, slipping a little in a spatter of blood from the mercenary captain's nose, and stared at the sudden slaughterhouse. "God," he muttered. "Now what do I do with 'em?"

CHAPTER NINE ✳ ✳ ✳

Elena and Mayhew stood waiting, looking at him expectantly. Miles suddenly realized he had not seen Baz Jesek in the fight—wait, there he was, pinned against the far wall. His dark eyes were like holes in his milky face, his breathing ragged.

"Are you hurt, Baz?" Miles cried in concern. The engineer shook his head, but did not speak. Their eyes met, and Jesek looked away. Miles knew then why he hadn't noticed him.

We're outnumbered two or three to one, Miles thought frantically. I can't spare a trained fighting man to funk—got to do something *right now* ... "Elena, Arde," he spoke, "go out in the corridor and close the door until I call you." They obeyed, looking baffled.

Miles walked up to the engineer. How do I do a heart transplant, he wondered, in the dark, by feel, without anesthetics? He moistened his lips and spoke quietly.

"We've got no choice. We have to capture their ship now. The best shot is to take their shuttle, make them think it's their own people coming back. That can only be done in the next few minutes.

"The only chance of escape for any of us is to take them before they get a squeak out. I'm going to assign the Sergeant and Daum to take their Nav and Com room, and prevent that. The next most vital section is engineering, with all the overrides."

Jesek turned his face away, like a man in pain or grief. Miles went on relentlessly.

"You're clearly the man for that one. So I'm assigning it to you and—" Miles took a breath, "and Elena."

The engineer turned his face back, if possible more drained than before. "Oh, no . . ."

"Mayhew and I will float, stunning anything that moves. Thirty minutes from now it will all be over, one way or another."

Jesek shook his head. "I can't," he whispered.

"Look, you're not the only one who's terrified. I'm scared witless."

Jesek's mouth twisted. "You don't look scared. You didn't even look scared when that mercenary pig decked you. You just looked pissed."

"That's because I've got forward momentum. There's no virtue in it. It's just a balancing act. I don't dare stop."

The engineer shook his head again, helplessly, and spoke through his teeth. "I *can't*. I've *tried*."

Miles barely kept his lips from curling back in a snarl of frustration. Wild threats cascaded through his mind—no, that wasn't right. Surely the cure for fear was not more fear.

"I'm drafting you," Miles announced abruptly.

"What?"

"I claim you. I'm—I'm confiscating you. I'm seizing your property—your training, that is—for the war effort. This is totally illegal, but since you're under a death sentence anyway, who cares? Get down on your knees and put your hands between mine."

Jesek's mouth fell open. "You can't—I'm not—nobody but one of the Emperor's designated officers can swear a vassal, and I was already sworn to him when I got my commission—and forsworn when—" he broke off.

"Or a Count or a Count's heir," Miles cut in. "I admit the fact that you're previously sworn to Gregor as an officer puts a wrinkle in it. We'll just have to change the wording around a bit."

"You're not . . ." Jesek stared. "What the hell are you, anyway? Who are you?"

"I don't even want to talk about it. But I really am a vassal secundus to Gregor Vorbarra, and I can take you for a leigeman, and I'm going to right now, because I'm in a hell of a hurry, and we can work out the details later."

"You're a lunatic! What the bloody hell do you think this is going to do?"

Distract you, thought Miles—and it's working already. "Maybe, but I'm a *Vor* lunatic. Down!"

The engineer fell to his knees, staring in disbelief. Miles captured his hands, and began.

"Repeat after me. I, Bazil Jesek, do testify I am, am, am a forsworn military vassal of Gregor Vorbarra, but I take service anyway under—under—" Bothari will be hot as hell if I break security, "under this lunatic in front of me—make that, this Vor lunatic—as an Armsman simple, and will hold him as my leige commander until my death or his releases me."

Jesek, looking hypnotized, repeated the oath verbatim.

Miles began. "I, uh—I better skip that part—I, a vassal secundus to Emperor Gregor Vorbarra, do accept your oath, and pledge you the protection of a leige-commander; this by my word as—well, by my word. There. You now have the dubious privilege of following my orders to the letter and addressing me as 'my lord', only you'd better not do it in front of Bothari until I get a chance to break the news to him gently. Oh, and one more thing . . ."

The engineer looked the question, bewildered.

"You're home. For what it's worth."

Jesek shook his head dizzily, and staggered to his feet. "Was that real?"

"Well—it's a little irregular. But from what I've read of our history, I can't help feeling it's closer to the original than the official version."

There was a knock on the door. Daum and Bothari had a prisoner, his hands fastened behind him. He was the pilot officer, by the silver circles on his temples and midforehead. Miles supposed that was why Bothari had picked him—he was bound to know all the recognition codes. The defiant set of the mercenary's head gave Miles a queasy premonition of trouble.

"Baz, take Elena and the Major and start hauling these guys to Hold #4, the one with nothing in it. They might wake up and get creative, so weld the door shut on 'em. Then unseal our own weapons cache, get the stunners and plasma arcs, and check out the mercenary shuttle. We'll meet you there in a few minutes."

When Elena dragged out the last unconscious body by the ankles—it was the mercenary captain, and she was noticeably not careful what his head bumped on the way—Miles shut the door and turned to his prisoner, held by Bothari and Mayhew.

"You know," he addressed the man apologetically, "I sure would appreciate it if we could skip all the preliminaries and go straight to your codes. It would save a lot of grief."

The mercenary's lips curled at this, sardonic-sour. "Sure it would—for you. No truth drugs, eh? Too bad, Shorty—you're out of luck."

Bothari tensed, eyes strangely alight; Miles restrained him with a small movement of one finger. "Not yet, Sergeant."

Miles sighed. "You're right," he said to the mercenary, "we have no drugs. I'm sorry. But we still must have your cooperation."

The mercenary snickered. "Stick it, Shorty."

"We don't mean to kill your friends," Miles added hopefully, "just stun them."

The man raised his head proudly. "Time's on my side. Whatever you can dish out, I can take. If you kill me, I can't talk."

Miles motioned Bothari aside. "This is your department, Sergeant," he said in a low voice. "Seems to me he's right. What do you think of trying to board them blind, no codes? Couldn't be any worse than if he gave us a false one. We could skip this—" a nervous wave of his hand indicated the mercenary pilot.

"It would be better with the codes," stated the Sergeant uncompromisingly. "Safer."

"I don't see how we can get them."

"I can get them. You can always break a pilot. If you will give me a free hand, my lord."

The expression on Bothari's face disturbed Miles. The confidence was all right, it was the underlying air of anticipation that put knots in his guts.

"You must decide now, my lord."

He thought of Elena, Mayhew, Daum and Jesek, who had followed him to this place—who wouldn't be here but for him . . . "Go ahead, Sergeant."

"You may wish to wait in the corridor."

Miles shook his head, belly-sick. "No. I ordered it. I'll see it through."

Bothari inclined his head. "As you will. I need the knife." He nodded toward the dagger Miles had retrieved from the unconscious mercenary captain and hung on his belt. Miles, reluctantly, drew it and handed it over. Bothari's face lightened a little at the beauty of the blade, its tensile flexibility and incredible sharpness. "They don't make them like that anymore," he muttered.

What are you planning to do with it, Sergeant? Miles wondered, but did not quite dare ask. If you tell him to drop his trousers, I'm going to stop this sesssion right now, codes or no codes . . . They returned to their prisoner, who was standing easy, still casually defiant.

Miles tried one more time. "Sir, I beg you to cooperate."

The man grinned. "I just don't buy you, Shorty. I'm not afraid of a little pain."

I am afraid, thought Miles. He stepped aside. "He's yours, Sergeant."

"Hold him still," said Bothari. Miles grasped the prisoner's right arm; Mayhew, looking puzzled, held the left.

The mercenary took in Bothari's face, and his grin slipped. One edge of Bothari's mouth turned upward, in a smile Miles had never seen before and immediately hoped he would never see again. The mercenary swallowed.

Bothari placed the tip of the dagger against the side of the silver button on the man's right temple and wrig-

gled it a little, to slip it beneath the edge. The mercenary's eyes shifted right, gone white-rimmed. "You
wouldn't dare . . ." he whispered. A drop of blood ringed
the circle in a quick blink. The mercenary inhaled
sharply, and began, "Wait—"

Bothari twisted the knife sideways, grasped the button between the thumb and fingers of his free hand, and
yanked. A ululating scream broke from the mercenary's
throat. He lunged convulsively from Miles's and Mayhew's
grasp and fell to his knees, mouth open, eyes gone huge
in shock.

Bothari dangled the implant before the man's eyes.
Hair-fine wires hung like broken spider legs from the
silver button body. He twirled it, with a glittering gleam
and a spatter of blood, thousands of Betan dollars worth
of viral circuitry and microsurgery turned instantly to
trash.

Mayhew, watching, went the color of oatmeal at this
incredible vandalism. The breath went out of him in a
tiny moan. He turned his back and went to lean against
the wall in a corner. After a moment, he bent over,
stifling vomiting.

I wish he hadn't witnessed that, thought Miles. I wish
I'd kept Daum instead. I wish . . .

Bothari squatted down to his victim's level, face to
face. He raised the knife again, and the mercenary pilot
recoiled, to bash into the wall and slide into a sitting
position, unable to retreat farther. Bothari placed the
dagger's point against the button on the man's forehead.

"Pain is not the point," he whispered hoarsely. He
paused, then added even more quietly, "Begin."

The man found his tongue abruptly, pouring out betrayal in his terror. There was, thought Miles, no question of clever subterfuge in the information tripping
frantically out of his mouth. Miles overcame his own
trembling belly to listen intently, carefully thoroughly,
that nothing be lost or missed or wasted. Unbearable,
that this sacrifice should be wasted.

When the man began to repeat himself, Bothari pulled
him cringing to his feet and frog marched him to the
shuttle hatch corridor. Elena and the others stared un-

certainly at the mercenary, a trickle of blood threading
down from his gored temple, but asked no questions. At
the slightest prodding from Bothari the captured pilot
officer, hasty and barely coherent, explained the internal layout of the light cruiser. Bothari pushed him aboard
and strapped him in a seat, where he collapsed and
burst into shocking sobs. The others looked away from
the prisoner uneasily, and chose seats as far from him
as possible.

Mayhew sat gingerly before the manual controls of
the shuttle, and flexed his fingers.

Miles slid in beside him. "Are you going to be able to
fly this thing?"

"Yes, my lord."

Miles took in his shaken profile. "You going to be all
right?"

"Yes, my lord." The shuttle's engines whined to life,
and they kicked away from the side of the RG132. "Did
you know he was going to do that?" Mayhew demanded
suddenly, low-voiced. He glanced back over his shoulder at Bothari and his prisoner.

"Not exactly."

Mayhew's lips tightened. "Crazy bastard."

"Look, Arde, you better keep this straight," murmured
Miles. "What Bothari does on my orders is my responsibility, not his."

"The hell you say. I saw the look on his face. He
enjoyed that. You didn't."

Miles hesitated, then repeated himself with a different emphasis, hoping to make Mayhew understand. "What
Bothari does is my responsibility. I've known it for a
long time, so I don't excuse myself."

"He *is* psychotic, then," hissed Mayhew.

"He keeps himself together. But understand—if you
have a problem about him, you see me."

Mayhew swore under his breath. "You're a pair, all
right."

Miles studied the mercenary craft in the forward
screens as they approached. It was a swift and powerful
small warship, well-armed. There was a bravura brilliance to its lines that suggested Illyrican make; it was

named, appropriately, the *Ariel*. No question that the lumbering RG132 would have had no chance of escaping it. He felt a twinge of envy at its deadly beauty, then realized with a start that if things went as planned, he was about to own it, or at least possess it. But the ambiguity of the methods poisoned his pleasure, leaving only a dry cold nervousness.

They came up without challenge or incident on the *Ariel's* shuttle hatch, and Miles floated aft to assist Jesek with locking on. Bothari bound his prisoner more securely to his seat, and loomed up beside Miles. Miles decided not to waste time arguing with him about precedence.

"All right," Miles conceded to his wordless demand. "You first. But I'm next."

"My reaction time will be quicker if my attention is not divided, my lord."

Miles snorted exasperation. "Oh, very well. You, then D—no. Then Baz." The engineer's eyes met his. "Then Daum, me, Elena, and Mayhew."

Bothari approved this schedule with a half-nod. The shuttle hatch sighed open, and Bothari slipped through. Jesek took a breath, and followed.

Miles paused only to whisper, "Elena, keep Baz moving forward as fast as you can. Don't let him stop."

From the ship ahead, he heard an exclamation—"Who the hell— !" and the quiet buzz of Bothari's stunner. Then he was through, into the corridor.

"Only one?" he asked Bothari, taking in the crumpled grey-and-white form on the floor.

"So far," replied the Sergeant. "We seem to have retained surprise."

"Good, let's keep it. Split, and move out."

Bothari and Daum melted down the first cross corridor. Jesek and Elena headed in the opposite direction. Elena cast one look backward; Jesek did not. Excellent, Miles thought. He and Mayhew took the third direction, and stopped before the first closed door. Mayhew stepped forward, in a kind of wobbly aggressiveness.

"Me first, my lord," he said.

God, it's contagious, thought Miles. "Go ahead."

Mayhew swallowed, and raised his plasma arc.

"Uh, wait a second, Arde." Miles pressed the palm lock. The door slid open smoothly. He whispered apologetically, "If it's not locked, you risk welding it shut that way . . ."

"Oh," said Mayhew. He gathered himself and burst through the aperture with a kind of war whoop, fanning the room with his stunner, then stopped. It was a storage area, and empty but for a few plastic crates strapped into place. No sign of the enemy.

Miles poked his head in for a glance around, and stepped back thoughtfully. "You know," he said as they started back up the corridor, "it might be better if we don't yell, going in. It's startling. It's bound to be a lot easier to hit people if they're not jumping around and ducking behind things."

"They do it that way on the vids," Mayhew offered.

Miles, who had originally been planning his own first rush very much along the lines just demonstrated, and for much the same reason, cleared his throat. "I guess it just doesn't look very heroic to sneak up behind somebody and shoot them in the back. I can't help thinking it would be more efficient, though."

They went up a lift tube, and came to another door. Miles tried the palm lock, and again the door slid open, revealing a darkened chamber. A dormitory with four bunks, three of them occupied. Miles and Mayhew tiptoed in, and took up can't-miss positions. Miles closed his fist, and they both fired at once. He fired again as the third figure began to lurch up from its bedclothes, reaching for a weapon hung in a holster by its bunk.

"Huh!" said Mayhew. "Women! That captain *was* a pig."

"I don't think they're prisoners," said Miles, switching on the light for a quick confirmation. "Look at the uniforms. They're part of the crew."

They withdrew, Miles very sober. Perhaps Elena had not been in as much danger as the mercenary captain had led them to believe. Too late now . . .

A low voice floated around the corner, growling, "Damn it, I warned that dumb son-of-a-bitch—" The speaker followed at a gallop, scowling and buckling on a holster belt, and ran headlong into them.

The mercenary officer reacted instantly, turning the accidental collision into a tackle. Mayhew received a kick to the abdomen. Miles was slammed into the wall, and found himself in a clutching, scrambling fight for possession of his own arsenal.

"Stun him, Arde!" he cried, muffled by an elbow to his teeth. Mayhew crawled after the stunner, rolled over, and fired. The mercenary slumped, and the nimbus of the bolt took Miles dizzily to his knees.

"Definitely better to catch them asleep," Miles mumbled. "Wonder if there's any more like him—her—"

"It," said Mayhew definitely, rolling the hermaphrodite soldier over to reveal the chiseled features of what could have been either a handsome young man or a strong-faced woman. Tangled brown hair framed the face and fell across the forehead. "Betan, by the accent."

"Makes sense," Miles gasped, and struggled back to his feet. "I think ..." He clutched the wall, head pounding, queer-colored lights scrambling his vision. Being stunned was not as painless as it looked. "We better keep moving ..." He leaned gratefully on Mayhew's supporting arm.

A dozen more chambers were checked, without flushing further quarry. They came eventually to Nav and Com, to find two bodies piled by the door and Bothari and Daum in calm possession.

"Engineering reports secure," Bothari said at once upon seeing them. "They stunned four. That makes seven."

"We got four," said Miles thickly. "Can you get their computers to cough up a roster, and see if that adds up to the total?"

"Already done, my lord," said Bothari, relaxing a little. "They all seem to be accounted for."

"Good." Miles more-or-less fell into a station chair, rubbing his twice-battered mouth.

Bothari's eyes narrowed. "Are you well, my lord?"

"Caught a little stunner flash. I'll be all right." Miles

forced himself to focus. What next? "I suppose we'd better get these guys locked up, before they wake up."

Bothari's face became mask-like. "They outnumber us three to one, and are technically trained. Trying to keep them all prisoner is bloody dangerous."

Miles looked up sharply, and held Bothari's eye. "I'll figure something out." He bit out each word emphatically.

Mayhew snorted. "What else can you do? Push 'em out the airlock?" The silence that greeted this joke turned his expression to sick dismay.

Miles shoved to his feet. "As soon as we've got 'em nailed down we'd better start both ships boosting for the rendezvous. The Oserans are bound to start looking for their missing ship pretty soon, even if they didn't get a distress signal out. Maybe Major Daum's people can take these guys off our hands, eh?"

He nodded to Daum, who gave a, "How should I know?" shrug. Miles left on rubbery legs to find Engineering.

The first thing Miles noticed upon entering the engineering section was the empty socket in the wall for the first aid kit. Fear flashed through him, and he searched the room for Elena. Surely Bothari would have reported casualties—wait, there she was, the bandager, not the bandagee.

Jesek was slumped heavily in a station chair, and Elena was applying something to a burn on his upper arm. The engineer was smiling up at Elena with a quite fatuous, Miles thought, expression of gratitude.

The smile ignited to a grin when he saw Miles. He stood—somewhat to Elena's annoyance, as she was trying to fasten the bandage at the time—and gave Miles a snappy Barrayaran regulation Service salute. "Engineering is secured, my lord," he intoned, and then gulped a giggle. Stifling hysteria, Miles realized. Elena pushed him exasperatedly back into his chair, where another strangled giggle escaped him.

Miles caught Elena's eye. "How did it go, your first combat experience? Ah . . ." he nodded toward Jesek's arm.

"We didn't run into anybody on the way down. Lucky, I guess," she explained. "We caught them by surprise, coming through the door, and stunned two right away. A third one had a plasma arc, and he ducked down behind those conduits over there. Then this woman jumped me—" a wave indicated an unconscious form in grey and white, disposed on the deck, "which probably saved my life, because the one with the plasma arc couldn't fire when we were all tangled up wrestling for my stunner." She smiled at Jesek with enthusiastic admiration. "Baz charged him, and knocked him out. I got a choke on mine, and then Baz stunned her, and it was all over. That took some nerve, charging a plasma arc with a stunner. The mercenary only got one shot off— that's what happened to Baz's arm. I don't think I would have dared, would you?"

Miles walked around the room during this recitation, mentally reconstructing the action. He stirred the inert body of the former plasma arc wielder with the toe of his boot, and thought of his own tally for the day—one tottering drunk and two sleeping women. Jealousy twinged. He cleared his throat thoughtfully and looked up. "No, I'd probably have taken my own plasma arc and tried to burn through the brackets on that overhead light bar, and drop it on him. Then either nail him after he was smashed or else stun him as he jumped out from under."

"Oh," said Elena.

Jesek's grin faded slightly. "I didn't think of that."

Miles kicked himself, mentally. Ass—what kind of commander tries to score points off a man who needs build up? A damned short-sighted one, obviously. This mess was only beginning. He amended himself immediately. "I might not have either, under fire. It's deceptively easy to second-guess somebody when you're not in the heat yourself. You did extremely well, Mr. Jesek."

Jesek's face sobered. The edge of hysterical glee faded, but left a residue of straightness in his spine. "Thank you, my lord."

Elena went off to examine one of the unconscious mercenaries, and he added to Miles in a low voice,

"How did you know? How did you know I could—hell, I didn't even know myself. I thought I could never face fire again." He stared voraciously at Miles, as though he were some mystic oracle, or talisman.

"I always knew," Miles lied cheerfuly. "From the first time I met you. It's in the blood, you know. There's more to being Vor than the right to tack a funny syllable on the front of your name."

"I always thought that was a load of manure," said Jesek frankly. "Now . . ." He shook his head in wonderment.

Miles shrugged, concealing secret agreement. "Well, you carry my shovel now, that's for damn sure. And speaking of work—we're going to stuff all these guys into their own brig, until we decide, uh, how to dispose of them. Is that wound going to incapacitate you, or can you make this ship go pretty soon?"

Jesek stared around. "They've got some pretty advanced systems . . ." he began doubtfully. His eye fell on Miles, standing straight as his limitations would allow before him, and his voice firmed. "Yes, my lord. I can."

Miles, feeling quite maniacally hypocritical, gave the engineer a firm commander's nod copied from observations of his father at Staff conferences and the dinner table. It seemed to work quite well, for Jesek collected himself and began an orienting survey of the systems around him.

Miles paused on the way out the door to repeat the instructions for confining the prisoners to Elena. She cocked her head at him when he finished.

"And how was *your* first combat experience?" she inquired, softly truculent.

He grinned involuntarily. "Educational. Very educational. Ah—did you two happen to yell, charging through the door here?"

She blinked. "Sure. Why?"

"Just a theory I'm working on . . ." He swept her a bow of good-humored mockery, and exited.

* * *

The shuttle hatch corridor was lonely and quiet, but for the soft susurrations of air circulation and other life support systems. Miles ducked through the dim shuttle tube and, free of the artificial gravity field of the larger ship's deck, floated forward. The mercenary pilot officer was still tied where they'd left him, his head and legs lolling in that strange bobbing fashion null-gee gave one. Miles cringed at the thought of having to explain the man's wound.

Miles's calculations about how to keep the man under control on the way to the brig were shattered when he came in view of his face. The mercenary's eyes were rolled back, his jaw slack; his face and forehead were mottled and flushed, and scorchingly hot to Miles's hesitant touch. His hands were waxen and icy, fingernails empurpled, pulse thready and erratic.

Horrified, Miles scrabbled at the knots binding him, then impatiently drew his dagger and cut the cords. Miles patted his face, on the side away from the dried streak of blood, but couldn't rouse him. The mercenary's body stiffened suddenly, and began to jerk and tremble, flailing in free fall. Miles ducked and swore, but his voice squeezed upwards to a squeak, and he clamped his jaw on it. Sickbay, then, get the man to sickbay, find the medtech and try to wake him up, or failing that, get Bothari, most experienced in first aid . . .

Miles wrestled the pilot officer through the shuttle's hatch. When he stepped from free fall into gravity he suddenly found out just how much the man weighed. Miles first tried to maneuver under him for a shoulder carry, to the imminent danger of his own bone structure. He staggered a few steps, then tried dragging him by the shoulders. Then the mercenary began to convulse again. Miles gave up and ran for sickbay and an antigrav stretcher, cursing the whole way, tears of frustration and fear in his voice.

It took time to get there, time to find the stretcher. Time to find Bothari on the ship's intercom and order him in a clipped fierce voice to report to sickbay with the medtech. Time to run back through the empty ship with the lift unit to the shuttle hatch corridor.

When Miles got there, the pilot officer had stopped breathing. His face was as waxy as his hands, his lips purple-blue as his nails, and the dried blood looked like a smear of colored chalk, dark and opaque.

Frantic haste made Miles's fingers seem thick and clumsy as he fitted the unit around the mercenary—he refused to think of it as "the mercenary's body"—and floated him off the floor. Bothari arrived at sickbay as Miles was positioning the mercenary over an examining table and releasing the lift unit.

"What's the matter with him, Sergeant?" asked Miles urgently.

Bothari glanced over the still form. "He's dead," he said flatly, and turned away.

"Not yet, damn it!" cried Miles. "We've got to be able to do something to revive him! Stimulants—heart massage—cryo-stasis—did you find the medtech?"

"Yes, but she was too heavily stunned to rouse."

Miles swore again, and began ransacking drawers for recognizable medications and equipment. They were disorganized, the labels on the outside having, apparently, no relation to the contents.

"It won't do any good, my lord," said Bothari, watching him impassively. "You'd need a surgeon. Stroke."

Miles rocked back on his heels, at last understanding what he had just seen. He pictured the implant wires, ripped through the man's brain, sliding against the rubbery covering of a major artery, slicing a fine groove in the heart-stressed tubule. Then the weakness propagated with every pulse until catastrophic failure filled the tissues with the killing hemorrhage.

Did this little sickbay even have a cryogenic chamber? Miles hastened around the room and into the next, searching. The freezing process would have to be started immediately, or brain death would be too far advanced to be reversed—never mind that he had only the vaguest idea of how patients were prepared for freezing, or how to operate the device, or . . .

There it was! A portable, a gleaming metal chamber on a float pallet looking faintly like some deep-sea probe. Miles's heart seemed to fill his throat. He approached it. Its power pack was empty, its gas canisters read fully discharged, and its control computer was laid open like some crudely dissected biological specimen. Out of order.

Bothari stood at rest, awaiting orders. "Do you require anything further, my lord? I would feel easier if I could supervise the weapons search of the prisoners myself." He gazed on the corpse with indifferent eyes.

"Yes—no . . ." Miles walked around the examining table at a distance. His eye was drawn to the dark clot on the pilot officer's right temple. "What did you do with his implant nexus?"

Bothari looked mildly surprised, and checked his pockets. "I still have it, my lord."

Miles held out his hand for the crushed silver spider. It weighed no more than the button it resembled, its smooth surface concealing the complexity of the hundreds of kilometers of viral circuitry packed within.

Bothari frowned a little, watching his face. "One casualty is not bad for an operation of this nature, my lord," he offered. "His life saved many, and not just on our side."

"Ah," said Miles, dry and cold. "I'll keep that in mind, when I come to explain to my father how it was we happened to torture a prisoner to death."

Bothari flinched. After a silence, he reiterated his interest in the ongoing weapons search, and Miles released him with a tired nod. "I'll be along shortly."

Miles puttered nervously around sickbay for a few more minutes, avoiding looking at the examining table. At last, moved by an obscure impulse, he fetched a basin, water, and a cloth, and washed the dried blood from the mercenary's face.

So this is the terror, he thought, that motivates those crazy massacres of witnesses one reads about. I understand them now. I liked it better when I didn't.

He drew his dagger and trimmed the trailing wires

from the silver button, and pressed it carefully back into place on the pilot officer's temple. After, until Daum came looking for him with some request for orders, he stood and meditated on the still, waxen features of the thing they'd made. But reason seemed to run backwards, conclusions swallowed in premises, and premises in silence, until in the end only silence and the unanswerable object remained.

CHAPTER TEN ✷ ✷ ✷

Miles gestured the injured mercenary captain ahead of him into sickbay with a little jab of his nerve disruptor. The deadly weapon seemed unnaturally light and easy in his hand. Something that lethal should have more heft, like a broadsword. Wrong, for murder to be so potentially effortless—one ought to at least have to grunt for it.

He would have felt happier with a stunner, but Bothari had insisted that Miles present a front of maximum authority when moving prisoners about. "Saves argument," he'd said.

The miserable Captain Auson, with two broken arms, nose a swollen blot on his face, did not look very argumentative. But the cat-like tension and calculating flicks of glance of Auson's first officer, the Betan hermaphrodite Lieutenant Thorne, reconciled Miles to Bothari's reasoning.

He found Bothari leaning with deceptive casualness against a wall within, and the mercenaries' frazzled-looking medtech preparing for her next customers. Miles had deliberately saved Auson for last, and toyed with a pleasantly hostile fantasy of ordering the Captain's arms, when set, immobilized in some anatomically unlikely position.

Thorne was seated to have a cut over one eye sealed, and to receive an injection against stunner-induced migraine. The lieutenant sighed as the medication took effect, and looked at Miles with less squinting curiosity. "Who the hell are you people, anyway?"

Miles arranged his mouth in what he hoped would be taken for a smile of urbane mystery, and said nothing.

"What are you going to do with us?" Thorne persisted.

Good question, he thought. He had returned to Cargo Hold #4 to find their first batch of prisoners well along to having one of the bulkheads apart and escape manufactured. Miles voiced no objection when Bothari prudently had them all stunned again for transport to the *Ariel's* brig. There, Miles found, the chief engineer and her assistants had nearly managed to sabotage the magnetic locks in their cells. Miles rather desperately had them all stunned again.

Bothari was right; it was an intrinsically unstable situation. Miles could hardly keep the whole crew stunned for a week or more, crammed in their little prison, without doing them serious physiological damage. Miles's own people were spread too thinly, manning both ships, guarding the prisoners around the clock—and fatigue would soon multiply error. Bothari's murderous and final solution had a certain logic to it, Miles supposed. But his eye fell on the silent sheeted form of the mercenary pilot officer in the corner of the room, and he shivered inwardly. Not again. He suppressed jittering panic at his abruptly enlarged troubles, and angled for time.

"It would be a favor to Admiral Oser to put you out now and let you walk home," he answered Thorne. "Are they all like you out there?"

Thorne said stonily. "The Oserans are a free coalition of mercenaries. Most captains are Captain-owners."

Miles swore, genuinely surprised. "That's not a chain of command. That's a damned committee."

He stared curiously at Auson. A shot of pain killer was at last unlocking the big man's attention from his own body, and he glowered back. "Is your crew sworn to you, then, or to Admiral Oser?" Miles asked him.

"Sworn? I hold the contracts of everybody on my ship, if that's what you mean," Auson growled. "Everybody." He frowned at Thorne, whose nostrils grew pinched.

"My ship," corrected Miles. Auson's mouth rippled in a silent snarl and he glared at the nerve disruptor but, as Bothari had predicted, did not argue. The medtech laid the deposed captain's arm in a brace, and began working over it with a surgical hand tractor. Auson paled, and became more withdrawn. Miles felt a slight twinge of empathy.

"You are, without a doubt, the sorriest excuse for soldiers I have seen in my career," Miles declaimed, trolling for reactions. One corner of Bothari's mouth twitched, but Miles ignored that one. "It's a wonder you're all still alive. You must choose your foes very carefully." He rubbed his own still-aching stomach, and shrugged. "Well, I know you do."

Auson flushed a dull red, and looked away. "Just trying to stir up a little action. We've been on this damned blockade duty a frigging *year*."

"Stir up action," Thorne muttered disgustedly. "You would."

I have you now. The certainty reverberated like a bell in Miles's mind. His idle dreams of revenge upon the mercenary captain vaporized in the heat of a new and more breathtaking inspiration. His eye nailed Auson, and he rapped out sharply, "How long has it been since your last General Fleet Inspection?"

Auson looked as if it had belatedly occurred to him that he ought to be limiting this conversation to names, ranks, and serial numbers, but Thorne replied, "A year and a half."

Miles swore, with feeling, and raised his chin aggressively. "I don't think I can take any more of this. You're going to have one now."

Bothari maintained an admirable stillness, against the wall, but Miles could feel his eyes boring through his shoulderblades with his sharpest what-the-hell-are-you-doing-now look. Miles did not turn.

"What the hell," said Auson, echoing Bothari's silence, "are you talking about? Who are you? I had you pegged for a smuggler for sure, when you let us shake you down without a squeak, but I'll swear we didn't miss—" he surged to his feet, causing Bothari's disruptor to snap to the aim. His voice edged upward in frustration. "You are a smuggler, damn it! I can't be that wrong. Was it the ship itself? Who'd want it? What the hell are you smuggling?" he cried plaintively.

Miles smiled coldly. "Military advisors."

He fancied he could see the hook of his words set in the mercenary captain and his lieutenant. Now to run in the line.

Miles began inspection, with some relish, in the sickbay itself, since he was fairly sure of his ground there. At disruptor point, the medtech produced her official inventory and began turning out drawers under Miles's intent eye. With a sure instinct Miles focused first on drugs capable of abuse, and immediately turned up some nicely embarrassing discrepancies.

Next was equipment. Miles itched to get to the cryogenic chamber, but his sense of showmanship held it for last. There were enough other breakdowns. Some of his grandfather's more acerbic turns of phrase, suitably edited, had turned the medtech's face to chalk by the time they arrived at the *piece de résistance*.

"And just how long has this chamber been out of commission, Medtech?"

"Six months," she muttered. "The repairs engineer kept saying he'd get to it," she added defensively at Miles's frown and raised eyebrows.

"And you never thought to stir him up? Or more properly, ask your superior officers to do so?"

"It seemed like there was plenty of time. We haven't used—"

"And in that six months your captain never once even ran an in-house inspection?"

"No, sir."

Miles swept Auson and Thorne with a gaze like a dash of cold water, then let his eye deliberately linger on the covered form of the dead man. "Time ran out for your pilot officer."

"How did he die?" asked Thorne, sharply, like a sword thrust.

Miles parried with a deliberate misunderstanding. "Bravely. Like a soldier." Horribly, like an animal sacrifice, his thought corrected. Imperative they don't figure that out. But, "I'm sorry," he added impulsively. "He deserved better."

The medtech was looking at Thorne, stricken. Thorne said gently, "The cryo chamber wouldn't have done much good for a disruptor blast to the head anyway, Cela."

"But the next casualty," Miles interposed, "might be some other injury." Excellent, that the excessively observant lieutenant had evolved a personal theory as to how the pilot officer happened to be dead without a mark on him. Miles was vastly relieved, not least because it freed him of having to dishonorably burden the medtech with a guilt not rightfully hers.

"I will send you the engineering technician later today," Miles went on. "I want every piece of equipment in here operating properly by tomorrow. In the meantime you can start putting this place in an order more like a military sickbay and less like a broom closet, is that understood, Medtech?" He dropped his voice to a whisper, like the hiss of a whip.

The medtech braced to attention, and cried, "Yes, sir!" Auson was flushed; Thorne's lips were parted in an expression very like appreciation. They left her pulling out drawers with trembling hands.

Miles motioned the two mercenaries ahead of him down the corridor, and fell behind for an urgent whispered conference with Bothari.

"You going to leave her unguarded?" Bothari muttered disapprovingly. "Madness."

"She's too busy to bolt. With luck, I may even be able to keep her too busy to run an autopsy on that Pilot Officer. Quick, Sergeant! If I want to fake a General Fleet Inspection, where's the best place to dig up dirt?"

"On this ship? Anywhere."

"No, really! The next stop has got to look bad. I can't fake the technical stuff, have to wait till Baz is ready for a break."

"In that case, try crew's quarters," suggested Bothari. "But why?"

"I want those two to figure we're some sort of mercenary super-outfit. I've got an idea how to keep them from combining to retake their ship."

"They'll never buy it."

"They *will* buy it. They'll love it. They'll eat it up. Don't you see, it saves their pride. We beat them—for now. Which do you think they'd rather believe, that we're great, or that they're a bunch of screw-ups?"

"Isn't it plain?"

"Just watch!" He skipped a silent dance step, composed his face to a mask of sternness, and strode after his prisoners, his boots ringing like iron down the corridor.

The crew's quarters were, from Miles's point of view, a delight. Bothari did the disassembling. His instinct for turning up evidence of slovenly habits and concealed vices was uncanny. Miles supposed he'd seen it all, in his time. When Bothari uncovered the expected bottles of the ethanol addict, Auson and Thorne took it as a matter of course; evidently the man was a known and tolerated borderline functional. The two kavaweed dopers, however, seemed to be a surprise to all. Miles promptly confiscated the lot. He left another soldier's remarkable collection of sexual aids *in situ*, however, merely inquiring of Auson, with a quirk of an eyebrow, if he were running a cruiser or a cruise ship? Auson fumed, but said nothing. Miles cordially hoped the captain might spend the rest of the day thinking up scathing retorts, too late to use.

Miles studied Auson's and Thorne's own chambers intently, for clues to their owners' personalities. Thorne's, interestingly, came closest to passing inspection. Auson appeared to brace himself for a rampage when they came at last to his own cabin. Miles smiled silkily, and had Bothari put everything away, after inspection, in better order than he'd found it. It was all those years as an officer's batman, perhaps; when they were done the room appeared quite transformed. From the evidence, or lack thereof, Auson himself appeared to have no serious vices beyond a natural indolence exacerbated by boredom into laziness.

The collection of exotic personal weapons picked up during this tour made an impressive pile. Miles had Bothari examine and test each one. He made an elaborate show of noting each substandard item and checking it off against a list of the owners. Exhilarated and inspired, he waxed wonderfully sarcastic; the mercenaries squirmed.

They inspected the arsenal. Miles took a plasma arc from a dusty rack, closing his hand over the control readouts on the grip.

"Do you store your weapons charged or uncharged?"

"Uncharged," muttered Auson, craning his neck slightly.

Miles raised his eyebrows and swung the weapon to point at the mercenary captain, finger tightening on the trigger. Auson went white. At the last instant, Miles flicked his wrist slightly to the left, and sent a bolt of energy sizzling past Auson's ear. The big man recoiled as a molten backsplash of plastic and metal sprayed from the wall behind him.

"Uncharged?" sang Miles. "I see. A wise policy, I'm sure."

Both officers flinched. As they exited, Miles heard Thorne mutter, "Told you so." Auson growled wordlessly.

Miles braced Baz privately before they began in engineering.

"You are now," he told him, "Commander Bazil Jesek of the Dendarii Mercenaries, Chief Engineer. You're rough and tough and you eat slovenly engineering technicians for breakfast, and you're *appalled* at what they've done to this nice ship."

"It's actually not too bad, near as I can tell," said Baz. "Better than I could do with such an advanced set of systems. But how am I going to make an inspection when they know more than I do? They'll spot me right away!"

"No, they won't. Remember, you're asking the questions, they're answering them. Say 'hm,' and frown a lot. Don't let it start going the other way. Look—didn't

you ever have an engineering commander who was a
real son-of-a-bitch, that everybody hated—but who was
always right?"

Baz looked confusedly reminiscent. "There was Lieutenant Commander Tarski. We used to sit around thinking up ways to poison him. Most of them weren't very
practical."

"All right. Imitate him."

"They'll never believe me. I can't—I've never been—I
don't even have a cigar!"

Miles thought a second, dashed off, and galloped back
moments later with a package of cheroots abstracted
from one of the mercenary's quarters.

"But I don't smoke," worried Baz.

"Just chew on it, then. Probably better if you don't
light it, God knows what it might be spiked with."

"Now, there's an idea for poisoning old Tarski that
might have worked—"

Miles pushed him along. "All right, you're an air
polluting son-of-a-bitch and you don't take 'I don't know'
for an answer. If I can do it," he uncorked his argument
of desperation, "you can do it."

Baz paused, straightened, bit off the end of the cheroot and spat it bravely on the deck. He eyed it a
moment. "I slipped on one of those damned disgusting
things once. Nearly broke my neck. Tarski. Right." He
clenched the cheroot between his teeth at an aggressive
angle, and marched into the main engineering bay.

Miles assembled the entire ship's company in their
own briefing room, and took center stage. Bothari, Elena,
Jesek and Daum waited in the wings, posted in pairs at
each exit, lethally armed.

"My name is Miles Naismith. I represent the Dendarii
Free Mercenary Fleet."

"Never heard of it," called a bold heckler from the
blur of faces around Miles.

Miles smiled acidly. "If you had, heads would roll in
my security department. We do not advertise. Recruit-
ment is by invitation only. Frankly," his gaze swept the
crowd, making eye contact, linking each face one by one

to its name and personal possessions, "if what I've seen so far represents your general standards, but for our assignment here you'd have gone right on not hearing of us."

Auson, Thorne, and the chief engineer, subdued and weary from fourteen hours of being dragged—raked—over every weld, weapon, tool, data bank, and supply room from one end of the ship to the other, had scarcely a twitch left in them. But Auson looked wistful at the thought.

Miles paced back and forth before his audience, radiating energy like a caged ferret. "We do not normally draft recruits, particularly from such dismal raw material. After yesterday's performance, I personally would have no compunction at disposing of you all by the swiftest means, just to improve the military tone of this ship." He scowled upon them fiercely. They looked nervous, uncertain; was there just the slightest hangdog shuffle there? Onward. "But your lives have been begged for you, upon a point of honor, by a better soldier than most of you can hope to be—" he glanced pointedly at Elena who, prepared, raised her chin and stood in a sort of parade rest, indicating to all the source of this unusual mercy.

Actually, Miles wondered if she wouldn't have personally shoved Auson, at least, out the nearest airlock. But having cast her in the role of "Commander Elena Bothari, my executive officer and unarmed combat instructor," it had occurred to him that he had the perfect set-up for a fast round of good guy-bad guy.

"—and so I have agreed to the experiment. To put it in terms you are familiar with—former Captain Auson has yielded your contracts to me."

That stirred them into outraged murmuring. A couple of them rose from their seats, a dangerous precedent. Fortunately, they hesitated, as if uncertain whether to start for Miles's throat first, or Captain Auson's. Before the ripple of motion could become an unstoppable tidal wave, Bothari brought his disruptor to aim with a good loud slap against his other hand. Bothari's lips were drawn back in a canine grimace, and his pale eyes blazed.

The mercenaries lost the moment. The ripple died. Those who had risen sat back down carefully, their hands resting plainly and demurely upon their knees.

Damn, thought Miles enviously, *I wish I could muster that much menace* ... The trick of it, alas, was that it was not a trick at all. Bothari's ferocity was palpably sincere.

Elena aimed her nerve disruptor in a white nervous grip, her eyes wide; but then, an obviously nervous person with a lethal weapon has a brand of menace all their own, and more than one mercenary spared a glance from the Sergeant to the other possible source of crossfire. A male mercenary attempted a prudent placating smile, palms out. Elena snarled under her breath, and the smile winked out hastily. Miles raised his voice and overrode the lingering whispers of confusion.

"By Dendarii regulation, you will all start at the same rank—the lowest, recruit-trainee. This is not an insult; every Dendarii, including myself, has started there. Your promotions will be by demonstrated ability—demonstrated to me. Due to your previous experience and the needs of the moment, your promotions will probably be much more rapid than usual. What this means, in effect, is that any one of you could find yourself the brevet captain of this ship within weeks."

The murmur became suddenly thoughtful. What this meant, in effect, thought Miles, was that he had just suceeded in dividing all the lower-ranking echelons from their former seniors. He nearly grinned as ambition visibly lit a scattering of faces. And had he ever lit a fire under those seniors—Thorne and Auson stared at each other in edgy speculation.

"Your new training will begin immediately. Those not assigned to training groups this shift will temporarily re-commence their old duties. Any questions?" He held his breath; his scheme pivoted on the point of a pin. He would know in a minute ...

"What's your rank?" asked a mercenary.

Miles decided to stay flexible. "You may address me

as Mr. Naismith." There, let them build theories on that.

"Then how do we know who to obey?" asked the original hard-eyed heckler.

Miles bared his teeth in a scimitar smile. "Well, if you disobey one of *my* orders, I'll shoot you on the spot. You figure it out." He drummed his fingers lightly on his holstered nerve disruptor. Some of Bothari's aura seemed to have rubbed off on him, for the heckler wilted.

A mercenary held up her hand, serious as a child at school.

"Yes, Trainee Quinn?"

"When do we get copies of the Dendarii regulations?"

Miles's heart seemed to stop. He hadn't thought of that one. It was such a reasonable request—the sort of commander Miles was trying to pass himself off as should know his regs by heart, or sleep with them under his pillow, or something. He produced a dry-mouthed smile, and croaked boldly, "Tomorrow. I'll have copies distributed to everyone." *Copies of what? I'll figure something out . . . .*

There was a silence. Then another voice from the back popped up. "What kind of insurance package does the, the Dendariis have? Do we get a paid vacation?"

And another: "Do we get any perqs? What's the pay scale?"

And yet another: "Will our pensions carry over from our old contracts? Is there a retirement plan?"

Miles nearly bolted from the room, confounded by this spate of practical questions. He had been prepared for defiance, disbelief, a concerted unarmed rush . . . He had a sudden maniac vision of Vorthalia the Bold demanding a whole-life policy from his Emperor at sword's point.

He gulped down total confusion, and forged ahead. "I'll distribute a brochure," he promised—he had a vague idea that sort of information came in brochures—"later. As for fringe benefits—" he barely managed to turn a glassy stare into an icy one. "I am permitting you to live. Further privileges will have to be earned."

He surveyed their faces. Confusion, yes, that was what

he wanted. Dismay, division, and most of all, distraction. Perfect. Let them, swirled upside-down in this gush of flim-flam, forget that their primary duty was to re-take their own ship. Forget it for just a week, keep them too busy to think for just a week, a week was all he needed. After that, they'd be Daum's problem. There was something else in their faces, though; he could not quite put his finger on it. No matter—his next task was to get off stage gracefully, and get them all moving. And get a minute alone with Bothari . . .

"Commander Elena Bothari has a list of your assignments. See her on your way out. Attention!" He put a snap in his voice. They shuffled raggedly to their feet, as if the posture were but dimly remembered. "Dismissed!" Yes, before they came up with any more bizarre questions and his invention failed him.

He caught a snatch of sotto voce conversation as he marched out.

"—homicidal runt lunatic . . ."

"Yes, but with a commander like that, there's a chance I might survive my next battle . . ."

He recognized the something-else in their faces suddenly—it was that same unnerving hunger he had seen in Mayhew's and Jesek's. It generated an unaccountable coldness in the pit of his belly.

He motioned Sergeant Bothari aside. "Do you still have that old copy of the Barrayaran Imperial Service regs that you used to carry around?" Bothari's bible, it was; Miles had sometimes wondered if the Sergeant had ever read another book.

"Yes, my lord." Bothari gave him a fishy stare, as if to say, Now what?

Miles sighed relief. "Good. I want it."

"What for?"

"Dendarii fleet regulations."

Bothari looked pole-axed. "You'll never—"

"I'll run it through the computer, make a copy—go through and chop out all the cultural references, change the names—it shouldn't take too long."

"My lord—those are the *old* regulations!" The flat

bass voice was almost agitated. "When those gutless slugs get a look at the old discipline parades—"

Miles grinned. "Yeah, if they saw the specs for those lead-lined rubber hoses, they'd probably faint dead away. Don't worry. I'll update them as I go along."

"Your father and the General Staff did that fifteen years ago. It took *them* two years."

"Well, that's what happens with committees."

Bothari shook his head, but told Miles where to find the old date disc among his things.

Elena joined the conference, looking nervous. But impressive, Miles thought; like a thoroughbred horse. "I've got them divided up into groups, by your list," she reported. "Now what?"

"Go ahead and take your group to the gym now and start the phys-ed class. General conditioning, then start teaching them what your father's taught you."

"I've never taught anybody before . . ."

He smiled up at her, willing confidence into her face, her eyes, her spine. "Look, you can probably kill the first two days just having them demonstrate what they know on each other, while you stand around and say "Um," and "Hm," and "God help us," and things like that. The important thing isn't to teach them anything, but to keep them busy, wear them out, don't give them time to think or plan or combine their forces. It's only for a week. If I can do it," he said manfully, "you can do it."

"I've heard that before somewhere," she muttered.

"And you, Sergeant—take your group and start them on weapons drills. If you run out of Barrayaran drills, the Oseran standard procedures are in the computers, you can filch some of them. Ride them. Baz will be running his people into the ground down in engineering—spring cleaning like they've never had before. And after I've gotten these regs straightened around, we can start quizzing them on those, too. Tire 'em out."

"My lord," said the Sergeant sternly, "there are twenty of them and four of us. At the end of the week, who do you think is going to be tireder?" He slipped into vehemence. "My first responsibility is your hide, damn it!"

"I'm thinking of my hide, believe me! And you can

best cover my hide by going out there and making *them* believe I'm a mercenary commander."

"You're not a commander, you're a bloody holovid director," muttered Bothari.

The editing job on the Imperial Regulations proved larger and more grueling than Miles had anticipated. Even the wholesale slaughter of such chapters as those detailing instructions for purely Barrayaran ceremonies such as the Emperor's Birthday Review left an enormous mass of material. Miles slashed into it, gutting almost as fast as he could read.

It was the closest look he had ever given to military regulations, and he meditated on them, deep in the night cycle. Organization seemed to be the key. To get huge masses of properly matched men and material to the right place at the right time in the right order with the swiftness required to even grasp survival—to wrestle an infinitely complex and confusing reality into the abstract shape of victory—organization, it seemed, might even outrank courage as a soldierly virtue.

He recalled a remark of his grandfather's—"More battles have been won or lost by the quartermasters than by any general staff." It had been apropos a classic anecdote about a quartermaster who had issued the young guerilla general's troops the wrong ammunition. "I had him hung by his thumbs for a day," Grandfather had reminisced, "but Prince Xav made me take him down." Miles fingered the dagger at his waist, and removed five screens of regulations about ship-mounted plasma weapons, obsolete for a generation.

His sclera were red and his cheeks hollow and grey with beard stubble at the end of the night cycle, but he had boiled his plagarization down into a neat, fierce little handbook for getting everybody's weapons pointed in the same direction. He pressed it into Elena's hands to be copied and distributed before staggering off to wash and change clothes, the better to present a front of eagle-eyed, as opposed to pie-eyed, command before his "new troops".

"Done," he murmured to her. "Does this make me a space pirate?"

She groaned.

Miles did his best to be seen everywhere that day cycle. He re-inspected sickbay, and gave it a grudging pass. He observed both Elena's and the Sergeant's "classes", trying to look as if he were noting every mercenary's performance with stern appraisal, and not in truth nearly falling asleep on his feet. He squeezed time for a private conversation with Mayhew, now manning the RG132 alone, to bring him up to date and bolster his confidence in the new scheme for holding the prisoners. He drew up some superficial written tests of his new "Dendarii Regulations" for Elena and Bothari to administer.

The mercenary pilot officer's funeral was in the afternoon, ship time. Miles made it a pretext for a rigorous inspection of the mercenaries' personal gear and uniforms; a proper parade. For the sake of example and courtesy, he turned himself and the Botharis out in the best clothes they had from his grandfather's funeral. Their somber brilliance artistically complimented the mercenaries' crisp grey-and whites.

Thorne, pale and silent, observed the sharp turnout with a strange gratitude. Miles was rather pale and silent himself, and breathed an inward sigh of relief when the pilot officer's body was at last safely cremated, his ashes scattered in space. Miles allowed Auson to conduct the brief ceremonies unhindered; his most soaring thespian hypocrisy, Miles felt, was not up to taking over this function.

He withdrew afterward to the cabin he had appropriated, telling Bothari he wanted to study the Oseran's real regulations and procedures. But his concentration was failing him. Odd flashes of formless movement occurred in his peripheral vision. He lay down but could not rest. He resumed pacing with his uneven stride, notions for fine-tuning his prisoner scheme tumbling through his brain but then escaping him. He was grateful when Elena interrupted him with a status report.

He confided to her, rather randomly, a half dozen of

his new ideas, then asked her anxiously, "Do they seem to be buying it? I'm not sure how I'm coming across. Are they going to accept orders from a kid?"

She grinned. "Major Daum seems to have taken care of that angle. Apparently he bought what you told him."

"Daum? What did I tell him?"

"About your rejuvenation treatment."

"My *what*?"

"He seems to think you were on leave from the Dendarii to go to Beta Colony for a rejuvenation treatment. Isn't that what you told him?"

"Hell no!" Miles paced. "I told him I was there for medical treatment, yes—thought it would account for this—" a vague wave of his hand indicating the peculiarities of his body, "combat injuries or something. But— there isn't any such thing as a Betan rejuvenation treatment! That's just a rumor. It's their public health system, and the way they live, and their genetics—"

"You may know it, but a lot of non-Betans don't. Daum seems to think you're not only older but, er, a lot older."

"Well, naturally he believes it, then, if he thought it up himself." Miles paused. "Bel Thorne must know better, though."

"Bel's not contradicting it." She smirked. "I think it has a crush on you."

Miles rubbed his hands through his hair, and over his numb face. "Baz must realize this rejuvenation rumor is nonsense, too. Better caution him not to correct anybody, though, it works to my advantage. I wonder what he thinks I am? I thought he'd have figured it out by now."

"Oh, Baz has his own theory. I—it's my fault, really. Father's always so worried about political kidnappers, I thought I'd better lead Baz astray."

"Good. What kind of fairy tale did you cook up for him?"

"I think you're right about people believing things they make up themselves. I swear I didn't plant any of this, I just didn't contradict it. He knows you're a Count's son, since you swore him in as an Armsman—aren't you going to get in trouble for that?"

Miles shook his head. "I'll worry about that if we live through this. Just so he doesn't figure out which Count's son."

"Well *I* think you did a good thing. It seems to mean a lot to him. Anyway, he thinks you're about his age. Your father, whoever he was, disinherited you, and exiled you from Barrayar to . . ." she faltered, "to get you out of sight," she finished, raising her chin bravely.

"Ah," said Miles. "A reasonable theory." He came to the end of a circuit in his pacing and stood absorbed, apparently, by the bare wall in front of him.

"You mustn't blame him for it—"

"I don't." He smiled a quick reassurance, and paced again.

"You have a younger brother who has usurped your rightful place as heir—"

He grinned in spite of himself. "Baz is a romantic."

"He's an exile himself, isn't he?" she asked quietly. "Father doesn't like him, but he won't say why . . ." She looked at him expectantly.

"I won't either, then. It's—it's not my business."

"But he's your leigeman now."

"All right, so it is my business. I just wish it weren't. But Baz will have to tell you himself."

She smiled at him. "I knew you'd say that." Oddly, the non-answer seemed to content her.

"How did your last combat class go? I hope they all crawled out on their hands and knees."

She smiled tranquilly. "Very nearly. Some of the technical people act like they never expected to do that kind of fighting. Others are awfully good—I've kind of got them working on the klutzy ones."

"That's just right," he approved eagerly. "Conserve your own energy, expend theirs. You've grasped the principle."

She glowed in his praise. "You've got me doing so many things I've never done before, new people, things I'd never dreamed of— "

"Yes ..." he stumbled. "I'm sorry I got you into this nightmare. I've been demanding so much of you—but I'll get you out. My word on it. Don't be scared."

Her mouth set in indignation. "I'm not scared! Well—some. But I feel more alive than I've ever been. You make anything seem possible."

The longed-for admiration in her eyes perturbed him. It was too much like hunger. "Elena—this whole thing is balanced on a hoax. If those guys out there wake up and realize how badly they have us outnumbered, we'll crash like—" he cut himself off. That wasn't what she needed to hear. He rubbed his eyes, fingertips pressing hard against them, and paced.

"It's not balanced on a hoax," she said earnestly. "You balance it."

"Isn't that what I said?" He laughed, shakily.

She studied him through narrowed eyes. "When was the last time you slept?"

"Oh, I don't know. I've lost track, with the ships on different clocks. That reminds me, got to get them on the same clock. I'll switch the RG132, that'll be easier. We'll all keep Oseran time. It was before the jump, anyway. A day before the jump."

"Have you had dinner?"

"Dinner?"

"Lunch?"

"Lunch? Was there lunch? I was getting things ready for the funeral, I guess."

She looked exasperated. "Breakfast?"

"I ate some of their field rations, when I was working on the regs last night—look, I'm short, I don't need as much as you overgrown types ..."

He paced on. Her face grew sober. "Miles," she said, and hesitated. "How did that pilot officer die? He looked, well, not all right, but he was alive in the shuttle. Did he jump you?"

His stomach did a roller-coaster flop. "My God, do you think *I* murdered—" But he had, surely, as surely as if he had held a disruptor to the man's head and fired. He had no desire to detail the events in the RG132's wardroom to Elena. They looped in his memory, violent images flashing over and over. Bothari's crime, his crime, a seamless whole . . .

"Miles, are you all right?" Her voice was alarmed. He realized he was standing still with his eyes shut. Tears were leaking between the lids.

"Miles, sit down! You're hyper."

"Can't sit down. If I stop I'll . . ." He resumed his circuit, limping mechanically.

She stared at him, her lips parted, then shut her mouth abruptly and slammed out the door.

Now he had frightened her, offended her, perhaps even sabotaged her carefully nurtured confidence . . . He swore at himself, savage. He was sinking in a black and sucking bog, gluey viscous terror sapping his vital forward momentum. He waded on, blindly.

Elena's voice again. "—bouncing off the walls. I think you'll have to sit on him. I've never seen him this bad . . ."

Miles looked up into the precious, ugly face of his personal killer. Bothari compressed his lips, and sighed. "Right. I'll take care of it."

Elena, eyes wide with concern but mouth calm with confidence in Bothari, withdrew. Bothari grasped Miles by the back of the collar and belt, frog-marched him over to the bed, and sat him down firmly.

"Drink."

"Oh, hell, Sergeant—you know I can't stand scotch. Tastes like paint thinner."

"I will," said Bothari patiently, "hold your nose and pour it down your throat if I have to."

Miles took in the flinty face and prudently choked down a slug from the flask, which he recognized vaguely as confiscated from mercenary stock. Bothari, with matter-of-fact efficiency, stripped him and slung him into bed.

"Drink again."

"Blech." It burned foully down his throat.

"Now sleep."

"Can't sleep. Too much to do. Got to keep them moving. Wonder if I can fake a brochure? I suppose death-gild is nothing but a primitive form of life insurance, at that. Elena can't possibly be right about Thorne. Hope to God my father never finds out about this—Sergeant, you won't . . . ? I thought of a docking drill with the RG132 . . ." His protests trailed off to a mumble, and he rolled over and slept dreamlessly for sixteen hours.

CHAPTER ELEVEN ✳ ✳ ✳

A week later, he was still in command.

Miles took to haunting the mercenary ship's control room as they neared their destination. Daum's rendezvous was a rare metals refinery in the system's asteroid belt. The factory was a mobile of chaotic structures strung together by girdering and powersats, winged by its vast solar collectors, junkyard art. A few lights winked, picking out bright reflections and leaving the rest in charitable dimness.

Too few lights, Miles realized as they approached. The place looked shut down. An off shift? Not likely; it represented too large an investment to let stand idle for the sake of its masters' biology. By rights the smelteries should be operating around the clock to feed the war effort. Tow ships with ore chunks should be jockying for docking space, outgoing freighters should be wheeling away with their military escorts in a traffic-control minuet . . .

"Are they still answering your recognition codes correctly?" Miles asked Daum. He barely kept himself from shifting from foot to foot.

"Yes." But Daum looked strained.

He doesn't like the looks of this either, Miles thought. "Shouldn't a strategically important installation like this be more actively guarded? Surely the Pelians and the Oserans have got to be trying to knock it out. Where are your picket ships?"

"I don't know." Daum moistened his lips, and stared into the screen.

"We have a live transmission now, sir," the mercenary communications officer reported.

A Felician colonel appeared in the viewscreen.

"Fehun! Thank God!" cried Daum. The tension melted in his face.

Miles let out his breath. For a horrible moment he'd been crushed by a vision of being unable to unload his prisoners along with Daum's cargo, and then what? He was quite as exhausted by the week as Bothari had predicted, and looked forward with a shiver of relief to its ending.

Lieutenant Thorne, coming on station, smiled and gave Miles a neat salute. Miles pictured the look on Thorne's face when the masquerade and betrayal were at last revealed. His ballooning anticipation turned to lead in his stomach. He returned the salute, and concealed his queasiness by turning to watch Daum's conversation. Maybe he could arrange to be elsewhere when the trap was sprung.

"—made it," Daum was saying. "Where is everybody? This place looks deserted."

There was a flash of static, and the military figure in the screen shrugged. "We drove off an attack by the Pelians a few weeks ago. The solar collectors were damaged. We're awaiting the repair crews now."

"How are things at home? Have we freed Barinth yet?"

Another flash of static. The colonel, seated behind his desk, nodded and said, "The war is going well."

The colonel had a tiny sculpture on his desk, Miles noticed, a mosaic horse cleverly formed of assorted scrap electronic parts soldered together, no doubt by some refinery technician in his off hours. Miles thought of his grandfather, and wondered what kind of horses they had on Felice. Had they ever slipped back enough technologically to have used horse cavalry?

"Great!" Daum chortled, avid upon his fellow Felician's face. "I took so long on Beta, I was afraid—so we're still in business! I'll buy you a drink when we get in, you old snake, and we'll toast the Premier together. How is Miram?"

Static. "The family is well," the colonel said gravely. Static. "Stand by for docking instructions."

Miles stopped breathing. The little horse, which had been on the colonel's right hand, was now on his left.

"Yes," agreed Daum happily, "and we can carry on without all this garbage on the channel. Is that you making the white noise?"

There was another blat of static. "Our communications equipment was damaged in an attack by the Pelians a few weeks ago." Now the horse was back on the right. White fuzz on the screen. "Stand by for docking instructions." Now the left. Miles felt like screaming.

Instead he motioned the communications officer to kill the channel.

"It's a trap," Miles said, the instant they were off transmission.

"What?" Daum stared. "Fehun Benar is one of my oldest friends! He wouldn't betray—"

"You haven't been talking to Colonel Benar. You've been having a synthesized conversation with a computer."

"But his voiceprint—"

"Oh, it really was Benar—pre-recorded. Something on his desk was flipping around between those blasts of static. They were being deliberately transmitted to cover the discontinuities—almost. Careless of somebody. They probably recorded his responses in more than one session."

"Pelians," grunted Thorne. "Can't do anything right . . ."

Daum's tan skin greyed. "He wouldn't betray—"

"They probably had a fair amount of time to prepare. There are—" Miles took a breath, "there are lots of ways to break a man. I bet there *was* an attack by the Pelians a few weeks ago—only it wasn't driven off."

It was over, then, surrender inevitable. The RG132 and its cargo would be confiscated, Daum taken prisoner of war, Miles and his liege-people interned, if they weren't shot outright. Barrayaran security would ransom him eventually, Miles supposed, with all due scandal. Then the Betan, Calhoun, with God-knew-what civil charges, then home at last to explain it all before the ultimate tribunal, his father. Miles wondered, if he waived his Class III diplomatic immunity on Beta Colony, could he be jailed there instead? But no, the Betans didn't jail offenders, they cured them.

Daum's eyes were wide, his mouth taut. "Yes," he hissed, convinced. "What do we do, sir?"

You're asking me? thought Miles wildly. Help, help, help . . . He stared around at the faces in the room, Daum, Elena, Baz, the mercenary technicians, Thorne and Auson. They gazed back with interested confidence, as if he were a goose about to lay a golden egg. Bothari leaned against the wall, his stance for once devoid of suggestions.

"They're asking why our transmission was interrupted," reported the communications officer urgently.

Miles swallowed, and produced his first cockatrice. "Pipe them some gooey music," he ordered, "and put a 'technical difficulties—please stand by' sign on the video."

The communications officer grinned and snapped to obey.

Well, that took care of the next ninety seconds . . .

Auson, his arms still immobilized, looked as sick as Miles felt. Doubtless he was not looking forward to explaining his humiliating capture to his admiral. Thorne was crackling with suppressed excitement. The lieutenant is about to get revenge for this week, mused Miles miserably, and knows it.

Thorne was standing at attention. "Orders, sir?"

My God, thought Miles, don't they realize they're free? And more wildly, with new rocketing hope—*They followed me home, Dad. Can I keep them?*

Thorne, experienced, knew the ship, soldiers, and equipment intimately, not with facile surface gloss but with true depth; more vital still, Thorne had forward momentum. Miles stood straight as he could and barked, "So, Trainee Thorne, you think you're fit to command a warship, eh?"

Thorne came to a stiffer attention, chin raised eagerly. "Sir!"

"We've been presented with a most interesting little tactical exercise,"—that was the phrase his father had used to describe the conquest of Komarr, Miles recalled—"I'm going to give you the chance at it. We can keep the Pelians on hold for about one more minute. As a commander, how would you handle this?" Miles folded his arms and tilted his head, in the style of a particularly intimidating proctor from his candidacy exams.

"Trojan horse," said Thorne instantly. "Ambush their ambush, and take the station from within—you do want it captured intact, don't you?"

"Ah," said Miles faintly, "that would be fine." He dredged his mind rapidly for some likely-sounding military-advisor-type noises. "But they must have some ships concealed around here somewhere. What do you propose to do about them, once you've committed yourself to defending an immobile base? Is the refinery even armed?"

"It can be, in a few hours," Daum put in, "with the maser scramblers we've got in the hold of the RG 132. Cannibalize the powersats—time permitting, even repair the solar collectors, to charge them—"

"Maser scramblers?" muttered Auson. "I thought you said you were smuggling military advisors . . ."

Miles quickly raised his voice and overrode this. "Remember that personnel are in short supply, and definitely not expendable right now." Particularly Dendarii officers . . . Thorne bore a thoughtful look; Miles was momentarily terrified that he'd overdone his critiqueing, causing Thorne to throw the problem back on him. "Convince me, then, Trainee Thorne, that taking a base is not tactically premature," Miles invited hastily.

"Yes, sir. Well, the defending ships we need to worry about are almost certainly Oseran. The Pelian ship-building capacity is way under par—they don't have the biotech for Jump ships at all. And we have all the Oseran codes and procedures, but they don't know a thing about our Dendarii ones. I think I—we, can take them."

Our Dendarii? Miles's mind echoed. "Very well, Trainee Thorne. Go ahead," he ordered in a fine loud decisive voice. "I won't interfere unless you get in over your head." He shoved his hands in his pockets by way of emphasis, also to keep from biting his nails.

"Take us into dock, then, without tipping them off," Thorne said. "I'll ready the boarding party. May I have Commander Jesek and Commander Bothari?"

Miles nodded; Sergeant Bothari sucked in his breath, but said nothing, duty-glued to Miles's back. Thorne, dazzled with visions of captaincy, dashed out, followed by the drafted "advisors". Elena's face shone with excitement. Baz rolled a rather soggy cigar stump between his teeth, and strode after her, eyes gleaming unreadably. There was color in his face, Miles noted.

Auson stood downcast, face furrowed with anger, shame, and suspicion. *There's a mutiny looking for a place to happen,* thought Miles. He lowered his voice for the big man's ear alone.

"May I point out, you're still on the sick list, Trainee Auson."

Auson waggled his arms. "I could've had these off day before yesterday, damn it."

"May I also point out, that while I've promised Trainee Thorne a command, I have not said of what ship. An officer must be able to obey as well as command. To each his own test, to each his own reward. I'll be watching you, too."

"There's only one ship."

"You're full of assumptions. A bad habit."

"You're full of—" Auson shut his mouth with a snap, and gave Miles a long, thoughtful stare.

"Tell them we're ready for docking instructions," Miles nodded to Daum.

Miles itched to be part of the fight, but discovered to his dismay the mercenaries had no space armor small enough to fit him. Bothari grunted frank relief. Miles then thought of going along in a simple pressure suit, if not at the front of the rush, then at least at the rear. Bothari nearly choked at the suggestion. "I swear I'll knock you down and sit on you if you go near those suits," he snarled.

"Insubordination, Sergeant," Miles hissed back.

Bothari glanced up the line at the mercenaries assembling in the armory to be sure he was not overheard. "I'm not hauling your body back to Barrayar to dump at my lord Count's feet like something the bloody cat caught." The Sergeant traded a driven glare for Miles's irritated frown.

Miles, in dim recognition of a man pushed to his limit, backed down grudgingly. "What if I'd passed my officer's training exams?" he asked. "You couldn't have stopped me from this sort of thing then."

"I'd have retired," Bothari muttered, "while I still had my honor."

Miles grinned involuntarily, and consoled himself with checking equipment and weapons for those who were going. The week of vigorous repair and refurbishment had clearly paid unexpected dividends; the combat group seemed to gleam with wicked efficiency. Now, Miles thought, we shall see if all this beauty is more than skin deep.

He took particular care over Elena's armor. Bothari arranged her comm leads himself before attaching her helmet, unnecessary business concealing most necessary rapid whispered instructions about how to handle herself in the only-half-familiar equipment.

"For God's sake, hang back," Miles told her. "You're supposed to be observing everybody's efficiency and reporting to me anyway, which you can't do if you're—" he swallowed the rest of his sentence, grisly visions of all the ways a beautiful woman could get mangled in combat skidding through his brain, "if you're in front," he substituted. Surely he'd been out of his scattered wits to let Thorne claim her.

Her features were framed in the helmet, hair drawn back and hidden so that the strong structure of her face sprang out, half knight, half nun. Her cheekbones were emphasized by the winged cheekpieces, ivory skin glowing in the tiny colored lights of her helmet readouts. Her lips were parted in exhilaration. They curved at

him. "Yes, my lord." Her eyes were bright and fearless.
"Thank you."

And more quietly, her gloved hand tightening on his
arm for emphasis, "Thank you, Miles—for the honor."
She had not quite mastered the touch of the servos, and
mashed his flesh to the bone. Miles, who would not
have moved to destroy the moment if she'd accidentally
torn his arm off, smiled back with no more than a blink
of pain. *God, what have I done?* he thought. *She looks
like a valkyrie* . . . .

He dropped back for a quick word with Baz.

"Do me a favor, Commander Jesek, would you? Stick
close to Elena and make sure she keeps her head down.
She's, uh, a little excited."

"Absolutely, my lord," Jesek nodded emphatically.
"I'd follow her anywhere."

"Um," said Miles. That hadn't been exactly what he'd
meant to convey.

"My lord," Baz added, then hesitated and lowered his
voice. "This, ah, commander business—you didn't mean
that as a real promotion, did you? It was for show,
right?" He jerked his head toward the mercenaries, now
being counted off into assault groups by Thorne.

"It's as real as the Dendarii Mercenaries," Miles replied, not quite able to manage an outright lie to his
leigeman.

Baz's eyebrows lifted. "And what does that mean?"

"Well . . . My fa—a person I knew once said that
meaning is what you bring to things, not what you take
from them. He was talking about Vor, as it happened."
Miles paused, then added, "Carry on, Commander Jesek."

Baz's eyes glinted amusement. He came to attention
and returned Miles an ironic, deliberate salute. "Yes,
sir—Admiral Naismith."

Miles, dogged by Bothari, returned to the mercenaries' tactics room to monitor the battle channels alongside Auson and the communications officer. Daum
remained posted in the control room with the engineering technician who was substituting for the dead pilot,
to guide them into the docking station. Now Miles re-

ally did chew his nails. Auson clicked the plastic immobilizers on his arms together in a nervous tattoo, the
limit of their motion. They caught each other, looking
sideways simultaneously.

"What would you give to be out there, Shorty?"

Miles hadn't realized his anguish was so transparent.
He did not even bother to be offended by the nickname.
"About fifteen centimeters of height, Captain Auson,"
he replied, wistfully frank.

The breath of a genuine laugh escaped the mercenary
officer, as if against his will. "Yeah." His mouth twisted
in agreement. "Oh, yeah . . ."

Miles watched, fascinated, as the communications officer began pulling in telemetry from the assault group's
battle armor. The holovid screen, split to display sixteen individuals' readouts at once, was a confetti-like
confusion. He framed a cautious remark, hoping to get
more information without revealing his own ignorance.

"Very nice. You can see and hear what each of your
men are seeing and hearing." Miles wondered which
information bits were the key ones. A trained person
could tell at a glance, he was sure. "Where was it built?
I've, ah—never seen this particular model."

"Illyrica," said Auson proudly. "The system came with
the ship. One of the best you can buy."

"Ah . . . Which one is Commander Bothari?"

"What was her suit number?"

"Six."

"She's at the upper right of the screen. See, there's
the suit number, keys for visual, audio, their suit-to-suit
battle channels, our ship-to-suit battle channels—we
can actually control the servos on any suit right from
here."

Both Miles and Bothari studied the display intently.
"Wouldn't that be a bit confusing for the individual, to
be suddenly overridden?" Miles asked.

"Well, you don't do that too often. It's supposed to be
for things like operating the suit medkits, pulling back
the injured . . . To tell the truth, I'm not completely
sold on that function. The one time I was on this end
and tried to pull out a wounded man, his armor was so

damaged by the blast that got him, it barely worked at all. I lost most of the telemetry—found out why, when we mopped up. His head had been blown off. I'd spent twenty frigging minutes walking a corpse back through the airlocks."

"How often have you used the system?" Miles asked.

Auson cleared his throat. "Well, twice, actually." Bothari snorted; Miles raised an eyebrow. "We were on that damned blockade duty so long," Auson hastened to explain. "Everybody likes a bit of easy work, sure, but . . . Maybe we were on it too long."

"That was my impression, too," Miles agreed blandly. Auson shifted uncomfortably, and returned his attention to his tactics displays.

They were on the verge of docking. The assault groups were poised, ready. The RG 132 was maneuvering into a parallel bay, lagging behind; the Pelians had cannily instructed the warship to dock first, no doubt planning to pick off the unarmed freighter at their leisure. Miles wished desperately that he'd had some pre-arranged code by which to warn Mayhew, still manning the freighter alone, what was up. But without scrambled communications channels he risked tipping their hand to the listening Pelians. Hopefully, Thorne's surprise attack would pull whatever troops were waiting away from the RG 132.

The moment's silence seemed to stretch unbearably. Miles finally managed to pick out the medical readouts from the battle armor. Elena's pulse rate was an easy 80 beats a minute. Jesek's, beside her, was running about 110. Miles wondered what his own was. Something astronomical, by the feel of it.

"Does the opposition have anything like this?" asked Miles suddenly, an idea beginning to boil up in his mind. Perhaps he could be more than an impotent observer . . . .

"The Pelians don't. Some of the more advanced ships in our—in the Oseran fleet do. That pocket dreadnought of Captain Tung's, for instance. Betan-built." Auson emitted an envious sigh. "He's got everything."

Miles turned to the communications officer. "Are you

picking up anything like that from the other side? Anybody waiting in the docking bay in battle armor?"

"It's scrambled," said the communications officer, "but I'd guess our reception committee to run about thirty individuals." Bothari's jaw tightened at this news.

"Thorne getting this?" asked Miles.

"Of course."

"Are they picking up ours?"

"Only if they're looking for it," said the communications officer. "They shouldn't be. We're tight-beamed and scrambled too."

"Two to one," muttered Auson unhappily. "Nasty odds."

"Let's try and even it up," said Miles. He turned to the communications officer. "Can you break their codes, get into their telemetry? You have the Oseran codes, don't you?"

The communications officer looked suddenly thoughtful. "It doesn't work exactly that way, but . . ." his sentence trailed off in his absorption with his equipment.

Auson's eye lit. "You thinking of taking over their suits? Walking them into walls, having them shoot each other—" the light went out. "Ah, hell—they've all got manual overrides. The second they figure out what's going on, they'll cut us off. It was a nice idea, though."

Miles grinned. "We won't let them figure it out, then. We'll be subtle. You think too much in terms of brute force, Trainee Auson. Now, brute force has never been my strong suit—"

"Got it!" the communications officer cried. The holovid plates threw up a second display beside the first. "There's ten of them over there with full-feedback armor. The rest seem to be Pelians—their armor only has comm links. But there are the ten."

"Ah! Beautiful! Here, Sergeant, take over our monitors." Miles moved to the new station and stretched his fingers, like a concert pianist about to play. "Now, I'll show you what I mean. What we want to do is simulate a lot of little, tiny suit malfunctions . . ." he zeroed in on one soldier. Medical telemetry—physiological support—there. "Observe."

He pinpointed the reservoir from the man's pilot relief tube, already half full. "Must be a nervous sort of
fellow—" He set it to backwash at full power, and checked
the audio transmitter. Savage swearing filled the air
briefly, overridden by a snarl calling for radio silence.
"Now, there is one distracted soldier. And there's not a
thing he can do about it until he gets somewhere he can
take the suit off."

Auson, beside him, choked with laughter. "You devious-
minded little bastard! Yes, yes!" He pounded his feet, in
lieu of his hands, and swung about in his own seat. He
called up the readings from another soldier, pecking out
the commands slowly with his few working fingertips.

"Remember," cautioned Miles, "subtle."

Auson, still cackling, muttered "Right." He bent over
his control panel. "There. There . . ." He sat up, grinning. "Every third servo command now operates on a
half-second time lag, and his weapons will fire ten de-
grees to the right of where he aims them."

"Very good," Miles applauded. "We'd better save the
rest until they're in critical positions, not tip our hand
with too much too soon."

"Right."

The ship was moving closer, closer to the docking
station. The enemy troops were preparing to board
through the normal flex tubes.

Suddenly, Thorne's assault groups exploded from the
dockside airlocks. Magnetic mines were hastily fired
onto the station hull, where they flared like sparks burning holes in a rug. Thorne's mercenaries jumped the
gap and poured through. The enemy's radio silence burst
into shocked chaos.

Miles hummed over his readouts. An enemy officer
turned her head to look over her shoulder, calling orders to her platoon; Miles promptly locked the helmet
in its position of maximum torsion, and the Oseran's
head perforce with it. He picked out another soldier, in
a corridor his own people had not yet reached, and
locked his suit's built-in heavy-duty plasma arc into
full-on. Fire flared wildly from the man's hand at his

surprised reflexive recoil, spraying floor, ceiling, and comrades.

Miles paused to glance over to Elena's readouts. A corridor was flowing past at high speed on the visual. It spun wildly as she used her suit's jets to brake. The artificial gravity was evidently now shut down in the docking station. An automatic air seal had clanged shut, blocking the corridor. She stopped her spin, aimed, and blasted a hole in it with her plasma arc. She flung herself through it as, at the same moment, an enemy soldier on the other side did likewise. They met in a confused scrambling grapple, servos screaming at the overload demands.

Miles searched frantically for the enemy among the ten readouts, but he was a Pelian. Miles had no access to his suit. His heart pounded in his ears. There was another view of the fight between Elena and the Pelian on the screens; Miles had a dizzy sense of being in two places at once, as if his atman had left his body, then realized he was looking at them through another Oseran's suit. The Oseran was raising his weapon to fire—he couldn't miss—

Miles called up the man's medkit and fired every drug in it into the man's veins at once. The audio transmitted a shuddering gasp; the heartbeat readout jumped crazily and then registered fibrillation. Another figure—Baz?—in the *Ariel's* armor rolled through the gash in the air seal, firing as he flew. The plasma washed over the Oseran, interrupting transmission.

"Son-of-a-bitch!" Auson screamed suddenly at Miles's elbow. "Whereinhell did *he* come from?"

Miles thought at first he was referring to the armored soldier, then followed the direction of Auson's gaze to another screen, showing space opposite the docking station.

Looming up behind them was a large Oseran warship.

CHAPTER TWELVE   ✳   ✳   ✳

Miles swore in frustration. Of course! Oseran full-feedback space armor logically implied an Oseran monitor nearby. He should have realized it instantly. Fool he was, to have simply assumed the enemy was being directed from inside the docking station. He ground his teeth in chagrin. He had totally forgotten, in the overwhelming excitement of the attack, in his particular terror for Elena, the first principle of larger commands: don't get balled up in the little details. It was no consolation that Auson appeared to have forgotten it too.

The communications officer hastily abandoned the game of suit sabotage and returned to his proper post. "They're calling for surrender, sir," he reported.

Miles licked dry lips, and cleared his throat. "Ah—suggestions, Trainee Auson?"

Auson gave him a dirty look. "It's that snob Tung. He's from Earth, and never lets you forget it. He has four times our shielding and firepower, three times our acceleration, three times our crew, and thirty years experience. I don't suppose you'd care to consider surrender?"

"You're right," Miles said after a moment. "I don't care for it."

The assault on the docking station was nearly over. Thorne and company were already moving into adjoining structures for the mopping-up. Victory swallowed

so swiftly by defeat? Unbearable. Miles groped vainly in
the pit of his inspiration for a better idea.

"It's not very elegant," he said at last, "but we're at
such incredibly short range, it's at least possible—we
could try to ram them."

Auson mouthed the words: my ship . . . He found his
voice. "My ship! The finest technology Illyrica will sell,
and you want to use it for a frigging medieval batter-
ing ram? Shall we boil some oil and fling it at 'em,
while we're at it? Throw a few rocks?" His voice went
up an octave, and cracked.

"I bet they wouldn't expect it," offered Miles, a little
quelled.

"I'll strangle you with my bare hands—" Auson, trying
to raise them, rediscovered the limits of his motion.

"Uh, Sergeant," Miles called, retreating before the rapidly breathing mercenary captain.

Bothari uncoiled from his chair. His narrow eyes
mapped Auson coldly, like a coroner planning his first
cut.

"It's got to be at least tried," Miles reasoned.

"Not with my ship you don't, you little—" Auson's
language sputtered into body language. His balance
shifted to free one foot for a karate kick.

"My God! Look!" cried the communications officer.

The RG 132, torpid, massive, was rolling away from
the docking station. Its normal space drives blared at
full power, giving it the usual acceleration of an ele-
phant swimming in molasses.

Auson dropped, unheeded, from Miles's attention. "The
RG 132, loaded, has four times the mass of that pocket
dreadnought," he breathed.

"Which is why it flies like a pig and costs a fortune
in fuel to move!" yelled Auson. "That pilot officer of
yours is crazy if he thinks he can outrun Tung—"

"Go, Arde!" cried Miles, jumping up and down. "Perfect! You'll pin him right up against that smelting unit—"

"He's not—" began Auson. "Son-of-a-bitch! He is!"

Tung, like Auson, was apparently late in divining the
bulk freighter's true intentions. Verniers began to flare,
to rotate the warship into position to thrust toward

open space. The dreadnought got one shot off, which was absorbed with little visible effect in the freighter's cargo area.

Then, almost in slow motion, with a kind of crazy majesty, the RG 132 lumbered into the warship—and kept going. The dreadnought was nudged into the huge smeltery. Projecting equipment and surface housings snapped and spun off in all directions.

Action calling for reaction, after an aching moment the smeltery heaved back. A wave of motion passed down its adjoining structures, like a giant's game of crack-the-whip. Smashed edges of the dreadnought were caught up on the smeltery, thoroughly entangled. Gaudy chemical fires gouted here and there into the vacuum.

The RG 132 drifted off. Miles stood before the tactics room screen and stared in stunned fascination as half the freighter's outer hull delaminated and peeled into space.

The RG 132 was the final detail to be mopped up in the capture of the metals refinery. Thorne's commandos smoked the last of the Oserans out of their crippled ship, and cleared the outlying structures of resisters and refugees. The wounded were sorted from the dead, prisoners taken under guard, booby traps detected and deactivated, atmosphere restored in key areas. Then, at last, the manpower and shuttles could be spared to warp the old freighter into the docking station.

A smudged figure in a pressure suit stumbled out of the flex tube into the loading bay.

"They're *bent*! They're *bent*!" cried Mayhew to Miles, pulling off his helmet. His hair stuck out in all directions, plastered by dried sweat.

Baz and Elena strode up to him, looking, with their helmets off, like a pair of dark knights after the tournament. Elena's hug pulled the pilot off his feet; from Mayhew's suffused look, Miles guessed she was still having a little trouble with her servos. "It was great, Arde!" she laughed.

"Congratulations," added Baz. "That was the most remarkable tactical maneuver I've ever seen. Beautifully calculated trajectory—your impact point was perfect. You hung him up royally, but without structural damage—I've just been over it—with a few repairs, we've captured ourselves a working dreadnought!"

"Beautiful?" said Mayhew. "Calculated? You're as crazy as *he* is—" he pointed at Miles. "As for damage—look at it!" He waved over his shoulder in the direction of the RG 132.

"Baz says they have the equipment to rig some sort of hull repairs at this station," Miles soothed. "It'll delay us here for a few more weeks, which I don't like any more than you do, but it can be done. God help us if anybody asks us to *pay* for it, of course, but with luck I should be able to commandeer—"

"You don't understand!" Mayhew waved his arms in the air. "They're *bent*. The Necklin rods."

The body of the jump drive, as the pilot and his viral control circuitry was its nervous system, was the pair of Necklin field generator rods that ran from one end of the ship to the other. They were manufactured, Miles recalled, to tolerances of better than one part in a million.

"Are you sure?" said Baz. "The housings—"

"You can stand in the housings and look up the rods and see the warp. Actually see it! They look like *skis!*" Mayhew wailed.

Baz let his breath trickle out in a hiss between his teeth.

Miles, although he thought he already knew the answer, turned to the engineer. "Any chance of repairing—?"

Baz and Mayhew both gave Miles much the same look.

"By God, you'd try, wouldn't you?" said Mayhew. "I can see you down there now, with a sledgehammer—"

Jesek shook his head regretfully. "No, my lord. My understanding is the Felicians aren't up to jump ship production on either the biotech or the engineering side. Replacement rods would have to be imported—Beta Colony would be closest—but they don't manufacture this model any more. They would have to be specially made, and shipped, and—well, I estimate it would take a year and cost several times the original value of the RG 132."

"Ah," said Miles. He stared rather blankly through the plexiports at his shattered ship.

"Couldn't we take the *Ariel*?" began Elena. "Break through the blockade, and—" she stopped, and flushed slightly. "Oh. Sorry."

The murdered pilot's ghost breathed a cold laugh in Miles's ear. "A pilot without a ship," he muttered under his breath, "a ship without a pilot, cargo not delivered, no money, no way home . . ." He turned curiously to Mayhew. "Why did you do it, Arde? You could have just surrendered peaceably. You're Betan, they'd have to have treated you all right . . ."

Mayhew looked around the docking bay, not meeting Miles's eyes. "Seemed to me that dreadnought was about to blow you all into the next dimension."

"True. So?"

"So—well—it didn't seem to me a, a right and proper Armsman ought to be sitting on his ass while that was going on. The ship itself was the only weapon I had. So I aimed it, and—" he mimed a trigger with his finger, and fired it.

He then inhaled, and added with more heat, "But you never warned me, never briefed—I swear if you ever pull a trick like that again, I'll, I'll—"

A ghostly smiled tinged Bothari's lips. "Welcome to my lord's service—Armsman."

Auson and Thorne appeared at the other end of the docking bay. "Ah, there he is, with the whole Inner Circle," said Auson. They bore down upon Miles.

Thorne saluted. "I have the final totals now, sir."

"Um—yes, go ahead, Trainee Thorne." Miles pulled himself to attentiveness.

"On our side, two dead, five injured. Injuries not too serious but for one bad plasma burn—she'll be needing a pretty complete facial regeneration when we get to proper medical facilities—"

Miles's stomach contracted. "Names?"

"Dead, Deveraux and Kim. The head burn was Elli—uh, Trainee Quinn."

"Go on."

"The enemy's total personnel were 60 from the *Triumph*, Captain Tung's ship—twenty commandos, the rest technical support—and 86 Pelians of whom 40 were military personnel and the rest techs sent to re-start the refinery. Twelve dead, 26 injured moderate-to-severe, and a dozen or so minor injuries.

"Equipment losses, two suits of space armor damaged beyond repair, five repairable. And the damages to the RG 132, I guess— " Thorne glanced up through the plexiports; Mayhew sighed mournfully.

"We captured, in addition to the refinery itself and the *Triumph*, two Pelian inner-system personnel carriers, ten station shuttles, eight two-man personal flitters, and those two empty ore tows hanging out beyond the crew's quarters. Uh—one Pelian armed courier appears to have—uh— gotten away." Thorne's litany trailed off; the lieutenant appeared to be watching Miles's face anxiously for his reaction to this last bit of news.

"I see." Miles wondered how much more he could absorb. He was growing numb. "Go on."

"On the bright side—"

There's a bright side? thought Miles.

"—we've found a little help for our personnel shortage problem. We freed 23 Felician prisoners—a few military types, but mostly refinery techs kept working at gunpoint until their Pelian replacements could arrive. A couple of them are a little messed up—"

"How so?" Miles began, then held up a hand. "Later. I'll—I'll be making a complete inspection."

"Yes, sir. The rest are able to help out. Major Daum's pretty happy."

"Has he been able to get in contact with his command yet?"

"No, sir."

Miles rubbed the bridge of his nose between thumb and forefinger, and squeezed his eyes shut, to contain the throbbing in his head.

A patrol of Thorne's weary commandos marched past,

moving a batch of prisoners to a more secure location. Miles's eye was drawn to a squat Eurasian of about fifty in torn Oseran grey-and-whites. In spite of his battered and discolored face and painful limp, he maintained a hard-edged alertness. That one looks like he could walk through walls *without* space armor, Miles thought.

The Eurasian stopped abruptly. "Auson!" he cried. "I thought you were dead!" He towed his captors toward Miles's group; Miles gave the anxious guard a nod of permission.

Auson cleared his throat. "Hello, Tung."

"How did they take your ship without—"the prisoner began, and stopped, as he assimilated Thorne's armor, Auson's—in light of his immobilized arms, decorative—sidearm, their lack of guards. His expression of amazement changed to hot disgust. He struggled for words. "I might have known," he choked at last. "I might have known. Oser was right to keep you two clowns as far away from the real combat as possible. Only the comedy team of Auson and Thorne could have captured *themselves*."

Auson's lips curled back in a snarl. Thorne flashed a thin, razor-edged smile. "Hold your tongue, Tung," it called, and added in an aside to Miles, "If you knew how many years I've been waiting to say that—"

Tung's face flushed a dark bronze-purple, and he shouted back, "Sit on it, Thorne! You're equipped for it—"

They both lunged forward simultaneously. Tung's guards clubbed him to his knees; Auson and Miles grabbed Thorne's arms. Miles was lifted off his feet, but between them they managed to check the Betan hermaphrodite.

Miles intervened. "May I point out, Captain Tung, that the—ah—comedy team has just captured you?"

"If half my commandos hadn't been trapped by that sprung bulkhead—" Tung began hotly.

Auson straightened, and smirked. Thorne stopped flexing on its feet. United at last, thought Miles, by the common enemy . . . Miles breathed a small. "Ha!", as he spotted his opportunity to finally put the disbelieving and suspicious Auson in the palm of his hand.

"Who the hell is that little mutant?" Tung muttered to his guard.

Miles stepped forward. "In fact, you have done so well, Trainee Thorne, that I have no hesitation in confirming you in your brevet command. Congratulations, Captain Thorne."

Thorne swelled. Auson wilted, all the old shame and rage crowding in his eyes. Miles turned to him.

"You have also served, Trainee Auson," Miles said, thinking, overlooking that understandable small mutiny in the tactics room . . . "Even while on the sick list. And for those who also serve, there is also a reward." He gestured grandly out the plexiport where a free-fall crew with cutting torches was just beginning to untangle the *Triumph* from its entrapment. "There is your new command. Sorry about the dents." He dropped his voice. "And perhaps next time you will not be so full of assumptions?"

Auson turned about, waves of bewilderment, astonishment, and delight breaking in his face. Bothari pursed his lips in appreciation of Miles's feudal ploy. Auson in command of his own ship must eventually wake to the fact that it *was* his own ship; Auson subordinate to Thorne must always be a potential focus for disaffection. But Auson in command of a ship held from Miles's hands became, ipso facto, Miles's man. Never mind that Tung's ship in either of their hands was technically grand theft of the most grandiose . . .

Tung took just slightly longer than Auson to understand the drift of the conversation. He began to swear; Miles did not recognize the language, but it was unmistakably invective. Miles had never seen a man actually foam at the lips before.

"See that this prisoner gets a tranquillizer," Miles ordered kindly as Tung was dragged away. An aggressive commander, Miles thought covetously. Thirty years experience—I wonder if I can do anything with him . . . ?

Miles looked around and added, "See the medtech and get those things taken off your arms, Captain Auson."

"Yes, sir!" Auson substituted a sharp nod for a curtailed attempt at a salute, and marched off, head held high. Thorne followed, to oversee further intelligence gathering from prisoners and the freed Felicians.

An engineering tech in want of supervision descended upon them instantly, to carry off Jesek. She grinned proudly at Miles. "Would you say we've earned our combat bonus today, sir?"

Combat bonus? Miles wondered blankly. He gazed around the station. Thinly spread but energetic activities of consolidation met his eye wherever he turned. "I should think so, Trainee Mynova."

"Sir," she paused shyly. "Some of us were wondering—just what is our pay schedule going to be? Bi-weekly or monthly?"

Pay schedule. Of course. His charade must continue—how long? He glanced out at the RG 132. Bent. Bent, and full of undelivered cargo, unpaid for. He'd have to keep going somehow, until they at least made contact with Felician forces. "Monthly," he said firmly.

"Oh," she said, sounding faintly disappointed. "I'll pass the word along, sir."

"What if we're still here in a month, my lord?" asked Bothari as she left with Jesek. "It could get ugly—mercenaries expect to be paid."

Miles rubbed his hands through his hair, and quavered with desperate assertiveness, "I'll figure something out!"

"Can we get anything to eat around here?" asked Mayhew plaintively. He looked drained.

Thorne popped back up at Miles's elbow. "About the counterattack, sir—"

Miles spun on his heel. "Where?" he demanded, looking around wildly.

Thorne looked slightly taken aback. "Oh, not yet, sir."

Miles slumped, relieved. "Please don't do that to me, Captain Thorne. Counterattack?"

"I'm thinking, sir, there's bound to be one. On account of the escaped courier, if nothing else. Shouldn't we start planning for it?"

"Oh, absolutely. Planning. Yes. You, ah—have an idea to present, do you?" Miles prodded hopefully.

"Several, sir." Thorne began to detail them, with verve;

Miles realized he was absorbing about one sentence in three.

"Very good, Captain," Miles interrupted. "We'll, uh, have a senior officer's meeting after—after inspection, and you can present them to everybody."

Thorne nodded contentedly, and dashed off, saying something about setting up a telecom listening post.

Miles's head spun. The jumbled geometries of the refinery, its ups and downs chosen, apparently, at random, did nothing to decrease his sense of disorientation. And it was all his, every rusty bolt, dubious weld, and stopped-up toilet in it . . .

Elena was observing him anxiously. "What's the matter, Miles? You don't look happy. We won!"

A true Vor, Miles told himself severely, does not bury his face in his leigewoman's breasts and cry—even if he is at a convenient height for it.

CHAPTER THIRTEEN   ✳   ✳   ✳

Miles's first tour of his new domain was rapid and exhausting. The *Triumph* was about the only encouraging part of it. Bothari lingered to go over the arrangements for keeping the horde of new prisoners secure with the overworked patrol assigned to that detail. Never had Miles seen a man wish more passionately to be twins; he half-expected Bothari to go into mitosis on the spot. The Sergeant grudgingly left Elena to be Miles's substitute bodyguard. Once out of sight, Miles instead put Elena to work as a real executive officer, taking notes. He did not trust even his own quick memory with the mass of new detail.

A combined sickbay had been set up in the refinery's infirmary, as the largest facility. The air was dry and cold and stale, like all recycled air, sweet with scented antiseptics overlaying a faint tang compounded of sweat, excrement, burnt meat, and fear. All medical personnel were drafted from the new prisoners, to treat their own wounded, requiring yet a couple more of Miles's thinly-spread troops as guards. They in turn were sucked in by the needs of the moment as assistant corpsmen. Miles watched Tung's efficient surgeon and staff at work, and let this pass, limiting himself to a quiet reminder to the guards of their primary duty. So long as Tung's medicos stayed busy it was probably safe.

Miles was unnerved by the catatonic Colonel Benar, and the two other Felician military officers who lay listlessly, barely responding to their rescue. Such little wounds, he thought, observing the slight chafing at wrists and ankles, and tiny discolorations under their skins marking hypospray injection points. By such little wounds we kill men ... The murdered pilot officer's ghost, perched on his shoulder like a pet crow, stirred and ruffled itself in silent witness.

Auson's medtech borrowed Tung's surgeon for the delicate placement of plastiskin that was to serve Elli Quinn for a face until she could be sent—how? when?—to some medical facility with proper regenerative biotech.

"You don't have to watch this," Miles murmured to Elena, as he stood discreetly by to observe the procedure.

Elena shook her head. "I want to."

"Why?"

"Why do you?"

"I've never seen it. Anyway, it was my bill she paid. It's my duty, as her commander."

"Well, then, it's mine, too. I worked with her all week."

The medtech unwrapped the temporary dressings. Skin, nose, ears, lips gone. Subcutaneous fat boiled away. Eyes glazed white and burst, scalp burned off—she tried to speak, a clotted mumble. Miles reminded himself that her pain nerves had been blocked. He turned his back abruptly, hand sneaking to his lips, and swallowed hard.

"I guess we don't have to stay. We're not really contributing anything." He glanced up at Elena's profile, which was pale but steady. "How long are you going to watch?" he whispered. And silently, to himself, for God's sake, it might have been you, Elena ...

"Until they're done," she murmured back. "Until I don't feel her pain anymore when I look. Until I'm hardened—like a real soldier—like my father. If I can block it from a friend, certainly I ought to be able to block it from the enemy—"

Miles shook his head in instinctive negation. "Look, can we continue this in the corridor?"

She frowned, but then took in his face, pursed her lips, and followed him without further argument. In the corridor he leaned against the wall, swallowing saliva and breathing deeply.

"Should I fetch a basin?"

"No. I'll be all right in a minute." *I hope* ... The minute passed without his disgracing himself. "Women shouldn't be in combat," he managed finally.

"Why not?" said Elena. "Why is that," she jerked her head toward the infirmary, "any more horrible for a woman than a man?"

"I don't know," Miles groped. "Your father once said that if a woman puts on a uniform she's asking for it, and you should never hesitate to fire—odd streak of egalitarianism, coming from him. But all my instincts are to throw my cloak across her puddle or something, not blow her head off. It throws me off."

"The honor goes with the risk," argued Elena. "Deny the risk and you deny the honor. I always thought you were the one Barrayaran male I knew who'd allow that a woman might have an honor that wasn't parked between her legs."

Miles floundered. "A soldier's honor is to do his patriotic duty, sure—"

"Or hers!"

"Or hers, all right—but all this isn't serving the Emperor! We're here for Tav Calhoun's ten percent profit margin. Or anyway, we were ..."

He gathered himself, to continue his tour, then paused. "What you said in there—about hardening yourself—"

She raised her chin. "Yes?"

"My mother was a real soldier, too. And I don't think she ever failed to feel another's pain. Not even her enemy's."

They were both silent for long after that.

The officers' meeting to plan for the counterattack was not so difficult as Miles had feared. They took over a conference chamber that had belonged to the refinery's senior management; the breathtaking panorama out the plexiports swept the entire installation. Miles growled, and sat with his back to it.

He quickly slid into the role of referee, controlling the

flow of ideas while concealing his own dearth of hard factual information. He folded his arms, and said "Um," and "Hm," but only very occasionally "God help us," because it caused Elena to choke. Thorne and Auson, Daum and Jesek, and the three freed Felician junior officers who had not been brain-drained did the rest, although Miles found he had to steer them gently away from ideas too much like those just demonstrated not to work for the Pelians.

"It would help a great deal, Major Daum, if you could reach your command," Miles wound up the session, thinking, How can you have misplaced an entire country, for God's sake? "As a last resort, perhaps a volunteer in one of those station shuttles could sneak on down to the planet and tell them we're here, eh?"

"We'll keep trying, sir," Daum promised.

Some enthusiastic soul had found quarters for Miles in the most luxurious section of the refinery, previously reserved, like the elegant conference chamber, for senior management. Unfortunately, the housekeeping services had been rather interrupted in the past few weeks. Miles picked his way among personal artifacts from the last Pelian to camp in the executive suite, overlaying yet another strata from the Felician he had evicted in his turn. Strewn clothing, empty ration wrappings, data discs, half-empty bottles, all well stirred by the flip-flops in the artificial gravity during the attack. The data discs, when examined, proved all light entertainment. No secret documents, no brilliant intelligence coups.

Miles could have sworn the variegated fuzzy patches growing on the bathroom walls moved, when he was not looking directly at them. Perhaps it was an effect of fatigue. He was careful not to touch them when he showered. He set the lights to maximum UV when he was done, and sealed the door, reminding himself sternly that he had not demanded the Sergeant's nocturnal company on the grounds that there were Things in his closet since he was four. Aching for sleep, he crawled into clean underwear brought with him.

Bed was a null-gee bubble, warmed womb-like by

infra-red. Null-gee sex, Miles had heard, was one of the high points of space travel. He'd never had a chance to try it, personally. Ten minutes of attempting to relax in the bubble convinced him he never would, either, although when heated the smells and stains that permeated the chamber suggested that a minimum of three people had tried it there before him recently. He crawled out hastily and sat on the floor until his stomach stopped trying to turn itself inside out. So much for the spoils of victory.

There was a splendid view out the plexiports of the RG 132's corrugated, gaping hull. Occasionally stress would release in some tortured flake of metal, and it would snap off spontaneously to stir the smattering of other wrinkled bits, clinging to the ship like dandruff. Miles stared at it for a time, then decided to go see if Sergeant Bothari still had that flask of scotch.

The corridor outside his executive suite ended in an observation deck, a crystal and chrome shell arched by the sweep of hard-edged stars in their powdered millions. Furthermore, it faced away from the refinery. Attracted, Miles wandered toward it.

Elena's voice, raised in a wordless cry, shot him out of somnolence into an adrenalin rush. It came from the observation deck; Miles broke into his uneven run.

He swarmed up the catwalk and spun one-handed around a gleaming upright. The dimmed observation deck was upholstered in royal-blue velvet that glowed in the starlight. Liquid-filled settees and benches in odd curving shapes seemed to invite the indolent recliner. Baz Jesek was spread-eagled backward over one, with Sergeant Bothari atop him.

The Sergeant's knees ground into the engineer's stomach and groin, and the great hands knotted about Baz's neck, twisting. Baz's face was maroon, his frantic words strangled inchoate. Elena, her tunic undone, galloped around the pair, hands clenching and unclenching in despair of daring to physically oppose Bothari. "No, Father! No!" she cried.

Had Bothari caught the engineer trying to attack her? Hot jealous rage shook Miles, dashed immediately by cold reason. Elena, of all women, was capable of defending herself; the Sergeant's paranoias had seen to that. His jealousy went ice green. He could let Bothari kill Baz . . .

Elena saw him. "Miles—my lord! Stop him!"

Miles approached them. "Get off him, Sergeant," he ordered. Bothari, his face yellow with rage, glanced sideways, then back to his victim. His hands did not slacken.

Miles knelt and laid his hand lightly on the corded muscles of Bothari's arm. He had the sick feeling it was the most dangerous thing he had done in his life. He dropped his voice to a whisper. "Must I give my orders twice, Armsman?"

Bothari ignored him.

Miles closed his hands tightly around the Sergeant's wrist.

"You don't have the strength to break my grip," Bothari snarled out of the corner of his mouth.

"I have the strength to break my own fingers trying," Miles murmured back, and threw all his weight into his pull. His fingernails went white. In a moment, his brittle joints would start to snap . . .

The Sergeant's eyes squeezed shut, his breath hissing in and out past his stained teeth. Then, with an oath, he sprang off Baz and shook free of Miles. He turned his back, chest heaving, blind eyes lost in infinity.

Baz writhed off the bench and fell to the carpet with a thump. He gulped air in a hoarse liquid choke, and spat up blood. Elena ran to him and cradled his head in her lap, heedless of the mess.

Miles staggered up and stood, catching his breath. "All right," he said at last, "What's going on here?"

Baz tried to speak, but it came out a gurgling bark. Elena was crying, no help there. "Damn it, Sergeant—"

"Caught her nuzzling that coward," Bothari growled, still with his back to them.

"He is not a coward!" Elena yelled. "He's as good a soldier as you. He saved my life today—" she turned to Miles. "Surely you saw it, my lord, on your monitors. There was an Oseran with a servo-aim locked on me—I thought it was all over—Baz shot him with his plasma arc. Tell him!"

She was talking about the Oseran he had slain with his own medkit, Miles realized. Baz had cooked a corpse, unknowing. *I saved you*, Miles cried inwardly. *It was me, it was me* . . . "That's right Sergeant," he heard himself saying. "You owe her life to your brother Armsman."

"That one is no brother to me."

"By my word, I say he is!"

"It's not proper—it's not right—I have to make it right. It has to be perfect—" Bothari swung around, narrow jaw working. In his life, Miles had never seen Bothari more agitated. I've put too much strain on him lately, he thought remorsefully. Too much, too fast, too out-of-control . . .

Baz croaked out words. "No . . . dishonor!" Elena hushed him, and lurched to her feet to face Bothari, fiercely.

"You and your military honor! Well, I've faced fire, and I've killed a man, and it was nothing but butchery. Any robot could have done it. There was nothing to it. It's all a sham, a hoax, a lie, a big put-on. Your uniform doesn't awe me any more, do you hear?"

Bothari's face was dark and rigid. Miles made shushing motions at Elena. He'd no objection to growing independence of spirit, but God in heaven, her timing was terrible. Couldn't she see it? No, she was too tangled up in her own pain and shame, and the new ghost clinging to her shoulder. She had not mentioned that she'd killed a man, earlier; but, Miles knew, there were reasons one might choose not to.

He needed Baz, he needed Bothari, he needed Elena, and he needed them all working together to get them home alive. Not, then, what he ached to cry out of his own anguish and anger, but what they needed to hear.

The first thing Elena and Bothari needed was to be parted until tempers cooled, lest they tear out each other's hearts. As for Baz—"Elena," said Miles, "Help Baz to the infirmary. See that the medtech checks him for internal injuries."

"Yes, my lord," she replied, emphasizing the official nature of the order with his title, for Bothari's benefit, presumably. She levered Baz to his feet, and pulled his arm across her shoulders, with an awkward venomous glower at her father. Bothari's hands twitched, but he said nothing and made no move.

Miles escorted them down the catwalk. Baz's breathing was growing slightly more regular, he saw with relief. "I think I'd better stay with the Sergeant," he murmured to Elena. "You two going to make it all right?"

"Thanks to you," said Elena. "I tried to stop him, but I was afraid. I couldn't do it." She blinked back last tears.

"Better this way. Everybody's edgy, too tired. Him too, you know." He almost asked her for a definition of "nuzzling", but stopped himself. She bore Baz off with tender murmurs that drove Miles wild.

He bit back his frustration and mounted again to the observation deck. Bothari still stood, grievously blank and inward. Miles sighed.

"You still have that scotch, Sergeant?"

Bothari started from his reverie, and felt his hip pocket. He handed the flask silently to Miles, who gestured at the benches. They both sat. The Sergeant's hands dangled between his knees, his head lowered.

Miles took a swallow, and handed the flask over. "Drink."

Bothari shook his head, but then took it and did so. After a time he muttered, "You never called me 'Armsman' before."

"I was trying to get your attention. My apologies."

Silence, and another swig. "It's the right title."

"Why were you trying to kill him? You know how badly we need techs."

A long pause. "He's not a right one. Not for her. Deserter . . ."

"He wasn't trying to rape her." It was a statement.

"No," lowly. "No, I suppose not. You never know."

Miles gazed around the crystal chamber, gorgeous in the sparked darkness. Superb spot for a nuzzle, and more. But those long white hands were down at the infirmary, probably laying cold compresses or something on Baz's brow. While he sat here getting drunk with the ugliest man in the system. What a waste.

The flask went back and forth again. "You never know," Bothari reiterated. "And she must have everything right, and proper. You see that, don't you, my lord? Don't you see it?"

"Of course. But please don't murder my engineer. I need him. All right?"

"Damn techs. Always coddled."

Miles let this pass, as an Old Service reflex complaint. Bothari had always seemed part of his grandfather's generation, somehow, although in fact he was a couple of years younger than Miles's father. Miles relaxed slightly, at this sign of a return to Bothari's normal—well, usual—state of mind. Bothari slipped into a reclining position on the carpet, shoulders against the settee.

"My lord," he added after a time. "You'd see to it, if I were killed—that she was taken care of, right. The dowry. And an officer, a fit officer. And a real go-between, a proper baba, to make the arrangements . . ."

Antique dream, thought Miles hazily. "I'm her leige-lord, by right of your service," he pointed out gently. "It would be my duty." *If I could only turn that duty to my own dreams.*

"Some don't pay much attention to their duty any more," Bothari muttered. "But a Vorkosigan—Vorkosigans never fail."

"Damn right," Miles mumbled.

"Mm," said Bothari, and slid down a little farther.

After a long silence, Bothari spoke again. "If I were killed, you wouldn't leave me out there, would you, my lord?"

"Huh?" Miles tore his attention from trying to make new constellations. He had just connected the dots into a figure dubbed, mentally, Cavalryman.

"They leave bodies in space sometimes. Cold as hell . . . God can't find them out there. No one could."

Miles blinked. He had never known the Sergeant concealed a theological streak. "Look, what's all this all of a sudden about getting killed? You're not going to—"

"The Count your father promised me," Bothari raised his voice slightly to override him, "I'd be buried at your lady mother's feet, at Vorkosigan Surleau. He promised. Didn't he tell you?"

"Er . . . The subject never came up."

"His word as Vorkosigan. Your word."

"Uh, right, then." Miles stared out the chamber's transparency. Some saw stars, it seemed, and some saw the spaces between them. Cold . . . "You planning on heaven, Sergeant?"

"As my lady's dog. Blood washes away sin. She swore it to me . . ." He trailed off, gaze never leaving the depths. Presently, the flask slipped from his fingers, and he began to snore. Miles sat cross-legged, watching over him, a small figure in his underwear against the black immensity, and very far from home.

Fortunately, Baz recovered quickly, and was back on the job the next day with the aid of a neck brace to ease his lacerated cervicals. His behavior to Elena was painfully circumspect whenever Miles was around, offering no further spur to his jealousy; but of course, where Miles was there also was Bothari, which perhaps accounted for it.

Miles began by flinging all their meager resources into getting the *Triumph* operational, overtly to fight the Pelians. Privately, he figured it was the only thing around big enough and fast enough for them to all pile into and successfully run like hell. Tung had two jump pilots; one of them at least might be persuaded to jump them out of Tau Verde local space altogether. Miles contemplated the consequences of turning up back at Beta Colony in a stolen warship with a kidnapped pilot officer, twenty or so unemployed mercenaries, a herd of bewildered refugee technicians, and no money for Tav Calhoun—or even for Betan shuttleport landing fees. The blanket of his Class III diplomatic immunity seemed to shrink to a bare fig leaf.

Miles's attempt to throw himself into the placement

and powering up of a selection of weapons from the RG
132's hold alongside the technicians was constantly interrupted by people wanting directions, or orders, or
organization, or, most frequently, authorization to seize
some piece of refinery equipment or resource or leftover military supplies for the work at hand. Miles blithely
authorized anything put in front of him, earning a reputation for brilliant decisiveness. His signature— "Naismith"—was developing into a nicely illegible flourish.

The personnel shortage was not, unfortunately, ame-
nable to like treatment. Double shifts that became triple shifts tended to end in loss of efficiency from
exhaustion. Miles took a stab at another approach.

Two bottles of Felician wine, quality unknown. A bottle of Tau Cetan liqueur, pale orange, not green, fortunately. Two nylon and plastic folding camp stools, a
small and flimsy plastic table. A half-dozen silvery strip-
packs of Felician delicacies—Miles hoped they were
delicacies—exact composition mysterious. The last glean-
ings of non-rotted fresh fruit from the refinery's damaged hydroponics section. It ought to be enough. Miles
loaded Bothari's arms with the looted picnic, gathered
up the overflow, and marched off toward the prison
section.

Mayhew raised an eyebrow as they passed him in a
corridor. "Where are you going with all that?"

"Courting, Arde," Miles grinned. "Courting."

The Pelians had left a makeshift brig, a storage area
hastily vented, plumbed, and partitioned into a series of
tiny, bleak metal boxes. Miles would have felt more
guilty about locking human beings in them if it had not
been a case of turn-about.

They surprised Captain Tung hanging by one hand
from the overhead light fixture and working, as yet
vainly, on levering its cover apart with a flattened snap
torn from his uniform jacket.

"Good afternoon, Captain," Miles addressed the dangling ankles with sunny good cheer. Tung scowled down
upon him, estimation in his eyes; measured Bothari,
found the sum of the calculation not in his favor, and

dropped to the floor with a grunt. The guard locked the door again behind them.

"What were you going to do with it if you got it apart?" Miles asked curiously, looking up.

Tung swore at him, like a man spitting, then clamped into recalcitrant silence. Bothari set up the table and stools, dumped out the groceries, and leaned against the wall by the door, skeptical. Miles sat down and opened a bottle of wine. Tung remained standing.

"Do join me, Captain," Miles invited cordially. "I know you haven't had supper yet. I was hoping we might have a little chat."

"I am Ky Tung, Captain, Oseran Free Mercenary Fleet. I am a citizen of the People's Democracy of Greater South America, Earth; my social duty number is T275-389-42-1535-1742. This 'chat' is over." Tung's lips flattened together in a granite slit.

"This is not an interrogation," Miles amplified, "which would be far more efficiently conducted by the medical staff anyway. See, I'll even give you some information." He rose, and bowed formally. "Permit me to introduce myself. My name is Miles Naismith." He gestured at the other stool. "Do, please, sit down. I spend enough time with a crick in my neck."

Tung hesitated, but finally sat, compromising by making it on the edge of his seat.

Miles poured wine, and took a sip. He groped for one of his grandfather's wine connoiseur phrases as a conversation opener, but the only one that sprang to his memory was "thin as piss", which didn't seem exactly inviting. He wiped the lip of the plastic cup on his sleeve, instead, and pushed it toward Tung. "Observe. No poison, no drugs."

Tung folded his arms. "The oldest trick in the book. You take the antidote before you come in."

"Oh," said Miles. "Yes, I suppose I could have done that." He shook a packet of rather rubbery protein cubes out between them, and eyed them almost as dubiously as Tung did. "Ah. Meat." He popped one in his mouth and chewed industriously. "Go ahead, ask me anything," he added around a mouthful.

Tung struggled with his resolve, then blurted, "My troops. How are they?"

Miles promptly detailed a list, by full name, of the dead, and of the wounded and their current medical status. "The rest are under lock and key, as you are; excuse me from mapping their exact locations for you—just in case you can do more with that light than I think you can."

Tung sighed sadness and relief, and absently helped himself to a protein cube.

"Sorry things got so messy," Miles apologized. "I realize how it must burn you to have your opponent blunder to victory. I'd have preferred something neater and more tactical myself, like Komarr, but I had to take the situation as I found it."

Tung snorted. "Who wouldn't? Who do you think you are? Lord Vorkosigan?"

Miles inhaled a lungful of wine. Bothari abandoned the wall to pound him, not very helpfully, on the back, and glare suspiciously at Tung. But by the time Miles had regained his breath he had regained his balance. He mopped his lips.

"I see. You mean Admiral Aral Vorkosigan of Barrayar. You, ah, confused me a bit—he's Count Vorkosigan, now."

"Oh, yeah? Still alive, is he?" remarked Tung, interested.

"Very much so."

"Have you ever read his book on Komarr?"

"Book? Oh, the Komarr report. Yes, I'd heard it had been picked up by a couple of military schools, off-planet—off Barrayar, that is."

"I've read it eleven times," Tung said proudly. "Most succinct military memoir I've ever seen. The most complex strategy laid out logically as a wiring diagram—politics, economics, and all—I swear the man's mind must operate in five dimensions. And yet I find most people haven't heard of it. It should be required reading—I test all my junior officers on it."

"Well, I've heard him say that war is the failure of

politics—I guess they've always been a part of his strategic thinking."

"Sure, when you get to that level—" Tung's ears pricked. "Heard? I didn't think he'd done any interviews—do you happen to remember where and when you saw it? Can copies be had?"

"Ah . . ." Miles trod a thin line. "It was a personal conversation."

"You've *met* him?"

Miles had the unnerving sensation of suddenly acquiring half a meter of height in Tung's eyes. "Well, yes," he admitted cautiously.

"Do you know—has he written anything like the Komarr Report about the Escobar invasion?" Tung asked eagerly. "I've always felt it should be a companion volume—defensive strategy next to offensive—get the other half of his thinking. Like Sri Simka's two volumes on Walshea and Skya IV."

Miles placed Tung at last; a military history nut. He knew the type very, very well. He suppressed an exhilarated grin.

"I don't think so. Escobar was a defeat, after all. He never talks about it much—I understand. Maybe a touch of vanity there."

"Mm," allowed Tung. "It was an amazing book, though. Everything that seemed so totally chaotic at the time revealed this complete inner skeleton—of course, it always seems chaotic when you're losing."

It was Miles's turn to prick his ears. "At the time? Were you at Komarr?"

"Yes, I was a junior lieutenant in the Selby Fleet, that Komarr hired—what an experience. Twenty-three years ago, now. Seemed like every natural weak point in mercenary-employer relations got blown up in our faces—and that was before the first shot was even fired. Vorkosigan's intelligence pathfinders at work, we learned later."

Miles made encouraging noises, and proceeded to pump this unexpected spring of reminiscence for all it was worth. Pieces of fruit became planets and satellites; variously shaped protein bits became cruisers, couriers, smart bombs and troop carriers. Defeated ships were eaten. The second bottle of wine introduced other well known mercenary battles. Miles frankly hung on Tung's words, self-consciousness forgotten.

Tung leaned back at last with a contented sigh, full of food and wine and emptied of stories. Miles, knowing his own capacity, had been nursing his own wine to the limits of politeness. He swirled the last of it around in the bottom of his cup, and essayed a cautious probe.

"It seems a great waste for an officer of your experience to sit out a good war like this, locked in a box."

Tung smiled. "I have no intention of staying in this box."

"Ah—yes. But there may be more than one way to get out of it, don't you see. Now, the Dendarii Mercenaries are an expanding organization. There's a lot of room for talent at the top."

Tung's smiled soured. "You took my ship."

"I took Captain Auson's ship, too. Ask him if he's unhappy about it."

"Nice try—ah—Mr. Naismith. But I have a contract. A fact that, unlike some, I remember. A mercenary who can't honor his contract when it's rough as well as when it's smooth is a thug, not a soldier."

Miles fairly swooned with unrequited love. "I cannot fault you for that, sir."

Tung eyed him with amused tolerance. "Now, regardless of what that ass Auson seems to think, I have you pegged as a hot-shot junior officer in over his head—and sinking fast. Seems to me it's you, not I, who's going to be looking for a new job soon. You seem to have at least an average grasp of tactics—and you *have* read Vorkosigan on Komarr—but any officer who can get Auson and Thorne hitched together to plow a straight line shows a genius for personnel. If you get out of this alive, come see me— I may be able to find something on the exec side for you."

Miles sat looking at his prisoner in open-mouthed appreciation of a chutzpah worthy of his own. Actually, it sounded pretty good. He sighed regret. "You honor me, Captain Tung. But I'm afraid I too have a contract."

"Pigwash."

"Beg pardon?"

"If you have a contract with Felice, it beats me where you got it. I doubt Daum was authorized to make any such agreement. The Felicians are as cheap as their counterparts the Pelians. We could have ended this war six months ago if the Pelians had been willing to pay the piper. But no—they chose to "economize" and only buy a blockade, and a few installations like this one— and for that, they act like they're doing us a favor. Peh!" Frustration edged his voice with disgust.

"I didn't say my contract was with Felice," said Miles mildly. Tung's eyes narrowed in puzzlement; good. The man's evaluations were entirely too close to the truth for comfort.

"Well, keep your tail down, son," Tung advised "In the long run more mercenaries have had their asses shot off by their contractors than by their enemies."

Miles took his leave courteously; Tung ushered him out with the panache of a genial host.

"Is there anything else you need?" asked Miles.

"A screwdriver," said Tung promptly.

Miles shook his head and smiled regretfully as the door was closed on the Eurasian. "Damned if I'm not tempted to send him one," said Miles to Bothari. "I'm dying to see what he thinks he can do with that light."

"Just what did all that accomplish?" asked Bothari. "He burned up your time with ancient history and didn't give away anything."

Miles smiled. "Nothing unimportant."

CHAPTER FOURTEEN ✳ ✳ ✳

The Pelians attacked from the ecliptic, opposite the sun, taking advantage of the scattered masses of the asteroid belt for what cover they provided. They came decelerating, telegraphing their intention to capture, not destroy; and they came alone, without their Oseran employees.

Miles laughed delight under his breath as he limped through the scramble of men and equipment in the refinery docking station corridors. The Pelians could scarcely be following his pet scenario more closely if he'd given them their orders himself. There had been some argument when he'd insisted on placing his farthest outlying pickets and his major weapons on the belt and not the planet side of the refinery. But it was inevitable. Barring subterfuge, a tactic currently exhausted, it was the Pelian's only hope of gaining a measure of surprise. A week ago, it would have done them some good.

Miles dodged some of his galloping troops hurrying to their posts. Pray God he would never find himself on foot in a retreat. He might as well volunteer for the rear guard in the first place, and save being trampled by his own side as well as by the enemy.

He dashed through the flex tube into the *Triumph*. The waiting soldier clanged the lock shut behind him, and hastily blew off the tube seals. As he'd guessed, he was

the last aboard. He made his way to the tactics room as
the ship maneuvered free of the refinery.

The *Triumph's* tactics room was noticeably larger than
the *Ariel's,* and quite as sleek. Miles quailed at the number of empty padded swivel chairs. A scant half of Auson's
old crew, even augmented by a few volunteer refinery
techs, made scarcely a skeleton crew for the new ship.

Holograph displays were up and working in all their
bright confusion. Auson looked up from trying to man
two stations at once with relief in his eyes.

"Glad you made it, my lord."

Miles slid into a station chair. "Me too. But please
just 'Mr. Naismith'. No 'my lord'."

Auson looked puzzled. "The others all call you that."

"Yes, but, um—it's not just a courtesy. It denotes a
specific legal relationship. You wouldn't call me 'my
husband' even if you heard my wife do so, eh? So what
have we got out here?"

"Looks like maybe ten little ships—all Pelian local
stuff." Auson studied his readouts, worry creasing his
broad face. "I don't know where our guys are. This sort
of thing should be just their style."

Miles correctly interpreted "our guys" to mean Auson's
former comrades, the Oserans. The slip of tongue did
not disturb him; Auson was committed, now. Miles
glanced sideways at him, and thought he knew exactly
why the Pelians hadn't brought their hired guns. For all
the Pelians knew to the contrary, an Oseran ship had
turned on them. Miles's eyes glittered at the thought of
the dismay and distrust that must now be reverberating
through the Pelian high command.

Their ship dove in a high arc toward their attackers.
Miles keyed Nav and Com.

"You all right, Arde?"

"For flying blind, deaf, dumb, and paralyzed, not
bad," Mayhew said. "Manual piloting is a pain. It's like
the machine is operating me. It feels awful."

"Keep up the good work," Miles said cheerfully. "Remember, we're more interested in herding them into
range of our stationary weapons than in knocking them
off ourselves."

Miles sat back and regarded the ever-changing displays. "I don't think they quite realize how much ordinance Daum brought. They're just repeating the same tactics the Felician officers reported they used the last time. Of course, it worked once . . ."

The lead Pelian ships were just coming into range of the refinery. Miles held his breath as though it could force his people to hold their fire. They were spread lonely, thin, and nervous out there. There were more weapons in place than Miles had personnel to man them, even with computer-controlled fire—especially since control systems had been plagued with bugs during installation that were still not all worked out. Baz had labored to the last instant—was still laboring, for all Miles knew, and Elena alongside him. Miles wished he could have justified keeping her beside himself, instead.

The lead Pelian spewed a glittering string of dandelion bombs, arcing toward the solar collectors. *Not again,* Miles groaned inwardly, seeing two weeks' repairs about to be wasted. The bombs puffed into their thousands of separate needles. Space was suddenly laced with threads of fire as the defense weaponry labored to knock them out. Should have fired an instant sooner. The Pelian ship itself exploded into pelting debris as someone on Miles's side scored a direct, perhaps lucky, hit. A portion of the debris continued on its former track and speed, almost as dangerous in its mindless momentum as the clever guided weapons.

The ships coming up behind it began to peel and swerve, shocked out of their bee-line complacency. Auson and Thorne in their respective ships now swung in from either side, like a pair of sheepdogs gone mad and attacking their flock. Miles beat his fist on the panel before him in a paroxysm of joy at the beauty of the formation. If only he'd had a third warship to completely box their flanks, none of the Pelians would make it home to complain. As it was, they were squeezed into a flat layer, carefully pre-calculated to present its maximum target area to the refinery's defenses.

Auson, beside him, shared his enthusiasm. "Lookatem!

Lookatem! Right down the gullet, just like you claimed they would—and Gamad swore you were crazy to strip the solar side—Shorty, you're a frigging genius!"

Miles's thrill was mitigated by the sober reflection of what names he'd have earned by guessing wrong. Relief made him dizzy. He leaned back in the station chair and let out a long, long breath.

A second Pelian ship burst into oblivion, and a third. A numeral buried in a crowded corner of Miles's readouts flipped quietly from a minus to a plus figure. "Ah ha!" Miles pointed. "We've got 'em now! They're starting to accelerate again. They're breaking off the attack."

Their momentum gave the Pelians no choice but to sweep through the refinery area. But all their attention now was on making it as fast a trip as possible. Thorne and Auson swung in behind to speed them on their way.

A Pelian ship corkscrewed past the installation, and fired—what? Miles's computers could present no interpretation of the—beam? Not plasma, not laser, not driven mass, for which the central factory was able to generate some shielding, the huge solar collectors necessarily being left to fend for themselves. It was not immediately apparent what damage it had done, or even if it were a hit. Strange . . .

Miles closed his hand gently around the Pelian ship's representation in his hologram, as if he could work sympathetic magic. "Captain Auson. Let's try and catch this one."

"Why bother? He's scooting for home with his buddies—"

Miles lowered his voice to a whisper. "That's an order."

Auson braced. "Yes, sir!"

Well, it works sometimes, Miles reflected.

The communications officer achieved a fully scrambled channel to the *Ariel*, and the new objective was transmitted. Auson, growing enthused, chortled at the chance to try his new ship's limits. The ghost imager, confusing the enemy's aim with multiple targets, proved particularly useful; through it they discovered the mystery beam's range limit and odd large time lag between shots. Recharging, perhaps? They bore down rapidly upon the fleeing Pelian.

"What's the script, Mr. Naismith?" Auson inquired. "Stop-or-we-blast-you?"

Miles chewed his lip thoughtfully. "I don't think that would work. I'd guess our problem is more likely to be keeping them from self-destructing when we get close. Threats would fall flat, I'm afraid. They're not mercenaries."

"Hm." Auson cleared his throat, and busied himself with his displays.

Miles suppressed a sardonic smile, for the sake of tact, and turned to his own readouts. The computers presented him with a clairvoyant vision of overtaking the Pelian, then paused, waiting politely on his merely human inspiration. Miles tried to think himself into the Pelian captain's skin. He balanced time lag, range, and the speed with which they could close on the Pelian at maximum red-line boost.

"It's close," he said, watching his holograph. The machine rendered a vivid and chilling display of what might happen if he missed bracketing his timing.

Auson glanced over his shoulder at the miniature fireworks, and muttered something about "—frigging suicidal . . .", which Miles chose to ignore.

"I want all our engineering people suited up and ready to board," Miles said at last. "They know they can't outrun us; my guess is they'll rig some go-to-hell with a time delay, all pile into their lifeboat shuttle, and try to blow the ship up in our faces. But if we don't waste time on the shuttle, and are quick enough getting in the back door as they go out the side, we might disarm it and take—whatever that was—intact."

Auson's lips puckered in worried disapproval at this plan. "Take all my engineers? We could blast the shuttle out of its clamps, when we get close enough to get the accuracy—trap them all aboard—"

"And then try to board a manned warship with four engineers and myself?" Miles interrupted. "No, thanks. Besides, cornering them just might trigger the sort of spectacular suicide move I want to prevent."

"What'll I do if you're not quick enough getting their booby-trap disarmed?"

A black grin stole over Miles's face. "Improvise."

The Pelians, it appeared, were not enough of a suicide squadron to spurn the thin chance of life their shuttle gave them. Into this narrow crack of time Miles and his technicians slipped, blasting their way, crude but quick, through the code-controlled airlock.

Miles cursed the discomfort of his over-large pressure suit. Loose places rubbed and skidded on his skin. Cold sweat, he discovered, was a term with a literal meaning. He glanced up and down the curving corridors of the unfamiliar dark ship. The engineering techs parted at a run, each to their assigned quadrant.

Miles took a fifth and less likely direction, to make a quick check of tactics room, crew's quarters and bridge for destructive devices and any useful intelligence left lying around. Blasted control panels and melted data stores met him everywhere. He checked the time; barely five minutes, and the Pelian shuttle would be safely beyond the range of, say, radiation from imploded engines.

A triumphant crow pierced his ears over his suit comm link. "I've done it! I've done it!" cried an engineering tech. "They had rigged an implosion! Chain reaction broken—I'm shutting down now."

Cheers echoed over the comm link. Miles sagged into a station chair on the bridge, heart lumping; then it seemed to stop. He keyed his comm link for a general broadcast, overriding and at volume. "I don't think we should assume there was only one booby-trap laid, eh? Keep looking for at least the next ten minutes."

Worried groans acknowledged the order. For the next three minutes the comm links transmitted only ragged breathing. Miles, dashing through the galley in search of the captain's cabin, inhaled sharply. A microwave oven, its control panel ripped out and hastily cross-wired, timer ticking away, had a high-pressure metal oxygen canister jammed into it. The nutrition techni-cian's personal contribution to the war effort, apparently. In two minutes it would have taken out the galley and most of the adjoining chambers. Miles tore it apart and ran on.

A tear-streaked voice hissed over the comm link. "Oh, shit. Oh, shit!"

"Where are you, Kat?"

"Armory. There's too many. I can't get them all! Oh, shit!"

"Keep working! We're on our way." Miles, taking the chance, ordered the rest of his crew to the armory on the double, and ran. A true light guided him as he arrived, overriding the infra-red display on the inside of his helmet faceplate. He swung into a storage chamber to find the tech crawling along a row of gleaming ordinance.

"Every dandelion bomb in here is set to go off!" she cried, sparing one glance at him. Her voice shook, but her hands never stopped patting out the reset codes. Miles, lips parted in concentration, watched over her shoulder and then began to repeat her movements on the next row. The great disadvantage to crying in fear in a space suit, Miles discovered, was that you could not wipe either your face or your nose, although the sonic cleaners on the inside of the faceplate saved that valuable informative surface from a sneeze. He sniffed surreptitiously. His stomach sent up a throat-burning, acid belch. His fingers felt like sausages. *I could be on Beta Colony right now—I could be home in bed—I could be home under my bed . . .*

Another tech joined them, Miles saw out of the corner of his eye. No one spared attention for social chit-chat. They worked together in silence broken only by the uneven rhythm of hyperventilation. His suit reduced his oxygen flow in stingy disapproval of his state of mind. Bothari would never have let him join the boarding party—maybe he shouldn't have ordered him to duty at the refinery. On to the next bomb—and the next—and the—there was no next. Finished.

Kat rose, and pointed to one bomb in the array. "Three seconds! Three seconds, and—" She burst into unabashed tears, and fell on Miles. He patted her shoulder clumsily.

"There, there—cry all you want. You've earned it—" He killed his comm link broadcast momentarily, and inhaled a powerful sniff.

Miles tottered out of his newly captured ship into the refinery docking station clutching an unexpected prize—a suit of Pelian battle armor nearly small enough to fit him. The plumbing, not surprisingly, was female, but Baz could surely convert it. He spotted Elena among his reception committee, and held it up proudly. "Look what I found!"

She wrinkled her nose in puzzlement. "You captured a whole ship just to get a suit of armor?"

"No, no! The other thing. The—the weapon, whatever it was. This is the ship whose shot penetrated your shielding—did it hit anything? What did it do?"

One of the Felician officers glowered—oddly, at Elena. "It punched a hole—well, not a hole—right through the prison section. It was losing air, and *she* let them all out."

His people, Miles noticed, were moving about in groups of three or more.

"We haven't got them half rounded up yet," the Felician complained. "They're hiding all over the station."

Elena looked distressed. "I'm sorry, my lord."

Miles rubbed his temples. "Uh. I suppose I'd better have the Sergeant at my back, then, for a while."

"When he wakes up."

"What?"

Elena frowned at her boots. "He was guarding the prison section alone, during the attack—he tried to stop me, from letting them out."

"Tried? And didn't succeed?"

"I shot him with my stunner. I'm afraid he's going to be rather angry—is it all right if I stick with you for a while?"

Miles pursed his lips in an involuntary silent whistle. "Of course. Were any prisoners—no, wait." He raised his voice. "Commander Bothari, I commend your initiative. You did the right thing. We are here to accomplish a specific tactical objective, not perpetrate mindless slaughter." Miles stared down the Felician junior lieutenant, what's his name, Gamad, who shrank under his gaze. He went on more quietly to Elena. "Were any prisoners killed?"

"Two, whose cells were actually penetrated by the electron orbital randomizer—"

"By the what?"

"Baz called it an electron orbital randomizer. And— and eleven asphyxiated that I couldn't get to in time." The pain in her eyes knifed him.

"How many would have died if you hadn't released them?"

"We lost air in the whole section."

"Captain Tung—?"

Elena spread her hands. "He's around here somewhere, I guess. He wasn't among the thirteen. Oh—one of his jump pilots was, though. And we haven't found the other one yet. Is that important?"

Miles's heart sank into his foaming stomach. He wheeled to the nearest mercenary. "Pass on this order at once. Prisoners are to be re-captured alive, with as little injury as possible." The woman hurried to obey. "If Tung's on the loose, you'd better stick by me," Miles told Elena. "Dear God. Well, I guess I'd better have a look at this hole that isn't a hole, then. Where did Baz come up with that jawbreaking name for it?"

"He said it's a Betan development from a few years back. It never sold very well, because all you have to do to defend from it is re-phase the mass shielding—he told me to tell you he was on it, and should have the shields reprogrammed by tonight."

"Oh." Miles paused, crushed. So much for his fantasy of returning the mystery beam to Barrayar to lay at the Emperor's feet, Captain Illyan agog, his father amazed. He'd pictured it as a splendid offering, proof of his military prowess. More like when the cat drags in a dead horned hopper, to be chased off with brooms. He sighed. At least he had a suit of space armor now.

Miles, Elena, Gamad, and an engineering tech started

toward the prison section, several structures down the linked chain of the refinery. Elena fell in beside Miles.

"You look so tired. Hadn't you better, uh, take a shower and get some rest?"

"Ah, yes, the stink of dried terror, well-warmed in a pressure suit." He grinned up at her, and tucked his helmet firmly under his arm, like a beheaded ghost. "Wait'll you hear about my day. What does Major Daum say about the defense nexus now? I suppose I'd better get a full battle report from him—he at least seems to have his thinking straight—" Miles eyed the back of the lieutenant in weary distaste.

Lieutenant Gamad, whose hearing was evidently keener than Miles had supposed, glanced back over his shoulder. "Major Daum's killed, sir. He and a tech were switching weapons posts, and their flitter was hit by high-speed debris—nothing left. Didn't they tell you?"

Miles stopped short.

"I'm the ranking officer here, now," the Felician added.

It took three days to ferret out the escaped prisoners from all the corners of the refinery. Tung's commandos were the worst. Miles eventually resorted to closing off sections and filling them with sleep gas. He ignored Bothari's irritated suggestion that vacuum would be more cost-effective. The bulk of the round-up duty fell naturally, if unjustly, to the Sergeant, and he was tight as a drawn bow-string with the tension of it.

When the final head count was made, Tung had seven of his men, including his other Pilot Officer, turned up missing. So did a station shuttle.

Miles moaned under his breath. There was no choice now but to wait for the laggard Felicians to come claim their cargo. He began to doubt whether the shuttle dispatched to try and reach Tau Verde before the counterattack had ever made it through the Oseran-controlled space between. Perhaps they should send another. With a draftee, not a volunteer, this time; Miles had his candidate all picked out.

Lieutenant Gamad, swollen with his newly inherited seniority, was inclined to challenge Miles's authority over the refinery, technically, it was true, Felician property. After Daum's cool, get the-job-done intensity, Miles suffered him ungladly. Gamad was quashed, however, when he overheard one of Miles's mercenaries address him as "Admiral Naismith." Miles was so delighted with the effect of the ersatz title on Gamad that he let it pass unchecked. Unfortunately, it spread; he found himself unable to retrieve the careful neutrality of "Mr. Naismith" thereafter.

Gamad was saved on the eighth day after the counterattack, when a Felician local space cruiser finally appeared on the monitors. Miles's mercenaries, twitchy and suspicious after repeated ambushes, were inclined to obliterate it first and sift the remains for positive I.D. after. But Miles at last established a measure of trust, and the Felicians came meekly to dock.

Two large, businesslike plastic crates on a float pallet riveted Miles's attention when the Felician officers entered the refinery conference chamber. The crates bore a pleasant resemblance, in size at least, to old sea pirates' treasure chests. Miles lost himself in a brief fantasy of glittering diadems, gold coins, and ropes of pearls. Alas that such gaudy baubles were treasures no more. Crystallized viral microcircuits, data packs, DNA splices, blank drafts on major planetary agricultural and mining futures; such was the tepid wealth men schemed upon in these degenerate days. Of course, there was still artwork. Miles touched the dagger at his belt, and was warmed, as by an old man's handclasp. He decided he would probably settle for a few of those blank drafts.

The pinched and harried Felician paymaster was speaking; "— must have Major Daum's manifest first, and physically check each item for damage in transit."

The Felician cruiser captain nodded wearily. "See my chief engineer, and draft as much help as you need. But make it quick." The captain turned a bloodshot and irritated eye on Gamad, trailing obsequiously. "Haven't you found that manifest yet? Or Daum's personal papers?"

"I'm afraid he may have had them on him when he was hit, sir."

The captain growled, and turned to Miles. "So, you're this mad galactic mutant I've been hearing about."

Miles drew himself up. "I am not a mutant! *Captain*." He drawled the last word out in his father's most sarcastic style, then took hold of his temper. The Felician clearly hadn't slept much the last few days. "I believe you have some business to conduct."

"Yes, mercenaries must have their pay, I suppose," sighed the captain.

"And physically check each item for damage in transit," Miles prodded with a pointed nod at the boxes.

"Take care of him, Paymaster," the captain ordered, and wheeled out. "All right, Gamad, show me this grand strategy of yours . . ."

Baz's eyes smoked. "Excuse me, my lord, but I think I'd better join them."

"I'll go with you," offered Mayhew. He clicked his teeth together gently, as if nibbling for a jugular.

"Go ahead." Miles turned to the paymaster, who sighed and shoved a data cartridge into the table-top viewer.

"Now—Mr. Naismith? is that correct? May I see your copy of the contract, please."

Miles frowned uneasily. "Major Daum and I had a verbal agreement. Forty thousand Betan dollars upon safe delivery of his cargo to Felice. This refinery is Felician territory, now."

The paymaster stared, astonished. "A verbal agreement? A verbal agreement is no contract!"

Miles sat up. "A verbal agreement is the most binding of contracts! Your soul is in your breath, and therefore in your voice. Once pledged it must be redeemed."

"Mysticism has no place—"

"It is not mysticism! It's a recognized legal theory!" On Barrayar, Miles realized.

"That's the first I've heard of it."

"Major Daum understood it perfectly well."

"Major Daum was in Intelligence. He specialized in galactics. I'm just Accounting Office—"

"You refuse to redeem your dead comrade's word? But you are real Service, no mercenary—"

The paymaster shook his head. "I have no idea what you're babbling about. But if the cargo is right, you'll be paid. This isn't Jackson's Whole."

Miles relaxed slightly. "Very well." The paymaster was no Vor, nor anything like one. Counting his payment in front of him was not likely to be taken as a mortal insult. "Let's see it."

The paymaster nodded to his assistant, who uncoded the locks. Miles held his breath in happy anticipation of more money than he'd seen in one pile in his life. The lids swung up to reveal stacks and stacks of tightly bundled, particolored pieces of paper. There was a long, long pause.

Miles slid off his leg-swinging perch on the conference table and picked out a bundle. Each contained perhaps a hundred identical, brightly engraved compositions of pictures, numbers, and letters in a strange cursive alphabet. The paper was slick, almost sleazy. He held one piece up to the light.

"What is it?" he asked at last.

The paymaster raised his eyebrows. "Paper currency. It's used commonly for money on most planets—"

"I know that! What currency is it?"

"Felician millifenigs."

"Millifenigs." It sounded faintly like a swear word. "What's it worth in real money? Betan dollars, or, say, Barrayaran Imperial marks."

"Who uses Barrayaran marks?" the paymaster's assistant muttered in puzzlement.

The paymaster cleared his throat. "As of the annual listing, millifenigs were pegged at 150 per Betan dollar on the Betan Exchange," he recited quickly.

"Wasn't that almost a year ago? What are they now?"

The paymaster found something to look at out the plexiports. "The Oseran blockade has prevented us from learning the current rate of exchange."

"Yeah? Well, what was the last figure you had, then?"

The paymaster cleared his throat again; his voice became strangely small. "Because of the blockade, you understand, almost all the information about the war has been sent by the Pelians."

"The rate, please."

"We don't know."

"The last rate," Miles hissed.

The paymaster jumped. "We really don't, sir. Last we heard, Felician currency had been, uh . . ." he was almost inaudible, "dropped from the Exchange."

Miles fingered his dagger. "And just what are these—millifenigs," he would have to experiment, he decided, to find just the right degree of venom to pronounce that word, "backed by?"

The paymaster raised his head proudly. "The government of Felice!"

"The one that's losing this war, right?"

The paymaster muttered something.

"You are losing this war, are you not?"

"Losing the high orbitals was just a set-back," the paymaster explained desperately. "We still control our own airspace—"

"Millifenigs," snorted Miles. "Millifenigs . . . Well, I want Betan dollars!" He glared at the paymaster.

The paymaster replied as one goaded in pride and turning at bay. "There are no Betan dollars! Every cent of it, yes, and every flake of other galactic currencies we could round up was sent with Major Daum, to buy that cargo—"

"Which I have risked my life delivering to you—"

"Which he died delivering to us!"

Miles sighed, recognizing an argument he could not win. His most frenetic posturing would not wring Betan dollars from a government that owned none. "Millifenigs," he muttered.

"I have to go," said the paymaster. "I have to initial the inventory—"

Miles flicked a hand at him, tiredly. "Yes, go."

The paymaster and his assistant fled, leaving him alone in the beautiful conference chamber with two crates of money. That the paymaster didn't even bother to set guard, demand receipt, or see it counted merely confirmed its worthlessness.

Miles piled a pyramid of the stuff before him on the conference table, and laid his head on his arms beside it. Millifenigs. He wandered momentarily in a mental calculation of its square area, if laid out in singles. He could certainly paper not only the walls, but the ceiling of his room at home, and most of the rest of Vorkosigan House as well. Mother would probably object.

He idly tested its inflammability, lighting one piece, planning to hold it until it burned down to his fingertips, to see if anything could hurt more than his stomach. But the doorseals clapped shut at the scent of smoke, a raucous alarm went off, and a chemical fire extinguisher protruded from the wall like a red, sardonic tongue. Fire was a real terror in space installations; the next step, he recalled, would be the evacuation of the air from the chamber to smother the flames. He batted the paper out hastily. Millifenigs. He dragged himself across the room to silence the alarm.

He varied his financial structure by building a square fort, with corner towers and an interior keep. The gate lintel had a tendency to collapse with a slight rustle. Perhaps he could pass on Pelian commercial shipping as a mentally retarded mutant, with Elena as his nurse and Bothari as his keeper, being sent to some off-planet hospital—or zoo—by rich relatives. He could take off his boots and socks and bite his toenails during customs inspections . . . But what roles could he find for Mayhew and Jesek? And Elli Quinn—liege-sworn or not, he owed her a face. Worse, he had no credit here—and somehow he doubted the exchange rate between Felician and Pelian currency would be in his favor.

The door sighed open. Miles quickly knocked his fort into a more random-appearing pile, and sat up straight, for the benefit of the mercenary who saluted and entered.

A self-conscious smile was pasted under the man's avid eyes. "Excuse me, sir. I'd heard a rumor that our pay had arrived."

Miles's lips peeled back in an uncontrollable grin. He forced them straight. "As you see."

Who, after all, could say what the exchange rate for millifenigs was—who could contradict any figure he chose to peg them at? As long as his mercenaries were in space, isolated from test markets, no one. Of course, when they did find out, there might not be enough pieces of him to go around, like the Dismemberment of Mad Emperor Yuri.

The mercenary's mouth formed an "o" at the size of the pile. "Shouldn't you set a guard, sir?"

"Just so, Trainee Nout. Good thinking. Ah—why don't you go fetch a float pallet, and secure this payroll in—er—the usual place. Pick two trustworthy comrades to relieve you on guard duty, around the clock."

"Me, sir?" The mercenary's eyes widened. "You'd trust me— "

What could you do? Steal it and go buy a loaf of bread? Miles thought. Aloud, he replied, "Yes, I would. Did you think I haven't been evaluating your performance these past weeks?" He prayed he'd got the man's name right.

"Yes, sir! Right away, sir!" The mercenary rendered him a perfectly unnecessary salute, and danced out as if he had rubber balls in his boots.

Miles buried his face in a pile of millifenigs and giggled helplessly, very close to tears.

He saw the millifenigs bundled back up and trundled safely to cold storage, then lingered in the conference chamber. Bothari should be seeking him out soon, when done turning the last of the prisoners over to Felician control.

The RG132, floating beyond the plexiports, was getting some attention at last. The hull was taking on the appearance of a half-finished patchwork quilt. Miles wondered if he'd ever get up the nerve to ride in it without a pressure suit on and his helmet at his elbow.

Jesek and Mayhew found him still gazing pensively across the installation. "We set them straight," the engineer declared, planting himself beside Miles. Savage contentment had replaced the burning indignation in his eyes.

"Hm?" Miles broke free of his moody reverie. "Set who straight about what?"

"The Felicians, and that greasy career-builder Gamad."

"About time somebody did that," Miles agreed absently. He wondered what the RG 132 might fetch if sold as an inner-system freighter. Not, preferably, for millifenigs. Or as scrap . . . No, he couldn't do that to Arde.

"Here they come now."

"Hm?"

The Felicians were back, the captain, the paymaster, and what looked like most of the ship's officers, plus some kind of space marine commander Miles had not seen before. From the captain's deference to him in the doorway, Miles guessed he must be the ranking man. A senior colonel, perhaps, or a young general. Gamad was notably absent. Thorne and Auson brought up the rear.

This time the captain came to attention, and saluted. "I believe I owe you an apology, Admiral Naismith. I did not fully understand the situation here."

Miles grasped Baz's arm and stood on tiptoe to his ear, whispering urgently between his teeth. "Baz, what have you been telling these people?"

"Just the truth," Baz began, but there was no time for further reply. The senior officer was stepping forward, extending his hand.

"How do you do, Admiral Naismith. I am General Halify. I have orders from my high command to hold this installation by whatever means necessary."

They shook hands, and were seated. Miles took the head of the table, by way of experiment. The Felician general seated himself earnestly and without demur on Miles's right. There was some interesting jostling for seats farther down the line.

"Since our second ship was lost to the Pelians on our way here, mine is the unenviable task of doing so with 200 men—half my complement," continued Halify.

"I did it with forty," Miles observed automatically. What was the Felician leading up to?

"Mine is also the task of stripping it of Betan ordinance to send back with Captain Sahlin here, to prosecute the war on what has unfortunately become the home front."

"That will make it more complicated for you," Miles agreed.

"Until the Pelians brought in galactics, our two sides were fairly matched. We thought we were on the verge of a negotiated settlement. The Oserans changed that balance."

"So I understand."

"What galactics can do, galactics can surely undo. We wish to hire the Dendarii Mercenaries to break the Oseran blockade and clear local space of all off-planet forces. The Pelians," he sniffed, "we can take care of ourselves."

I'm going to let Bothari finish strangling Baz . . . "A bold offer, General. I wish I could take you up on it. But as you must know, most of my forces are not here."

The general clasped his hands intensely before him on the table. "I believe we can hold out long enough for you to send for them."

Miles glanced at Auson and Thorne, down the expanse of darkly gleaming plastic. Not, perhaps, the best time to explain just how long a wait that would be . . .

"We would have to run the blockade to do so, and at the moment all my jump ships are disabled."

"Felice has three commercial jump ships left, besides the ones that were trapped outside the blockade when it began. One is very fast. Surely, in combination with your warships, you might get it through."

Miles was about to make a rude reply, when it hit him—here was escape, being offered on a platter. Pile his leige-people into the jump ship, have Thorne and Auson run him through the blockade, and thumb his nose to Tau Verde IV and all its denizens forever. It was risky, but it could be done—was in fact the best idea he'd had all day—he sat up, smiling suavely. "An interesting proposition, General." He must not appear too eager. "Just how do you propose to pay for my services? The Dendarii do not work cheaply."

"I'm authorized to meet whatever terms you ask. Within reason, of course," General Halify added prudently.

"To put it bluntly, General, that's a load of—millifenigs. If Major Daum had no authority to hire outside forces, neither do you."

"They said, by whatever means necessary." The general's jaw set. "They'll back me."

"I'd want a contract in writing, signed by somebody who can properly be shaken down—uh, held responsible, after. Retired generals' incomes are not notoriously vast."

A spark of amusement flared briefly in Halify's eye, and he nodded. "You'll get it."

"We must be paid in Betan dollars. I understood you were fresh out."

"If the blockade is broken, we can get off-planet currencies again. You'll get them."

Miles pressed his lips together firmly. He must not break down into howls of laughter. Yet here he sat, a man with an imaginary battle fleet negotiating for its services with a man with an imaginary budget. Well, the price was certainly right.

The general extended his hand. "Admiral Naismith, you have my personal word on it. May I have yours?"

His humor shattered in a thousand frozen shards, swallowed in a cold vast emptiness that used to be his belly. "My word?"

"I understand it has some meaning to you."

You understand entirely too much . . . "My word. I see." He had never yet broken his word. Almost eighteen, and he still preserved that virginity. Well, there was a first time for everything. He accepted the general's handclasp. "General Halify, I'll do my best. My word on it."

CHAPTER FIFTEEN ✳ ✳ ✳

The three ships dove and wove in an intricate evasion pattern. Around them, twenty more darted, as if hawks hunted in packs. The three ships sparked, blue, red, yellow, then dissolved in a brilliant rainbow glare.

Miles leaned back in his station chair in the *Triumph's* tactics room and rubbed his bleary eyes. "Scratch that idea." He vented a long sigh. If he couldn't be a soldier, perhaps he had a future as a designer of fireworks displays.

Elena drifted in, munching a ration bar. "That looked pretty. What was it?"

Miles held up a didactic finger. "I have just discovered my twenty-third new way to get killed this week." He waved toward the holograph display. "That was it."

Elena glanced across the room to her father, apparently asleep, on the friction matting. "Where is everybody?"

"Catching sleep. I'm just as glad not to have an audience while I attempt to teach myself first-year tactics. They might begin to doubt my genius."

She gave him an odd look. "Miles—how serious are you about this blockade busting?"

He glanced up to the outside screens, which showed the same boring view of what might be called the backside of the metals refinery they had displayed since the ship had been parked after the counterattack. The *Triumph* was now being dubbed Miles's flagship. With the arrival of the Felician forces, filling the refinery's crews quarters, he had decamped, secretly relieved, from the squalid luxury of the executive suite to the more restful austerity of Tung's former quarters.

"I don't know. It's been two weeks since the Felicians promised us that fast courier to leg on out of here, and they haven't produced it yet. We're going to at least have to break through the blockade . . ." He hastened to erase the worry in her face. "At least it gives me something to do while we wait. This machine is more fun than chess or Strat-O any day."

He hopped up, and gestured her with a courtly bow toward the next station chair. "Look, I'll teach you how to operate it. Show you a game or two. You'll be good."

"Well . . ."

He introduced her to a couple of elementary tactics patterns, demystifying them by calling them "play." "Captain Koudelka and I used to play something like this." She caught on quickly. It had to be some kind of criminal injustice, that Ivan Vorpatril was even now deeply engaged in officer's training for which Elena could not even be considered.

He went through his half of the patterns automatically, while his mind circled again around his real life military dilemma. This was just the sort of thing he would have been taught how to do at the Imperial Service Academy, he thought with an inward sigh. There was probably a book on it. He wished he had a copy; he was getting mortally tired of having to re-invent the wheel every fifteen minutes. Although it was just barely possible there *was* no way for three small warships and a battered freighter to take out an entire mercenary fleet. The Felicians could offer little assistance, beyond the use of the refinery as a base. Of course, Miles's presence there benefited them at least as much as their support did him, as Pelian-repellant.

He glanced up at Elena, and pushed the importunate strategic hassles from his mind. Her strength and sharpness were blooming these days, in her new challenges. All she'd ever needed was a chance, it seemed. Baz shouldn't have it all his own way. He glanced over to see if Bothari was really asleep, and screwed up his courage. The tactics room with its swivel chairs was not well-arranged for nuzzling, but he would try. He went to her shoulder, and leaned over it, manufacturing some helpful instruction.

"Mr. Naismith?" blatted the intercom. It was Captain Auson, calling from Nav and Com. "Put the outside channels on, I'm coming down."

Miles snapped out of his haze, cursing silently. "What's up?"

"Tung's back."

"Uh, oh. Better scramble everybody."

"I am."

"What's he brought? Can you tell yet?"

"Yes, it's strange. He's standing just out of range in what looks like a Pelian inner-system passenger ship, maybe a little troop-carrier or something, and saying he wants to talk. With you. Probably a trick."

Miles frowned, mystified. "Well, pipe it down, then. But keep scrambling."

In moments the Eurasian's familiar face appeared, larger than life. Bothari was now up, at his usual post by the door, silent as ever; he and Elena didn't talk much since the incident in the damaged prison section. But then, they never had.

"How do you do, Captain Tung. We meet again, I see." The subtle vibrations of the ship changed, as it powered up and began to move into open space.

"We do indeed." Tung smiled, tight and fierce. "Is that job offer still open, son?"

The two shuttles sandwiched themselves together, belly to belly like a pair of mismatched limpets, in space midway between their mother ships. There the two men met face-to-face in privacy, but for Bothari, tense and discreet just out of earshot, and Tung's pilot, who remained equally discreetly aboard Tung's shuttle.

"My people are loyal to me," said Tung. "I can place them at your service, every one."

"You realize," Miles pointed out mildly, "that if you wished to re-take your ship, that would be an ideal ploy. Load my forces with yours, and strike at will. Can you prove you're not a Trojan Horse?"

Tung sighed agreement. "Only as you proved that memorable lunch was not drugged. In the eating."

"Mm." Miles pulled himself back down into his seat in the gravityless shuttle, as if he could so impose orientation on body and mind. He offered Tung a soft-drink bulb, which Tung accepted without hesitation or comment. They both drank, Miles sparingly; his stomach was already starting to protest null-gee. "You also realize, I cannot give you your ship back. All I have to offer at the moment is a captured Pelian putt-putt, and perhaps the title of Staff Officer."

"Yes, I understand that."

"You'll have to work with both Auson and Thorne, without bringing up, um, past frictions."

Tung looked less than enthusiastic, but he replied, "If I have to, I can even do that." He snapped a squirt of fruit juice out of the air. Practice, thought Miles enviously.

"My payroll, for the moment, is entirely in Felician millifenigs. Do you, ah—know about millifenigs?"

"No, but at a guess from the Felician's strategic situation, I'd suppose they'd make an eye-catching toilet paper."

"That's about right." Miles frowned. "Captain Tung. After going to a great deal of trouble to escape two weeks ago, you have gone to what looks like an equal amount of trouble to return to join what can only be described as the losing side. You know you can't have your ship back, you know your pay is at best problematical—I can't believe it's all for my native charm. Why?"

"It wasn't that much trouble. That delightful young lady—remind me to kiss her hand—let me out," observed Tung.

"That 'delightful young lady' is Commander Bothari to you, sir, and considering what you owe her, you can bloody well confine yourself to saluting her," snapped Miles, surprising himself. He swallowed a squirt of fruit drink to hide his confusion.

Tung raised his eyebrows, and smiled. "I see."

Miles dragged his mind back to the present. "Again. Why?"

Tung's face hardened. "Because you are the only force in local space with a chance of giving Oser a prick in the ass."

"And just when did you acquire this motivation?"

Hard, yes, and inward. "He violated our contract. In the event of losing my ship in combat, he owed me another command."

Miles jerked his chin up, inviting Tung to go on.

Tung's voice lowered. "He had a right to chew me out, yes, for my mistakes—but he had no right to humiliate me before my people . . ." His hands were clenched, ivory-knuckled, on the arms of his seat. His drink bulb floated away, forgotten.

Miles's imagination filled in the picture. Admiral Oser, angry and shocked at this sudden defeat after a year of easy victories, losing his temper, mishandling Tung's hot damaged pride—foolish, that, when it would have been so easy to turn that pride redoubled to his own service—yes, it rang true.

"And so you come to my hand. Ah—with all your officers, you say? Your pilot officer?" Escape, escape in Tung's ship possible again? Escape from the Pelians and Oserans, thought Miles soberly. It's escape from the Dendarii that's beginning to look difficult.

"All. All but my communications officer, of course."

"Why 'of course'?"

"Oh, that's right, you don't know about his double life. He's a military agent, assigned to keep watch on the Oseran fleet for his government. I think he wanted to come—we've gotten to know each other pretty well these past six years—but he had to follow his primary orders." Tung chuckled. "He apologized."

Miles blinked. "Is that sort of thing usual?"

"Oh, there's always a few, scattered through all the mercenary organizations." Tung gave Miles a sharp look. "Haven't you ever had any? Most captains throw them out as soon as they catch on, but I like them. They're generally extremely well-trained, and more trustworthy than most, as long as you're not fighting anybody they know. If I'd had occasion to fight the Barrayarans, God forbid, or any of their—well, the Barrayarans are not particularly troubled with allies—I'd have been sure to drop him off somewhere first."

"B—" choked Miles, and swallowed the rest. Ye gods. Had he been recognized? If the man were one of Captain Illyan's agents, almost certainly. And what the devil had the man made of the recent events, seen from the Oseran point of view? Miles could kiss goodbye any hope of keeping his late adventures secret from his father, then.

His fruit drink seemed to slosh, viscous and nasty, on the roof of his stomach. Damn null-gee. He'd better wind this up. A mercenary Admiral didn't need a reputation for space sickness to go with his more obvious disabilities. Miles wondered briefly how many key command decisions in history had been flicked out in the compelling urgency of some like biological necessity.

He stuck out his hand. "Captain Tung, I accept your service."

Tung took it. "Admiral Naismith—it is Admiral Naismith now, I understand?"

Miles grimaced. "So it would appear."

A half-suppressed grin turned one corner of Tung's mouth. "I see. I shall be pleased to serve you, son."

When he had left, Miles sat eyeing his drink bulb for a moment. He gave it a squeeze, and it snapped. Bright red fruit drink marinated his eyebrows, chin, and tunic front. He swore under his breath, and floated off in search of a towel.

The *Ariel* was late. Thorne, accompanied by Arde and Baz, was supposed to be escorting the Betan weapons through to Felician-controlled airspace, and then bringing the fast jump courier back, and they were late. It took two days for Miles to persuade General Halify to relinquish Tung's old crew from their cells; after that, there was nothing to do but watch and wait, and worry.

Five days behind schedule, both ships appeared in the monitors. Miles got Thorne on the com, and demanded, with an edge in his voice, the reason for the delay.

Thorne positively smirked. "It's a surprise. You'll like it. Can you meet us now in the docking bay?"

A surprise. God, now what? Miles was at last beginning to sympathize with Bothari's stated taste for being bored. He stalked to the docking bay, nebulous plans for bracing his laggard subordinates rotating in his brain.

Arde met him, grinning and bouncing on his heels. "Just stand right here, my lord." He raised his voice. "Go ahead, Baz!"

"Hup, hup, hup!" There came a great shuffling thumping from the flex tube. Out of it marched, double-time, a ragged string of men and women. Some wore uniforms, both military and civilian types, others civilian clothes in a wild assortment of various planetary fashions. Mayhew directed them into a standard square formation, where they stood more-or-less to attention.

There was a group of a dozen or so black-uniformed Kshatryan Imperial mercenaries who formed their own tight little island in the sea of color; on closer look, their uniforms, though clean and mended, were not all complete. Odd buttons, shiny seats and elbows, lop-worn boot heels—they were long, long from their distant home, it seemed. Miles's temporary fascination with them was shattered at the appearance of two dozen Cetagandan ghem fighters, variously dressed, but all with full formal face paint freshly applied, looking like an array of Chinese temple demons. Bothari swore, and clapped his hand to his plasma arc at the sight of them. Miles motioned him to parade rest.

Freighter and passenger liner tech uniforms, a white-skinned, white-haired man in a feathered g-string—Miles, taking in the polished bandolier and plasma rifle he also bore, was not inclined to smile—a dark-haired woman in her thirties of almost supernatural beauty, engrossed with directing a crew of four techs—she glanced toward him, then frankly stared, a very odd look on her face. He stood a little straighter. *Not a mutant, ma'am,* he thought irritably. When the flex tube emptied at last, perhaps a hundred people stood before him in the docking bay. Miles's head whirled.

Thorne, Baz, and Arde all appeared at his elbow, looking immensely pleased with themselves.

"Baz—" Miles opened his hand in helpless supplication. "What is this?"

Jesek stood to attention. "Dendarii recruits, my lord!"

"Did I ask you to collect recruits?" He had never been that drunk, surely. . .

"You said we didn't have enough personnel to man our equipment. So I applied a little forward momentum to the problem, and—there you are."

"Where the devil did you get them all?"

"Felice. There must be two thousand galactics trapped there by the blockade. Merchant ship personnel, passengers, business people, techs, a little of everything. Even soldiers. They're not all soldiers, of course. Not yet."

"Ah." Miles cleared his throat. "Hand-picked, are they?"

"Well . . ." Baz scuffed his boot on the deck, and studied it, as if looking for signs of wear. "I gave them some weapons to field-strip and reassemble. If they didn't try to shove the plasma arc power cartridge in the nerve disruptor grip slot, I hired 'em."

Miles wandered up and down the rows, bemused. "I see. Very ingenious. I doubt I could have done better myself." He nodded toward the Kshatryans. "Where were they going?"

"That's an interesting story," put in Mayhew. "They weren't exactly trapped by the blockade. Seems some local Felician magnate of the, uh, sub-economy, had hired them for bodyguards a few years ago. About six months back they botched the job, rendering themselves unemployed. They'll do about anything for a ride out of here. I found them myself," he added proudly.

"I see. Ah, Baz—Cetagandans?" Bothari had not taken his eyes from their gaudy fierce faces since they had exited the flex tube.

The engineer turned his hands palm-outwards. "They're *trained.*"

"Do they realize that some Dendarii are Barrayaran?"

"They know I am, and with a name like Dendarii, any Cetagandan would have to make the connection. That mountain range made an impression on them during the Great War. But they want a ride out of here too. That was part of the contract, you see, to keep the price down—almost everybody wants to be discharged outside Felician local space."

"I sympathize," muttered Miles. The Felician fast courier floated outside the docking station. He itched for a closer look. "Well—see Captain Tung, and arrange quarters for them all. And, uh, training schedules . . ." Yes, keep them busy, while he—slipped away?

"Captain Tung?" said Thorne.

"Yes, he's a Dendarii now. I've been doing some recruiting too. Should be just like a family reunion for you—ah, Bel," he fixed the Betan with a stern eye, "you are now comrades in arms. As a Dendarii, I expect you to remember it."

"Tung." Thorne sounded more amazed than jealous. "Oser will be foaming."

Miles spent the evening running his new recruits' dossiers into the *Triumph's* computers, by hand, by himself, and by choice, the better to familiarize himself with his leigemen's human grab-bag. They were in fact well chosen; most had previous military experience, the rest invariably possessed some arcane and valuable technical specialty.

Some were arcane indeed. He stopped his monitor to study the face of the extraordinarily beautiful woman who had stared at him in the docking bay. What the devil had Baz been about to hire a banking comm link security specialist as a soldier of fortune? To be sure, she might want off-planet badly enough—ah. Never mind. Her resume explained the mystery; she had once held the rank of ensign in the Escobaran military space forces. She'd had an honorable medical discharge after the war with Barrayar nineteen years ago. Medical discharges must have been a fad then, Miles mused, thinking of Bothari's. His amusement drained away, and he felt the hairs on his arms stir.

Great dark eyes, clean square line of jaw—her last

name was Visconti, typically Escobaran. Her first name was Elena.

"No," whispered Miles to himself firmly. "Not possible." He weakened. "Anyway, not *likely* . . ."

He read the resume again more carefully. The Escobaran woman had come to Tau Verde IV a year ago to install a comm link system her company had sold to a Felician bank. She must have arrived just days before the war started. She listed herself as unmarried with no dependents. Miles swung around in his chair with his back to the screen, then found himself sneaking another look from the corner of his eye. She had been unusually young to be an officer during the Escobar-Barrayar war— some sort of precocious hot-shot, perhaps. Miles caught himself up ironically, wondering when he'd started feeling so middle-aged.

But if she were, just possibly, his Elena's mother, how had she got mixed up with Sergeant Bothari? Bothari had been pushing forty then, and looked much the same as now, judging from vids Miles had seen from his parents' early years of marriage. No accounting for taste, maybe.

A little reunion fantasy blossomed in his imagination, unbidden, galloping ahead of all proof. To present Elena not merely with a grave, but with her longed-for mother in the flesh—to finally feed that secret hunger, sharper than a thorn, that had plagued her all her life, twin to his own clumsy hunger to please his father—that would be a heroism worth stretching for. Better than showering her with the most fabulous material gifts imaginable— he melted at the picture of her delight.

And yet—and yet . . . it was only a hypothesis. Testing it might prove awkward. He had realized the Sergeant was not being strictly truthful when he'd said he couldn't remember Escobar, but it might be partly so. Or this woman might be somebody else altogether. He would make his test in private then, and blind. If he were wrong, no harm done.

Miles held his first full senior officers' meeting the next day, partly to acquaint himself with his new henchmen, but mostly to throw the floor open to ideas for blockade-busting. With all this military and ex-military talent around, there had to be someone who knew what they were doing. More copies of the "Dendarii regulations" were passed out, and Miles retired after to his appropriated cabin on his appropriated flagship, to run the parameters of the Felician courier through the computer one more time.

He had upped the courier's estimated passenger capacity for the two-week run to Beta Colony from a crowded four to a squeezed five by eliminating several sorts of baggage and fudging the life-support back-up figures as much as he dared; surely there had to be something he could do to boost it to seven. He also tried very hard not to think about the mercenaries, waiting eagerly for his return with reinforcements. And waiting. And waiting . . .

They should not linger here any longer. The *Triumph's* tactics simulator had shown that thinking he could break the Oserans with 200 troops was pure megalomania. Still . . . No. He forced himself to think reasonably.

The logical person to leave behind was Elli Quinn of the slagged face. She was no leigewoman of his, really. Then a toss-up between Baz and Arde. Taking the engineer back to Beta Colony would expose him to arrest and extradition; leaving him here would be for his own good, yessir. Never mind that he had been selflessly busting his tail for weeks to serve Miles's every military whim. Never mind what the Oserans would do to all their deserters and everyone associated with them when they finally caught up with them, as they inevitably must. Never mind that it would also most handily sever Baz's romance with Elena, and wasn't that very possibly the real reason. . . ?

Logic, Miles decided, made his stomach hurt.

Anyway, it was not easy to keep his mind on his work just now. He checked his wrist chronometer. Just a few more minutes. He wondered if it had been silly to lay in that bottle of awful Felician wine, concealed now with four glasses in his cupboard. He need only bring it out if, if, if . . .

He sighed and leaned back, and smiled across the cabin at Elena. She sat on the bed in companionable silence, screening a manual on weapons drills. Sergeant Bothari sat at a small fold-out table, cleaning and recharging their personal weapons. Elena smiled back, and removed her audio bug from her ear.

"Do you have your physical training program figured out for our, uh, new recruits?" he asked her. "Some of them look like it's been a while since they've worked out regularly."

"All set," she assured him. "I'm starting a big group first thing next day-cycle. General Halify is going to lend me the refinery crew's gym." She paused, then added, "Speaking of not working out for a while—don't you think you'd better come too?"

"Uh . . ." said Miles.

"Good idea," said the Sergeant, not looking up from his work.

"My stomach—"

"It would be a good example to your troops," she added, blinking her brown eyes at him in feigned, he was sure, innocence.

"Who's going to warn them not to break me in half?"

Her eyes glinted. "I'll let you pretend you're instructing them."

"Your gym clothes," said the Sergeant, blowing a bit of dust out of the silvered bell-muzzle of a nerve disruptor and nodding to his left, "are in the bottom drawer of that wall compartment."

Miles sighed defeat. "Oh, all right." He checked his chronometer again. Any minute now.

The door of the cabin slid open; it was the Escobaran woman, right on time. "Good day, Technician Visconti," he began cheerfully. His words died on his lips as she raised a needler and held it in both hands to aim.

"Don't anybody move!" she cried.

An unnecessary instruction; Miles, at least, was frozen in shock, mouth open.

"So," she said at last. Hatred, pain, and weariness trembled her voice. "It is you. I wasn't sure at first. You. . ."

She was addressing Bothari, Miles guessed, for her needler was aimed at his chest. Her hands shook, but the aim never wavered.

The Sergeant had caught up a plasma arc when the door slid open. Now, incredibly, his hand fell to his side, weapon dangling. He straightened slightly by the wall, out of his firing semi-crouch.

Elena sat cross-legged, an awkard position from which to jump. Her hand viewer fell forgotten to the bed. The audio emitted a thin tinny sound, small as an insect, in the silence.

The Escobaran woman's eyes flicked for a moment to Miles, then back to their target. "I think you'd better know, Admiral Naismith, just what you have hired for your bodyguard."

"Uh . . . Why don't you give me your needler, and sit down, and we'll talk about it—" He held out an open hand, experimentally inviting. Hot shivers that began in the pit of his stomach were radiating outward; his hand shook foolishly. This wasn't the way he'd rehearsed this meeting. She hissed, her needler swinging toward him. He recoiled, and her aim jerked back to Bothari.

"That one," she nodded at the Sergeant, "is an ex-Barrayaran soldier. No surprise, I suppose, that he should have drifted into some obscure mercenary fleet. But he was Admiral Vorrutyer's chief torturer, when the Barrayarans tried to invade Escobar. But maybe you knew that—" her eyes seemed to peel Miles, like flensing knives, for a moment. A moment was quite a long time, at the relativistic speed at which he was now falling.

"I—I—" he stammered. He glanced at Elena; her eyes were huge, her body tense to spring.

"The Admiral never raped his victims himself—he preferred to watch. Vorrutyer was Prince Serg's cata-mite, perhaps the Prince was jealous. He applied more inventive tortures himself, though. The Prince was waiting, since his particular obsession was pregnant women, which I supose Vorrutyer's group was obliged to supply—"

Miles's mind screamed through a hundred unwanted connections, no, no, no . . . So, there was such a thing as latent knowledge. How long had he known not to ask questions he didn't want to hear the answers to? Elena's face reflected total outrage and disbelief. God help him to keep it that way. His stunner lay on Bothari's table, across their mutual line of fire; did he stand a chance of leaping for it?

"I was eighteen years old when I fell into their hands. Just graduated, no war lover, but wishing to serve and protect my home—that was no war, out there, that was some personal hell, growing vile in the Barrayaran high command's unchecked power—" She was close to hysteria, as if old cold dormant terrors were erupting in a swarm more overwhelming than even she had anticipated. He had to shut her up somehow—

"And that one," her finger was tight on the trigger of the needler, "was their tool, their best show-maker, their pet. The Barrayarans refused to turn over their war criminals, and my own government bargained away the justice that should have been mine for the sake of the peace settlements. And so he went free, to be my nightmare for the past two decades. But mercenary fleets dispense their own justice. Admiral Naismith, I demand this man's arrest!"

"I don't—it's not—" began Miles. He turned to Bothari, his eyes imploring denial—make it not be true—"Sergeant?"

The explosion of words had spattered over Bothari like acid. His face was furrowed with pain, brow creased with an effort of—memory? His eyes went from his daughter to Miles to the Escobaran, and a sigh went out of him. A man descending forever into hell, vouchsafed one glimpse of paradise, might have such a look on his face. "Lady . . ." he whispered. "You are still beautiful."

Don't goad her, Sergeant! Miles screamed silently.

The Escobaran woman's face contorted with rage and fear. She braced herself. A stream, as of tiny silver raindrops, sang from the shaking weapon. The needles burst against the wall all around Bothari in a whining shower of spinning, razor-sharp shards. The weapon jammed. The woman swore, and scrabbled at it. Bothari, leaning against the wall, murmured, "Rest now," Miles was not sure to whom.

Miles sprang for his stunner as Elena leaped for the Escobaran. Elena struck the needler sliding across the room and had the woman's arms hooked behind her, twisting in their shoulder sockets with the strength of her terror and rage, by the time he'd brought the stunner to aim. But the woman was resistless, spent. Miles saw why as he spun back to the Sergeant.

Bothari fell like a wall toppling, as if in pieces at the joints. His shirt displayed four or five tiny drops of blood only, scarcely a nosebleed's worth. But they were obliterated in a sudden red flood from his mouth as he convulsed, choking. He writhed once on the friction matting, vomiting a second scarlet tide across the first, across Miles's hands, lap, shirt front, as he scrambled on hands and knees to kneel by his bodyguard's head.

"Sergeant?"

Bothari lay still, watchful eyes stopped and open, head twisted, the blood flung from his mouth soaking into the friction matting. He looked like some dead animal, smashed by a vehicle. Miles patted Bothari's chest frantically, but could not even find the pinhole entrance wounds. Five hits—Bothari's chest cavity, abdomen, organs, must be sliced and stirred to hamburger, within . . .

"Why didn't he fire?" wailed Elena. She shook the Escobaran woman. "Wasn't it charged?"

Miles glanced at the plasma arc's readouts in the Sergeant's stiffening hand. Freshly charged, Bothari had just done it himself.

Elena took one despairing look at her father's body, and snaked a hand around the Escobaran woman's throat, catching her tunic. Her arm tightened across the woman's windpipe.

Miles rocked back on his heels, his shirt, trousers, hands soaked in blood. "No, Elena! Don't kill her!"

"Why not? Why not?" Tears were swarming down her ravaged face.

"I think she's your mother." Oh, God, he shouldn't have said that . . .

"You believe those horrible things—" she raged at him. "Unbelieveable lies—" But her hold slackened.

"Miles—I don't even know what some of those words mean . . ."

The Escobaran woman coughed, and twisted her head around, to stare in astonishment and dismay over her shoulder. "This is that one's spawn?" she asked Miles.

"His daughter."

Her eyes counted off the features of Elena's face. Miles did too; it seemed to him the secret sources of Elena's hair, eyes, elegant bone structure, stood before him.

"You look like him." Her great brown eyes held a thin crust of distaste over a bog of horror. "I'd heard the Barrayarans had used the fetuses for military research." She eyed Miles in confused speculation. "Are you another? But no, you couldn't be . . ."

Elena released her, and stood back. Once, at the summer place at Vorkosigan Surleau, Miles had witnessed a horse trapped in a shed burn to death, no one able to get near it for the heat. He had thought no sound could be more heart-piercing than its death screams. Elena's silence was. She was not crying now.

Miles drew himself up in dignity. "No, ma'am. Admiral Vorkosigan saw them all safely delivered to an orphanage, I believe. All but . . ."

Elena's lips formed the word, "lies," but there was no more conviction in her. Her eyes sucked at the Escobaran woman with a hunger that terrified Miles.

The door of the cabin slid open again. Arde Mayhew sauntered in, saying, "My lord, do you want these assignments—God almighty!" He nearly tripped, stopping short. "I'll get the medtech, hang on!" He dashed back out.

Elena Visconti approached Bothari's body with the caution one would use toward a freshly-killed poisonous reptile. Her eyes locked with Miles's from opposite sides of the barrier. "Admiral Naismith, I apologize for inconveniencing you. But this was no murder. It was the just execution of a war criminal. It was just," she insisted, her voice edged with passion. "It was." Her voice fell away.

It was no murder, it was a suicide, Miles thought. He

could have shot you where you stood at any time, he was that fast. "No . . ."

Her lips thinned in despair. "You call me a liar too? Or are you going to tell me I enjoyed it?"

"No . . ." He looked up at her across a vast gulf, one meter wide. "I don't mock you. But—until I was four, almost five years old, I couldn't walk, only crawl. I spent a lot of time looking at people's knees. But if there was ever a parade, or something to see, I had the best view of anybody because I watched it from on top the Sergeant's shoulder."

For answer, she spat on Bothari's body. A spasm of rage darkened Miles's vision. He was saved from a possibly disastrous action by the return of Mayhew and the medtech.

The medtech ran to him. "Admiral! Where are you hit?"

He stared at her stupidly a moment, then glanced down at himself, realizing the red reason for her concern. "Not me. It's the Sergeant." He brushed ineffectually at the cooling stickiness.

She knelt by Bothari. "What happened? Was it an accident?"

Miles glanced up at Elena where she stood, just stood, arms wrapped around herself as if she were cold. Only her eyes traveled, back and forth from the Sergeant's crumpled form to the harsh straightness of the Escobaran. Back and forth, finding no rest.

His mouth was stiff; he made it move by force of will. "An accident. He was cleaning the weapons. The needler was set on auto rapid-fire." Two true statements out of three.

The Escobaran woman's mouth curled in silent triumph and relief. She thinks I have endorsed her justice, Miles realized. Forgive me . . .

The medtech shook her head, running a hand scanner over Bothari's chest. "Whew. What a mess."

A sudden hope rocketed through Miles. "The cryo chambers—what's their status?"

"All filled, sir, after the counterattack."

"When you triage for them, how—how do you choose?"

"The least messed-up ones have the best hope of re-vival. They get first choice. Enemies last, unless Intelli-gence throws a fit."

"How would you rate this injury?"

"Worse than any I've got on ice now, except two."

"Who are the two?"

"A couple of Captain Tung's people. Do you want me to dump one?"

Miles paused, searching Elena's face. She was staring at Bothari's body as if he were some stranger, wearing her father's face, who had suddenly unmasked. Her dark eyes were like deep caverns; like graves, one for Bothari, one for himself.

"He hated the cold," he muttered at last. "Just—get a morgue pack."

"Yes, sir." She exited, unhurried.

Mayhew wandered up, to stare bemused and bewil-dered on the face of death. "I'm sorry, my lord. I was just beginning to like him, in a kind of weird way."

"Yes. Thank you. Go away." Miles looked up at the Escobaran woman. "Go away," he whispered.

Elena was turning around and around between the dead and the living, like a creature newly caged discov-ering that cold iron sears the flesh. "Mother?" she said at last, in a tiny voice not at all like her own.

"You keep away from me," the Escobaran woman snarled at her, low-voiced and pale. "Far away." She gave her a look of loathing, contemptuous as a slap, and stalked out.

"Um," said Arde. "Maybe you should come somewhere and sit down, Elena. I'll get you a, a drink of water or something." He plucked at her anxiously. "Come away now, there's a good girl."

She suffered herself to be led, with one last look over her shoulder. Her face reminded Miles of a bombed-out city.

Miles waited for the medtech, in deathwatch for his first leigeman, afraid, and growing more so, unaccus-tomed. He had always had the Sergeant to be afraid for him. He touched Bothari's face; the shaved chin was rough under his fingertips.

"What do I do now, Sergeant?"

CHAPTER SIXTEEN ✳ ✳ ✳

It was three days before he cried, worried that he could not cry. Then, in bed alone at night, it came as a frightening uncontrollable storm lasting hours. Miles judged it a just catharsis, but it kept repeating on succeeding nights, and then he worried that it would not stop. His stomach hurt all the time now, but especially after meals, which he therefore scarcely touched. His sharp features sharpened further, molding to his bones.

The days were a grey fog. Faces, familiar and unfamiliar, badgered him for directions, to which his reply was an invariable, laconic, "Suit yourself." Elena would not talk to him at all. He was stirred to fear she was finding comfort in Baz's arms. He watched her covertly, anxious. But she seemed not to be finding comfort anywhere.

After a particularly formless and inconclusive Dendarii staff meeting Arde Mayhew took him aside. Miles had sat silent at the head of the table, seemingly studying his hands, while his officers' voices had croaked on meaningless as frogs.

"God knows," whispered Arde, "I don't know much about being a military officer." He took an angry breath. "But I do know you can't drag 200 and more people out on a limb with you like this and then go catatonic."

"You're right," Miles snarled back, "you don't know much."

He stamped off, stiff-backed, but shaken inside with

the justice of Mayhew's complaint. He slammed into his cabin just in time to throw up in secret for the fourth time that week, the second since Bothari's death, resolve sternly to take up the work at hand immediately and no more nonsense, and fall across his bed to lay immobile for the next six hours.

He was getting dressed. Men who'd done isolated duty all agreed, you had to keep the standards up or things went to hell. Miles had been awake three hours now, and had his trousers on. In the next hour he was either going to try for his socks, or shave, whichever seemed easier. He contemplated the pig-headed masochism of the Barrayaran habit of the daily shave versus, say, the civilized Betan custom of permanently stunning the hair follicles. Perhaps he'd go for the socks.

The cabin buzzer blatted. He ignored it. Then the intercom, Elena's voice: "Miles, let me in."

He lurched to a sitting position, nearly blacking himself out, and called hastily, "Come!", which released the voice-lock.

She picked her way in across strewn clothing, weapons, equipment, disconnected chargers, rations wrappers, and stared around, wrinkling her nose in dismay. "You know," she said at last, "if you're not going to pick this mess up yourself you ought to at least choose a new batman."

Miles stared around too. "It never occurred to me," he said humbly. "I used to imagine I was a very neat person. Everything just put itself away, or so I thought. You wouldn't mind?"

"Mind what?"

"If I got a new batman."

"Why should I care?"

Miles thought it over. "Maybe Arde. I've got to find something for him to do, sooner or later, now he can't jump anymore."

"Arde?" she repeated dubiously.

"He's not nearly as slovenly as he used to be."

"Mm." She picked up a hand-viewer that was lying

upside-down on the floor, and looked for a place to set it. But there was only one level surface in the cabin that held no clutter or dust. "Miles, how long are you going to keep that coffin in here?"

"It might as well be stored here as anywhere. The morgue's cold. He didn't like the cold."

"People are beginning to think you're strange."

"Let 'em think what they like. I gave him my word once that I'd take him back to be buried on Barrayar, if—if anything happened to him out here."

She shrugged angrily. "Why bother keeping your word to a corpse? It'll never know the difference."

"I'm alive," Miles said quietly, "and I'd know."

She stalked around the cabin, lips tight. Face tight, whole body tight—"I've been running your unarmed combat classes for ten days now. You haven't come to a single session."

He wondered if he ought to tell her about throwing up the blood. No, she'd drag him off to the medtech for sure. He didn't want to see the medtech. His age, the secret weakness of his bones—too much would become apparent on a close medical examination.

She went on. "Baz is doing double shifts, reconditioning equipment, Tung and Thorne and Auson are running their tails off organizing the new recruits—but it's all starting to come apart. Everybody's spending all their time arguing with everybody else. Miles, if you spend another week holed up in here, the Dendarii Mercenaries are going to start looking just like this cabin."

"I know, I've been to the staff meetings. Just because I don't say anything doesn't mean I'm not listening."

"Then listen to them when they say they need your leadership."

"I swear to God, Elena, I don't know what for." He ran his hands through his hair, and jerked up his chin. "Baz fixes things, Arde runs them, Tung and Thorne and Auson and their people do the fighting, you keep them all sharp and in condition—I'm the one person who doesn't do anything real at all." He paused. "They say? What do you say?"

"What does it matter what I say?"

"You came . . ."

"They asked me to come. You haven't been letting anyone else in, remember? They've been pestering me for days. They act like a bunch of ancient Christians asking the Virgin Mary to intercede with God."

A ghost of his old grin flitted across his mouth. "No, only with Jesus. God is back on Barrayar."

She choked, then buried her face in her hands. "Damn you for making me laugh!" she said, muffled.

He rose to capture her hands and make her sit beside him. "Why shouldn't you laugh? You deserve laughter, and all good things."

She did not answer, but stared across the room at the oblong silver box resting in the corner, at the bright scars on the far wall. "You never doubted her accusations," she said at last. "Not even for the first instant."

"I saw a lot more of him than you ever did. He practically lived in my back pocket for seventeen years."

"Yes . . ." her eyes fell to her hands, now twisting in her lap. "I suppose I never did see more than glimpses. He would come to the village at Vorkosigan Surleau and give Mistress Hysop her money once a month—he'd hardly ever stay more than an hour. Looking three meters tall in that brown and silver livery of yours. I'd be so excited, I couldn't sleep for a day before or after. Summers were heaven, because when your mother asked me up the lake to the summer place to play with you, I'd see him all day long." Her hands tightened to fists, and her voice broke. "And it was all *lies*. Faking glory, while all the time underneath was this—cess-pit."

He made his voice more gentle than he had ever known he could. "I don't think he was lying, Elena. I think he was trying to forge a new truth."

Her teeth were clenched and feral. "The *truth* is, I am a madman's rape-bred bastard, my mother is a murderess who hates the very shape of my shadow—I can't believe I've inherited no more from them than my nose and my eyes—"

There it was, the dark fear, most secret. He started in

recognition, and dove after it like a knight pursuing a dragon underground. "No! You're not them. You are you, your own person—totally separate—innocent—"

"Coming from you, I think that's the most hypocritical thing I've ever heard."

"Huh?"

"What are you but the culmination of your generations? The flower of the Vor—"

"Me?" He stared in astonishment. "The culmination of degeneration, maybe. A stunted weed . . ." He paused; her face seemed a mirror of his own astonishment. "They do add up, it's true. My grandfather carried nine generations on his back. My father carried ten. I carry eleven—and I swear that last one weighs more than all the rest put together. It's a wonder I'm not squashed even shorter. I feel like I'm down to about half a meter right now. Soon I'll disappear altogether."

He was babbling, knew he was babbling. Some dam had broken in him. He gave himself over to the flood and boiled on down the sluice.

"Elena, I love you, I've always loved you—" She leaped like a startled deer, he gasped and flung his arms around her. "No, listen! I love you, I don't know what the Sergeant was but I loved him too, and whatever of him is in you I honor with all my heart, I don't know what is truth and I don't give a damn anymore, we'll make our own like he did, he did a bloody good job I think, I can't live without my Bothari, marry me!" He spent the last of his air shouting the last two words, and had to pause for a long inhalation.

"I can't marry you! The genetic risks—"

"I am *not* a mutant! Look, no gills—" he stuck his fingers into the coners of his mouth and spread it wide, "no antlers— " he planted his thumbs on either side of his head and wriggled his fingers.

"I wasn't thinking of your genetic risks. Mine. *His.* Your father must have known what he was—he'll never accept—"

"Look, anybody who can trace a blood relationship with Mad Emperor Yuri through two lines of descent has no room to criticize anybody else's genes."

"Your father is loyal to his class, Miles, like your grandfather, like Lady Vorpatril—they could never accept me as Lady Vorkosigan."

"Then I'll present them with an alternative. I'll tell them I'm going to marry Bel Thorne. They'll come around so fast they'll trip over themselves."

She sat back helplessly and buried her face in his pillow, shoulders shaking. He had a moment of terror that he'd broken her down into tears. Not break down, build up, and up, and up . . . But, "*Damn* you for making me laugh!" she repeated. "Damn you . . ."

He galloped on, encouraged. "And I wouldn't be so sure about my father's class loyalties. He married a foreign plebe, after all." He dropped into seriousness. "And you cannot doubt my mother. She always longed for a daughter, secretly—never paraded it, so as not to hurt the old man, of course—let her be your mother in truth."

"Oh," she said, as if he had stabbed her. "Oh . . ."

"You'll see, when we get back to Barrayar—"

"I pray to God," she interrupted him, voice intense, "I may never set foot on Barrayar again."

"Oh," he said in turn. After a long pause he said, "We could live somewhere else. Beta Colony. It would have to be pretty quietly, once the exchange rate got done with my income—I could get a job, doing—doing—doing something."

"And on the day the Emperor calls you to take your place on the Council of Counts, to speak for your district and all the poor sods in it, where will you go then?"

He swallowed, struck silent. "Ivan Vorpatril is my heir," he offered at last. "Let him take the Countship."

"Ivan Vorpatril is a jerk."

"Oh, he's not such a bad sort."

"He used to corner me, when my father wasn't around, and try to feel me up."

"What! You never said—"

"I didn't want to start a big flap." She frowned into the past. "I almost wish I could go back in time, just to boot him in the balls."

He glanced sideways at her, considerably startled. "Yes," he said slowly, "you've changed."

"I don't know what I am anymore. Miles, you must believe me—I love you as I love breath—"

His heart rocketed.

"But I can't be your annex."

And crashed. "I don't understand."

"I don't know how to put it plainer. You'd swallow me up the way an ocean swallows a bucket of water. I'd disappear in you. I love you, but I'm terrified of you, and of your future."

His bafflement sought simplicity. "Baz. It's Baz, isn't it?"

"If Baz had never existed, my answer would be the same. But as it happens—I have given him my word."

"You—" the breath went out of him in a "ha,"—"Break it," he ordered.

She merely looked at him, silently. In a moment he reddened, and dropped his eyes in shame.

"You own honor by the ocean," she whispered. "I have only a little bucketful. Unfair to jostle it—my lord."

He fell back across his bed, defeated.

She rose. "Are you coming to the staff meeting?"

"Why bother? It's hopeless."

She stared down at him, lips thinned, and glanced across to the box in the corner. "Isn't it time you learned to walk on your own feet—cripple?"

She ducked out the door just in time to avoid the pillow he threw at her, her lips curving just slightly at this spasmodic display of energy.

"You know me too bloody well," he whispered. "Ought to keep you just for security reasons."

He staggered to his feet and went to shave.

He made it to the staff conference, barely, and sagged into his usual seat at the head of the table. It was a full meeting, held therefore in the roomy refinery conference chamber. General Halify and an aide sat in. Tung and Thorne and Auson, Arde and Baz, and the five men and women picked to officer the new recruits ringed the table. The Cetagandan ghem-captain sat opposite the

Kshatryan lieutenant, their growing animosity threatening to equal the three-way rivalry among Tung, Auson, and Thorne. The two united only long enough to snarl at the Felicians, the professional assassin from Jackson's Whole, or the retired Tau Cetan major of commandos, who in turn sniped at the ex-Oserans, making the circle complete.

The alleged agenda for this circus was the preparation of the final Dendarii battle-plan for breaking the Oseran blockade, hence General Halify's keen interest. His keenness had been rather blunted this last week by a growing dismay. The doubt in Halify's eyes was an itch to Miles' spirit; he tried to avoid meeting them. *Bargain rates, General,* Miles thought sulkily to him. *You get what you pay for.*

The first half hour was spent knocking down, again, three unworkable pet plans that had been advanced by their owners at previous meetings. Bad odds, requirements of personnel and material beyond their resources, impossibilities of timing, were pointed out with relish by one half of Miles's group to the other, with opinions of the advancers' mentalities thrown in gratis. This rapidly degenerated into a classic slanging match. Tung, who normally suppressed such, was one of the principals this time, so it threatened to escalate indefinitely.

"Look, damn it," shouted the Kshatryan lieutenant, banging his fist on the table for emphasis, "we can't take the wormhole direct and we all know it. Let's concentrate on something we can do. Merchant shipping—we could attack that, a counter-blockade—"

"Attack neutral galactic shipping?" yelped Auson. "Do you want to get us all hung?"

"Hanged," corrected Thorne, earning an ungrateful glare.

"No, see," Auson bulled on, "the Pelians have little bases all over this system we could have a go at. Like guerilla warfare, attacking and fading into the sands—"

"What sands?" snapped Tung. "There's nothing to hide your ass behind out there—the Pelians have our home address. It's a miracle they haven't given up all hope of capturing this refinery and flung a half-c meteor shower through here already. Any plan that doesn't work quickly won't work at all—"

"What about a lightning raid on the Pelian capital?" suggested the Cetagandan captain. "A suicide squadron to drop a nuclear in there—"

"You volunteering?" sneered the Kshatryan. "That might almost be worthwhile."

"The Pelians have a trans-shipping station in orbit around the sixth planet," said the Tau Cetan. "A raid on that would—"

"—take that electron orbital randomizer and—"

"—you're an idiot—"

"—ambush stray ships—"

Miles's intestines writhed like mating snakes. He rubbed his hands wearily over his face, and spoke for the first time; the unexpectedness of it caught their attention momentarily.

"I've known people who play chess like this. They can't think their way to a checkmate, so they spend their time trying to clear the board of the little pieces. This eventually reduces the game to a simplicity they can grasp, and they're happy. The perfect war is a fool's mate."

He subsided, elbows on the table, face in his hands. After a short silence, expectation falling into disappointment, the Kshatryan renewed the attack on the Cetagandan, and they were off again. Their voices blurred over Miles. General Halify began to push back from the table.

No one noticed Miles's jaw drop, behind his hands, or his eyes widen, then narrow to glints. "Son-of-a-bitch," he whispered. "It's *not* hopeless."

He sat up. "Has it occurred to anyone yet that we're tackling this problem from the wrong end?"

His words were lost in the din. Only Elena, sitting in a corner across the chamber, saw his face. Her own face turned like a sunflower toward him. Her lips moved silently: Miles?

Not a shameful escape in the dark, but a monument. That's what he would make of this war. Yes . . .

He pulled his grandfather's dagger from its sheath and spun it in the air. It came down and stuck point-first in the center of the table with a ringing vibration. He climbed up on the table and marched to retrieve it.

The silence was sudden and complete, but for a mutter from Auson, in front of whom the dagger had landed, "I didn't think that plastic would scratch . . ."

Miles yanked the dagger out, resheathed it, and strode up and down the tabletop. His leg brace had developed an annoying click recently, which he'd meant to have Baz fix; now it was loud in the silence. Locking attention, like a whisper. Good. A click, a club on the head, whatever worked was fine by him. It was time to get their attention.

"It appears to have escaped you gentlemen, ladies, and others, that the Dendarii's appointed task is not to physically destroy the Oserans, but merely to eliminate them as a fighting force in local space. We need not blunt ourselves attacking their strengths."

Their upturned faces followed him like iron filings drawn to a magnet. General Halify sank back in his seat. Baz's face, and Arde's, grew jubilant with hope.

"I direct your attention to the weak link in the chain that binds us—the connection between the Oserans and their employers the Pelians. *There* is where we must apply our leverage. My children," he stood gazing out past the refinery into the depths of space, a seer taken by a vision, "we're going to hit them in the payroll."

The underwear came first, soft, smooth-fitting, absorbent. Then the connections for the plumbing. Then the boots, the piezo-electric pads carefully aligned with points of maximum impact on toes, heels, the ball of the foot. Baz had done a beautiful job adjusting the fit of the space armor. The greaves went on like skin to Miles's uneven legs. Better than skin, an exoskeleton, his brittle bones at last rendered technologically equal to anyone's.

Miles wished Baz were by him at this moment, to take pride in his handiwork, although Arde was doing his best to help Miles ooze into the apparatus. Even more passionately Miles wished himself in Baz's place.

Felician intelligence reported all still quiet on the Pelian home front. Baz and his hand-picked party of techs, starring Elena Visconti, must have penetrated the planetside frontier successfully and be moving into place for their blow. The killing blow of Miles's strategy. The keystone of his arching ambitions. His heart had nearly broken, sending them off alone, but reason ruled. A commando raid, if it could be so called, delicate, technical, invisible, would not benefit from so conspicuous and low-tech a piece of baggage as himself. He was better employed here, with the rest of the grunts.

He glanced up the length of his flagship's armory. The atmosphere seemed a combination of locker room, docking bay, and surgery—he tried not to think about surgeries. His stomach twinged, a probe of pain. Not now, he told it. Later. Be good, and I promise I'll take you to the medtech, later.

The rest of his attack group were arming and armoring themselves as he was. Techs checked out systems to a quiet undercurrent of colored lights and small audio signals as they probed here, there; the quiet undercurrent of voices was serious, attentive, concentrated, almost meditative, like an ancient church before the services began. It was well. He caught Elena's eye, two soldiers down the row from himself, and smiled reassuringly, as if he and not she were the veteran. She did not smile back.

He probed his strategy as the techs did their systems. The Oseran payroll was divided into two parts. The first was an electronic transfer payment of Pelian funds into an Useran account in the Pelian capital, out of which the Oseran fleet purchased local supplies. Miles's special plan was for that. The second half was in assorted galactic currencies, primarily Betan dollars. This was the cash profit, to be divided among Oser's captain-owners to carry out of Tau Verde local space to their various destinations when their contracts at last expired. It was delivered monthly to Oser's flagship on its blockade station. Miles corrected his thought with a small grin—*had* been delivered monthly.

They had taken the first cash payroll in midspace with devastating ease. Half of Miles's troops were Oserans, after all; several had even done the duty before. Presenting themselves to the Pelian courier as the Oseran pick-up had required only the slightest of adjustments in codes and procedures. They were done and far out of range before the real Oserans arrived. The transcript of the subsequent dispatches between the Pelian courier and the Oseran pick-up ship was a treasure for Miles. He kept it stored atop Bothari's coffin in his cabin, beside his grandfather's dagger. *More to come, Sergeant,* he thought. *I swear it.*

The second operation, two weeks later, had been crude by comparison, a slugging match between the new, more heavily-armed Pelian courier and Miles's three warships. Miles had prudently stepped aside and let Tung direct it, confining his comments to an occasional approving "Ah." They gave up maneuvering to board upon the approach of four Oseran ships. The Oserans were taking no chances with this delivery.

The Dendarii had blasted the Pelian and its precious cargo into its component atoms, and fled. The Pelians had fought bravely. Miles burned them a death-offering that night in his cabin, very privately.

Arde connected Miles's left shoulder joint, and began to run through the checklist of rotational movements of all the joints from shoulder to fingertips. His ring finger was running about 20% weak. Arde opened the pressure plate under his left wrist and pinned the tiny power-up control.

His strategy . . . By the third attempted hijacking, it was clear the enemy was learning from experience. Oser sent a convoy practically to the planet's atmosphere for the pick-up. Miles's ships, hovering out of range, had been unable to even get near. Miles was forced to use his ace-in-the-hole.

Tung had raised his eyebrows when Miles asked him to send a simple paper message to his former communications officer. "Please cooperate with all Dendarii requests," it read, signed, meaninglessly to the Eurasian, with the Vorkosigan seal concealed in the hilt of Miles's grandfather's dagger. The communications officer had been a fountain of intelligence ever since. Bad, to so endanger one of Captain Illyan's operatives, worse to risk their best eye in the Oseran fleet. If the Oserans ever figured out who had microwaved the money, the man's life was surely forfeit. To date, though, the Oserans held only four packing cases of ashes and a mystery.

Miles felt a slight change in gravity and vibration; they must be moving into attack formation. Time to get his helmet on, and make contact with Tung and Auson in the tactics room. Elena's tech fitted her helmet. She opened her faceplate, spoke to the tech; they collaborated on some minor adjustment.

If Baz was keeping his schedule, this was surely Miles's last chance with her. With the engineer out of the way, there was no one to usurp his hero's role. The next rescue would be his. He pictured himself, blasting menacing Pelians right and left, pulling her out of some tactical hole—the details were vague. She would have to believe he loved her then. His tongue would magically untangle, he'd finally find the right words after so many wrong ones, her snowy skin would warm in the heat of his ardor and bloom again . . .

Her face, framed by her helmet, was cold, austere in profile, the same blank winter landscape she had exhibited to the world since Bothari's death. Her lack of reaction worried Miles. True, she had had her Dendarii duties to distract her, keep her moving—not like the self-indulgent luxury of his own withdrawal. At least with Elena Visconti gone, she was spared those awkward meetings in the corridors and conference rooms, both women pretending fiercely to cold professionalism.

Elena stretched in her armor, and gazed pensively into the black hole of her plasma arc muzzle built into the right arm of her suit. She slipped on her glove, covering the blue veins like pale rivers of ice in her wrist. Her eyes made Miles think of razors.

He stepped to her shoulder, and waved away her tech. The words he spoke weren't any of the dozens he had rehearsed for the occasion. He lowered his voice to whisper.

"I know all about suicide. Don't think you can fool me."

She started, and flushed. Frowned at him in fierce scorn. Snapped her faceplate shut.

Forgive, whispered his anguished thought to her. It is necessary.

Arde lowered Miles's helmet over his head, connected his control leads, checked the connections. A lacework of fire netted, knotted, and tangled in Miles's gut. Damn, but it was getting hard to ignore.

He checked his comm link with the tactics room. "Commodore Tung? Naismith here. Roll the vids." The inside of his faceplate blurred with color, duplicate readouts of the tactics room telemetry for the field commander. Only communications, no servo links this time. The captured Pelian armor had none, and the old Oseran armor was all safely on manual override. Just in case somebody else out there was learning from experience.

"Last chance to change your mind," Tung said over the comm link, continuing the old argument. "Sure you wouldn't rather attack the Oserans after the transfer, farther from the Pelian bases? Our intelligence on them is so much more detailed . . ."

"No! We have to capture or destroy the payroll before the delivery. Taking it after is strategically useless."

"Not entirely. We could sure use the money."

And how, Miles reflected glumly. It would soon take scientific notation to register his debt to the Dendarii. A mercenary fleet could hardly burn money faster if the ships ran on steam power and the funds were shoveled directly into their furnaces. Never had one so little owed so much to so many, and it grew worse by the hour. His stomach oozed around his abdominal cavity like a tortured amoeba, throwing out pseudopods of pain and the vacuole of an acid belch. You are a psychosomatic illusion, Miles assured it.

The assault group formed up and marched to the waiting shuttles. Miles moved among them, trying to touch each person, call them by name, give them some personal word; they seemed to like that. He ordered their ranks in his mind, and wondered how many gaps there would be when this day's work was done. Forgive . . . He had run out of clever solutions. This one was to be done the old hard way, head-on.

They moved through the shuttle hatch corridors into the waiting shuttle. This must surely be the worst part, waiting helplessly for Tung to deliver them like cartons of eggs, as fragile, as messy when broken. He took a deep breath, and prepared to cope with the usual effects of zero-gee.

He was totally unprepared for the cramp that doubled him over, snatched his breath away, drained his face to a paper-whiteness. Not like this, it had never come on like this before—. He redoubled into a ball, gasping, lost his grasp on his grip-strap, floated free. Dear God, it was finally happening—the ultimate humiliation—he was going to throw up in a space suit. In moments, everyone would know of his hilarious weakness. Absurd, for a would-be Imperial officer to get space-sick. Absurd, absurd, he had always been absurd. He had barely the presence of mind to hit his ventilator controls to full power with a jerk of his chin, and kill his broadcast—no need to treat his mercenaries to the unedifying sound of their commander retching.

"Admiral Naismith?" came an inquiry from the tactics room. "Your medical readouts look odd—telemetry check requested."

The universe seemed to narrow to his belly. A wrenching rush, gagging and coughing, another, another. The ventilator could not keep up. He'd eaten nothing this day, where was it all coming from?

A mercenary pulled him out of the air, tried to help him straighten his clenched limbs. "Admiral Naismith? Are you all right?"

He opened Miles's faceplate, to Miles's gasp of "No! Not in here—"

"Son-of-a-bitch!" The man jumped back, and raised his voice to a piercing cry. "Medtech!"

You're overreacting, Miles tried to say; I'll clean it up myself . . . Dark clots, scarlet droplets, shimmering crimson globules, floated past his confused eyes, his secret spilled. It appeared to be pure blood. "No," he whimpered, or tried to. "Not *now* . . ."

Hands grasped him, passed him back to the shuttle hatch he had entered moments before. Gravity pressed him to the corridor deck—who the devil had upped it to three-gee?—hands pulled his helmet off, plucked at his carefully-donned carapace. He felt like a lobster supper. His belly wrung itself out again.

Elena's face, nearly as white as his now, circled above him. She knelt, tore off her servo glove and gripped his hand, flesh to flesh at last. "Miles!"

Truth is what you make it . . . "Commander Bothari!" he croaked, as loud as he could. A ring of frightened faces huddled around him. His Dendarii. His people. For them, then. All for them. All. "Take over."

"I can't!" Her face was pale with shock, terrified. God, Miles thought, I must look just like Bothari, spilling his guts. It's not that bad, he tried to tell her. Silver-black whorls sparkled in his vision, blotting out her face. No! Not yet—

"Leige-lady. You can. You must. I'll be with you." He writhed, gripped by some sadistic giant. "You are true Vor, not I . . . Must have been changelings, back there in those replicators." He gave her a death's head grin. "Forward momentum—"

She rose then, determination crowding out the hot terror in her face, the ice that had run like water transmuted to marble.

"Right, my lord," she whispered. And more loudly, "Right! Get back there, let the medtechs do their job—" she drove away his admirers. He was flipped efficiently onto a float pallet.

He watched his booted feet, dark and distant hillocks, waver before him as he was borne aloft. Feet first, it would have to be feet first. He barely felt the prick of the first I.V. in his arm. He heard Elena's voice, raised tremblingly behind him.

"All right you clowns! No more games. We're going to win this one for Admiral Naismith!"

Heroes. They sprang up around him like weeds. A carrier, he was seemingly unable to catch the disease he spread.

"Damn it," he moaned. "Damn it, damn it, damn it. . ." He repeated this litany like a mantra, until the medtech's second sedative injection parted him from his pain, frustration, and consciousness.

CHAPTER SEVENTEEN   ✱   ✱   ✱

He wandered in and out of reality, like being lost in the Imperial Residence when he was a boy, trying various doors, some leading to treasures, others to broom closets, but none to familiarity. Once he awoke to Tung, sitting beside him, and worried about it; shouldn't the mercenary be in the tactics room?

Tung eyed him with affectionate concern. "You know, son, if you're going to last in this business, you have to learn to pace yourself. We almost lost you there."

It sounded like a good dictum; perhaps he'd have it calligraphed for the wall of his bedroom.

Another time, Elena. How had she come to sickbay? He'd left her in the shuttle. Nothing stayed where you put it . . .

"Damn it," he mumbled apologetically, "things like this never happened to Vorthalia the Bold."

She raised a thoughtful eyebrow. "How do you know? The histories of those times were all written by minstrels and poets. You try and think of a word that rhymes with 'bleeding ulcer'."

He was still dutifully trying when the greyness swallowed him again.

Once, he woke alone and called over and over for Sergeant Bothari, but the Sergeant didn't come. It's just like the man, he thought petulantly, underfoot all the time and then gone on long leave just when he needed him. The medtech's sedative ended that bout with consciousness, not in Miles's favor.

It was an allergic reaction to the sedative, the surgeon told him later. His grandfather came, and smothered him with a pillow, and tried to hide him under the bed. Bothari, bloody-chested, and the mercenary pilot officer, his implant wires somehow turned inside out and waving about his head like some strange brachiated coral, watched. His mother came at last and shooed away the deadly ghosts like a farm wife clucking to her chickens. "Quick," she advised Miles, "calculate the value of e to the last decimal place, and the spell will be broken. You can do it in your head if you're Betan enough."

Miles waited eagerly all day for his father, in this parade of hallucinatory figures; he had done something extremely clever, although he could not quite remember what, and he ached for a chance at last to impress the Count. But his father never came. Miles wept with disappointment.

Other shadows came and went, the medtech, the surgeon, Elena and Tung, Auson and Thorne, Arde Mayhew, but they were distant, figures reflected on lead glass. After he had cried for a long time, he slept.

When he woke again, the little private room off the sickbay of the *Triumph* was clear and unwavering in outline, but Ivan Vorpatril sat beside his bed.

"Other people" Miles groaned, "get to hallucinate orgies and giant cicadas and things. What do I get? Relatives. I can see relatives when I'm conscious. It's not fair . . ."

Ivan turned worriedly to Elena, who was perched on the end of the bed. "I thought the surgeon said the antidote would have cleared him out by now."

Elena rose, and bent over Miles in concern, long white fingers across his brow. "Miles? Can you hear me?"

"Of course I can hear you." He suddenly realized the absence of another sensation. "Hey! My stomach doesn't hurt."

"Yes, the surgeon blocked off some nerves during the

repair operation. You should be completely healed up inside within a couple of weeks."

"Operation?" He attempted a surreptitious peek down the shapeless garment he seemed to be occupying, looking for he knew not what. His torso seemed to be as smooth, or lumpy, as ever, no important body parts accidently snipped off—"I don't see any dotted lines."

"He didn't cut. It was all shoving things down your gullet, and hand-tractor work, except for installing the biochip on your vagus nerve. A bit grotesque, but very ingenious."

"How long was I out?"

"Three days. You were—"

"Three days! The payroll raid—Baz—" he lunged convulsively upward; Elena pushed him back down firmly.

"We took the payroll. Baz is back, with his whole group. Everything's fine, except for you almost bleeding to death."

"Nobody dies of ulcers. Baz back? Where are we, anyway?"

"Docked at the refinery. I didn't think you could die of ulcers either, but the surgeons says holes in your body with blood pouring out are the same whether they're on the inside or the outside, so I guess you can. You'll get a full report—" she pushed him back down again, looking exasperated, "but I thought you'd better see Ivan privately first, without all the Dendarii standing around."

"Uh, right." He stared in bewilderment at his big cousin. Ivan was dressed in civilian gear, Barrayaran-style trousers, a Betan shirt, but Barrayaran regulation Service boots.

"Do you want to feel me, to see if I'm real?" Ivan asked cheerfully.

"It wouldn't do any good, you can feel hallucinations, too. Touch them, smell them, hear them ..." Miles shivered. "I'll take your word for it. But Ivan—what are you doing here?"

"Looking for you."

"Did Father send you?"

"I don't know."

"How can you not know?"

"Well, he didn't talk to me personally—look, are you sure Captain Dimir hasn't arrived yet, or got any messages to you, or anything? He had all the dispatches and secret orders and things."

"Who?"

"Captain Dimir. He's my commanding officer."

"Never heard of him. Or from him."

"I think he works out of Captain Illyan's department," Ivan added helpfullly. "Elena thought you might have heard something that you didn't have time to mention, maybe."

"No . . ."

"I don't understand it," sighed Ivan. "They left Beta Colony a day ahead of me in an Imperial fast courier. They should have been here a week ago."

"How was it you travelled separately?"

Ivan cleared his throat. "Well, there was this girl, you see, on Beta Colony. She invited me home—I mean, Miles, a Betan! I met her right there in the shuttleport, practically the first thing. Wearing one of those sporty little sarongs, and nothing else—" Ivan's hands were beginning to wave in dreamy discriptive curves; Miles hastened to cut off what he knew could be a lengthy digression.

"Probably trolling for galactics. Some Betans collect them. Like a Barrayaran getting banners of all the provinces." Ivan had such a collection at home, Miles recalled. "So what happened to this Captain Dimir?"

"They left without me." Ivan looked aggrieved. "And I wasn't even late!"

"How did you get here?"

"Lieutenant Croye reported you'd gone to Tau Verde IV. So I hitched a ride with a merchant vessel bound for one of those neutral countries down there. The Captain dropped me off here at this refinery."

Miles's jaw dropped. "Hitched—dropped you off—do you realize the risks—"

Ivan blinked. "She was very nice about it. Er—motherly, you know."

Elena studied the ceiling, coolly disdainful. "That pat on the ass she gave you in the shuttle tube didn't look exactly maternal to me."

Ivan reddened."Anyway, I got here." He brightened. "And ahead of old Dimir! Maybe I won't be in as much trouble as I thought."

Miles ran his hands through his hair. "Ivan—would it be too much trouble to begin at the beginning? Assuming there is one."

"Oh, yeah, I guess you wouldn't know about the big flap."

"Flap? Ivan, you're the first word we've had from home since we left Beta Colony. The blockade, you know—although you seem to have passed through it like so much smoke . . ."

"The old bird was clever, I'll give her that. I never knew older women could—"

"The flap," Miles rerouted him urgently.

"Yes. Well. The first report we had at home, from Beta Colony, was that you had been kidnapped by some fellow who was a deserter from the Service—"

"Oh, ye gods! Mother—what did Father—"

"They were pretty worried, I guess, but your mother kept saying that Bothari was with you, and anyway somebody at the Embassy finally thought to talk with your Grandmother Naismith, and she didn't think you'd been kidnapped at all. That calmed your mother down a lot, and she, um, sat on your father—anyway, they decided to wait for further reports."

"Thank God."

"Well, the next reports were from some military agent here in Tau Verde local space. Nobody would tell me what was in them—well, nobody would tell my mother, I guess, which make sense when you think about it. But Captain Illyan was running in circles between Vorkosigan House and General Headquarters and the Imperial Residence and Vorhartung Castle twenty-six hours a day for while. It didn't help that all the information they got was three weeks out of date, either—"

"Vorhartung Castle?" murmured Miles in surprise. "What does the Council of Counts have to do with this?"

"I couldn't figure it either. But Count Henri Vorvolk was pulled out of class at the Academy three times to attend secret committee sessions at the Counts, so I cornered him—seems there was some fantastic rumor going around that you were in Tau Verde local space building up your own mercenary fleet, nobody knew why—at least, I thought it was a fantastic rumor—" Ivan stared around at the little sickbay cubicle, at the ship it implied. "Anyway, your father and Captain Illyan finally decided to send a fast courier to investigate."

"Via Beta Colony, I gather. Ah—did you happen to run across a fellow named Tav Calhoun while you were there?"

"Oh, yeah, the crazy Betan. He hangs around the Barrayaran Embassy—he has a warrant for your arrest, which he waves at whoever he can catch going in or out. The guards won't let him in anymore."

"Did you actually talk to him?"

"Briefly. I told him there was a rumor you'd gone to Kshatryia."

"Really?"

"Of course not. But it was the farthest place I could think of. The clan," Ivan said smugly, "should stick together."

"Thanks . . ." Miles mulled this over, "I think." He sighed. "I guess the best thing to do is wait for your Captain Dimir, then. He might at least be able to give us a ride home, which would solve one problem." He looked up at his cousin. "I'll explain it all later, but I have to know some things now—can you keep your mouth shut a while? Nobody here is supposed to know who I really am." A horrid thought shook Miles. "You haven't been going around asking for me by name, have you?"

"No, no, just Miles Naismith," Ivan assured him. "We knew you were traveling with your Betan passport. Anyway, I just got here last night, and practically the first person I met was Elena."

Miles breathed relief, and turned to Elena. "You say Baz is out there? I've got to see him."

She nodded, and withdrew, walking a wide circle around Ivan.

"Sorry to hear about old Bothari," Ivan offered when she'd left. "Who'd have thought he could do himself in cleaning weapons after all these years? Still, there's a bright side—you've finally got a chance to make time with Elena, without him breathing down your neck. So it's not a dead loss."

Miles exhaled carefully, faint with rage and reminded grief. *He does not know*, he told himself. *He cannot know* . . . "Ivan, one of these days somebody is going to pull out a weapon and plug you, and you're going to die in bewilderment, crying, 'What did I say? What did I say?'"

"What did I say?" asked Ivan indignantly.

Before Miles could go into detail, Baz entered, flanked by Tung and Auson, Elena trailing. The chamber was jammed. They all seemed to be grinning like loons. Baz waved some plastic flimsies triumphantly in the air. He was lit like a beacon with pride, scarcely recognizable as the man Miles had found five months ago cowering in a garbage heap.

"The surgeon says we can't stay long, my lord," he said to Miles, "but I thought these might do for a get-well wish."

Ivan started slightly at the honorific, and stared covertly at the engineer.

Miles took the sheets of printing. "Your mission—were you able to complete it?"

"Like clockwork—well, not exactly, there were some bad moments in a train station—you should see the rail system they have on Tau Verde IV. The engineering— magnificent. Barrayar missed something by going from horseback straight to air transport—"

"The *mission*, Baz!"

The engineer beamed. "Take a look. Those are the transcripts of the latest dispatches between Admiral Oser and the Pelian high command."

Miles began to read. After a time, he began to smile. "Yes . . . I'd understood Admiral Oser had a remarkable command of invective when, er, roused . . ." Miles's gaze crossed Tung's, blandly. Tung's eyes glinted with satisfaction.

Ivan craned his neck. "What are they? Elena told me about your payroll heists—I take it you managed to mess up their electronic transfer, too. But I don't understand—won't the Pelians just re-pay, when they find the Oseran fleet wasn't credited?"

Miles's grin became quite wolfish. "Ah, but they *were* credited—eight times over. And now, as I believe a certain Earth general once said, God has delivered them into my hand. After failing four times in a row to deliver their cash payment, the Pelians have demanded the electronic overpayment be returned. And Oser," Miles glanced at the flimsies, "is refusing. Emphatically. That was the trickiest part, calculating just the right amount of overpayment. Too little, and the Pelians might have just let it go. Too much, and even Oser would have felt bound to return it. But just the right amount . . ." he sighed, and cuddled back happily into his pillow. He would have to commit some of Oser's choicest phrases to memory, he decided. They were unique.

"You'll like this, then, Admiral Naismith." Auson, bursting with news, erupted at last. "Four of Oser's independent Captain-owners took their ships and jumped out of Tau Verde local space in the last two days. From the transmissions we intercepted, I don't think they'll be coming back, either."

"Glorious," breathed Miles. "Oh, well done . . ."

He looked to Elena. Pride there, too, strong enough even to nudge out some of the pain in her eyes. "As I thought—intercepting that fourth payroll was vital to the success of the strategy. Well done, Commander Bothari."

She glowed back at him, hesitantly. "We missed you. We—took lot of casualties."

"I anticipated we would. The Pelians had to be laying for us, by then." He glanced at Tung, who was making a small shushing gesture at Elena. "Was it much worse than we'd calculated?"

Tung shook his head. "There were moments when I was ready to swear she didn't know she was beaten.

There are certain situations into which you do not ask mercenaries to follow you—"

"I didn't ask anyone to follow me," said Elena. "They came on their own." She added in a whispered aside to Miles, "I just thought that was what boarding battles were like. I didn't know it wasn't supposed to be that bad."

Tung spoke to Miles's alarmed look. "We would have paid a higher price if she hadn't insisted you'd put her in charge and refused to withdraw when I ordered. Then we would have paid much for nothing—that ratio works out to infinity, I believe." Tung gave Elena a nod of judicious approval, which she returned gravely. Ivan looked rather stunned.

A low-voiced argument penetrated from the corridor; Thorne, and the surgeon. Thorne was saying, "You've got to. This is vital—"

Thorne towed the protesting surgeon into the cubicle. "Admiral Naismith! Commodore Tung! Oser's *here*!"

"What!"

"With his whole fleet—what's left of it—they're just out of range. He's asking permission to dock his flagship."

"That can't be!" said Tung. "Who's guarding the wormhole?"

"Yes, exactly!" cried Thorne. "Who?" They stared at each other in elated, wild surmise.

Miles sprang to his feet, fought off a wave of dizziness, clutched his gown behind him. "Get my clothes," he enunciated.

Hawk-like, Miles decided, was the word for Admiral Oser. Greying hair, a beak of a nose, a bright, penetrating stare, fixed now on Miles. He had mastered the look that makes junior officers search their consciences, Miles thought. He stood up under it, and gave the real mercenary Admiral a slow smile, there in the docking bay. The sharp, cold, recycled air was bitter in his nostrils, like a stimulant. You could get high on it, surely.

Oser was flanked by three of his Captain-employees and two of his Captain-owners, and their seconds. Miles trailed the whole Dendarii staff, Elena on his right hand, Baz on his left.

Oser looked him up and down. "Damn," he murmured. "Damn . . ." He did not offer his hand, but stood and spoke; deliberate, rehearsed cadences.

"Since the day you entered Tau Verde local space, I've felt your presence. In the Felicians, in the tactical situation turning under me, in the faces of my own men—" his glance passed over Tung, who smiled sweetly, "even in the Pelians. We have been grappling in the dark, we two, at a distance, long enough."

Miles's eyes widened. My God, is Oser about to challenge me to single combat? Sergeant Bothari, help! He jerked his chin up, and said nothing.

"I don't believe in prolonging agonies," said Oser. "Rather than watch you enspell the rest of my fleet man by man—while I still possess a fleet to offer—I understand the Dendarii Mercenaries are looking for recruits."

It took Miles a moment to realize he had just heard one of the most stiff-necked surrender speeches in history. *Gracious. We are going to be gracious as hell, oh, yes . . .* He held out his hand; Oser took it.

"Admiral Oser, your understanding is acute. There's a private chamber, where we can work out the details. . ."

General Halify and some Felician officers were watching at a distance from a balcony overlooking the docking bay. Miles's glance crossed Halify's. *And so my word to you, at least, is redeemed.*

Miles marched across the broad expanse, the whole herd, all Dendarii now, strung out behind him. Let's see, Miles thought, the Pied Piper of Hamlin led all the rats into the river—he looked back—and all the children he led to a mountain of gold. What would he have done if the rats and the children had been inextricably mixed?

CHAPTER EIGHTEEN   ✳   ✳   ✳

Miles reclined on a liquid-filled settee in the refinery's darkside observation chamber, hands behind his head, and stared into the depths of a space no longer empty. The Dendarii fleet glittered and winked, riding at station in the vacuum, a constellation of ships and men.

In his bedroom at the summer place at Vorkosigan Surleau, he had owned a mobile of space warships, classic Barrayaran military craft held in their carefully balanced arrangement by nearly invisible threads of great tensile strength. Invisible threads. He pursed his lips, and blew a puff of breath toward the crystalline windows as if he might set the Dendarii ships circling and dancing.

Nineteen ships of war and over 3000 troops and techs. "Mine," he said experimentally. "All mine." The phrase did not produce a suitable feeling of triumph. He felt more like a target.

In the first place, it was not true. The actual ownership of those millions of Betan dollars worth of capital equipment out there was a matter of amazing complexity. It had taken four solid days of negotiations to work out the "details" he had so casually waved his hand over in the docking bay. There were eight independent captain-owners, in addition to Oser's personal possession of eight ships. Almost all had creditors. At least ten percent of "his" fleet turned out to be owned by the

First Bank of Jackson's Whole, famous for its numbered accounts and discreet services; for all Miles knew, he was now contributing to the support of gambling rackets, industrial espionage, and the white slave trade from one end of the wormhole nexus to the other. It seemed he was not so much the possessor of the Dendarii mercenaries as he was their chief employee.

The ownership of the *Ariel* and the *Triumph* was made particularly complex by Miles's capture of them in battle. Tung had owned his ship outright, but Auson had been deeply in debt to yet another Jackson's Whole lending institution for the *Ariel*. Oser, when still working for the Pelians, had stopped payments after its capture, and left the, what was it called?—Luigi Bharaputra and Sons Household Finance and Holding Company of Jackson's Whole Private Limited—to collect on its insurance, if any. Captain Auson had turned pale upon learning that an inquiry agent from said company would be arriving soon to investigate.

The inventory alone was enough to boggle Miles's mind, and when it came to the assorted personnel contracts—his stomach would hurt if it still could. Before Oser had arrived, the Dendarii had been due for a tidy profit from the Felician contract. Now the profit for 200 must be spread to support 3000.

Or more than 3000. The Dendarii kept ballooning. Another free ship had arrived through the wormhole just yesterday, having heard of them through God-knew-what rumor mill, and excited would-be recruits from Felice managed to turn up with each new ship from the planet. The metals refinery was operating as a refinery again, as control of local space fell into the hands of the Felicians; their forces were even now gobbling up Pelian installations all over the system.

There was talk of re-hiring to Felice, to blockade the wormhole in turn for the former underdogs. The phrase, "Quit while you're winning," popped unbidden into Miles's mind whenever this subject came up; the proposal secretly appalled him. He itched to be gone from here before the whole house of cards collapsed. He should be keeping reality and fantasy separate in his own mind, at least, even while mixing them as much as possible in others.

Voices whispered from the catwalk, reflected to his ear by some accident of acoustics. Elena's alto captured his attention.

"You don't have to ask him. We're not on Barrayar, we're never going back to Barrayar—"

"But it will be like having a little piece of Barrayar to take with us," Baz's voice, gentle and amused as Miles had never heard it, followed. "A breath of home in airless places. God knows I can't give you much of that 'right and proper' your father wanted for you, but all the pittance I can command shall be yours."

"Mm." Her response was unenthusiastic, almost hostile. All references to Bothari seemed to fall on her like hammer blows to dead flesh these days, a muffled thud that sickened Miles but brought no response from Elena herself.

They emerged from the catwalk, Baz close behind her. He smiled at his liege-lord in shy triumph. Elena smiled too, but not with her eyes.

"Deep meditation?" she inquired lightly. "It looks more like staring out the window and biting your nails to me."

He struggled upright, causing the settee to slither under him, and responded in kind. "Oh, I just told the guard that to keep the tourists out. I actually came up here for a nap."

Baz grinned at Miles. "My lord. I understand, in the absence of other relations, that Elena's legal guardianship has fallen to you."

"Why—so it has. I haven't had much time to think about it, to tell you the truth." Miles stirred uneasily at this turn in the conversation, not quite sure just what was coming.

"Right. Then as her liege-lord and guardian, I formally request her hand in marriage. Not to mention the rest of her." His silly smile made Miles long to kick him in the teeth. "Oh, and as my liege-commander, I request your permission to marry, uh, 'that my sons may serve you, lord.' " Baz's abbreviated version of the formula was only slightly scrambled.

You're not going to have any sons, because I'm going to chop your balls off, you lamb-stealing, double-crossing, traitorous—he got control of himself before his emotion showed as more than a drawn, lipless grin. "I see. There—there are some difficulties." He marshalled logical argument like a shield-wall, protecting his craven, naked rage from the sting of those two honest pairs of brown eyes.

"Elena is quite young, of course—" he abandoned that line at the ire that lit her eye, as her lips formed the soundless word, You—!

"More to the point, I gave my own word to Sergeant Bothari to perform three services for him in the event of his death. To bury him on Barrayar, to see Elena betrothed with all correct ceremony, and, ah—to see her married to a suitable officer of the Barrayaran Imperial Service. Would you see me forsworn?"

Baz looked as stunned as if Miles had kicked him. His mouth opened, closed, opened again. "But—aren't I your leige-sworn Armsman? That's certainly the equal of an Imperial officer—hell, the Sergeant was an Armsman himself! Has—has my service been unsatisfactory? Tell me how I have failed you, my lord, that I may correct it!" His astonishment turned to genuine distress.

"You haven't failed me," Miles's conscience jerked the words from his mouth. "Uh . . . But of course, you've only served me for four months, now. Really a very short time, although I know it seems much longer, so much has happened . . ." Miles floundered, feeling more than crippled; legless. Elena's furious glower had chopped him off at the knees. How much shorter could he afford to get in her eyes? He trailed off weakly. "This is all very sudden . . ."

Elena's voice dropped to a gravelled register of rage. "How dare you—" her voice burst in her indrawn breath like a wave, formed again, "What do you owe—what can anybody owe *that*?" she asked, referring, Miles realized, to the Sergeant. "I was not his chattel and I am not yours, either. Dog in the manger— "

Baz's hand closed anxiously on her arm, stemming the breakers crashing across Miles. "Elena—maybe this isn't the best time to bring it up. Maybe later would be better." He glanced at Miles's stony face, and winced, confusion in his eyes.

"Baz, you're not going to take this seriously—"

"Come away. We'll talk about it."

She forced her voice back to its normal timbre. "I'll meet you at the bottom of the catwalk. In a minute."

Miles nodded a dismissal to Baz for emphasis.

"Well . . ." the engineer left, walking slowly, and looking back over his shoulder in worry.

They waited, by unspoken agreement, until the soft sound of his steps had gone. When she turned, the anger in her eyes had been displaced by pleading.

"Don't you see, Miles? This is my chance to walk away from it all. Start new, fresh and clean, somewhere else. As far away as possible."

He shook his head. He'd have fallen to his knees if he'd thought it would do any good. "How can I give you up? You're the mountains and the lake, the memories—you have them all. When you're with me, I'm at home, wherever I am."

"If Barrayar was my right arm, I'd take a plasma arc and burn it off. Your father and mother knew what he was all the time, and yet they sheltered him. What are they, then?"

"The Sergeant was doing all right—doing well, even, until . . . You were to be his expiation, don't you see it—"

"What, a sacrifice for his sins? Am I to form myself into the pattern of a perfect Barrayaran maiden like trying to work a magic spell for absolution? I could spend my whole life working out that ritual and not come to the end of it, damn it!"

"Not the sacrifice," he tried to tell her. "The altar, perhaps."

"Bah!" She began to pace, leopardess on a short chain. Her emotional wounds seemed to work themselves open and bleed before his eyes. He ached to staunch them.

"Don't you see," he launched himself again, passionate

with conviction, "you'd do better with me. Acting or reacting, we carry him in us. You can't walk away from him any more than I can. Whether you travel toward or away, he'll be the compass. He'll be the glass, full of subtle colors and astigmatisms, through which all new things will be viewed. I too have a father who haunts me, and I know."

She was shaken, and shaking. "You make me," she stated, "feel quite ill."

As she stalked away, Ivan Vorpatril emerged from the catwalk. "Ah, there you are, Miles."

Ivan circled warily around Elena as they passed, his hands moving in an unconscious protective gesture toward his crotch. One corner of Elena's mouth turned venomously upward, and she tilted her head in a polite nod. He acknowledged the greeting with a fixed and nervous smile. So much, thought Miles sadly, for his chivalrous plans to protect Elena from Ivan's unwanted attentions.

Ivan settled himself beside Miles with a sigh. "Have you heard anything from Captain Dimir yet?"

"Not a thing. Are you sure they were coming to Tau Verde, and not suddenly ordered somewhere else? I don't see how a fast courier could be two weeks late."

"Oh, God," said Ivan, "do you think that's possible? I'm going to be in so much trouble—"

"I don't know." Miles tried to assuage his alarm. "Your original orders were to find me, and so far you're the only one who seems to have succeeded in carrying them out. Mention that, when you ask Father to get you off the hook."

"Ha," muttered his cousin. "What's the use of living with a system of inherited power if you can't have a little nepotism now and then? Miles, your father doesn't do favors for *anybody*." He gazed out at the Dendarii fleet, and added elliptically, "That's impressive, y'know?"

Miles was insensibly cheered. "Do you really think so?" He added facetiously, "Do you want to join? It seems to be the hot new fashion around here."

Ivan chuckled. "No, thanks. I have no desire to diet for the Emperor. Vorloupulous's law, y'know."

Miles's smile died on his lips. Ivan's chuckle drained away like something going down the sink. They stared at each other in stunned silence.

"Oh, *shit* . . ." said Miles at last. "I forgot about Vorloupulous's law. It never even crossed my mind."

"Surely nobody could interpret this as raising a private army," Ivan reassured him feebly. "Not proper livery and maintenance. I mean, they're not leige-sworn to you or anything—are they?"

"Only Baz and Arde," said Miles. "I don't know how Barrayaran law would interpret a mercenary contract. They're not for life, after all—unless you happen to be killed . . ."

"Who is that Baz fellow, anyway?" asked Ivan. "He seems to be your right-hand man."

"I couldn't have done this without him. He was an Imperial Service engineer, before he—" Miles choked himself off, "quit." Miles tried to guess what the laws might be about harboring deserters. He hadn't, after all, originally intended to be caught doing so. Upon reflection, his nebulous plan for returning home with Baz and begging his father to arrange some sort of pardon began to feel more and more like a man falling from an aircraft making plans to land on that soft fluffy cloud rushing up below him. What looked solid at a distance might well turn to fog at closer range.

Miles glanced at Ivan. Then he gazed at Ivan. Then he stared at Ivan. Ivan blinked back in innocent inquiry. There was something about that cheerful, frank face that made Miles hideously uneasy.

"You know," Miles said at last, "the more I think about your being here, the weirder it seems."

"Don't you believe it," said Ivan. "I had to work for my passage. That old bird was the most insatiable—"

"I don't mean your getting here—I mean your being sent in the first place. Since when do they pull first-year cadets out of class and send them on Security missions?"

"I don't know. I assumed they wanted somebody who could identify the body or something."

"Yes, but they've got almost enough medical data on me to build a new one. That idea only makes sense if you don't think about it too hard."

"Look, when a General Staff Admiral calls a cadet in the middle of the night and says go, you go. You don't stop to debate with him. He wouldn't appreciate it."

"Well—what did your recorded orders say?"

"Come to think of it, I never saw my recorded orders. I assumed Admiral Hessman must have given them to Captain Dimir personally."

Miles decided his uneasiness stemmed from the number of times the phrase "I assumed" was turning up in this conversation. There was something else—he almost had it . . . "Hessman? Hessman gave you your orders?"

"In person," Ivan said proudly.

"Hessman doesn't have anything to do with either Intelligence or Security. He's in charge of Procurement. Ivan, this is getting screwier and screwier."

"An Admiral is an Admiral."

"This Admiral is on my father's shit list, though. For one thing, he's Count Vordrozda's pipeline to Imperial Service Headquarters, and Father hates his officers getting involved in party politics. Father also suspects him of peculating Service funds, some kind of sleight-of-hand in shipbuilding contracts. At the time I left home, he was itchy enough to put Captain Illyan on it personally, and you know he wouldn't waste Illyan's talents on anything minor."

"All that's way over my head. I've got enough problems with navigational math."

"It shouldn't be over your head. Oh, as a cadet, sure but you're also Lord Vorpatril. If anything happened to me, you'd inherit the Countship of our district from my father."

"God forbid," said Ivan. "I want to be an officer, and travel around, and pick up girls. Not chase around through those mountains trying to collect taxes from homicidal illiterates and keep chicken-stealing cases from turning into minor guerilla wars. No insult intended, but your district is the most intractable on Barrayar. Miles, there are people back behind Dendarii Gorge who live in *caves*." Ivan shuddered. "And they *like* it."

"There are some great caves back there," Miles agreed. "Gorgeous colors when you get the right light on the rock formations." Homesick remembrance twinged through him.

"Well, if I ever inherit a Countship, I'm praying it will be of a city," Ivan concluded.

"You're not in line for any I can think of," grinned Miles. He tried to recapture the thread of their conversation, but Ivan's remarks made lines of inheritance map themselves in his head. He traced his own descent through his Grandmother Vorkosigan to Prince Xav to Emperor Dorca Vorbarra himself. Had the great Emperor ever forseen what a turn his law, that finally broke the private armies and the private wars of the Counts forever, would give his great-great-grandson?

"Who's your heir, Ivan?" Miles asked idly, staring out at the Dendarii ships, but dreaming of the Dendarii Mountains. "Lord Vortaine, isn't it?"

"Yeah, but I expect to outlive the old boy any minute. His health wasn't too good, last I heard. Too bad this inheritance thing doesn't work backwards, I'd be in for a bundle."

"Who does get his bundle?"

"His daughter, I guess. His titles go to—let me think— Count Vordrozda, who doesn't even need 'em. From what I've heard of Vordrozda, he'd rather have the money. Don't know if he'd go as far as marrying the daughter to get it, though, she's about fifty years old."

They both gazed into space.

"God," said Ivan after a while, "I hope those orders Dimir got when I ducked out weren't to go home or something. They'll think I've been AWOL for three weeks—there won't be enough room on my record for all the demerits. Thank God they've eliminated the old-style discipline parades."

"You were there when Dimir got his orders? And you didn't stick around to see what they were?" asked Miles, astonished.

"It was like pulling teeth to get that pass out of him. I

didn't want to risk it. There was this girl, you see—I wish now I'd taken my beeper."

"You left your comm link?"

"There was this girl—I really did almost really forget it. But he was opening the stuff by then, and I didn't want to go back in and get nabbed."

Miles shook his head hopelessly. "Can you remember anything unusual about the orders? Anything out of the ordinary?"

"Oh, sure. It was the damndest packet. In the first place, it was delivered by an Imperial Household courier in full livery. Lessee, four data discs, one green for Intelligence, two red for Security, one blue for Operations. And the parchment, of course."

Ivan had the family memory, at least. What would it be like to have a mind that retained nearly everything, but never bothered to put it any kind of order? Exactly like living in Ivan's room, Miles decided. "Parchment?" he said. *"Parchment?"*

"Yeah, I thought that was kind of unusual."

"Do you have any idea how bloody—" he surged up, sat back down, squeezed his temples with the heels of his hands in an effort to get his brain into motion. Not only was Ivan an idiot, but he generated a telepathic damping field that turned people nearby into idiots too. He would point this out to Barrayaran Intelligence, who would make of his cousin the newest weapon in their arsenal—if anyone could be found who could remember what they were doing once they closed on him ... "Ivan, there are only three kinds of thing written on parchment any more. Imperial edicts, the originals of the official edicts from the Council of Counts and from the Council of Ministers, and certain orders from the Council of Counts to their own members."

"I know that."

"As my father's heir, I am a cadet member of that Council."

"You have my sympathy," said Ivan, his gaze wandering back to the window. "Which of those ships out there is the fastest, d'you think, the Illyrican cruiser or the—"

"Ivan, I'm psychic," Miles announced suddenly. "I'm so psychic, I can tell what color the ribbon was on that parchment without even seeing it."

"I know what color it was," said Ivan irritably. "It was— "

"Black," Miles cut across him. "Black, you idiot! And you never thought to mention it!"

"Look, I have to take that stuff from my mother and your father, I don't have to take it from you, too—" Ivan paused. "How did you know?"

"I know the color because I know the contents." Miles rose to pace uncontrollably back and forth. "You know them too, or you would if you ever stopped to think. I've got a joke for you. What's white, taken from the back of a sheep, tied up with black bows, shipped thousands of light years, and lost?"

"If that's your idea of a joke, you're weirder than—"

"Death." Miles's voice fell to a whisper, making Ivan jump. "Treason. Civil war. Betrayal, sabotage, almost certainly murder. Evil . . ."

"You haven't had any more of that sedative you're allergic to, have you?" asked Ivan anxiously.

Miles's pacing was becoming frenetic. The urge to pick Ivan up and shake him, in the hope that all that information floating randomly around inside his head would start to polymerize into some chain of reason, was almost overwhelming.

"If Dimir's courier ship's Necklin rods were sabotaged during the stopover at Beta Colony, it would be weeks before the ship was missed. For all the Barrayaran embassy would know, it left on its mission, made the jump—no way for Beta Colony to know if it came out the other side or not. What a *thorough* way to get rid of the evidence." Miles imagined the dismay and terror of the men aboard as the jump began to go wrong, as their bodies began to run and smear like watercolors in the rain—he forced his mind back to abstract reason.

"I don't understand. Where d'you think Dimir is?" asked Ivan.

"Dead. Quite thoroughly dead. You were meant to be quite thoroughly dead too, but you missed the boat." A high, wheeing laugh escaped Miles. He took hold of himself, literally, wrapping his arms around his torso. "I guess they figured if they were going to all that trouble to get rid of that parchment, they'd throw you in at the same time. There's a certain economy in the plot—you might expect it from a mind that ended up in Procurement."

"Back up," demanded Ivan. "What do you figure the parchment was, anyway—and who the devil are 'they'? You're beginning to sound as paranoid as old Bothari."

"The black ribbon. It had to have been a capital charge. An Imperial order for my arrest on a capital charge laid in the Council of Counts. The charge? You said it yourself. Violation of Vorloupulous's law. Treason, Ivan! Now ask yourself—who would benefit by my conviction for treason?"

"Nobody," said Ivan promptly.

"All right," Miles rolled his eyes upward. "Try it this way. Who would suffer by my conviction for treason?"

"Oh, it would destroy your father, of course. I mean, his office overlooks the Great Square. He could stand at his window and watch you starve to death every working day." An embarrassed laugh escaped Ivan. "It would have to about drive him crazy."

Miles paced. "Take his heir, by execution or exile, break his morale, bring him down and his Centrist coalition with him—or— force him to make the false charges real, attempting my rescue. Then bring him down for treason as well. What a demonic fork!" His intellect admired the plot's abstract perfection, even while rage at its cruelty nearly took his breath away.

Ivan shook his head. "How could anything like that get this far and not be quashed by your father? I mean, he may be famous for impartiality, but there are limits even for him."

"You saw the parchment. If Gregor himself had been worked over into a state of suspicion . . ." Miles spoke slowly. "A trial clears as well as convicts. If I showed up voluntarily, it would go a long way toward proving I had no treasonable intent. That cuts both ways, of course—if I don't show, it's a strong presumption of guilt. But I could hardly show up if I weren't informed it was taking place, could I?"

"The Council of Counts is such a cantankerous body of old relics," argued Ivan. "Your plotters would be taking an awful chance they could swing the vote their way. Nobody would want to get caught voting for the losing side in something like that. Either way, there'd be blood drawn at the end."

"Maybe they were forced. Maybe my father and Illyan finally moved in on Hessman, and he figured the best defense would be a counterattack."

"So what's in it for Vordrozda? Why doesn't he just throw Hessman to the wolves?"

"Ah," said Miles. "There I'm . . . I really wonder if I haven't gone a little *paro*, but—follow this chain. Count Vordrozda, Lord Vortaine, you, me, my father—who is my father heir to?"

"Your grandfather. He's dead, remember? Miles, you can't convince me that Count Vordrozda would knock off five people to inherit the Dendarii Province. He's the Count of Lorimel, for God's sakes! He's a rich man. Dendarii would drain his purse, not fill it."

"Not my grandfather. We're talking about another title altogether. Ivan, there is a large faction of historically-minded people on Barrayar who claim, defensibly, that the salic bar to Imperial inheritance has no foundation in Barrayaran law or custom. Dorca himself inherited through his mother, after all."

"Yes, and your father would like to ship every one of that faction off to, er, summer camp."

"Who is Gregor's heir?"

"Right now, nobody, which is why everybody is on his back to marry and start swiving—"

"If salic descent were allowed, who *would* be his heir?"

Ivan refused to be stampeded. "Your father. Everybody knows that. Everybody also knows he wouldn't touch the Imperium with a stick, so what? This is pretty wild, Miles."

"Can you think of another theory that will account or the facts?"

"Sure," said Ivan, happily continuing the role of devil's advocate. "Easy. Maybe that parchment was addressed to someone else. Damir took it to him, which is why he hasn't shown up here. Have you ever heard of Occam's Razor, Miles?"

"It sounds simpler, until you start to think about it. Ivan, listen. Think back on the exact circumstances of your midnight departure from the Imperial Academy, and that dawn lift-off. Who signed you out? Who saw you go? Who do you know, for certain, who knows where you are right now? Why didn't my father give you any personal messages for me—or my mother or Captain Illyan either, for that matter?" His voice became insistant. "If Admiral Hessman took you off to some quiet, isolated place right now and offered you a glass of wine with his own hands, would you drink it?"

Ivan was silent for a long, thoughtful time, staring out at the Dendarii Free Mercenary Fleet. When he turned back to Miles, his face was painfully somber. "No."

CHAPTER NINETEEN   ✳   ✳   ✳

He tracked them down finally in the crew's mess of the *Triumph*, now parked in Docking Bay 9. It was an off-hour for meals, and the mess was nearly empty but for a few die-hard caffeine addicts swilling an assortment of brews.

They sat, dark heads close, opposite each other. Baz's hand lay open, palm-up, on the small table as he leaned forward. Elena's shoulders were hunched, her hands shredding a napkin in her lap. Neither looked happy.

Miles took a deep breath, carefully adjusted his own expression to one of benevolent good cheer, and sauntered up to them. He no longer bled inside, the surgeon had assured him. Couldn't prove it now. "Hi."

They both started. Elena, still hunched, shot him a look of resentment. Baz answered with a hesitant, dismayed "My lord?" that made Miles feel very small indeed. He suppressed an urge to turn tail and slither out under the door.

"I've been thinking over what you said," Miles began, leaning against an adjoining table in a pose of nonchalance. "Your arguments made a lot of sense, when I came to really examine them. I've changed my opinion. For what it's worth, you're welcome to my blessing."

Baz's face lit with honest delight. Elena's posture opened like a daylily in sudden noon, and as suddenly closed again. The winged brows drew down in puzzlement. She looked at him directly, he felt, for the first time in weeks. "Really?"

He supplied her with a chipper grin. "Really. And we shall satisfy all the forms of etiquette, as well. All it takes is a little ingenuity."

He pulled a colored scarf from his pocket, secreted there for the occasion, and walked around to Baz's side of the table. "We'll start over, on the right foot this time. Picture, if you will, this banal plastic table bolted to the floor before you as a starlit balcony, with a pierced lattice window crawling with those little flowers with the long sharp thorns that make you itch like fire, behind which is, rightly and properly, concealed your heart's desire. Got that? Now—Armsman Jesek, speaking as your liege lord, I understand you have a request."

Miles's pantomime gestures cued the engineer. Baz leaned back with a grin, and picked up his lead.

"My lord I ask your permission and aid to wed the first daughter of Armsman Konstantine Bothari, that my sons may serve you."

Miles cocked his head, and smirked. "Ah, good, we've all been watching the same vid dramas, I see. Yes, certainly, Armsman; may they all serve me as well as you do. I shall send the Baba."

He flipped the scarf into a triangle and tied it around his head. Leaning on an imaginary cane, he hobbled arthritically over to Elena's side of the table, muttering in a cracked falsetto. Once there, he removed the scarf and reverted to the role of Elena's liege lord and guardian, and grilled the Baba as to the suitability of the suitor she represented. The Baba was sent bobbing back twice to Baz's liege commander, to personally check and guarantee his a) continued employment prospects and b) personal hygiene and absence of head-lice.

Muttering obscene little old lady imprecations, the Baba returned at last to Elena's side of the table to conclude her transaction. Baz by this time was cackling with laughter at assorted Barrayaran in-jokes, and Elena's smile had at last reached her eyes.

When his clowning was over and the last somewhat

scrambled formula was completed, Miles hooked a third chair into its floor bolts and fell into it.

"Whew! No wonder the custom is dying out. That's exhausting."

Elena grinned. "I've always had the impression you were trying to be three people. Perhaps you've found your calling."

"What, one-man shows? I've had enough of them lately to last a lifetime." Miles sighed, and grew serious. "You may consider yourselves well and officially betrothed, at any rate. When do you plan to register your marriage?"

"Soon," said Baz, and "I'm not sure," said Elena.

"May I suggest tonight?"

"Why—why . . ." stammered Baz. His eyes sought his lady's. "Elena? Could we?"

"I . . ." she searched Miles's face. "Why, my lord?"

"Because I want to dance at your wedding and fill your bed with buckwheat groats, if I can find any on this benighted space station. You may have to settle for gravel, they've got plenty of that. I'm leaving tomorrow."

Three words should not be so hard to grasp as all that. . .

"What?" cried Baz.

"Why?" repeated Elena in a shocked whisper.

"I have some obligations to pursue," Miles shrugged. "There's Tav Calhoun to pay off, and—and the Sergeant's burial." And, very possibly, my own . . .

"You don't have to go in person, do you?" protested Elena. "Can't you send Calhoun a draft, and ship the body? Why go back? What is there for you?"

"The Dendarii Mercenaries," said Baz. "How can they function without you?"

"I expect them to function quite well, because I am appointing you, Baz, as their commander, and you, Elena, as his executive officer—and apprentice. Commodore Tung will be your chief of staff. You understand that, Baz? I'm going to charge you and Tung jointly with her training, and I expect it to be the best."

"I—I—" gasped the engineer. "My lord, the honor—I couldn't—"

"You'll find that you can, because you must. And

besides, a lady should have a dowry worthy of her. That's what a dowry is for, after all, to provide for the bride's support. Bad form for the bridegroom to squander it, note. And you'll still be working for me, after all."

Baz looked relieved. "Oh—you'll be coming back, then. I thought—never mind. When will you return, my lord?"

"I'll catch up with you sometime," Miles said vaguely. Sometime, never . . . "That's the other thing. I want you to clear out of Tau Verde local space. Pick any direction away from Barrayar, and go. Find employment when you get there, but go soon. The Dendarii Mercenaries have had enough of this Tweedledum-and-Tweedledee war. It's bad for morale when it gets too hard to remember which side you're working for this week. Your next contract should have clearly defined objectives that will weld this motley bunch into a single force, under your command. No more committee warfare. Its weaknesses have been amply demonstrated, I trust—"

Miles went on with instructions and advice until he began to sound like a pint-sized Polonius in his own ears. There was no way he could anticipate every contingency. When the time came to leap in faith, whether you had your eyes open or closed or screamed all the way down or not made no practical difference.

His heart cringed from his next interview even more than from the last, but he forced his feet to carry him to it anyway. He found the comm link technician at work at the electron microscope bench of the *Triumph's* engineering repairs section. Elena Visconti frowned at his gesture of invitation, but turned the work over to her assistant and came slowly to Miles's side.

"Sir?"

"Trainee Visconti. Ma'am. Can we take a walk?"

"What for?"

"Just to talk."

"If it's what I think, you may as well save your breath. I can't go to her."

"I'm not any more comfortable talking about it than you are, but it's an obligation I cannot honorably evade."

"I've spent eighteen years trying to put what happened

at Escobar behind me. Must I be dragged through it again?"

"This is the last time, I promise. I'm leaving tomorrow. The Dendarii fleet will follow soon after. All you short-contract people will be dropped off at Dalton Station, where you can take ship for Tau Ceti or wherever you want. I suppose you'll be going home?"

She fell in reluctantly beside him, and they paced down the corridor. "Yes, my employers will doubtless be astonished at how much back pay they owe me."

"I owe you something myself. Baz says you were outstanding on the mission."

She shrugged. "Straightforward stuff."

"He didn't mean just your technical efforts. Anyway, I didn't want to leave Elena—my Elena—up in the air like this, you see," he began. "She ought to at least something, to replace what was taken from her. Some little crumb of comfort."

"The only thing she lost was some illusion. And believe me, Admiral Naismith, or whatever you are, the only thing I could give her would be another illusion. Maybe if she didn't look so much like him . . . Anyway, I don't want her following me around, or showing up at my door."

"Whatever Sergeant Bothari was guilty of, she is surely innocent."

Elena Visconti rubbed her forehead wearily with the back of her hand. "I'm not saying you're not right. I'm just saying I *can't*. For me, she radiates nightmares."

Miles chewed his lip gently. They turned out of the *Triumph* into a flex tube and walked across the quiet docking bay. Only a few techs were busy at some small tasks.

"An illusion . . ." he mused. "You could live a long time on an illusion," he offered. "Maybe even a lifetime, if you're lucky. Would it be so difficult, to do a few days—even a few minutes—of acting? I'm going to have to dip some Dendarii funds anyway to pay for a dead ship, and buy a lady a new face. I could make it worth your time."

He regretted his words immediately at the loathing

that flashed across her face, but the look she finally gave him was ironically thoughtful.

"You really care about that girl, don't you?"

"Yes."

"I thought she was making time with your chief engineer."

"Suits me."

"Pardon my slowness, but that does not compute."

"Association with me could be lethal, where I'm going next. I'd rather she were travelling in the opposite direction."

The next docking bay was busy and noisy with a Felician freighter being loaded with ingots of refined rare metals, vital to the Felician war industries. They avoided it, and searched out another quiet corridor. Miles found himself fingering the bright scarf in his pocket.

"He dreamed of you for eighteen years too, you know," he said suddenly. It wasn't what he meant to say. "He had this fantasy. You were his wife, in all honor. He held it so hard, I think it was real to him, at least part of the time. That's how he made it so real for Elena. You can touch hallucinations. Hallucinations can even touch you."

The Escobaran woman, pale, paused to lean against the wall and swallow. Miles pulled the scarf from his pocket and crumpled it anxiously in his hands; he had an absurd impulse to offer it to her, heaven knew what for—a basin?

"I'm sorry," Elena said at last. "But the very thought that he was pawing over me in his twisted imagination all these years makes me ill."

"He was never an easy person . . ." Miles began inanely, then cut himself off. He paced, frustrated, two steps, turn, two steps. He then took a gulp of air, and flung himself to one knee before the Escobaran woman.

"Ma'am. Konstantine Bothari sends me to beg your forgiveness for the wrongs he did you. Keep your revenge, if you will—it is your just right—but be satisfied," he implored her. "At least give me a death-offering to burn for him, some token. I give him aid in this as his go-between by my right as his leige lord, his friend, and, as he was a father's hand, held over me in protection all my life, as his son."

Elena Visconti was backed up against the wall as though cornered. Miles, still on one knee, shuffled back a step and shrank into himself, as if to crush all hint of pride and coercion to the deck.

"Damned if I'm not starting to think you're as weird— you're no Betan," she muttered. "Oh, do get up. What if somebody comes down this corridor?"

"Not until you give me a death-offering," he said firmly.

"What do you want from me? What's a death-offering?"

"Something of yourself, that you burn, for the peace of the soul of the dead. Sometimes you burn it for friends or relatives, sometimes for the souls of slain enemies, so they don't come back to haunt you. A lock of hair would do." He ran his hand over a short gap in his own crown. "That wedge represents twenty-two dead Pelians last month."

"Some local superstition, is it?"

He shrugged helplessly. "Superstition, custom—I've always thought of myself as an agnostic. It's only lately that I've come to—to need for men to have souls. Please. I won't bother you any more."

She blew out her breath in troubled exasperation. "Well—well . . . Give me that knife in your belt, then. But get up."

He rose, and handed her his grandfather's dagger. She sawed off a short curl. "Is that enough?"

"Yes, that's fine." He took it in his palm, cool and silken like water, and closed his fingers over it. "Thank you."

She shook her head. "Crazy . . ." Wistfulness stole over her face. "It allays ghosts, does it?"

"It is said," replied Miles gently. "I'll make it a proper offering. My word on it." He inhaled shakily. "And as I have given you my word, I'll bother you no more. Excuse me, ma'am. We both have other duties."

"Sir."

They passed through the flex tube to the *Triumph*,

turned each away. But the Escobaran woman looked back over her shoulder.

"You are mistaken, little man," she called softly. "I believe you're going to bother me for a long time yet."

Next he searched out Arde Mayhew.

"I'm afraid I never was able to do you the good I intended," Miles apologized. "I have managed to find a Felician shipmaster who will buy the RG132 for an inner-system freighter. He's offering about a dime on the dollar, but it's cash up front. I thought we could split it."

"At least it's an honorable retirement," sighed Mayhew. "Better than having Calhoun tear it to pieces."

"I'm leaving for home tomorrow, via Beta Colony. I could drop you off, if you want."

Mayhew shrugged. "There's nothing on Beta for me." He looked up more sharply. "What happened to all this leigeman stuff? I thought I was working for you."

"I—don't really think you'd fit in on Barrayar," said Miles carefully. The pilot officer must not follow him home. Betan or no, the deadly bog of Barrayaran politics could suck him down without a bubble, in the vortex of his leige lord's fall. "But you could certainly have a place with the Dendarii Mercenaries. What rank would you like?"

"I'm no soldier."

"You could re-train, something on the tech side. And they'll certainly need back-up pilots, for sub-light, and the shuttles."

Mayhew's forehead wrinkled. "I don't know. Driving a shuttle and so on was always the scut work, something you did so you could jump. I don't know that I want to be so close to ships. It would be like standing outside the bakery hungry, with no credit card to go in and buy." He looked greyly depressed.

"There's one more possibility."

Mayhew's brows lifted in polite inquiry.

"The Dendarii Mercenaries are going to be outward bound, looking for work on the fringes of the wormhole nexus. The RG ships were never all accounted for—it's possible one or two might still be junked out there somewhere. The Felician shipmaster would be willing to lease the RG132, although for a lot less money. If you could find and salvage a pair of RG Necklin rods—"

Mayhew's back straightened from a slump that had looked to be permanent.

"I don't have time to go hunting all over the galaxy for spare parts," Miles went on. "But if you'd agree to be my agent, I'll authorize Baz to release Dendarii funds to buy them, if you find any, and a ship to bring them back here. A quest, as it were. Just like Vorthalia the Bold and the search for Emperor Xian Vorbarra's lost scepter." Of course, in the legend Vorthalia never actually *found* the scepter . . .

"Yeah?" Mayhew's face was brightening with hope. "It's a long shot—but I guess it is just barely possible. . ."

"That's the spirit! Forward momentum."

Mayhew snorted. "Your forward momentum is going to lead all your followers over a cliff someday." He paused, beginning to grin. "On the way down, you'll convince 'em all they can fly." He stuck his fists in his armpits, and waggled his elbows. "Lead on, my lord. I'm flapping as hard as I can."

The docking bay, its every second light bar extinguished, provided an illusion of night in the unmarked changeless time of space. Those lights that remained on threw a dull illumination like shimmering puddles of mercury, that gave vision without color. The sounds of the loading, small thumps and clanks, carried in the silence, and voices muted themselves.

The Felician fast courier pilot grimaced as Bothari's coffin was carried past him and vanished into the flex tube. "When we've stripped baggage down to practically a change of underwear each, it seems deuced gaudy to bring that."

"Every parade needs a float," remarked Miles absently, indifferent to the pilot's opinion. The pilot, like his ship, was merely a courtesy loan from General Halify. The general had been reluctant to authorize the expenditure, but Miles had hinted that if his emergency run

to Beta Colony failed to bring him to a certain mysterious appointment on time, the Dendarii Mercenaries just
might be forced to look for their next contract from the
highest bidder here in Tau Verde local space. Halify had
reflected only briefly before making all haste to speed
him on his way.

Miles shifted from foot to foot, anxious to be gone
before the bright activities marking day-cycle began.
Ivan Vorpatril appeared, carefully clutching a valise
whose mass was most certainly not wasted on clothes.
Stripes on the docking bay deck, placed to aid organization in loading and unloading complex cargoes, made
pale parallels. Ivan blinked, and walked down one line
toward them with dignified precision only slightly spoiled
by a list that precessed like an equinox. He hove to by
Miles.

"What a wedding party," he sighed happily. "For an
impromptu out in the middle of nowhere, your Dendarii
came up with quite a spread. Captain Auson is a splendid fellow."

Miles smiled bleakly. "I thought you two would get
along well."

"You kind of disappeared about halfway through. We
had to start the drinking without you."

"I wanted to join you," said Miles truthfully, "but I
had a lot of last-minute things to work out with Commodore Tung."

"Too bad." Ivan smothered a belch, gazed across the
docking bay, and muttered, "Now, I can see your wanting to bring a woman along, two weeks in a box and all
that, but did you have to pick one that gives me
nightmares?"

Miles followed his gaze. Elli Quinn, escorted by Tung's
surgeon, was making her slow blind way toward them.
Her crisp grey-and-whites outlined the body of an athletic
young woman, but above the collar she was a bad dream
of an alien race. The hairless uniformity of the bland
pink bulb of a head was broken by the black hole of
a mouth, two dark slits above it for a nose, and a dot on
either side marking the entrances to the ear canals.

Only the right one still vented sound into her darkness. Ivan stirred uneasily, and looked away.

Tung's surgeon took Miles aside for last minute instructions for her care during the journey, and some acerbic advice on Miles's treatment of his own still-healing stomach. Miles patted his hip flask, now filled with medication, and faithfully swore to drink 30 cc's every two hours. He placed the injured mercenary's hand on his arm, and stood on tiptoe to her ear. "We're all set, then. Next stop Beta Colony."

Her other hand patted the air, then found his face for a brief touch. Her damaged tongue tried to form words in her stiff mouth; on the second try Miles correctly interpreted them as "Thank you, Admiral Naismith." Had he been any tireder, he might have wept.

"All right," Miles began, "let's get out of here before the bon voyage committee wakes up and delays us another two hours—" but he was too late. Out of the corner of his eye he saw a willowy form sprinting across the docking bay. Baz followed at a saner pace.

Elena arrived out of breath. "Miles!" she accused. "You were going to leave without saying goodbye!"

He sighed, and twitched a smile at her. "Foiled again." Her cheeks were flushed, and her eyes sparkled from the exertion. Altogether desirable . . . he had hardened his heart for this parting. Why did it hurt worse?

Baz arrived. Miles bowed to each. "Commander Jesek. Commodore Jesek. You know, Baz, perhaps I should have appointed you an Admiral. Those names could get confusing over a bad comm link—"

Baz shook his head, smiling. "You have piled enough honors on me, my lord. Honors, and honor, and much more—" his eyes sought Elena. "I once thought it would take a miracle to make a nobody into a somebody once again." His smile broadened. "I was right. And I thank you."

"And I thank you," said Elena quietly, "for a gift I never expected to possess."

Miles obediently cocked his head in an angle of inquiry. Did she mean Baz? Her rank? Escape from Barrayar?

"Myself," she explained.

It seemed to him there was a fallacy in her reasoning somewhere, but there was no time to unravel it. Dendarii were invading the docking bay through several entrances, in twos and threes and then in a steady stream. The lights came up to full day-cycle power. His plans for slipping away quietly were disintegrating rapidly.

"Well," he said desperately, "goodbye, then." He shook Baz's hand hastily. Elena, her eyes swimming, grabbed him in a hug just short of bone-crushing. His toes sought the floor indignantly. Altogether too late . . .

By the time she put him down, the crowd was gathering, hands reaching to shake his hand, to touch him, or just reaching, as if to warm themselves. Bothari would have had a spasm; Miles rendered the Sergeant's spirit an apologetic salute, in his mind.

The docking bay was now a seething sea of people. It rang to babble, and cheers, and cheerful hoots, and foot stamping. These soon picked up rhythm; a chant. "Naismith! Naismith! Naismith . . ."

Miles raised his hands in helpless acquiescence, cursing under his breath. There was always some idiot in a crowd to start these things. Elena and Baz between them hoisted him to their shoulders, and he was cornered. Now he would have to come up with a bloody farewell speech. He lowered his hands; rather to his surprise, they quieted. He flung his hands back up; they roared. He lowered them slowly, like an orchestra director. The silence became absolute. It was terrifying.

"As you can see, I am high because you all have raised me up," he began, pitching his voice to carry to the last and least. A gratified chuckle ran through them. "You have raised me up on your courage, tenacity, obedience, and other soldierly virtues," that was it, stroke them, they were eating it up—although surely he owed as much to their confusion, bad-tempered rivalry, greed, ambition, indolence, and gullibility—pass on, pass on—"I can do no less than to raise you up in return. I hereby revoke your provisional status, and declare you a permanent arm of the Dendarii Mercenaries."

The cheering, whistling, and foot stomping shook the docking bay. Many were Oser's latecomers, curious, along for the ride, but practically all of Auson's original crew were there. He picked out Auson himself, beaming, and Thorne, tears streaming down cheeks.

He raised his arms for silence again, and got it. "I am recalled on urgent affairs for an indefinite period. I request and require that you obey Commodore Jesek as you would me." He glanced down to meet Baz's up-turned gaze. "He will not desert you."

He could feel the engineer's shoulder tremble beneath him. Absurd of Baz to look so exalted—Jesek, of them all, knew Miles was a fake . . . "I thank you all, and bid you farewell."

His feet hit the deck with a thump as he slid down. "And may God have mercy upon me, amen," he mut-tered under his breath. He backed toward the flex tube, and escape, smiling and waving.

Jesek, blocking the press, spoke to his ear. "My lord. For my curiosity—before you go, may I be permitted to know what house I serve?"

"What, you haven't figured that out yet?" Miles looked to Elena in astonishment.

Bothari's daughter shrugged. "Security."

"Well—I'm not going to shout it out in this crowd, but if you ever go shopping for livery, which doesn't seem too bloody likely—choose brown and silver."

"But—" Baz ground to a halt, there in the crowd, a little knot of personal silence. "But that's—" He paled.

Miles smiled, wickedly gratified. "Break him in gently, Elena."

The silence in the flex tube sucked at him, refuge; the noise in front of him beat on his senses, for the Dendarii had taken up their chant again, Naismith, Naismith, Naismith. The Felician pilot escorted Elli Quinn aboard, Ivan following. The last person Miles saw as he waved and backed into the tube was Elena. Making her way toward her through the crowd, her face drawn and grave and thoughtful, was Elena Visconti.

*   *   *

The Felician pilot bolted the hatch and blew the tube seals, and went ahead of them to Nav and Com.

"Whew," remarked Ivan respectfully. "You sure got them going. You have to be higher than I am now just on psychic waves or something."

"Not really," Miles grimaced.

"Why not? I sure would be." There was an undercurrent of envy in Ivan's voice.

"My name isn't Naismith."

Ivan opened his mouth, closed it, studied him sideways. The screens were up in Nav and Com, showing the refinery and space around them. The ship pulled away from the docking bay. Miles tried to keep that particular slot in the row of docking bays in sight, but soon became confused; fourth or fifth from the left?

"Damn." Ivan thrust his thumbs through his belt, and rocked on his heels. "It still knocks me flat. I mean, here you come into this place with nothing, and in four months you turn their war completely around and end up with all the marbles on top of it."

"I don't want all the marbles," said Miles impatiently. "I don't want any of the marbles. It's death for me to be caught with marbles in my possession, remember?"

"I don't understand you," Ivan complained. "I thought you always wanted to be a soldier. Here you've fought real battles, commanded a whole fleet of ships, wiped the tactical map with fantastically few losses—"

"Is that what you think? That I've been playing soldier? Peh!" Miles began to pace restlessly. He paused, and lowered his head in shame. "Maybe I did. Maybe that was the trouble. Wasting day after day, feeding my ego, while all the time back home Vordrozda's pack of dogs were running my father to ground—staring out the damn *window* for five days while they're *killing* him—"

"Ah," said Ivan. "So that's what's got the hair up you. Never fear," he comforted, "we'll get back all right." He blinked, and added in a much less definite tone, "Miles—assuming you're right about all this—what is it we're going to *do*, once we get back?"

Miles's lips drew back in a mirthless grin. "I'll figure something out."

He turned to watch the screens, thinking silently, *But you are mistaken about the losses, Ivan. They were enormous.*

The refinery and the ships around it dwindled to a scattered constellation of specks, sparks, water in the eyes, and gone.

CHAPTER TWENTY   *   *   *

The Betan night was hot, even under the force dome that shielded the suburb of Silica. Miles touched the silver circles on his midforehead and temples, praying that his sweat was not loosening their glue. He had passed through Betan customs on the Felician pilot's doctored I.D.'s; it would not do for his supposed implant contact to go sliding down his nose.

Artistically bonsai'd mesquite and acacia trees, picked out with colored spotlights, surrounded the low dome that was the pedestrian entrance to his grandmother's apartment complex. The old building pre-dated the community force shield, and was therefore entirely underground. Miles hooked Elli Quinn's hand over his arm, and patted it.

"We're almost there. Two steps down, here. You'll like my grandmother. She supervises life support equipment maintenance at the Silica University Hospital—she'll know just who to see for the best work. Now here's a door . . ."

Ivan, still clutching the valise, stepped through first. The cooler interior air caressed Miles's face, and relieved him at least of his worries about his fake implant contacts. It had been nerve-wracking, crossing Customs with a false I.D., but using his real ones would have guaranteed instant entanglement in Betan legal proceedings, entailing God-knew-what delays. Time drummed in his head.

"There's a lift tube there," Miles began to Elli, then choked on an oath, recoiling. Popping out of the Up tube in the foyer was the very man he least wanted to see on his touch-and-go planetary stopover.

Tav Calhoun's eyes started from his head at the sight of Miles. His face turned the color of brick. "You!" he cried. "You—you—you—" He swelled, stuttering, and advanced on Miles.

Miles tried a friendly smile. "Why, good evening, Mr. Calhoun. You're just the man I wanted to see—"

Calhoun's hands clenched on Miles's jacket. "Where is my ship?"

Miles, borne backwards to the wall, felt suddenly lonely for Sergeant Bothari. "Well, there was a little problem with the ship," he began placatingly.

Calhoun shook him. "Where is it? What have you goons done with it?"

"It's stuck at Tau Verde, I'm afraid. Damage to the Necklin rods. But I've got your money." He essayed a cheerful nod.

Calhoun's hold did not slacken. "I wouldn't touch your money with a hand-tractor!" he growled. "I've been given the royal run-around, lied to, followed, had my comconsole tapped, had Barrayaran agents questioning my employees, my girlfriend, her wife—I found out about that damned worthless hot land, by the way, you little mutant—I want blood. You're going to *therapy*, because I'm calling Security right now!"

A plaintive mumble came from Elli Quinn, which Miles's practiced ear translated as, "What's happening?"

Calhoun noticed her in the shadows for the first time, jumped, shrugged, then turned on his heel and shot over his shoulder to Miles, "Don't you move! This is a citizen's arrest!" He headed for the public comconsole.

"Grab him, Ivan!" Miles cried.

Calhoun twisted away from Ivan's clutch. His reflexes were quicker than Miles had expected for so beefy a body. Elli Quinn, head cocked to one side, slid into his path in two smooth sideways steps, her ankles and knees flexing. Her hands found his shirt. They whirled for a dizzy instant like a pair of dancers, and suddenly

Calhoun was doing spectacular cartwheels. He landed flat on his back on the pavement of the foyer. The air went out of him in a booming whoosh. Elli, sitting, spun around, clamped one leg across his neck, and put his arm in a lock.

Ivan, now that his target was no longer moving, took over and achieved a creditable come-along hold. "How did you do that?" he asked Elli, astonishment and admiration in his voice.

She shrugged. "Used to practice with eyes covered," she mumbled, "to sharpen balance. It works."

"What do we do with him, Miles?" asked Ivan. "Can he really have you arrested, even if you offer to pay him?"

"Assault!" croaked Calhoun. "Battery!"

Miles straightened his jacket. "I'm afraid so. There was some fine print in that contract—look, there's a janitor's closet on the second level. We better take him down there, before somebody comes through here."

"Kidnapping," gurgled Calhoun, as Ivan dragged him to the lift tube.

They found a coil of wire in the roomy janitor's closet. "Murder!" shrieked Calhoun as they approached him with it. Miles gagged him; his eyes rolled whitely. By the time they finished all the extra loops and knots just in case, the salvage operator began to resemble a bright orange mummy.

"The valise, Ivan," Miles ordered.

His cousin opened it, and they began stuffing Calhoun's shirt and sarong rope with bundles of Betan dollars.

"... thirty-eight, thirty-nine, forty thousand," Miles counted.

Ivan scratched his head. "Y'know, there's something backwards about this ..."

Calhoun was rolling his eyes and moaning urgently. Miles ungagged him for a moment.

"—plus ten percent!" Calhoun panted.

Miles gagged him again, and counted out another four thousand dollars. The valise was much lighter now. They locked the closet behind them.

*   *   *

"Miles!" His grandmother fell on him ecstatically.
"Thank God, Captain Dimir found you, then. The Embassy people have been terribly worried. Cordelia says
your father didn't think he could get the date for the
challenge in the Council of Counts put off a third time—"
She broke off as she saw Elli Quinn. "Oh, my."

Miles introduced Ivan, and named Elli hastily as a
friend from off-planet with no connections and no place
to stay. He quickly outlined his hopes for leaving the
injured mercenary in his grandmother's hands. Mrs.
Naismith assimilated this at once, merely remarking,
"Oh, yes, another of your strays." Miles silently called
down blessings upon her.

His grandmother herded them to her living room.
Miles sat on the couch with a twinge, remembering
Bothari. He wondered if the Sergeant's death would
become like a veteran's scar, echoing the old pain with
every change of weather.

As if reflecting his thought, Mrs. Naismith said,
"Where's the Sergeant, and Elena? Making reports at
the Embassy? I'm surprised they let you out even to
visit me. Lieutenant Croye gave me the impression they
were going to hustle you aboard a fast courier for
Barrayar the instant they laid hands on you."

"We haven't been to the Embassy yet," confessed
Miles uneasily. "We came straight here."

"Told you we should have reported in first," said
Ivan. Miles made a negative gesture.

His grandmother glanced at him with a new penetrating concentration. "What's wrong, Miles? Where is
Elena?"

"She's safe," replied Miles, "but not here. The Sergeant was killed two, almost three months ago now. An
accident."

"Oh," said Mrs. Naismith. She sat silent a moment,
sobered. "I confess I never did understand what your
mother saw in the man, but I know he will be sadly
missed. Do you want to call Lieutenant Croye from
here?" She tilted her head at Miles, and added, "Is that
where you've been for the last five months? Training to

be a jump pilot? I shouldn't have thought you'd have to do it in secret, surely Cordelia would have supported you—"

Miles touched a silver circle in embarrassment. "This is a fake. I borrowed a jump pilot's I.D. to get through customs."

"Miles . . ." Impatience thinned her lips, and worry creased twin verticals between her eyebrows. "What's going on? Is this more to do with those ghastly Barrayaran politics?"

"I'm afraid so. Quickly—what have you heard from home since Dimir left here?"

"According to your mother, you're scheduled to be challenged in the Council of Counts on some sort of trumped-up treason charge, and very soon."

Miles gave Ivan a short I-told-you-so nod; Ivan began nibbling on a thumbnail.

"There's evidently been a lot of behind-the-scenes maneuvering—I didn't understand half of her message discs. I'm convinced only a Barrayaran could figure out how their government works. By all right reason it should have collapsed years ago. Anyway, most of it seemed to revolve around changing the substance of the charge from treason by violation of something called Vorloupulous's law to treason by intent to usurp the Imperial throne."

"What!" Miles shot to his feet. The heat of terror flushed through him. "This is pure insanity! I don't want Gregor's job! Do they think I'm out of my mind? In the first place, I'd need to command the loyalty of the whole Imperial Service, not just some grubby free mercenary fleet—"

"You mean there really *was* a mercenary fleet?" His grandmother's eyes widened. "I thought it was just a wild rumor. What Cordelia said about the charges makes more sense, then."

"What did Mother say?"

"That your father went to a great deal of trouble to goad this Count Vor-what's-his-name—I can never keep all those Vor-people straight—"

"Vordrozda?"

"Yes, that was it."

Miles and Ivan exchanged wild looks.

"To goad Vordrozda to up the charge from the minor to the major, while appearing publicly to want just the opposite. I didn't understand what difference it made, since the penalty's the same."

"Did Father succeed?"

"Apparently. At least as of two weeks ago, when the fast courier that arrived yesterday left Barrayar."

"Ah." Miles begn to pace. "Ah. Clever, clever—maybe. . ."

"I don't understand it either," complained Ivan. "Usurpation is a much worse charge!"

"But it happens to be one I'm innocent of. And furthermore, it's a charge of intent. About all I'd have to do is show up to disprove it. Violating Vorloupulous's law is a charge of fact—and in fact, although not in intent, I'm guilty of it. Given that I showed up for my trial, and spoke the truth as I'm sworn to, it'd be a lot harder to wriggle out of."

Ivan finished his second thumbnail. "What makes you think your innocence or guilt is going to have anything to do with the outcome?"

"I beg your pardon?" said Mrs. Naismith.

"That's why I said, maybe," explained Miles. "This thing is so damned political—how many votes d'you suppose Vordrozda will have sewn up in advance, before any evidence or testimony is even presented? He's got to have some, or he'd never have dared to float this in the first place."

"You're asking me?" said Ivan plaintively.

"You . . ." Miles eye fell on his cousin. "You . . . I am absolutely convinced you are the key to this thing, if only I can figure out how to fit you into the lock."

Ivan looked as if he were trying, and failing, to picture himself as a key to anything. "Why?"

"For one thing, until we report in somewhere, Hessman and Vordrozda will think you're dead."

"What?" said Mrs. Naismith.

Miles explained about the disappearance of Captain Dimir's mission. He touched his forehead, and added to

Ivan, "And that's the real reason for this, besides Calhoun, of course."

"Speaking of Calhoun," said his grandmother, "he's been coming around here regularly, looking for you. You'd best be on the lookout for him, if you really mean to stay covert."

"Uh," said Miles, "thanks. Anyway, Ivan, if Dimir's ship was sabotaged, it would have to have taken somebody on the inside to do it. What's to keep whoever doesn't want me to show up for my trial from trying again, if we so-conveniently place ourselves in his hands by popping up at the Embassy?"

"Miles, your mind is crookeder than your bac—I mean—anyway, are you sure you're not catching Bothari's disease?" said Ivan. "You're making me feel like I've got a bulls-eye painted on my back."

Miles grinned, feeling bizarrely exhilarated. "Wakes you up, doesn't it?" It seemed to him he could hear the gates of reason clicking over in his own brain, cascading faster and faster. His voice took on a faraway tone. "You know, if you're trying to take a roomful of people by surprise, it's a lot easier to hit your targets if you don't yell going through the door."

They kept the rest of the visit almost as brief as Miles had hoped. They emptied out the valise onto the living room floor, and Miles counted out piles of Betan dollars to clear his various Betan debts, including his grandmother's original "investment". Rather bemusedly, she agreed to be his agent for the task of distribution.

The largest pile was for Elli Quinn's new face. Miles gulped when his grandmother quoted him the approximate price for the best work. When he was finished, he had one meager wad of bills left in his hand.

Ivan snickered. "By God, Miles, you've made a profit. I think you're the first Vorkosigan to do so in five generations. Must be that bad Betan blood."

Miles weighed the dollars, wryly. "It's getting to be a kind of family tradition, isn't it? My father gave away 275,000 marks the day before he left the Regency, just so he would have the exact financial balance as the day he took it up sixteen years earlier."

Ivan raised his eyebrows. "I never knew that."

"Why do you think Vorkosigan House didn't get a new roof last year? I think that was the only thing Mother regretted, the roof. Otherwise, it was kind of fun, figuring out where to bury the stuff. The Imperial Service orphanage picked up a packet."

For curiosity, Miles stole a moment and punched up the financial exhange on the comconsole. Felician millifenigs were listed once again. The exchange rate was 1,206 millifenigs to the Betan dollar, but at least they were listed. Last week's rate had been 1,459 to the dollar.

Miles's growing sense of urgency propelled them toward the door.

"If we can have a one-day head start in the Felician fast courier," he told his grandmother, "that should be enough. Then you can call the Embassy and put them out of their misery."

"Yes." She smiled. "Poor Lieutenant Croye was convinced he was going to spend the rest of his career as a private doing guard duty someplace nasty."

Miles paused at the door. "Ah—about Tav Calhoun—"

"Yes?"

"You know that janitor's closet on the second level?"

"Vaguely." She looked at him in unease.

"Please be sure somebody checks it tomorrow morning. But don't go up there before then."

"I wouldn't dream of it," she assured him faintly.

"Come on, Miles," Ivan urged over his shoulder.

"Just a second."

Miles darted back inside to Elli Quinn, still seated obediently in the living room. He pressed the wad of leftover bills into her palm, and closed her fingers over it.

"Combat bonus," he whispered to her. "For upstairs just now. You earned it."

He kissed her hand and ran after Ivan.

CHAPTER TWENTY-ONE ✳ ✳ ✳

Miles banked the lightflyer in a gentle, demure turn around Vorhartung Castle, resisting a nervous urge to slam it directly down into the courtyard. The ice had broken on the river winding through the capital city of Vorbarr Sultana, running a chill green now from the snows melting in the Dendarii Mountains far to the south. The ancient building straddled high bluffs; the lightflyer rocked in the updraft puffing from the river.

The modern city spread out for kilometers around was bright and noisy with morning traffic. The parking areas near the castle were jammed with vehicles of all descriptions, and knots of men in half-a-hundred different liveries. Ivan, beside Miles, counted the banners snapping in the cold spring breeze on the battlements.

"It's a full Council session," said Ivan. "I don't think there's a banner missing—there's even Count Vortala's, and I don't think he's been to one in years. Must have been carried in. Ye gods, Miles! There's the Emperor's banner—Gregor must be inside."

"You could figure that from all the fellows on the roof in Imperial livery with the anti-aircraft plasma guns," observed Miles. He flinched inwardly. One such weapon was swivelling to follow their track even now, like a suspicious eye.

Slowly and carefully, he set the lightflyer down in a painted circle outside the castle walls.

"Y'know," said Ivan thoughtfully, "We're going to

look a pair of damn fools busting in there if it turns out they're all having a debate on water rights or something."

"That thought has crossed my mind," Miles admitted. "It was a calculated risk, landing in secret. Well, we've both been fools before. There won't be anything new or startling in it."

He checked the time, and paused a moment in the pilot's seat, bent his head down, and breathed carefully.

"You feeling sick?" asked Ivan, alarmed. "You don't look so good."

Miles shook his head, a lie, and begged forgiveness in his heart for all the harsh things he'd once thought about Baz Jesek. So this was the real thing, paralyzing funk. He wasn't braver than Baz after all—he'd just never been as scared. He wished himself back with the Dendarii, doing something simple, like defusing dandelion bombs. "Pray to God this works," he muttered.

Ivan looked even more alarmed. "You've been pushing this surprise-scheme on me for the last two weeks—all right, so you've convinced me. It's *too late* to change your mind!"

"I haven't changed my mind." Miles rubbed the silver circles loose from his forehead, and stared up at the great grey wall of the castle.

"The guards are going to notice us, if we just keep sitting here," Ivan added after a time. "Not to mention the hell that's probably breaking loose back at the shuttleport right now."

"Right" said Miles. He dangled now at the end of a long, long chain of reason, swinging in the winds of doubt. Time to drop to solid ground.

"After you," said Ivan politely.

"Right."

"Any time now," added Ivan.

The vertigo of free fall ... he popped the doors and clambered to the pavement.

They strode up to quartet of armed guards in Imperial livery at the castle gate. One's fingers twitched into a devil's horns, down by his side; he had a countryman's face. Miles sighed inwardly. Welcome home. He settled on an incisive nod, by way of greeting.

"Good morning, Armsmen. I am Lord Vorkosigan. I understand the Emperor has commanded me to appear here."

"Damn joker," began a guard, loosening his truncheon. A second guard grasped his arm, staring shocked at Miles.

"No, Dub—it really *is*!"

They underwent a second search in the vestibule of the great chamber itself. Ivan kept trying to peek around the door, to the annoyance of the guard charged with being the final check against weapons carried into the presence of the Emperor. Voices wafted from the council chamber to Miles's straining ear. He identified Count Vordrozda's, pitched to a carrying nasality, rhythmic in the cadences of formal debate.

"How long has this been going on?" Miles whispered to a guard.

"A week. This was to be the last day. They're doing the summing up now. You're just in time, my lord." he gave Miles an encouraging nod; the two guard captains finished a sotto voce argument, "—but he's *supposed* to be here!"

"You sure you wouldn't rather be in Betan therapy?" muttered Ivan.

Miles grinned blackly. "Too late now. Won't it be funny if we've arrived just in time for the sentencing?"

"Hysterical. You'll die laughing, no doubt," growled Ivan.

Ivan, approved by the guard, started for the door. Miles grabbed him. "Sh, wait! Listen."

Another identifiable voice; Admiral Hessman.

"What's he doing here?" whispered Ivan. "I thought this thing was closed and sealed to the Counts alone."

"Witness, I'll bet, just like you. Sh!"

". . . If our illustrious Prime Minister knew nothing of this plot, then let him produce this 'missing' nephew," Vordrozda's voice was heavy with sarcasm. "He says he cannot. And why not? I submit it is because Lord Vorpatril was dispatched with a secret message. What message? Obviously, some variation of 'Fly for your life—all is revealed!' I ask you—is it reasonable that a plot of this magnitude could have been advanced so far by a son with no knowledge by his father? Where did those missing 275,000 marks, whose fate he so adamantly refuses to disclose, go but to secretly finance the operation? These repeated requests for delays are simply smokescreen. If Lord Vorkosigan is so innocent, why is he not here?" Vordrozda paused dramatically.

Ivan tugged Miles's sleeve. "Come on. You'll never get a better straight line than that if you wait all day."

"You're right. Let's go."

Stained glass windows high in the east wall splashed the heavy oak flooring of the chamber with colored light. Vordrozda stood in the speaker's circle. Upon the witness bench, behind it, sat Admiral Hessman. The gallery above, with its ornately carved railings, was indeed empty, but the rows of plain wooden benches and desks that ringed the room below were jammed with men.

Formal liveries in a wild assortment of hues peeked out beneath their scarlet and silver robes of office, but for a sprinkling of robeless men who wore the red and blue parade uniform of active Imperial service. Emperor Gregor, on his raised dais to the left of the room, also wore Imperial service uniform. Miles gulped down a sharp spasm of stage fright. He wished he'd stopped at Vorkosigan House to change; he still wore the plain dark shirt, trousers, and boots he'd stood in when leaving Tau Verde. He estimated the distance to the center of the chamber as about a light-year.

His father sat, looking entirely at home in his red-and-blues, behind his desk in the first row not far from Vordrozda. Count Vorkosigan leaned back, his legs stretched out and crossed at the ankles, arms draped along the backrest, yet looking no more casual than a tiger stalking his prey. His face was sour, murderous, concentrated on Vordrozda; Miles wondered briefly if the old slanderous sobriquet, 'the Butcher of Komarr', that had once attached to his father might have some basis in fact after all.

Vordrozda, in the speaker's circle, was the only one directly facing the darkened entrance arch. He was the first to see Miles and Ivan. He had just opened his mouth to continue; it hung there, slack.

"That's just the question I propose to make you answer, Count Vordrozda—and you, Admiral Hessman," Miles called. Two light-years, he thought, and limped forward.

The chamber stirred to murmurs and cries of astonishment. Of all the men's reactions, Miles searched for only one.

Count Vorkosigan snapped his head around, saw Miles. He inhaled, and his arms and legs drew in. He sat for a moment with his elbows on his desk, face buried in his hands. He rubbed his face, hard; when he raised it again, it was flushed and furrowed, blinking.

When did he grow to look so old? Miles grieved. Was his hair always that grey? Has he changed so much, or is it I? Or both?

Count Vorkosigan's eye fell on Ivan, and his face cleared to stunned exasperation. "Ivan, you idiot! Where have you been?"

Ivan glanced at Miles and rose to the occasion, bowing toward the witness bench. "Admiral Hessman sent me to find Miles, sir."

"I did. Somehow, I don't think that was what he really had in mind."

Vordrozda turned in the circle to glare furiously at Hessman, who was goggling at Ivan. "You—" Vordrozda hissed at the Admiral, voice venomous with rage. He caught himself up almost instantly, straightening his crouch, relaxing his hands from clawed rakes to elegant curves once again.

Miles swept a bow to the encircling assemblage, ending it on one knee in the direction of the dais. "My leige and my lords. I would have been here sooner, but my invitation was lost in the mail. To attest this I wish to call Lord Ivan Vorpatril as my witness."

Gregor's young face stared down at him, stiff, dark eyes troubled and distant. The Emperor's gaze turned in bewilderment to his new advisor, standing in the speaker's circle. His old advisor, Count Vorkosigan, looked wonderfully enlightened; his lips drew back in a tigerish smile.

Miles too glanced at Vordrozda from the corner of his eye. Now, he thought, instantly, is the time to push. By the time the Lord Guardian of the Circle admits Ivan with all due ceremony, they will have recovered. Give them sixty seconds to confer on the bench, and they will concoct new lies of utmost reasonableness, leaving it their word against ours in the hideous gamble of a stacked Council vote. Hessman, yes, it was Hessman he must put the wind up. Vordrozda was too supple to stampede. Strike now, and cleave the conspiracy in half.

He swallowed, cleared his locked throat, and swung to his feet. "I challenge Admiral Hessman, here before you, lords, on charges of sabotage, murder, and attempted murder. I can prove he ordered the sabotage of Captain Dimir's Imperial fast courier, resulting in the horrible deaths of all aboard her; I can prove his intent that my cousin Ivan have been among them."

"You are out of order," cried Vordrozda. "These insane charges do not belong in the Council of Counts. You must make them in a military court, if you make them at all, traitor."

"Where Admiral Hessman, most conveniently, must stand them alone, since you, Count Vordrozda, cannot be tried there," said Miles immediately.

Count Vorkosigan was tapping his fist softly on his desk, leaning forward urgently toward Miles; his lips formed a silent litany, yes, go, go . . .

Miles, encouraged, raised his voice. "He will stand alone, and he will die alone, since he has only his own unwitnessed word that his crimes were by your order. They were unwitnessed, were they not, Admiral? Do you really think that Count Vordrozda will be so overcome by emotions of loyalty to a comrade as to endorse that word?"

Hessman was dead white, breathing heavily, stare flicking back and forth between Vordrozda and Ivan. Miles could see the panic blossoming in his eyes.

Vordrozda, straddling the circle, gestured jerkily at Miles. "My lords, this is not a defense. He merely hopes to camouflage his guilt by these wild counter-accusations, and totally out of order at that! My Lord Guardian, I appeal to you to restore order!"

The Lord Guardian of the Circle began to rise, stopped, speared by a penetrating stare from Count Vorkosigan. He sank back weakly to his bench. "This is certainly very irregular . . ." he managed, then ran down. Count Vorkosigan smiled approvingly.

"You haven't answered my question, Vordrozda," called Miles. "Will you speak for Admiral Hessman?

"Subordinates have committed unauthorized excesses throughout history," began Vordrozda.

He twists, he turns, he's going to torque away—no! I can twist too. "Oh, you admit he is your subordinate, do you now?"

"He is nothing of a sort," snapped Vordrozda. "We have no connection but common interest in the good of the Imperium."

"No connection, Admiral Hessman; do you hear that? How does it feel to be stabbed in the back with such surpassing smoothness? I wager you can scarcely feel the knife going in. It will be like that right up to the end, you know."

Hessman's eyes bulged. He sprang to his feet. "No, it won't," he snarled. "You started this, Vordrozda. If I'm going down I'll take you with me!" He pointed at Vordrozda. "He came to me at Winterfair, wanting me to pass him the latest Imperial Security intelligence about Vorkosigan's son—"

"Shut up!" ground out Vordrozda desperately, fury firing his eyes at being so needlessly taken from behind, "Shut up—" His hand snaked under his scarlet robe, emerged with a glitter. Locked the needler's aim on the babbling Admiral. Stopped. Vordrozda stared down at the weapon in his hand as though it were a scorpion.

"Who now is out of order?" mocked Miles softly.

Barrayar's aristocracy still maintained its military tone. Drawing a deadly weapon in the presence of the Emperor struck a deep reflex. Twenty or thirty men started up from their benches.

Only on Barrayar, Miles reflected, would pulling a loaded needler start a stampede *toward* one. Others ran between Vordrozda and the dais. Vordrozda abandoned Hessman and whirled to face his real tormentor, raising the weapon. Miles stood stock still, transfixed by the needler's tiny dark eye. Fascinating, that the pit of hell should have so narrow an entrance . . .

Vordrozda was buried in an avalanche of tackling bodies, their scarlet robes flapping. Ivan had the honor of the first hit, taking him in the knees.

Miles stood before his Emperor. The chamber had quieted, his late accusers hustled out under arrest. Now he faced his true tribunal.

Gregor sighed uneasily, and motioned the Lord Guardian of the Circle to his side. They conferred briefly.

"The Emperor requests and requires a recess of one hour, to examine the new testimony. For witness, Count Vorvolk, Count Vorhalas."

They all filed into the private chamber behind the dais, Gregor, Count Vorkosigan, Miles and Ivan, and Gregor's curious choice of witnesses. Henri Vorvolk was one of Gregor's few age-mates among the Counts, and a personal friend. Nucleus of a new generation of cronies, Miles supposed. No surprise that Gregor should desire his support. Count Vorhalas . . .

Vorhalas was Miles's father's oldest and most implacable enemy, since the deaths of his two sons on the wrong side of Vordarian's Pretendership eighteen years before. Miles eyed him queasily. The Count's son and heir had been the man who'd fired the soltoxin gas grenade through the window of Vorkosigan House one night, in a tangled attempt at vengeance for the death of his younger brother. He had been executed in turn for his treason. Had Count Vorhalas seen in Vordrozda's conspiracy an opportunity to complete the job, revenge in perfect symmetry, a son for a son?

Yet Vorhalas was known as a just and honest man— Miles could as easily picture him uniting with his father in disdain of Vordrozda's mushroom upstart plot. The two had been enemies so long, and outlived so many friends and foes, their enmity had almost achieved a kind of harmony. Still, no one would dare accuse Vorhalas of favoritism in witness to the former Regent.

Now the two men exchanged nods, like a pair of fencers en garde, and took seats opposite each other.

"So," said Count Vorkosigan, grown serious and intense, "What really happened out there, Miles? I've had Illyan's reports—until lately—but somehow they all seemed to raise more questions than they answered."

Miles was diverted moment. "Isn't his agent still sending? I promise you, I didn't interfere with his duties—"

"Captain Illyan is in prison."

"What!"

"Awaiting trial. He was included in your conspiracy charges."

"That's absurd!"

"Not at all. Most logical. Who, moving against me, would not take the precaution first of taking away my eyes and ears, if they could?"

Count Vorhalas nodded a tactician's approval and agreement, as if to say, Just how I'd have done it myself.

Miles's father's eyes narrowed with dry humor. "It's a learning experience for him to be on the other end of the process of justice for a time. No harm done. I admit, he is a trifle annoyed with you at the moment."

"The question," said Gregor distantly, "was whether the Captain served me, or my Prime Minister." Bitter uncertainty still lingered in his eyes.

"All who serve me serve you, through me," Count Vorkosigan stated. "It is the Vor system at work. Streams of experience, all flowing together, combining at last in a river of great power. Yours is the final confluence." It was the closest to flattery Miles had ever heard his father come, a measure of his unease. "You do Simon Illyan an injustice to suspect him. He has served you all your life, and your grandfather before you."

Miles wondered what sort of tributary he now constituted—the Dendarii Mercenaries included some very odd headwaters indeed. "What happened. Well, sir . . ." he paused, groping along the chain of events to some starting point. Truly, it began at a wall not 100 kilometers outside Vobarr Sultana. But he launched his account at his meeting with Arde Mayhew on Beta Colony. He stumbled in fearful hesitation, took a breath, then went on in an exact and honest description of his meeting with Baz Jesek. His father winced at the name. The blockade, the boarding, the battles—self-forgetfulness overcame him during his enthusiastic description of these; at one point he looked up to realize he had the Emperor playing the part of the Oseran fleet, Henri Vorvolk Captain Tung, and his father the Pelian high command. Bothari's death. His father's face grew drawn and inward at this news. "Well," he said after a time, "he is released from a great burden. May he find his ease at last."

Miles glanced at the Emperor, and edited out the Escobaran woman's accusations about Prince Serg. From the sharp and grateful look Count Vorkosigan gave him, Miles gathered that was the correct thing to do. Some truths come in too fierce a flood for some structures to withstand; Miles had no wish to witness another devastation like Elena Bothari's.

By the time he reached the account of how he broke the blockade at last, Gregor's lips were parted in fascination, and Count Vorkosigan's eyes glinted with appreciation. Ivan's arrival, and Miles's deductions from it—he was reminded of the hour, and reached for his hip flask.

"What is that?" asked his father, startled.

"Antacid. Uh—want some?" he offered politely.

"Thank you," said Count Vorkosigan. "Don't mind if I do." He took a grave swig, so straight-faced even Miles was not sure if he was laughing.

Miles gave a brief, bald account of the thinking that led him to return in secret, to attempt to surprise Vordrozda and Hessman. Ivan endorsed all he had been eyewitness to, giving Hessman the lie. Gregor looked disturbed at having his assumptions about his new friends turned so bluntly inside-out. Wake up Gregor, thought Miles. You of all men cannot afford the luxury of comfortable illusions. No, indeed, I have no desire to trade places with you.

Gregor was downcast by the time Miles finished. Count Vorkosigan sat at Gregor's right hand, backwards on a plain chair as usual, and gazed at his son with a pensive hunger.

"Why, then?" asked Gregor. "What did you think to make of yourself, when you raised up such force, if not Emperor—if not of Barrayar, perhaps of someplace else?"

"My leige," Miles lowered his voice. "When we played together in the Imperial Residence in the winters, when did I ever demand any part except that of Vorthalia the loyal? You know me—how could you doubt? The Dendarii Mercenaries were an accident. I didn't plan them—they just happened, in the course of scrambling from crisis to crisis. I only wantd to serve Barrayar, as my father before me. When I couldn't serve Barrayar, I wanted—I wanted to serve something. To—" he raised his eyes to his father's, driven to a painful honesty, "to make my life an offering fit to lay at his feet." He shrugged. "Screwed up again."

"Clay, boy." Count Vorkosigan's voice was hoarse but clear. "Only clay. Not fit to receive so golden a sacrifice." His voice cracked.

For a moment, Miles forgot to care about his coming trial. He lidded his eyes, and stored tranquillity away in his heart's most secret recesses, to pleasure him in some lean and desperate future hour. Fatherless Gregor swallowed, and looked away, as if ashamed. Count Vorhalas stared at the floor discomfited, like a man accidently intruding onto some private and delicate scene.

Gregor's right hand moved hesitantly to touch the shoulder of his first and most loyal protector. "I serve Barrayar," he offered. "It's justice is my duty. I never meant to dispense injustice."

"You were ring-led, boy," Count Vorkosigan muttered, to Gregor's ear alone. "Never mind. But learn from it."

Gregor sighed. "When we played together, Miles, you always beat me at Strat-O. It was because I knew you that I doubted."

Miles knelt, head bowed, and spread his arms. "Your will, my leige."

Gregor shook his head. "May I always endure such treason as that." He raised his voice to his witnesses. "Well, my lords? Are you satisfied that the substance of Vordozda's charge, intent to usurp the Imperium, is false and malicious? And will you so testify to your peers?"

"Absolutely," said Henri Vorvolk with enthusiasm. Miles gauged that the second-year cadet had fallen in love with him about halfway through his account of his adventures with the Dendarii Mercenaries.

Count Vorhalas remained cool and thoughtful. "The usurpation charge does indeed appear false," the old man agreed, "and by my honor I will so testify. But there is another treason here. By his own admission, Lord Vorkosigan was, and indeed remains, in violation of Vorloupulous's law, treason in its own right."

"No such charge," said Count Vorkosigan distantly, "has been laid in the Council of Counts."

Henri Vorvolk grinned. "Who'd dare, after this?"

"A man of proven loyalty to the Imperium, with an academic interest in perfect justice, might so dare," said Count Vorkosigan, still dispassionate. "A man with nothing to lose, might dare—much. Might he not?"

"Beg for it, Vorkosigan," whispered Vorhalas, his coolness slipping. "Beg for mercy, as I did." His eyes shut tight, and he trembled.

Count Vorkosigan gazed at him in silence for a long moment. Then, "As you wish," he said, and rose, and slid to one knee before his enemy. "Let it lay, then, and I will see the boy does not trouble those waters any more."

"Still too stiff-necked."

"If it please you, then."

"Say, 'I beg of you.' "

"I beg of you," repeated Count Vorkosigan obediently. Miles searched for tensions of rage in his father's backbone, found none; this was something old, older than himself, between the two men, labyrinthine; he could scarcely penetrate its inward places. Gregor looked sick, Henri Vorvolk bewildered, Ivan terrified.

Vorhalas's hard stillness seemed edged with a kind of ecstasy. He leaned close to Miles's father's ear. "Shove it, Vorkosigan," he whispered. Count Vorkosigan's head bowed, and his hands clenched.

He sees me, if at all, only as a handle on my father . . .

Time to get his attention. "Count Vorhalas," Miles's voice flexed across the silence like a blade. "Be satisfied. For if you carry this through, at some point you are going to have to look my mother in the eye and repeat that. Dare you?"

Vorhalas wilted slightly. He frowned at Miles. "Can your mother look at you, and not understand desire for vengeance?" He gestured at Miles's stunted and twisted frame.

"Mother," said Miles, "calls it my great gift. Tests are a gift, she says, and great tests are a great gift. Of course," he added thoughtfully, "it's widely agreed my mother is a bit strange . . ." He trapped Vorhalas's gaze direct. "What do you propose to do with your gift, Count Vorhalas?"

"Hell," Vorhalas muttered, after a short, interminable silence, not to Miles but to Count Vorkosigan. "He's got his mother's eyes."

"I've noticed that," Count Vorkosigan murmured back. Vorhalas glared at him in exasperation.

"I am not a bloody saint," Vorhalas declared, to the air generally.

"No one is asking you to be," said Gregor, anxiously soothing. "But you are my sworn servant. And it does not serve me for my servants to be ripping up each other instead of my enemies."

Vorhalas sniffed, and shrugged grudgingly. "True, my liege." His hands unclenched, finger by finger, as if releasing some invisible possession. "Oh, get up," he added impatiently to Count Vorkosigan. The former Regent rose, quite bland again.

Vorhalas glared at Miles. "And just how, Aral, do you propose to keep this gifted young maniac and his accidental army under control?"

Count Vorkosigan measured out his words slowly, drop by drop, as though pursuing some delicate titration. "The Dendarii Mercenaries are a genuine puzzle." He glanced at Gregor. "What is your will, my liege?"

Gregor jerked, startled out of spectatorhood. He looked, rather pleadingly, at Miles. "Organizations do grow and die. Any chance of them just fading away?"

Miles chewed his lip. "That hope has crossed my mind, but—they looked awfully healthy when I left. Growing."

Gregor grimaced. "I can hardly march my army on them and break them up like old Dorca did—it's definitely too long a walk."

"They themselves are innocent of any wrongdoing," Miles hastened to point out. "They never knew who I was—most of them aren't even Barrayaran."

Gregor glanced uncertainly at Count Vorkosigan, who studied his boots, as if to say, You're the one who itched to make your own decisions, boy. But he did add, aloud, "You are just as much Emperor as Dorca ever was, Gregor. Do what you will."

Gregor's gaze returned to Miles for a long moment. "You couldn't break your blockade, within its military context. So you changed the context."

"Yes, sir."

"I cannot change Dorca's law . . ." said Gregor slowly. Count Vorkosigan, who had begun to look uneasy, relaxed again. "It saved Barrayar."

The Emperor paused a long time, awash in bafflement. Miles knew just how he felt. Miles let him stew a few moments more, until the silence was stretched taut with expectation, and Gregor was starting to get that desperate glazed look Miles recognized from his candidacy orals, of a man caught without the answer. Now.

"The Emperor's Own Dendarii Mercenaries," Miles said suggestively.

"What?"

"Why not?" Miles straightened, and turned his hands palm-out. "I'd be delighted to give them to you. Declare them a Crown Troop. It's been done."

"With horse cavalry!" said Count Vorkosigan. But his face was suddenly much lighter.

"Whatever he does with them will be a legal fiction anyway, since they are beyond his reach," Miles bowed apologetically to Gregor. "He may as well arrange it to his own maximum convenience."

"Whose maximum convenience?" inquired Count Vorhalas dryly.

"You were thinking of this as a private declaration, I trust," said Count Vorkosigan.

"Well, yes—I'm afraid most of the mercenaries would be, uh, rather disturbed to hear they'd been drafted into the Barrayaran Imperial Service. But why not put them in Captain Illyan's department? Their status would have to remain covert then. Let him figure out something useful to do with 'em. A free mercenary fleet secretly owned by Barrayaran Imperial Security."

Gregor looked suddenly more reconciled; indeed, intrigued. "That might be practical . . ."

Count Vorkosigan's teeth glinted in a white flash of a grin, instantly supressed. "Simon," he murmured, "will be overjoyed."

"Really?" said Gregor dubiously.

"You have my personal guarantee." Count Vorkosigan sketched a bow, sitting.

Vorhalas snorted, and eyed Miles. "You're too bloody clever for your own good, you know, boy?"

"Exactly, sir," said Miles agreeably, in a mild hysteria of relief, feeling lighter by 3000 soldiers and God knew how many tons of equipment. He had done it—the last piece glued back in its place . . .

". . . dare play the fool with me," muttered Vorhalas. He raised his voice to Count Vorkosigan. "That only answers half my question, Aral."

Count Vorkosigan studied his fingernails, eyes alight. "True, we can't leave him running around loose. I, too, shudder to think what accidents he might commit next. He should doubtless be confined to an institution, where he would be forced to labor all day long under many watchful eyes." He paused thoughtfully. "May I suggest the Imperial Service Academy?"

Miles looked up, mouth open in an idiocy of sudden hope. All his calculations had been concentrated on wriggling out from under Vorloupulous's law. He'd scracely dared even to dream of life afterwards, let alone such reward as this . . .

His father lowered his voice to him. "Assuming it's not beneath you—Admiral Naismith. I never did get to congratulate you on your promotion."

Miles reddened. "It was all just fakery, sir. You know that."

"All?"

"Well—mostly."

"Ah, you grow subtle, even with me ... But you have tasted command. Can you go back to subordination? Demotions are a bitter meat to swallow." An old irony played around his mouth.

"You were demoted, after Komarr, sir ..."

"Broken back to Captain, yes."

One corner of Miles's mouth twisted up. "I have a bionic stomach now, that can digest anything. I can handle it."

Count Vorhalas raised skeptical brows. "What sort of ensign do you think he will make, Admiral Vorkosigan?"

"I think he will make a terrible ensign," said Count Vorkosigan frankly. "But if he can avoid being strangled by his harried superiors for—er—excessive initiative, I think he might be a fine General Staff officer someday."

Vorhalas nodded reluctant agreement. Miles's eyes blazed up like bonfires, in reflection to his father's.

After two days of testimony and behind the-scenes maneuvering, the Council vote was unanimous for acquittal. For one thing, Gregor took his place by right as Count Vorbarra and cast a resounding "innocent" as the fourth vote called, instead of the usual abstention customary for the Emperor. The rest swung meekly into line.

Some of Count Vorkosigan's older political opponents looked as if they'd rather spit, but only Count Vorhalas voted an abstention. Then, Vorhalas had never been of Vordrozda's party, and had no taint of association to wash off.

"Ballsy bastard." Count Vorkosigan exchanged a familiar salute across the chamber with his closest enemy. "I wish they all had his backbone, if not his opinions."

Miles sat quietly, absorbing this most mitigated triumph. Elena would have been safe, after all.

But not happy. Hunting hawks do not belong in cages, no matter how much a man covets their grace, no matter how golden the bars. They are far more beautiful soaring free. Heartbreakingly beautiful.

He sighed, and rose to go wrestle with his destiny.

The vinyards garlanding the terraced slopes of the long lake above Vorkosigan Surleau were misted with new green. The surface of the water glittered in a warm breath of air, a spatter of silver coins. It had once been a custom somewhere to put coins on the eyes of the dead, Miles had read, for their journey; it seemed appropriate. He imagined the sun-coins sinking to the bottom of the lake, there to pile up and up until they broke the surface, a new island.

The clods of earth were cold and wet yet, winter lingering beneath the surface of the soil. Heavy. He tossed a shovelful shoulder-high from the hole he dug.

"Your hands are bleeding," observed his mother. "You could do that in five seconds with a plasma arc."

"Blood," said Miles, "washes away sin. The Sergeant said so."

"I see." She made no further demur, but sat in companionable silence, her back against a tree, watching the lake. It was her Betan upbringing, Miles supposed; she never seemed to tire of the delight of water open to the sky.

He finished at last. Countess Vorkosigan gave him a hand up out of the pit. He took up the control lead of the float pallet, and lowered the oblong box, waiting patiently all this time, into its rest. Bothari had always waited patiently for him.

Covering it back up was quicker work. The marker his father had ordered was not yet finished; hand-carved, like the others in this family plot. Miles's grandfather lay not far away, next to the grandmother Miles had never known, dead decades before in Barrayaran civil strife. His eye lingered a moment, uncomfortably, on a double space reserved next to his grandfather, above the slope and perpendicular to the Sergeant's new grave. But that burden was yet to come.

He placed a shallow beaten copper bowl upon a tripod at the foot of the grave. In it he piled juniper twigs from the mountains, and a lock of his own hair. He then pulled a colored scarf from his jacket, carefully unfolded it, and placed a curl of finer dark hair among the twigs. His mother added a clipping of short grey hair, and a thick, generous tress of her own red roan, and withdrew to a distance.

Miles, after a pause, laid the scarf beside the hair. "I'm afraid I made a most improper Baba," he whispered in apology. "I never meant to mock you. But Baz loves her, he'll take good care of her . . . My word was too easy to give, too hard to keep. But there. There." He added flakes of aromatic bark. "You shall lie warm here, watching the long lake change its faces, winter to spring, summer to fall. No armies march here, and even the deepest midnights aren't wholly dark. Surely God won't overlook you, in such a spot as this. There will be grace and forgiveness enough, old dog, even for you." He lit the offering. "I pray you will spare me a drink from that cup, when it overflows for you."

EPILOGUE ✳ ✳ ✳

The emergency docking drill was called in the middle of the night cycle, naturally. He'd probably have timed it that way himself, Miles thought, as he scrambled through the corridors of the orbital weapons platform with his fellow cadets. This four-week stint of orbital and free-fall training was due to end tomorrow for his group, and the instructors hadn't pulled anything nasty for at least four days. Not for him the galloping anticipation of upcoming leave planetside that had formed the bulk of the conversation in the officer's mess last night. He had sat quietly, meditating on all the marvelous possibilities for a grand finale.

He arrived at his assigned shuttle hatch corridor at the same moment as his co-trainee and the instructor. The instructor's face was a mask of neutrality. Cadet Kostolitz looked Miles over sourly.

"Still carrying that obsolete pig-sticker, eh?" said Kostolitz, with an irritated nod at the dagger at Miles's waist.

"I have permission," said Miles tranquilly.

"D'you sleep with it?"

A small, bland smile. "Yes."

Miles considered the ongoing problem of Kostolitz. The accidents of Barrayaran history guaranteed he would be dealing with class-consciousness in his officers throughout his Imperial Service career, aggressive like Kostolitz's or in more subtle forms. He must learn to handle it not merely well, but creatively, if his officers were ever to give him their best.

He had the uncanny sensation of being able to look through Kostolitz the way a doctor saw through a body with his diagnostic viewers. Every twist and tear and emotional abrasion, every young cancer of resentment growing from them, seemed red-lined in his mind's eye. Patience. The problem displayed itself with ever-increasing clarity. The solution would follow, in time, with opportunity. Kostolitz could teach him much. This docking drill might prove interesting after all.

Kostolitz had acquired a thin green armband since they had last been paired, Miles saw. He wondered what wit among the instructors had come up with that idea. The armbands were rather like getting a gold star on your paper in reverse; green represented injury in drills, yellow represented death, in the judgment of whatever instructor was umpiring the simulated catastrophe. Very few cadets managed to escape these training cycles without a collection of them. Miles had encountered Ivan Vorpatril yesterday, sporting two greens and a yellow, not as bad as the unfortunate fellow he'd seen at mess last night with five yellows.

Miles's own undecorated sleeve was attracting a bit more attention from the instructors than he really wanted, lately. The notoriety had a pleasant flip-side; some of the more alert among his fellow cadets vied quietly to have Miles in their groups, as armband-repellent. Of course, the very most alert were now avoiding him like a plague, realizing he was beginning to draw fire. Miles grinned to himself, in happy anticipation of something really sneaky and underhanded coming up. Every cell of his body seemed awake and singing.

Kostolitz, with a stifled yawn and a last growl at Miles's upper-class decorative blade, took the starboard side of the shuttle and began working forward with his checklist. Miles took the port side, ditto. The instructor floated between them, watching sharply over their shoulders. He'd got one good thing out of his adventures with the Dendarii Mercenaries, Miles reflected; his free-fall nausea had vanished, an unexpected side-benefit of the

work Tung's surgeon had done on his stomach. Small
favors.

Kostolitz was working swiftly, Miles saw from the
corner of his eye. They were being timed. Kostolitz
counted emergency breath masks through the plexi-
glass of their case and hurried on. Miles almost called a
suggestion to him, then clamped his jaw. It wouldn't be
appreciated. Patience. Item. Item. Item—first aid kit,
correctly in its wall socket. Automatically suspicious,
Miles unlocked it and checked to see that all its contents were indeed intact. Tape, tourniquets, plastic bandage, IV tubing, meds, emergency oxygen—no surprises
concealed there. He ran a hand along the bottom of the
case, and caught his breath—plastic explosive? No, only
a wad of chewing gum. Shucks.

Kostolitz was finished and waiting impatiently as
Miles arrived up front. "You're slow, Vorkosigian."
Kostolitz jammed his report panel into the read-slot,
and slid into the pilot's seat.

Miles eyed an interesting bulge in the instructor's
breast pocket. He patted his own pockets, and essayed a
helpless smile. "Oh, sir," he chirped politely to the
instructor, "I seem to have misplaced my light-pen.
May I borrow yours?"

The instructor disgorged it unwillingly. Miles lidded
his eyes. In addition to the light-pen, the instructor's
pocket contained three emergency breath-masks, folded.
An interesting number, three. Anyone on a space station
might carry a breath mask in his pocket as a matter of
course, but three? Yet they had a dozen breath-masks
ready to hand, Kostolitz had just checked them—no.
Kostolitz had just *counted* them.

"Your light pens are standard issue," said the instructor coldly. "You're supposed to hang onto them. You
careless characters are going to bring the Accounting
Office down on us all, one of these days."

"Yes, sir. Thank you, sir." Miles signed his name with
a flourish, made to pocket the pen, came up with two.
"Oh, here's mine. Sorry, sir."

He entered his report, and strapped himself into the
co-pilot's chair. With his seat at the limit of its forward

adjustment, he could just reach the foot controls. Imperial equipment was not so flexible as the mercenaries' had been. No matter. He schooled himself to strict attention. He was still awkward in his handling of shuttle controls. But a bit more practice, and he would never be at the mercy of a shuttle pilot for transporation again.

It was Kostolitz's turn now, though. Miles was pressed into his padded seat by the acceleration as the shuttle popped free of its clamps and began to boost toward its assigned station. Breath masks. Check lists. Assumptions. The chip on Kostolitz's shoulder. Assumptions . . . Miles's nerves extended themselves, spider-patient, questing. Minutes crept by.

A sharp report, and a hissing, came from the rear of the cabin. Miles's heart lurched and began to pound violently, in spite of his anticipation. He swung around and took it in at a glance, as when a strobe-flash of lightning betrays the secrets of the dark. Kostolitz swore violently. Miles breathed, "Ha!"

A jagged hole in the paneling on the starboard side of the shuttle was pouring out a thick green gas; a coolant line had snapped, as from a meteor hit. The "meteor" was undoubtedly plastic explosive, since the stuff was streaming into and not out of the cabin. Besides, the instructor was still seated, watching them. Kostolitz leaped for the case of emergency breath masks.

Miles dove instead for the controls. He snapped the atmosphere circuit from recycle to exterior venting, and in one pauseless motion fired the shuttle's attitude verniers at maximum boost. After a groaning moment, the shuttle began to turn, then spin, around an axis through the center of the cabin. Miles, the instructor, and Kostolitz were thrown forward. The coolant gas, heavier than their atmosphere mix, began to pile up against the back wall of the cabin in noxious billows under the influence of this simplest of artificial gravities.

"You crazy bastard!" screamed Kostolitz, scrabbling at a breath mask. "What are you doing?"

The instructor's expression was first an echo of Kostolitz's, then suddenly enlightened. He eased back into the seat he had begun to shoot out of, hanging on tightly and observing, his eyes crinkling with interest.

Miles was too busy to reply. Kostolitz would figure it out shortly, he was sure. Kostolitz donned a breath mask, attempted to inhale. He snatched it off his face and threw it aside, and grabbed up the second of the three he'd brought forward. Miles climbed up the wall toward the first aid kit.

The second breath mask curved past him. Empty reservoirs, no doubt. Kostolitz had counted the breath masks without checking their working condition. Miles levered the first aid kit open and pulled out IV tubing and two Y-connectors. Kostolitz threw aside the third breath mask and began climbing back up the starboard wall toward the case of breath masks. The coolant gas made an acrid, burning stench in Miles's nostrils, but its harmful concentrations remained in the other end of the cabin, for now.

A cry of rage and fear, interrupted by coughing, came from Kostolitz as he began pawing through breath masks, checking their condition readouts at last. Miles's lips drew back in a wicked grin. He pulled his grandfather's dagger from its sheath, cut the IV tubing into four pieces, inserted the Y-connectors, sealed them with blobs of plastic bandage, jammed the hookah-like apparatus into the single outlet of the emergency medical oxygen canister, and skidded back to the instructor.

"Air, sir?" He offered a hissing end of IV tubing to the officer. "I suggest you breathe in through your mouth and out through your nose."

"Thank you, Cadet Vorkosigan," said the instructor in a fascinated tone, taking it. Kostolitz, coughing, eyes rolling desperately, fell back toward them, barely managing not to put his feet through the control panel. Miles blandly handed him a tube. He sucked on it, eyes wide and watering, not, Miles thought, only from the effects of the coolant gas.

Clenching his air-tube between his teeth, Miles began to climb the starboard wall. Kostolitz started after him, then discovered that both he and the instructor had been issued short tethers. Miles uncoiled tubing behind

him; yes, it would reach, although just barely. Kostolitz
and the instructor could only watch, breathing in yoga-
like cadence.

Miles reversed his hold as he passed the midpoint of
the cabin and centrifugal force began to pull him toward
the pooling green gas slowly filling the shuttle
from the back wall. He counted down wall panels, 4a,
4b, 4c—that should be it. He popped it open, and found
the manual shut-off valves.That one? No, that one. He
turned it. It slipped in his sweating hand.

The panel door on which he rested his weight gave
way with a sudden crack, and he swung out over the
evilly heaving green gas. The oxygen tube ripped from
his mouth and flapped around wildly. He was saved
from yelping only by the fact that he was holding his
breath. The instructor, forward, lurched futilely, tied to
his air supply. But by the time he'd fumbled his pocket
open, Miles had swallowed, achieved a more secure grip
on the wall, and recovered his tube in a heart-stopping
grab. Try again. He turned the valve, hard, and the
hissing from the hole in the wall a meter astern of him
faded to an elfin moan, then stopped.

The tide of green gas began to recede and thin at last,
as the cabin ventilators labored. Miles, shaking only
slightly, climbed back to the front end of the shuttle
and strapped himself into his co-pilot's seat without
comment. Comment would have been awkward around
his oxygen tube anyway.

Cadet Kostolitz, in his role as pilot, returned to his
controls. The atmosphere cleared at last. He stopped
the spin and aimed the damaged shuttle slowly back
toward dock, paying strict and subdued attention to
engine temperature readouts. The instructor looked extremely thoughtful, and only little pale.

The chief instructor himself was waiting in the shuttle hatch corridor of the orbital station when they docked,
along with a repairs tech. He smiled cheerily, turning
two yellow armbands absently in his hands.

Their own instructor sighed, and shook his head dolefully at the armbands. "No."

"No?" queried the chief instructor. Miles was not sure if it was with amazement or disappointment.

"No."

"This I've got to see." The two instructors ducked into the shuttle, leaving Miles and Kostolitz alone a moment.

Kostolitz cleared his throat. "That, ah—blade of yours came in pretty handy after all."

"Yes, there are times when a plasma arc beam isn't nearly as suitable for cutting," Miles agreed. "Like when you're in a chamber full of inflammable gas."

"Oh, hell," Kostolitz seemed suddenly struck. "That stuff *will* go off, mixed with oxygen. I almost . . ." He cut himself off, cleared his throat again. "You don't miss much, do you?" A sudden suspicion filled his face. "Did you know about this set up in advance?"

"Not exactly. But I figured something must be up when I counted the three breath masks in the instructor's pocket."

"You—" Kostolitz paused, turned. "Did you really lose track of your light-pen?"

"No."

"Hell," Kostolitz muttered again. He scuffed around the corridor a moment, hunched, red, dismally recalcitrant.

Now, thought Miles. "I know a place you can buy good blades, in Vorbarr Sultana," he said with nicely calculated diffidence. "Better than standard issue stuff. You can get a real bargain there sometimes, if you know what to look for."

Kostolitz stopped. "Oh, yeah?" He began to straighten, as though being relieved of a weight. "You, ah—I don't suppose . . ."

"It's kind of a hole-in-the-wall. I could take you there sometime, during leave, if you're interested."

"Really? You'd—you'd—yes, I'd be interested." Kostolitz feigned a casual air. "Sure." He looked suddenly much more cheerful.

Miles smiled.